MW01715296

NO ENEMY BUT TIME

Other books by Evelyn Wilde Mayerson

SANJO

IF BIRDS ARE FREE

NO ENEMY BUT TIME

Evelyn Wilde Mayerson

DOUBLEDAY & COMPANY, INC.
GARDEN CITY, NEW YORK
1983

While all fiction contains autobiographical elements, the characters in this book are invention, and any resemblance to actual persons, living or dead, is purely coincidental.

Lines from "In Memory of Eva Gore-Booth and Con Markiewicz" are reprinted by permission of Macmillan Publishing Co., Inc. and A. P. Watt Ltd. from *Collected Poems* of W. B. Yeats. Copyright 1933 by Macmillan Publishing Co., Inc., renewed 1961 by Bertha Georgie Yeats.

Lines from *I Couldn't Sleep a Wink Last Night* by Jimmy McHugh and Harold Adamson. Copyright 1943 T. B. Harms Company. Copyright renewed. (c/o The Welk Music Group, Santa Monica, CA 90401). International copyright secured. All rights reserved. Used by permission.

Library of Congress Cataloging in Publication Data
Mayerson, Evelyn Wilde.
No enemy but time.
I. Title.
PS3563.A9554N6 1983 813'.54
ISBN: 0-385-17966-9 AACR2
Library of Congress Catalog Card Number 82-45260

Copyright © 1983 by Evelyn Wilde Mayerson
ALL RIGHTS RESERVED
PRINTED IN THE UNITED STATES OF AMERICA
FIRST EDITION

To the eager young men and women
of World War II, who put aside
their lives and changed the world.

I would like to express my gratitude for the assistance of the reference staff of the University of Miami library, the Miami *Herald*, the Miami Historical Association, and members of the Miami Beach Hotel Association. I also wish to acknowledge Colonel Leo Schmidt, USAFR, Commander William Williams IV, USNR, and the Research Division of the Albert F. Simpson Historical Research Center of the United States Air Force for invaluable information, time, and memories.

The innocent and the beautiful
Have no enemy but time.

—William Butler Yeats

NO ENEMY BUT TIME

1

Twenty-five years before, the land had been a swamp, a black, oozy mire, crisscrossed with stilting and archlike mangrove roots under which shrimp and snapper spawned and thrived, until it was rescued from its primordial state by an entrepreneur in plus fours. With visions of polo fields, he hacked away the mangroves and covered their stubs with dirt sucked from the bay bottom. Despite losses of a few unlucky men and mules drowned while trying to escape the mosquitoes, the morass turned into a three-mile-long island of ghostly sugar whiteness, barren and sterile, until the entrepreneur hauled in topsoil from the Everglades and hired droves of stooped and patient Italian laborers, who had not heard about the mosquitoes, to set in the grass seeds by hand.

By 1941, without cemeteries or resident blacks, except for live-in domestics, who were required to carry work permits to get on the island, Miami Beach was a lush resort, a semitropical pastiche of pastel mansions in peach and pale butter yellow, rose-colored sidewalks flanked by pink and white oleander, bougainvillaea trailing over the high stone walls, jewel thieves climbing over the bougainvillaea, palm trees brought in from Hawaii, polo grounds, tattered hangers-on called Birddogs, looking to make a mark, and hotels, one after another, including thirty-one new ones, each trying to outdo those of the year before. They lined Collins Avenue, peculiar buildings of garish and uncertain architecture, looking out like eccentrics over the coarse coral sand to an ocean ribboned with the pale green Gulf Stream and the dark blue of the Labrador Current.

At November's end, the city had successfully negotiated the hurricane season, a strange time of low barometric pressure, when the prudent, remembering the storm of 1936, which swept everything off the Florida Keys into the ocean, boarded up their windows and bought candles, and listened to the radio for the latest advisory, and fatalists smeared themselves with concoctions of baby oil and iodine and baked in the sun.

Now, with hurricanes out of the way for another year, the city anticipated the winter season, a period of less than four months in which everyone, with the patience of pelicans waiting for fish, looked to the tourist for a score. This year's expectations were especially high, specifically, two million tourists expected to leave close to two hundred million dollars. Everyone had a little more money to spend, the summer season had been the most successful in the city's short history, and the war in Europe, spreading like an Everglades fire out of control, was something most people wanted to forget, including reports of German U-boats sinking American ships somewhere near Iceland and aerial photos of rubble that the newspaper said was Rotterdam.

The trains were running, the horses were running, and so were the dolphins, the barracudas, and the Northerners. One of the hotels to which they fled, distinguished from its neighbors by the vaulting pagoda roof of its driveway, was built closer to the water than it should have been, according to the specifications of the not too strictly enforced building code, so that the beach beyond its seawall was only twenty to forty feet in depth, depending on the tide.

This morning, warm for the end of November, two tanned and sandy-haired children, plastered with yellow foam, splashed in its surf. The boy dived into the foam over and over again, coming up with handfuls of light brown seaweed whose small air bladders he popped between his fingers. His name was Freddie and he was eight. His ten-year-old sister, Hilary, wore the same navy blue trunks as he, although she was encumbered with a cotton halter tied over her undeveloped chest like a bandage. It slipped with each wave and Hilary spent most of her time hiking it up. A biplane, trailing a long streamer that read "I'd Walk A Mile For

A Camel," sputtered and coughed in the pale blue sky above them.

Watching the children was a flock of sandpipers, ready to skitter away at a moment's notice, and a tall, skinny pool boy named Lenny, who stood in the doorway of a shack built precariously on top of the seawall.

"Your mother's yelling for you to come for breakfast!" he shouted.

Hilary wrinkled her nose, a habit her father said would make her look like a bulldog. "I didn't hear her," she replied, not counting as serious any parental injunction issued by a third party.

Lenny shrugged and thrust his head into the doorway. "I gotta go," he said to someone inside the shack, which tilted on its side and then righted itself.

"No, I mean it," he said to the interior of the listing shack. "I gotta set up."

Suddenly a woman came through the door, hoisting with a thumb the strap of a black latex swimsuit that packed her body in like a shiny sausage. She was a New Yorker who had recently remarried her second furrier, preferring things to be warm, which is why she was in Florida in the first place. Hilary wondered why Mrs. Steinfeld was up so early. Most guests did not come down to the beach until ten. She pretended to swim, walking with her hands on the shell-lined bottom and kicking her feet. Grown-ups did things differently when they thought they weren't being watched. Mrs. Steinfeld obliged.

"Will I see you tonight?" she asked.

The pool boy hefted a dozen mats over his pimply shoulders. "I don't know," he said.

"I have tickets to the dog track," she said, her hand hooked into the waistband of his swim trunks.

"Check me later. I'll let you know. I'm not crazy about the dogs. It's kind of stupid to watch them yap around a fake rabbit, and anyway, I can get all the dog passes I want from the bell captain."

Mrs. Steinfeld removed her hand from his trunks and rolled her hair more tightly upon the cotton rat that lay coiled on her forehead, tucking the ends in with her pointed bright red nails.

"You're not the only one," she said. "There are plenty of others."

"Sure," he replied, slapping the mats over the wooden beach chairs.

The children scrambled over the coral-rock seawall. Freddie scraped his knee on one of its sharp extrusions, and Hilary's halter came undone and hung about her waist. As she tied it behind her, causing her shoulder blades to stick out like chicken wings, she was unconcerned that the pool boy, who was also unconcerned, had seen her without it.

"Why don't you use the steps?" asked the pool boy.

"That's no fun," said Freddie. "Who can't walk the steps?"

"You kids got a screw loose," said the pool boy. "You know that?"

"And you got gaposis," said Hilary.

The pool boy fumbled with the buttons of his swim trunks while Hilary slipped off a rubber band and squeezed out water from the dripping braid. "Hello, Mrs. Steinfeld," she said.

"Tell your mother to cut your hair," said Mrs. Steinfeld. "Braids make you look like a German. You're an American, aren't you?"

Hilary nodded. The question had never come up before. While she pondered it, her halter fell again. She dropped the rubber band to yank it up.

Mrs. Steinfeld held on with the tenacity of a terrier. "Well then, the last thing you want to look like is a Nazi. They're very bad people. Murderers. You know what they did to Poland and France and Belgium and Holland? They ran right over them. Don't they teach you that in school?"

Hilary nodded again while she searched for the rubber band, now lost forever in the sparkling silica. Everyone knew about the Nazis. The teacher talked about them in current events among other things including Louis Lepke Buchalter, who was going to die in the electric chair.

Hilary wondered where there was country for children of Miami Beach to hide in case the Nazis came. Probably the Everglades, where Jimmy Tiger had his alligator camp. There, concealed under straw-thatched chickees, they could sit with the Seminoles and help them stitch multicolored skirts, while Jimmy Tiger let out the alligators to eat up the Nazis.

Hilary thought about Mrs. Steinfeld's question. She did not condone the takeover of Poland and France, much less Holland which had wooden shoes and tulips, and which she could, with a slight spin of the globe, find with her eyes shut, a trick that made her schoolmates call her a show-off. The rubber band lay next to a cellophane wrapper.

She picked it up and snapped it over the end of her braid wondering why Mrs. Steinfeld was so mad at her. "Come on," she said to Freddie, "let's go."

Freddie was staring out over the ocean. Hilary could see nothing, only a pair of narrow-winged terns, diving headlong into the water.

"What's out there?" she asked.

"A tiny ship," he said. "It goes smooth."

"It can't go smooth," said Hilary. "It has to go on the waves, like this." She moved her hand up and down.

"This one didn't," he replied, "this one went smooth."

Hilary took Freddie's hand and raced with him barefoot over the concrete pool deck, stopping to spin him into statues, while Lenny, the pool boy, yelled after them not to run on the concrete.

Mel stood chalking odds on a blackboard in the bookie cabana. He was a former lot salesman who used to wear a white knicker suit, had once controlled 10,000 acres of Florida land for five hundred dollars, and who had lost, according to his calculations, a quarter of a million dollars in the land boom bust of '27.

"Hey, kid," he called, "how about taking this to 311?" He held out an envelope.

"I can't," replied Hilary.

"What about him?" Mel pointed to her brother.

"Freddie can't do it either. Not now, anyhow. We have to go for breakfast."

"Too bad. There's fifty cents for you."

Hilary stopped. Fifty cents would buy a *Captain Marvel* comic book, a movie ticket, three ropes of licorice, and a barrette. She turned to Freddie. "Tell Ma I'm changing into shorts."

Freddie fixed his solemn eyes upon her. "That's a lie."

"It's not really a lie because I'm going to change afterward. I'll split with you. Forty cents for me, a dime for you."

"That's a no-fair split."

"Okay. A quarter for each."

"Don't take a long time," he said. "Ma read the note from my teacher."

"I told you not to give it to her before Monday morning."

"I didn't give it to her. She found it," yelled Freddie, running to the dining room. Hilary turned toward Mel.

"Who's this for, anyway?"

"Mr. Radner, from Philadelphia. He's waiting for Tropical to open. Some of these guys will bet on anything. Yesterday it was how many times Ramon the busboy dropped his tray. Today it's how many times the Jap ambassador is pictured on the front page. Those Japs sure got lousy teeth. Must be all that rice sticks in their teeth and pushes them out."

The front door of 311 was wide open. Hilary knocked on the louvered inner door. She shivered in her wet trunks. A woman in a robe, her hair short and curled about her head in crisp waves like a run of "i's" one had to make in penmanship, opened the door. She looked very tired. Hilary noticed how her eyelids fell over her eyes. She wondered how the woman could see. Inside, a man sat on the bed in white shorts that blossomed over his hairy legs, the telephone squashed against his ear. "I don't care if you call it a palmetto bug," he shouted, "I call it a cockroach. It came up this morning, as big as a rat, right from the drain into my bathtub. My wife is afraid to sit on the toilet." He motioned to the woman and pointed to a handful of change that lay on the bureau. The woman handed a quarter to Hilary.

Hilary's nose began to run and she wiped it with the edge of her hand.

"Don't do that," said the woman. "Use a handkerchief. You should carry one. Always."

Hilary came up to the woman's shoulders. The place between her huge breasts was creased. Hilary wondered how old you had to be before your breasts wrinkled. She also wondered how old you had to be to have breasts. Obviously it was not ten. There was no point in asking that question of her mother, who would have only pointed her to a book called *Growing Up*, which purported to have the answers, but really, when you came right down to it, did not. Once she asked her mother what rape meant. Her mother said to look it up. *Growing Up* made no mention of it. She tried the dictionary, which only said, cryptically, carnal knowledge. It was clear that neither grown-ups nor books were anxious to dispense information. One was forced to find out for oneself.

"Mel said fifty cents," she said.

"What's the matter now?" bellowed the man.

"She wants fifty cents," said the woman.

"Then give it to her. Jesus, do I have to do everything?"

The dining room, which overlooked the pool through great glass windows, was packed. Every seat was taken. The overflow strained against velvet ropes. Mrs. Steinfeld, wearing a terry-cloth robe over her latex suit, sat with her son, Rudy, and sectioned his grapefruit. Rudy was the same age as Freddie and had a float designed to look like Mickey Mouse that he would parade with to the beach, holding it over his head, and making sure that everyone had seen it, then flop on the water, surrounded by Mickey's loving arms. Hilary had once asked him if Freddie could use it. Rudy had said no. Hilary was determined to get him. She shot him a look, one of the looks she learned from Marco, the salad man, where you narrowed your eyes and glared at your enemy through the slits. Marco had said that in his country, such a look was guaranteed to send men scurrying to their mothers.

Rudy was unintimidated, possibly because he was already with his mother, and ate the grapefruit, which his mother continued to section, while Mrs. Templeton, the social hostess, generally acknowledged to have class, since she was a gentile who had gone to college, came to take her name for the shuffleboard tournament.

Someone tapped Hilary on the shoulder. It was Vicky Sue, a pretty waitress from Baton Rouge who wore a bright red lipstick called Firedrill. "Better hustle your ass in there, baby," she said. "Your ma is really pissed."

She pushed through the swinging doors and entered the steaming kitchen where waitresses and busboys scurried over the wooden decking, shouting orders and heaving trays of clattering plates into the sinks, while dishwashers yelled at the busboys to stack their glasses, and cooks yelled at the waitresses to pick up.

Freddie was seated on a high stool behind the salad counter, bent over his breakfast, while the salad man, Marco, cut radishes into roses. Behind Freddie stood their mother, Ilona, wearing a long white apron, her brown hair tucked neatly into a chenille net she called a snood. Ilona was holding a piece of paper in her hand and yelling at Freddie who pulled his neck into his shoulders like a turtle.

"I don't know why you didn't do good in school. All you have to do is pay attention to the teacher. You're not slow. Nobody in our family was ever slow. I don't want to get any more notes that say you stare out of windows. You understand?"

Freddie mashed his eggs and pushed them from one side of his plate to the other. Tears fell from his lids and dripped onto his round, tanned cheeks.

"Do you?"

He nodded and continued to look miserable.

Hilary grabbed a stool and slid it next to her brother's. Marco winked at her and sliced off a petal.

"And you," said Ilona, "running around like a maniac. When your grandmother and your aunt Margit and your cousin Dieter come to this country, things will be different. I'll tell you that. A lot different. You won't be running wild, you and your brother." Something about the way she said it sounded unsure.

Hilary's grandmother and aunt Margit had been coming from Europe for the past four years. Ilona had sent them money, a little each month for their fares. Now they were waiting for a visa which was expected any day, or so Ilona had conjectured. The problem was, no one was sure where they were coming from. While they had waited, each country into which they had fled fell to the Germans. With Holland and France occupied, that left only a few places. Ilona had a letter, folded and unfolded so many times it had begun to tear at the corner. The letter had said that they were running out of languages and money.

"Maybe they're in Lisbon," Hilary's father had said. "We would have heard," Ilona had replied. "No news is good news," he had said.

Hilary pictured her grandmother as soft and warm with a big, deep lap, enough to accommodate a ten-going-on-eleven, where you could nestle and rest your head and talk about the olden times. She preferred this image to the photograph of the pinch-faced, unsmiling woman with her hair in a bun.

Hilary's father, wearing a puffy, dome-shaped chef's cap that rose over his head like bread dough, waved from the steam table. He was tall to begin with, but his turbinate headgear made him loom over everyone in the kitchen. He looked something like Hilary, only he was better-favored. His teeth, for example, were not as big in his mouth, his ears didn't stick out, and his hands and feet seemed to fit in better with the rest of him. Hilary waved back. A waitress leaned over the counter to whisper something to him. He laughed.

Ilona looked, then turned back, a tiny furrow creasing the space between her eyebrows. "Ten o'clock is too late to come in for breakfast," she shouted. "You saw what's going on in the dining room, and it isn't even December yet. I don't have time for this." She crumpled the note and tossed it onto a garbage can full of eggshells.

"The teachers like you to come to school," said Hilary.

"The customers like you to substitute blueberry muffins for toast but that doesn't mean they're going to get it. I can't come to school," said Ilona. "You think all I have to do is come to school? I have to work. I want you to tell her for me. You go in my place and say, my mother said my brother's not slow. And don't be wishy-washy when you say it. Look right in her eye and say, my mother said. Maybe she speaks too fast. Maybe that's why he's not getting the work. Maybe she should slow down."

Ilona reached into Freddie's orange juice and plucked out pulp with her fingers, flinging it after the crumpled note.

"Can I cut my hair?" asked Hilary, deciding it was time to draw fire from her brother.

"What?"

"My hair. Can I cut it? Nobody wears braids anymore."

"No. You can't cut it. It's neat this way. It's nice. It suits you and it's out of your eyes."

"They cut hair out of your eyes."

"You can't count on that. Sometimes they do. Sometimes they don't. Remember Mrs. Shimmel."

Mrs. Shimmel had had a permanent that scorched and singed her hair, leaving her with an enduring smell of fire. Hilary couldn't see the relationship between a haircut and a permanent. Somehow it was connected for Ilona. The analogue was lost to Hilary. She slipped a quarter into Freddie's hand.

"How about curls? Shirley Leone's mother makes her curls. Every morning. She winds them around her finger."

"If Shirley Leone's mother wants to make curls for you every morning, it's okay with me."

It was one of those arguments that sounded like a win but was really a lose. Freddie continued to cry after Ilona left to check on the walk-in icebox; not full-scale crying, just a quiet seeping of tears and an occasional sniffle.

"Stop crying," said Hilary. "She's not even going to school."

"I can't help it," he said, "it's coming out of my eyes."

"Think about the quarter," she said.

Gus, the baker, passed the salad counter carrying a tray of rolls. Gus was German and had bristles on his face, long stray hairs that somehow had escaped his razor. He wore an undershirt and a baker's cap, and his accent was as thick as his strudel.

"Tomorrow," he whispered to Freddie, "I make you a cookie with your name on it."

By the time they reached the two adjoining hotel rooms that they called home for most of the year, everything was in an uproar. Ilona, with wisps of hair poking out of every hole in her snood, had torn off the linens of the beds and had thrown them into a heap. Boxes lay everywhere piled high with buckets, spades, balls, sieves, roller skates, a tin gadget of Freddie's that sent water pouring down a chute into a dipper, comics, baseball cards in cigar boxes, two outgrown Dydee dolls that Ilona made Hilary keep for her own children, Monopoly money, a post office set that had never been unsealed, and Freddie's American Flyer train and tracks, boxed in hope of the day when the family would live in a regular house and have space to set it up.

"Where's my shoebox?" asked Hilary.

"I can't worry about shoeboxes," said Ilona. "Help your brother pick up the wet bathing suits."

"It's got to be here somewhere," said Hilary. "I had it yesterday."

"What are you looking for?" asked Frank.

"My shoebox. The one with all my free coupons so I can send away for things."

"Oh, that one," said Ilona. She waved a hand. "It's in there someplace. I took out the Zonite coupon. It's not for you."

Suddenly, as though inspired, Ilona whipped a sheet off the floor and began to tack it to the ceiling, dividing her room in half, while Frank, his cigar now a butt, pushed a double bed next to the window for Hilary and Freddie, then, as per Ilona's continued instructions, ducked beneath the sheet to push their own nearer to the door in case a burglar came in the middle of the night, although he argued that a burglar who had to depend on them for a living would hang himself on the cord of the venetian blind.

"You know how to make a venetian blind?" asked Freddie. "You stick him in the eye."

No one laughed, not even Hilary, who was still angry with her mother for throwing away her Zonite coupon which had promised to reveal intimate feminine secrets for the price of a 3-cent stamp.

Winona, the black maid from housekeeping, came to ask if she could make up the room for the guests who had checked in and were waiting in the lobby. Ilona said ten more minutes, and Winona said she would help.

"You got this room fixed up real nice," said Winona, carrying wet laundry from the shower rod of one room to the shower rod of the next. "Get you some curtains instead of them blinds, you can make it real homelike. You'd be surprised."

Things began to escalate. The front desk called to ask what was taking so long and Frank dropped the box that contained Freddie's water chute. Freddie started yelling when he bent inside to look and found the chute collapsed and the dipper twisted.

Within minutes the move was made. Everything they owned was packed, stacked, hung, draped, and shoved into one room. Hilary studied the narrow aisle between the boxes and the beds and the sheet that dipped from the ceiling, and concluded that Mr. Davis was mean to rent out their room; she said so. Winona, trying to bend back the twisted dipper, told them about the concert Marian Anderson gave on the steps of the Lincoln Memorial because the DAR would not let her use their hall.

Did Winona think they should sleep at the Lincoln Memorial? Probably not. Her meaning was hidden in the story.

"I would have punched them in the nose," said Hilary.

"That's an awful lot of noses," said Winona.

"Well, anyhow, that's what I would've done."

"Seems like she done it anyway," said Winona, "with her singing."

When Winona left to make up their old beds, Ilona chased Hilary and Freddie into the hall so she could restore order. Hilary gave their old room one last peek. Winona had already smoothed the bedspreads and was bringing in fresh towels. This meant they couldn't listen to the radio until midnight anymore, or wade into the surf in the dark while they imagined that monsters were swimming to get them, although the latter was really for Freddie's benefit, since Hilary no longer believed in monsters.

"What do you want to do?" she asked Freddie. "Jelly doors or stuffing?"

The latter meant shoving newspapers underneath the outer and inner louvered doors of the hotel rooms. Properly wedged, the jammed doors could neither be opened nor closed. Freddie considered the choice. It was a question of inventory.

"Jelly doors," he replied.

They spent the rest of the afternoon running through upper floors, smearing doorknobs with orange marmalade from tiny packets that they got from the dining room, hiding in the corners whenever they heard footsteps, and waiting for a guest to enter his room. At first Hilary was halfhearted. It was only when Mr. Franklin, a natty accountant from Chicago, wiped his jellied hand on his white sharkskin slacks, and ran down to the front desk with orange rind hanging from his pants, that she got into it. They followed after him, past Mrs. Radner, the lady with the tired eyelids, on her way back to Philadelphia, her creased breasts hidden behind a printed jacket whose pocket contained a handkerchief pinned like a blossom, and progressed all the way to the front desk, in time to hear the red-jacketed room clerk say to Mr. Franklin, "That's no reason for name calling."

That night, squashed in their new bed against the windowsill, they listened to Charlie McCarthy on the radio. "He's really a wooden dummy," said Hilary.

"How do you know?" asked Freddie. "You never saw him."

"Edgar Bergen is a ventriloquist. That's how I know. You can't be a ventriloquist without a dummy."

"Oh," said Freddie. "I still like him."

Winona came by on her way home to bring them extra pillows. She was taking one for her own son, Lionel. "You folks ought to use something else beside marmalade," she said. "It takes a long time to get that sticky mess off of all them doors."

Hilary watched her leave, the pillow stuffed beneath her dress, the skin around her eyes tinged with a deep slate gray. Hilary suddenly felt sad. "Next time let's do stuffing," she said.

Freddie, who had leaned over to sit with his ear to the radio, didn't answer.

Charlie McCarthy was telling how he would put one over on Mr. Bergen, when the guests in their old room began banging on the wall in a steady, rhythmic knocking.

"I think they're sending us a message," said Hilary. She raced for her Girl Scout Handbook, hidden in one of the boxes, and looked for the section on Morse Code. Then she banged on the wall. "Who are you?" she tapped. "And what do you want?"

2

Hilary stood beneath the feathery foliage of a tamarind, a huge tree imported from across the bay with long, flat pods and a red-and-yellow snail hanging from it like a fragile gem. She wore the white webbed belt of a crossing guard. The belt and a whistle—her own idea—suspended from a lanyard which she blew for minor infractions, indicated her authority. Hilary decided when people crossed and when they waited on the sidewalk, and her jurisdiction, absent the override of a teacher, was absolute. It even included parents, although they seldom paid attention and crossed when they felt like it.

Hilary was grumpy despite her favorite smell of pine needles warming in the sun. It had to do with not being able to find anything. Her comics were lost, hidden beneath Freddie's pajamas, the best starfish she had ever found was missing one of its points, and worse, she had to speak to Freddie's teacher.

She was thinking these thoughts, including how much she hated sleeping behind a sheet and sharing a bed with Freddie, who kicked, when she saw Rudy in the midst of a small crowd waiting to cross. He wore clean, freshly starched shorts and shirt and the Vaselined pompadour of early morning.

"You had to move," he shouted from across the street. "You got in trouble and you had to move. My mother said!"

The decision was an impulsive one, but Hilary made it. It was clearly the moment and probably what Mr. Lonzo meant when Hilary heard him say to Frank, when you got your enemy by the balls, don't forget to squeeze.

Hilary signaled with an elaborate wave of her hand for the crowd to cross. "All except you!" she shouted, pointing at Rudy and blowing her whistle.

"What do you mean?" he shouted back.

"You can't go yet."

"Why not? They're going."

"Because I said so."

Rudy scuffed the toes of his Buster Browns against the sidewalk. "I don't care what you say. I'm crossing anyway."

"It's against the law!" yelled Hilary, her palm up. "You can get in a lot of trouble. Especially tourists who don't live here. If they find out you broke the law, they won't let you stay in school."

Rudy stood as if rooted, weaving in the direction of the street, like a flower to the sun, yet firmly planted on the rose-tinted concrete. "Well, when can I cross?"

"Maybe never."

Rudy looked like he might cry. "I'm telling my mother."

"Tell her," shouted Hilary. "Tell her you're a selfish pig who won't share his Mickey Mouse float and I'll tell all the kids you don't even know how to cut your own grapefruit."

Rudy bent to pick up a fallen pod from the tamarind, but figuring that it had limited range, dropped it and selected instead a pebble. He hesitated for a moment, then hurled it. The pebble landed in the middle of the street. Rudy bent down to get another pebble. It too landed in the middle of the street. Soon he had a small mound, except for one that made it almost to the gutter.

A teacher, one of those assigned to spot a putsch in the making, walked briskly from the schoolyard. She was portly, her front and rear jutting out like two shelves and the garters around which her stockings were rolled, sunken in the flesh of her knees. Her name was Miss Daly and she taught the sixth grade.

"What's going on here?" asked Miss Daly.

"He's throwing rocks at me," said Hilary.

"Are you throwing rocks?"

"She won't let me cross," said Rudy.

"Of course she won't let you cross. Not when you throw rocks. You can put out people's eyes that way."

Miss Daly took Rudy's arm, holding it up as if it were broken, and led him across the street toward the principal's office. Hilary watched them go.

The warning bell rang and Hilary crossed the street, running past a cluster of pink and white periwinkles growing wild beside the schoolyard, toward the pine frame bungalow that housed the third grade. She skipped as she ran, her braids flying behind her, her cotton socks falling to her ankles.

Freddie was already seated behind a little wooden desk near the back of the bungalow, looking miserable, even when Hilary walked in. His teacher, wearing a sweater draped across her shoulders, was writing on the freshly washed blackboard with soft yellow chalk.

Hilary pulled up her socks. "Miss Carmichael, can I talk to you?" she asked.

Miss Carmichael turned, peered at Hilary over her glasses, then turned back to the blackboard, neatly rolling yellow "l's." "May, not can. What is it, Hilary?"

"My mother got your note." Hilary clasped her hands behind her back.

"When is she coming to see me?" asked Miss Carmichael.

Hilary twisted her hands into a knot. "She can't."

"She can't? I don't understand that at all. This is a very serious matter."

"She knows," said Hilary. "It's just that she can't come. She's working."

"So what?" challenged Miss Carmichael. "I'm working, and I assure you that if I had a child and a teacher called for a meeting, I would certainly make every effort to be there."

Hilary shifted to her other foot.

"Is there more?" asked Miss Carmichael.

Hilary swallowed. "My mother wants me to tell you something else."

"What is it?"

"She said that nobody in our family was ever slow. That Freddie's not slow."

"Yes?"

Hilary dug her nails into her palms. "That maybe you speak too fast."

The color in Miss Carmichael's face rose like mercury in a thermometer. Her sweater fell off her shoulders. She bent to retrieve it. "And you tell your mother that I am at the end of my rope with your brother. He pays no attention, his mind wanders, and I no longer have the patience to find busy work for him when the other children are learning to read. Go to your classroom."

"He reads," said Hilary. "Freddie reads."

"That is very interesting. I have never seen him do so," said Miss Carmichael. "What does he read?"

"He sorts out the racing form for my father. He can read all the months and all the dates, except sometimes he has trouble telling the difference between June and July on account of they both start with JU and they both have four letters."

Somehow, without touching them, Miss Carmichael pinched her nostrils shut. "Recognizing dates on a racing form is hardly a skill I am interested in teaching. It is not reading. Tell your mother that I intend to file a full report, and that I will discuss this with the principal very thoroughly."

Hilary glanced at Freddie. He was gouging his desk with a ruler. There was nothing else Hilary could do. She had a bad taste in her mouth, like metal. The jubilant feeling was gone.

On her way out, Hilary passed Miss Daly, who came in leading Rudy by the arm. A faint line of sweat beaded Miss Daly's upper lip. "This young man was throwing stones, Helen. He has already been to see Mr. Detwiler."

"Thank you," said Miss Carmichael. "Take your seat, Rudy. I am very surprised that you would do such a thing."

Rudy's head hung like that of a puppet whose strings had been cut. He brushed past Hilary, knocking her with his shoulder.

"You'd think that with all that's going on, they'd behave better, wouldn't you?" asked Miss Daly. "Can you imagine those cunning English children in their knee socks throwing rocks like Neanderthals? I can't. Their only concern is whether or not they'll ever see their parents again."

The P.A. began to crackle, and the principal's voice came on to announce that President Roosevelt was addressing Congress, and that any moment would come on the air to speak to the nation. There was a pause, more crackling, then President Roosevelt's familiar voice, sounding very grave, as he had done on the Monday before when he spoke of the Japanese sneak attack on Pearl Harbor and called it a date that would live in infamy. This time the

President spoke of powerful and resourceful gangsters who had banded together to make war on the whole human race, and explained that now the United States included Germany and Italy among its enemies, and that the war, which had begun days earlier with Japan, would be a global war, that it would cover the entire earth, and that every man, woman, and child alive, would be involved.

Shirley Leone was an acknowledged beauty. She had shiny black sausage curls that sprung about her pretty, round-cheeked face, black eyes, and thick lashes like the fringe of a shawl. She was also Hilary's best friend, although she disclaimed this relationship during school and would only acknowledge it when the bus let them off at the hotel.

As they entered the lobby of the Flamingo Arms, Winona was explaining to Mr. Davis that she had been detained all that day in the police station for failing to have her work permit on her person. Mr. Davis wore a short-sleeved white shirt and bow tie, and had freckles on his scalp. You could see the freckles when he bent to think, as he now was doing. He said that he believed her and that under the serious circumstances of the day, it was easy to see why she had forgotten it, and he might have done so himself, if he had been required to carry one.

Winona turned away. With a great sigh she picked up her net tote bag, then saw Hilary. "Hello, sugar," she said.

"Who's that?" asked Shirley Leone. "Your maid?"

Hilary waited until they were out of earshot. "Yes," she said, hoping that Winona had not heard her.

"Our maid steals liquor," said Shirley. "My mother has to lock up the cabinet."

"That's nothing," said Hilary, "my father has to lock up the whole bar."

"How can he do that?" asked Shirley. "How can he lock up the whole room? It doesn't even have a door."

"He has this chain in the wall, with a lock as big as your head. He just pulls it across."

"I don't believe that," said Shirley, "and I can tell when you're lying, Hilary. Your eyes get funny." Hilary quickly regretted her overreach.

The lobby buzzed with urgent bombinate murmurings of guests

who sat back in cushioned damask, some with their arms folded, some holding newspapers with headlines that announced that the East was crippled by snow and cold, speaking of what the declaration of war against Germany and Italy meant. Mr. Samuelson said that he had fought during the Great War in France. "That makes this the second world war," he said. No one picked up on that, and Mr. Samuelson said it again, this time raising his voice a little and adding that he had narrowly missed getting gassed, so that it would carry better and with more punch.

Hilary climbed over everyone's legs and whispered in his ear. "Mel wants his twenty dollars," she said.

Mr. Samuelson dug deep into his pocket and pulled out a bill. She tucked it into her lunch box. "I'm glad you didn't get gassed," she said.

"Where are we going now?" asked Shirley. "I thought we were going to the beach."

"One more stop," said Hilary.

The bell station was having its own conversation. Mack the bellhop was telling the bell captain that the Japanese were cross-eyed, which affliction would prevent them from seeing their targets straight. The bell captain asked him how he explained Pearl Harbor. "That was easy," said Mack. "They had nothing else to hit. No buildings, no nothing. Of course they're gonna hit them ships. How could they miss?"

Mack had come to Miami because he wanted to be a jockey. The trainers told him they had all the short fellows they needed, except one who said that if anything came up, he would give him a call. On this slender thread, Mack waited, hanging around the paddock on his time off, and coming back with in-the-know stories of horses with ailments like hockhives, and trainers who were definitely making their push in the seventh race on Friday.

Hilary hit the bell. "Front," she said.

"Don't do that, Eleanor," said the bell captain.

"Hilary. My name is Hilary. How come you always say Eleanor?"

"I don't know, they sound alike."

Hilary took out two bills from her lunch box and handed them to Mack. "Did they say you could be a jockey yet?"

"Not yet. Boy, these smell from pickles. You ought to keep them separate."

The bell captain looked over Hilary's head. "All I can say is, this country's in big trouble. Big trouble. And don't forget that 311 wants ice." His attention was arrested. "Hubba hubba," he said.

Mack whistled softly.

Mickey Biscayne stood in the lobby surrounded by suitcases and boxes. She was twenty-two and until the week before had been a dancer in the Pago Pago, a nightclub in which men guests were given fezzes to wear, women guests were given swizzle sticks, and the club photographer, also the cigarette girl, made matchbook covers from customers' pictures. Mickey was not tall enough to have been a showgirl, one of those stately, inaccessible beauties costumed in towering headdresses of feathers and glitter. Instead, she was a pony, a dancer on the line, whose costume was brief and cute, the most recent one of which was a rhinestoned "V," front and back, which she kept as a souvenir. Now, waiting for a bellhop, she wore a pale blue suit with square padded shoulders, a flared ruffle on the jacket called a peplum, and white high heels. The seams on her stockings were perfectly straight, as was her nose, and the space between her soft green eyes was wide, giving her forehead a serene look.

Everyone turned to look at her. The bell captain signaled for Mack to pick up her bags. Mack smiled over his chinstrap and expertly lifted them, shifting them under his arm in order to pick up the boxes, but became galvanized by her seams and allowed one of the boxes to open and spill its contents on the terrazzo floor.

Hilary watched her kneel to pick up her strewn bibelots, which included an iron, a pair of patent leather tap shoes, and a small ceramic poodle. One of her stockings began a run that laddered down her leg. With her long blond shining pageboy curving over her neck, she was the most beautiful girl Hilary had ever seen in real life, by definition not counting movie stars and comic-book heroines like Brenda Starr.

"Hi," said Mickey, tying the opened box with a cord.

"Are you checking in?" asked Hilary.

"Sure am."

"What room did they give you? I know them all. Are you ocean front or what?"

"Three-eleven," said Mickey. "Is it any good? It sounds like an 'or what' to me." She smiled. Her teeth were not the perfect Chiclets of the Ipana ads. There was a tiny gap between the two in front, but somehow, it looked right, like a space to whistle through. Hilary hoped her teeth would have a space between them. Right now, they were crowding each other out of her mouth.

"You can't be checking into 311," said Hilary. "That belongs to Mr. Radner and I don't think he's checked out yet."

Mickey smiled again. "I know," she said.

Mack had all the boxes and suitcases neatly in hand, giving his short arms a rounded look, like those of a gorilla. He walked away and she followed after. "My name is Mickey," she called behind her. "What's yours?"

"Hilary."

"Don't take any wooden nickels, Hilary."

"Your first time in Miami?" asked Mack.

Hilary stared after her. Sibylline and knowing, Mickey had more style than even Gomez, the dark and passionate dance teacher whose name was really Levine. Mickey's perfume lingered in the air like a veil. Hilary stood under it for a moment, inhaling as much of it as she could.

"What are you doing?" asked Shirley. "What is it, a fire?"

"Never mind. Wait here."

Hilary ran to the front desk where the red-jacketed room clerk was filling out his cards.

"Is Mr. Radner still in 311?" she asked.

"Last I know, unless he skipped."

"Did that girl check into the same room?"

"Yes."

"Is she his daughter?"

The room clerk smiled. "You ever see the three monkeys?" he asked. "See no evil, hear no evil, speak no evil, that's good advice for anyone." He rapped his cards sharply on the marble counter.

Hilary wondered what could be evil about a girl more beautiful than Glinda the Good or Veronica Lake—sweet-smelling, clear-eyed, with the softest voice she ever heard.

"Come on! You think I want to wait here all day?" yelled Shirley.

By the time they had put on their bathing suits, Freddie had his trunks on and was waiting in the hall. They tried to ignore his banging on the door.

"Is this your room or your brother's?" asked Shirley.

"It's everybody's room," said Hilary.

"You mean your mother and daddy and your brother?"

Hilary nodded.

"You're lying again. I told you I could tell. Why is there a sheet hanging from the ceiling?"

Hilary decided to test Shirley's fallibility. "We're playing stage."

"You mean like a show?"

"Yes." Hilary tied her halter behind her. "Everyone sings and dances. We have a good time." Shirley Leone didn't bat an eye.

"You don't have anything on top," said Shirley, whose own top was beginning to swell.

Hilary tied her halter faster. She noticed that Shirley was also getting hair between her legs. It was sparse, like the bristles on Gus's face. It didn't look very good. Hilary hoped that when she got hers, it would look better.

The banging started again.

"Why does he have to play with us?" asked Shirley.

"Because he's my brother."

"I have a brother and he doesn't play with me."

After they were chased off the beach by gloved coastguardsmen who were unrolling barbed wire, they decided to play Gone With the Wind. Freddie was happy with his part, because he got to be Rhett Butler, chewing on one of Frank's cigars, and strutting back and forth in a straw panama. The only problem was that Shirley refused to play unless she was Scarlett O'Hara, for which part she said she was clearly suited because of her curls. This left only the parts of Mammy or Melanie for Hilary. Either way Hilary lost. If she was Mammy, Shirley ordered her about, telling her to do such things as, "Get in there and get that bathroom clean, and that means the mildew," and if she was Melanie, Shirley shouted at her, "Go raise your pack of mealy-mouthed brats." The game ended when the doorman sent Mack to say that Shirley's father had come for her, and that his maroon fluid-drive De Soto was blocking the driveway.

Later that evening the hotel twinkled on the ocean front in an extended row of brilliants that rimmed the coastline. The lobby was jammed, the men wearing jeweled cuff links, the women wearing sequined silk and satin lobby dresses, extravagant and elegant creations in which they paraded up and down, turning this way and that. Gomez and her partner Lipschutz, a lanky somber man who looked like Lincoln, sat behind a desk recruiting rhumba lessons. A fur thief conferred with his client, on a flocked velvet loveseat, advising him not to make a selection too hastily but to take his time. Discrimination, he cautioned, was the keynote to a good fur. They watched a woman in a silver fox shrug while the client made notes.

Mickey Biscayne, as graceful and lithe as the moonvine that draped behind the diving board, was there on Mr. Radner's arm. Her cheeks were flushed and her pageboy not as smooth as it had been earlier.

Hilary waved. "That's her," she said.

Mickey waved back and was about to come toward her when Mr. Radner, a cigar clamped between his teeth, led her by her upper arm into the cocktail lounge where the Living Gas Range was about to perform.

"Who are you waving to?" asked Ilona.

"My new friend, over there with Mr. Radner."

Frank waggled his eyebrows at Ilona.

"Oh," said Ilona. "She's not your friend. Shirley Leone is your friend. That one is a loose woman."

Hilary filed the concept away as she did her most recent insight that raisins were really grapes. Shoelaces got loose. Bowels got loose. People, apparently, could also get loose.

Rudy's mother, looking very angry, stood at the front desk talking to Mr. Davis. Mr. Davis called to them. "Can I have a word with you, Frank?" he asked. Ilona smoothed her skirt and followed Frank to the marble counter. Mr. Davis spoke with his head down, then they all turned to look at Hilary.

"What did you do?" asked Freddie.

"I got even with Rudy for not lending you his Mickey Mouse float."

"I don't like that float. Stop thinking I like things when I don't, Hilary. I'm not a baby. You act like I'm a baby."

"Like when?"

"Like when you came to see my teacher."

"Ma made me do that. It wasn't my idea. You heard her. You were there when she told me to do it."

"I wish everyone would just leave me alone," he said.

Ilona was very angry when she returned. Tiny blue veins throbbed at her temple. "They're our guests," she said. "You have to treat them accordingly."

"What's accordingly?" asked Freddie.

"With respect," said Frank. "You have to be nice to guests. They're our bread and butter. You understand?"

Hilary understood. It meant that from now on Rudy would be unbearable. She nodded.

"All right, then," said Frank. "Tomorrow I want you to apologize to Rudy. First thing. You go to him at breakfast and you say, in front of his mother, I'm sorry. You got that?"

She did. It was going to be a terrible humiliation, like when Clark Kent, who could not reveal his true identity, was forced to shine the shoes of Snakeface. "Why can't I just say it to Rudy?"

"It's his mother that made the complaint," said Frank.

"It's very important that she hear you say it."

"She's not going to like my hair again," said Hilary.

"What has that got to do with anything?" asked Ilona. "Talk sense, will you please?"

"It's late," said Frank. "The kid is tired. Get them to bed. I'm going to check on the kitchen."

While they changed into their pajamas, Ilona put tape around the edges of the venetian blinds. "That's so no light gets out," she said.

"How come?" asked Freddie.

Ilona turned away. "There's a war on," she said. Her eyes were wet and she snipped another piece of tape.

Hilary ran for one last look out the window, before her mother could seal them all. Everything was ghostly pale. Behind the diving board trailed the vine which had lain limp all day, now blossoming with large white flowers. A sentry in canvas leggings pointed his fixed bayonet at the ocean. She could see his silhouette but not make out his face. Searchlights fingered over the water.

"Okay," said Ilona. "You had your look." She taped the last window shut.

Hilary heard the sounds of the surf as it pounded the beach and the chirping of crickets under their window.

"When will we be able to see outside at night again?" she asked.

"Who knows?" said Ilona. "Anyway, children don't have to see outside at night. Children are supposed to sleep at night."

"Ma," said Hilary, "how come you don't wear lipstick?"

"Lipstick takes time to put on and take off," said Ilona. "You don't just smear it on your mouth. You have to take a pinky and do it right."

"Did you used to wear lipstick and smear it with your pinky?" asked Hilary.

"Only in this country. On the other side nice girls don't wear lipstick and rouge, although once I saw a countess in the town where I lived, I was as close to her as I am to you, and she had mascara on her lashes, each lash just so, top and bottom."

"Tell me more," said Hilary, "about the countess. Did you have to bow to her?"

"I'm scared," said Freddie.

Ilona kissed his forehead. "It's silly to be scared," she said. "Cats are scared. Didn't you ever hear people say, scaredy cat? People aren't scared."

"I am," said Hilary. "I'm scared too."

"You're too big," said Ilona, closing the door behind her.

Hilary waited for the sound of her footsteps to disappear at the end of the hall, then for Freddie to fall asleep. His mouth had slightly opened. Hilary wanted to kiss his cheek where his curly hair, damp from perspiration, lay in tendrils. She decided against it. Instead, she knelt on the bed and carefully peeled the corner of the tape, one little place, less than a thumbnail's breadth, but big enough to see out of.

She stared at the night and the rolling searchlight dappled surf, thinking about Mickey, about how quickly you could get into trouble, how she was too old for some things, and too young for others, and how long it was taking to reach eleven.

When Ilona entered the kitchen through the swinging doors, Frank was sitting on the butcher block, his hands clasped about his knees, telling one of his stories, while two waitresses, Margie and Vicky Sue, who had her arm around his shoulder, leaned over him and smiled. Margie began to laugh even before he came to the punch line. Everyone stiffened except Frank. Vicky Sue dropped her arm.

Ilona tied her apron tighter about her tiny waist and went to check the walk-in icebox. A quick look inside at the smoking blocks of ice confirmed that it had stopped melting. She closed it shut with a decisive slide of the bolt and looked about her as if she were mentally checking a list. The garbage cans had all been emptied and scoured. Marco was hosing down the planking with sudsy water.

"Watch it, missus," he called.

Ilona stepped aside to wait for Frank. She smoothed her hair and took off her apron, then touched her lips. They were dry and cracked. Frank continued to lean back on the butcher block, his deep voice intoning, with perfect timing, the next punch line. Everyone screamed with laughter.

After they closed the kitchen for the night, Ilona walked silently with Frank to their room. It was dark. Sounds of maracas and castanets came from the patio. They switched on the light, their movements casting monstrous images on the sheet. Ilona went behind it to see to the sleeping children. She tucked their bedclothes under their chins, pulling out their hands to rest on the sheet, and pasting back the strip of tape that had come loose.

"They won't be able to sleep together much longer," she said.

"Stop pressuring me."

"It's not a pressure, Frank. It's just something to consider."

"I've considered it. Don't nag."

Ilona sighed. She unpinned her snood and her rich brown hair tumbled out. She brushed it and tied it back with a ribbon.

"I'm thinking of buying lipstick," she said. "What kind do you think I should get?"

"I don't know," replied Frank. "Get what you like."

"It's what you like that counts, Frank. I could get red or pink."

"God, I'm tired."

He lay back in his stockinged feet. Ilona leaned over him and brushed the hair back from his eyes.

"I'm tired, Ilona."

"So am I."

"No, I mean, I'm really tired. I mean, I can't. Not with them so close. I'm sorry. I just can't."

Ilona's eyes became wet for the second time that night. She lay beside him, fitting herself into the curves of his body, swallowing her grief so that the children would not hear. She thought of the little girl on the other side of the sheet and was sorry that she had not kissed her as she had the boy. She must remember that the child could not help it that she looked so much like him.

"Tell you what," he said. "You can massage the back of my neck. Will you do that for me? My head is so tight it feels like it's going to snap off."

Ilona began to knead the back of his neck, easing down the ligaments with her fingers. "Who do you think is prettier," she asked, "Margie, or Vicky Sue?"

"Vicky," he said. "You have to try harder to say the V when you're supposed to."

"What did I say?"

"You said Wicky."

"You didn't answer my question."

"Neither," he said. "They've both been around too much. It begins to show on a woman's face. A man can tell every time if a woman's been around too much."

"What does my face look like?"

He smiled. "Like you haven't been around."

"But I'm a married woman."

"That's not being around."

"What about the Army, Frank? They won't take you, will they?"

"My draft card says 3-A. They don't want me unless Miami's invaded, and don't look like that. The Japs aren't interested in palm trees. They got plenty of their own. They want the kids. Like Lenny."

"Can you imagine anyone wanting Lenny." Her face sobered. "My sister wrote that they sent my uncle's ashes from Dachau and a bill for 150 marks. What do you think is happening? On the other side?"

"They're waiting, just like we are. To see what the big guys are going to do. The little guys like us, we wait. It's the big guys who make all the moves."

"I'll never see them again."

"You'll see them again. Everyone says the war will be over in a few months at the most."

"How can they be so sure?"

"It stands to reason. Look, the Japanese can't fight. They proved that by their sneak attack. They couldn't fight in the open like stand-up guys; they had to do it in secret. It was the only way they could win. And the Germans, there's a whole ocean between us and the Germans." He turned to kiss her cheek. "Don't worry about your mother and Margit, and Dieter. They're okay. Honest, would I lie to you?"

3

In January some of the kids started calling Hilary Dumbo after the baby elephant in the Disney cartoon. It was because of her ears. Rudy started it, and it spread over the school, with the speed of chicken pox. It was hard to pretend that it didn't hurt. Instead of things getting better, as she had expected they would when she drew nearer eleven, things grew worse. Despite the fact that she and Billy Connaught were the only ones who could somersault over the horse, or even that, having beaten Frances Simmons in the run off, she would represent North Beach Elementary in the city spelling finals, it was becoming increasingly apparent that there was something wrong with her. Just about the time that the Dumbo thing started, Shirley Leone mysteriously and without explanation stopped being her best friend.

Hilary sat in assembly, one of a string of daily assemblies, trying to get Shirley's eye, and trying to figure out how friendship changed overnight, one minute yes, one minute no, for no reason. Like the beach. She had gone down that morning before breakfast, the time when the birds probed the seaweed-filled rills for worms and crabs cast up by the tide, and found the sand covered with black tar. There had been no warning, no globs the day before, just suddenly, overnight, the entire beach oozing with pitch and a few unfortunate oil-slicked gulls flopping about on their webbed feet, struggling to free their coated feathers. She finally caught Shirley's eye, but Shirley had turned to Jackie Snyder to whisper something.

Today Mr. Detwiler announced that he was going to talk about rumors. His starched collar made him hold his head up high, forcing him to peer down his nose at the assembly.

"If you know something," he said, "keep it to yourself. If you hear something, stop its circulation with you. Don't pass it on. Even"—his voice dropped—"even if you see a submarine destroyed or captured"—here everyone turned to pop their eyes wide at each other—"keep it to yourself. Let the enemy guess what happened."

Billy Connaught carried out a poster. It showed a beautiful blond woman who looked like Mickey, with upswept hair, lounging on a couch. Behind her stood admiring servicemen.

"Read it, Billy," said Mr. Detwiler, easing his collar with his finger.

"She's not so dumb," said Billy. "A slip of the lip can sink a ship."

"Thank you, Billy," said Mr. Detwiler.

The assembly was over. Everyone filed outside for a demonstration of how to put out an incendiary bomb. A fallen log took the place of the bomb. Mr. Detwiler, tiptoeing about, took great pains to show everyone that he was not going to touch the log, not even allowing his jacket to brush it as that would cause it to explode and destroy an entire city block. Instead, he would render it harmless with a pail of sand. All the kids in the fifth and sixth grades were given a bucketful of sand each, in turn, in order to show that they also knew how to put out an incendiary bomb.

"Here, Dumbo," said Frances Simmons to Hilary. "Your turn."

Hilary lifted the pail and slung its contents in the direction of the log. "I before E," she said to Frances, "except after C."

When everyone had had a turn with the bucket (Sorrell Myers took two), Mr. Detwiler called Hilary to his side and gave her a lecture on the improper use of power. He told of how power corrupts, and a lot of other things she didn't understand, then told her that if she were to become a good crossing guard, one that did not misuse her power, she was helping the war effort because that freed up some policeman who could now chase fifth columnists with a clear mind.

Mr. Detwiler put his hands on her shoulders. "We're counting on you," he said.

Despite the cold snap, the guests lay immobile in the sun, soaking up its warmth like batteries storing electricity. Even if the day had been warmer they wouldn't be swimming. The beach was full of tar and floating in the pool was a purple man-of-war with long dangling tentacles capable of causing excruciatingly painful stings on contact. Lenny was trying to fish it out. No one knew how it had gotten there. It was too large to have gotten in through the filtering system, and while Hilary and Freddie had been prime suspects, it was ascertained that the time it had been thrown in, they were at school. It was a mystery. Mrs. Portman said it must have crawled in from the beach.

Hilary recognized Mickey Biscayne even though Mickey's eyes were covered with cotton pads. Her oil-slicked body shone taut and gleaming, like the coating on a pudding. Mickey lay isolated next to a hibiscus bush, the other women at a distance, the men glancing at her covertly when they thought their wives were not looking, and poking each other with their elbows.

"Hi, Mickey," said Hilary.

"Is that you, kid? Drag a lounge over for yourself."

"There's no more lounges."

"Where's Lenny?" Mickey peeled off the cotton pads with one hand and reached for her bathing-suit straps with the other.

"He's over there, fishing something out of the deep end," said Hilary.

"Sit here then, next to me." Mickey smelled like a coconut. She turned on her stomach and lay her face on the wooden slats. "Tell me what you did today," she said.

The question was seldom asked of Hilary unless part of a specific fact finding, the object of which was to find out who did something bad. Hilary warmed to it. She leaned forward. "Well, we're studying about Australia in geography. They have Stone Age people there, just like thousands of years ago."

"I don't think anybody knows about what happened thousands of years ago," said Mickey. "Ask someone what they had for supper last week, you see how silly the whole thing is." She looked bored. Hilary discarded the soft goods for the hard stuff.

"They don't just have aborigines, they have a lot of other

things in Australia," said Hilary, "they have koala bears and a duckbilled platypus. It's oviparous."

Mickey poured witch hazel onto her eye pads. "That's nice," she said.

"What are you doing that for?"asked Hilary.

"To make my eyes shine. It's one of my beauty tricks."

Hilary watched her press the excess moisture from the pads. "What happens when people have big ears? Is there a trick for that?"

"You mean nosy people?" asked Mickey.

"No, I mean big. Like funny."

"Well, if they're a woman, they cut their hair and wear it over their ears, and if they're a man, well, look at Clark Gable."

"What if they can't cut their hair?" asked Hilary. "Then what?"

"Who."

"People."

"Then," said Mickey, snapping off a hibiscus and tucking it behind Hilary's ear, "they tuck a flower behind their ear. That way people notice only the flower."

A woodpecker bobbed on a nearby palm. It looked like a toy of Freddie's that you put in a dish of water.

"Lady Esther sent me a free sample of powder," said Hilary, trying not to smile. She hoped the flower would stay.

"You must have a flame if you're interested in powder."

"You mean boys? I don't like boys."

"You'll change your mind."

"No I won't."

Mickey laughed. "That's what everyone says. You'll see." She leaned on her elbow. "I'm beginning to roast. Do you think your mother will let you go to a movie with me?"

"Sure," said Hilary.

"Better find out," said Mickey, "before you say sure."

Hilary ran to the kitchen, grabbing a toothpick from the cashier that she tried to wedge between her front teeth. Ilona was near the bakery, reading a letter aloud to Gus, who was shoveling loaves of rye bread onto a tray.

Ilona's face was flushed, her brown eyes sparkling. When she saw Hilary, she waved the onionskin. "This is from England," she said, "from a stranger, someone I have never met, someone who has seen your aunt Margit and your grandmother, and your cousin Dieter. They are in Denmark. Where is your father? I want to tell him."

"I haven't seen him," said Hilary. "How did they get to Denmark?"

"He says they took a taxicab to Holland. He doesn't say how they got from Holland to Denmark. But they are all right. Some family has taken them in. Some wonderful family with a good heart and a spare room. I can't read this all, some of it is torn, my mother has pains in her side"—Ilona frowned—"but Margit thinks it is just fright and grief. Over my uncle." She folded the letter. "They're alive."

"I always liked the Danes," said Gus.

"When can they come?" asked Hilary.

Ilona sighed. "They can't come. They can't get out of Denmark. People can't just leave Europe. It isn't like going from Florida to Georgia. They have to have exit visas, and entry permits, and papers, and even if they get them, no one can travel anywhere. Borders are closed and ships shoot other ships. I thought you understood that. How come you're so smart in some things and so stupid in others?"

Even her mother was beginning to notice. Hilary shifted her weight to her other foot. "Ma, can I go to the movies?"

Ilona looked disgusted with her. "Go to the movies, but take Freddie."

"Why? This isn't a picture for Freddie."

"If it isn't a picture for Freddie, it isn't a picture for you, and don't do that to your teeth. You'll separate them."

Hilary found Freddie holding a garbage can which came to his chest while Lenny shoveled strips of beach and dumped them into the can.

"We're going to the movies with Mickey," she said, "and we're not going to say anything about it."

"That's lying," said Freddie.

"No it's not. We're not going to say we're *not* going with Mickey. We just don't say we *are* going with her. Do you want to come or not?"

Freddie set the can upright. "I'll help you later," he said to Lenny who pursed his lips with the resignation of a factotum and continued to shovel the beach.

They were in time for the four o'clock show, a time of day when the theater was filled with schoolchildren, tired pairs of women shoppers, and a few stray, isolated males scattered here and there like buckshot.

On the way in, Hilary looked to see who was looking at them, or more correctly, who was looking at Mickey. It was like being with a movie star. They were given popcorn with extra butter, and the usher flashlighted them all the way to their seats.

The picture was called *Claudia*. It was a story of a childlike bride who bravely pretended to her mother that she does not know the truth about her mother's coming death.

"Why is it so secret?" asked Hilary.

"You just don't talk about dying, that's all."

"They talk about it in the paper," said Hilary. "Lots of soldiers and sailors have died. Hundreds."

"That's different. That's war. You don't say it about civilians."

"What do you say?"

"You say they went to heaven, or that they passed on."

Freddie spilled his popcorn. Mickey gave him money for another box and he went to get it, crawling over the legs of a group of boys who were throwing Jujubes into the next row.

"Why does David say she's his child?" asked Hilary. "She's his wife."

"That's because men think of their wives as little girls. They like it like that. See, even if a woman's smart, if she acts like a little girl, she gets anything she wants. It's all in knowing how."

"Like me, you mean?"

"Not exactly," said Mickey.

Everything went smoothly. Freddie didn't say anything about Mickey, although he could not look Ilona in the eye. Hilary felt a little guilty but not very. It was the kind of guilt that one could easily chase away with a solid, well-thought-out justification. Ilona stood by the sinks instructing a new dishwasher that glasses were to be drained dry and did not have to be toweled.

"Ma," said Hilary, "if you were dying, would you want me to know you knew I knew?"

The issue was academic. Ilona's death was unthinkable, as was her own death, both as remote as a duckbilled platypus.

"How can you ask such a thing?"

"Don't get mad," said Hilary.

"I'm not mad. I just don't understand where you get these questions from. Why do you always ask what I can't answer?"

She undid the end of one of Hilary's braids, replaited it, and slipped back the rubber band. "I liked it better when you asked me why the sky was blue."

"Your answer was wrong," said Hilary. "I found out later in science. It's refraction of color bands."

"It sounded right when I said it," said Ilona. "It satisfied you. What did I tell you anyway? I forgot."

"You said God painted the sky with a big brush."

"What do I know about skies?" Ilona had a faraway look.

"Are you thinking of Denmark?"

"I'm thinking you have to go someplace else. We have special things to get ready for. I don't want you making me any crazier than I'm going to be."

The night was chilly and everyone sat around the patio in sweaters talking about Joe Louis who knocked out Max Baer in the first round in Madison Square Garden, then turned around and enlisted in the Army. Hilary, Freddie, Frank, and Mel, who was wearing the insignia of a block warden, were sitting on the edge of the patio at an umbrella table with the umbrella folded for the night. The patio lights had been screened, but the moon was bright enough to cast a gleam upon everything, including the ghostly pale blossoms of the moonvine.

In addition to Mel's job of bookmaking, he had volunteered to prepare people for air raids, encourage them to keep windows on the ocean side of the hotel sealed with tape, dim patio lights, paint the bottom half of their headlights, salvage what they could, conserve what they had, and not hoard. He took his job seriously.

He was telling Frank that he should save fat to make bullets, and that even though he would get a monthly allotment, it was his duty to start conserving sugar. "They're also talking of rationing meat," he said.

"Never happen," said Frank. "The people will never go for it. One thing America is used to is steak and chops. We're a land of steak and chops.

"You hear anything about tires, Mel? I can't get any," said Frank. "One of my tires is bald and the spare is just as bad. One service station told me he could make new grooves, and everywhere I went, they all wanted to patch it, but there's not a tire in the whole town. I even went over to Miami, drove all the way to Ojus, no tires. The only way to get new tires is to get a new car."

"I didn't hear anything about tires," said Mel, "but it stands to reason. They need rubber for tanks and gas masks, and a whole lot of things." He turned to the children. Hilary was examining a scab on her knee, deciding whether or not to peel it off.

"You kids can do your bit too, you know, save rubber bands and make a ball out of it, tie paper in bales, collect tin cans, coat hangers, tinfoil, you know, from chewing gum and cigarettes, any kind of scrap, save all that stuff and take it down to the salvage center."

"They're having a contest at school for the class who buys the most war bonds," said Hilary. "I have four stamps pasted on the front page of my book. In six months, counting tips for payoffs and collections, minus movies and comics, I'll have enough stamps to fill it."

"I don't like her running your collections," said Frank. "Payoffs, okay, but not collections. People can get nasty."

"What's going on in there?" asked Mel, pointing to the dining room with its drawn blinds.

"The big shots are having a meeting," said Frank. "Every hotel man on the beach."

"What's up?"

"I can't talk about it."

"Sounds serious. Got any action for me tomorrow?"

Frank reached into his pocket and took out a bill. "Here's ten across the board. Hasty Bananas in the fifth." Mel pocketed the bill. "Give my regards to Ilona." He climbed the stairs to the roof to talk to the plane spotter who stood with binoculars looking for enemy aircraft.

"I gotta go inside," said Frank. "You kids get to bed. What's that hanging on your ear?"

"A flower," said Hilary.

"I almost swatted it. I didn't know what the hell it was. Where'd you get that idea anyway, it looks like something Gomez would do."

"Mickey gave it to me."

"I don't want you hanging around with Mickey. For one thing, she's too old for you. For another, she's a kept woman. She's not someone I want you to run around with."

"What's a kept woman?" She pulled the scab all the way off her knee. Her knee began to bleed.

"Mr. Radner keeps her. She's his mistress. Never mind. She's bad."

"Is Mr. Radner bad too, then?"

"No, it's different for men."

Sol Radner was a self-made man. His advice to everyone was that he pulled himself up by his jockstrap and he expected everyone else to do the same. He asked no favors, nor did he grant them. But he was a fair man. If he got, he gave. Given this unencumbered philosophy, life for him was simple.

He had seen Mickey Biscayne one night in the Pago Pago, and asked her to his table. She said she couldn't do that. He said what about his hotel room? That she said she could do. He found out that she had four major qualifications. She was young, she was beautiful, she was clean, and she was appreciative. It was no wonder that he asked her if she wanted to live more or less on a permanent basis in the hotel room with him. He would be gone from time to time, to make sure his brother-in-law wasn't stealing him blind in the family business in Philadelphia, to keep his wife happy, and to make the kind of side deals one could only make in person. In the meantime, she could move in. She would no longer have to work at the Pago Pago, and she could have all the spending money, within reason, that she needed. In exchange, she would be available upon his return, which was more or less hit-or-miss, since he was never sure when he could squeeze four or five unaccountable days together.

Mickey, for her part, did not have a bad deal. Work at the Pago Pago was hard. They danced from nine in the evening until three in the morning, often arduous routines that kept them in rehearsal four hours every day, and left them after each performance, alternately sweating and shivering back stage. And while she was waiting to be discovered, as Lana Turner and a few others had been, the reality was that she had been dancing for four years and no one had ever singled her out of the line. As a dancer, she was one of the worst, as a looker, she was somewhere in the middle, and other than the trumpet player who waggled his horn at her nightly, she was just one of many pretty women, not particularly distinguishable except for a mole on her shoulder that Mr. Radner said she should have looked at by a doctor.

Mickey was unprepared to do anything else. She had not gone to secretarial school, and ever since her mother had been sick, growing wan and marasmic from some unnamed ailment that caused her to smell like chocolate and show every bone in her wrist, Mickey had never wanted to be a nurse. The only thing left to be was a stewardess, impossible since her vision was not twenty-twenty, or a receptionist, which paid less than dancing, and worse, which had working hours during sun time, her favorite time of the day.

Her greatest qualification was that she was sweet. She figured that she'd better trade on that while she could. Mr. Radner, from all the evidence, looked like a man who could pay well for geniality.

Mickey thought about a husband and children, but she did not associate homemaking with Mr. Radner. That was someday, a little later, when she was ready to pack it all in, with some nice sweet guy like her father, who maybe owned a filling station, not like the truck driver she had married when she was sixteen who spent his nights oiling his gun collection until he left, as he put it, to tend to business, and was never heard from again. Next time, when she was ready, she would find a little house somewhere with some guy who would help her stake tomatoes in the backyard, and take her out to dinner Saturday night, and then, when she was really over the hill, thirty-three or so, have a few kids.

They had just made love. Being forty-seven, Mr. Radner was not too demanding, except for a request for a testimonial from time to time and some rather routine sexual activities that left her with his black curly chest hairs all over her body. Mickey was in the bathroom, as she put it, "fixing herself."

Mr. Radner called in. "I got a question for you. What do you spend so much time with that kid for?" he asked. "Every time I look outside, whenever I come back from the track, there she is."

"You mean Hilary?"

"How the hell should I know her name? I mean the skinny kid with the braids and the big ears."

"Don't say that, Sol. Don't say she has big ears."

"Why not? It's the truth. She can't hear me. You're not answering my question."

Mickey came out of the bathroom wearing a slip. Her makeup had been freshly applied, as Mr. Radner had told her he liked women to look as though they just stepped out of a bandbox. "I don't know. I like her. She's someone to talk to."

"Why are you holding your eyes wide open like that?" he asked.

"My mascara is drying," she said.

"You don't have people to talk to? The cabanas are full of people. Plenty of nice, sociable women."

"I try, Sol."

"Maybe you don't try hard enough. Ask them questions, ask them where they come from, ask them how they like the weather, ask them to go shopping with you. I treat you right, you can always go shopping." He came behind her and put his hands on her breasts as if he were feeling fruit. "Don't I?"

"What, Sol?"

"Treat you right?"

It was a cue. Mickey did not miss it. She allowed her eyes to roll about in her head as if she were becoming frenzied, accelerated her breathing, and rubbed against him. "You know it, baby," she said.

He opened the blind with one hand and peeked out. "I wonder what's going on over there. They got the place closed off."

"I don't know. You want to get dressed and go out? We could go to the Brook Club. I was real lucky at roulette last time."

"You sappy broad," he said, "they were using you for a shill. You dressed up the table is all. The dealer could've spun you out any time he wanted. Forget the Brook Club. I'd rather go for a corned beef sandwich. There's a new place gives you all the pickles and cole slaw you want."

Mickey put on a peasant skirt and blouse. She wondered what they were doing at the Pago Pago. "How long will you be gone this time?"

"I just got here. Now you want to know when I'm leaving? Why? What's on your mind?"

"Nothing, baby. I just like to know."

Mr. Radner tucked his shirt into his pants. "Two, three weeks. I have to see to my business, and then I have to register at the draft board."

"Don't take this the wrong way," said Mickey, "but aren't you kind of old? I mean, to be drafted?"

"Every man up to the age of sixty-four has to register. If you read something more than the comics you'd know, same as me. That puts me smack in the middle. They'll never take me, though, if that's what you're worried about. I have a trick knee."

Frank and the second cook had outdone themselves. Pompano en papillote for 150—150 perfectly browned steaming paper bags on every plate—had been presented like favors to the hotel owners of Miami Beach, who sat in the closed-off dining room, leaning back in a haze of smoke, discussing Joe Louis, the best season they ever had, and the rumor.

The rumor was that the Army Air Corps wanted the hotels of Miami Beach for barracks. It was, of course, unthinkable.

Mr. Davis, who had a calming influence, was addressing the group. Dressed in a jacket befitting the occasion, he stood with folded arms, trying to remember not to bend his head as he did when he was thinking.

"There's nothing to worry about as I see it, gentlemen, and I have Major McDermott's assurances, a fine man, first rate, they don't make them any better, they only want a few hotels, a handful. They're willing to pay, they don't want them for nothing, and so no one's going to get hurt."

"Why do they have to come here?" asked Mr. Franklin, whose hotel was one of the newest. "The tourists aren't going to like seeing all that marching and whatever else they're going to do. It reminds them of what they came here to forget. Now they have to see it where they take their vacation."

"And," shouted Mr. Fullman, "if I may have the floor, let's not forget about the fair sex. What are we talking about here? We're talking about soldiers. The women will not feel safe, not with all those women-hungry men around, you know how men are in wartime."

"My kid is in the service," said Mr. Ornstein. "I don't think your attitude is very patriotic."

"No one can accuse me of being unpatriotic," said Mr. Fullman. "My help has the silverware arranged in a V, for God's sakes, at every meal, so don't accuse me of not being 100 percent for the war effort. I go on record."

"We have no secretary today," said Mr. Davis.

"I go on record in a way of speaking."

"It's a free country," shouted another. "They can't make us do it. It's in the Constitution. The Bill of Rights says it very clear. Nobody has to quarter soldiers."

"That's in your home," said Mr. Davis. "That only applies to the place where you live. Not where you earn your living, a commercial enterprise like a hotel. That's an entirely different matter. Now, Mr. Lonzo, who many of you know, has come here to say a few words."

Mr. Lonzo, a stocky, dapper man in a pinstriped suit, nodded, then walked to the podium. A retired gangster who had gone legit, he was connected somehow to Mr. Davis, who was in his debt, since it was he who gave Mr. Davis the cash he had needed to buy the hotel. It was said that Mr. Lonzo was a powerful man, that even when he was in the penitentiary, many years before, men waited in line to see him.

He was flanked by two janissaries in navy blazers (one with French cuffs halfway to his elbow), who dropped away at the last moment like a sea wake to take posts against the wall. "Everyone take it easy," he said. "Stay calm. Everything will be all right. We let them take a few hotels. Cooperate. Show that we're patriotic. A gesture. Finish."

"But which one of us?" asked another. "Who's going to have to give up his hotel?"

"There's no way to know," said Mr. Lonzo. "The main thing is stay calm."

"We'll be an army camp. Drunken soldiers in the streets, running after the women."

"I got it on good authority that we don't have to worry about that score. I got it on good authority that they're giving them saltpeter, and as far as what they ask, everybody has to change a little. Go with the times. Pitch in. I got a friend, used to make bedspreads. He makes mosquito netting. I know another guy used to bottle soft drinks, now his people are loading shells with explosives, and you all know Phil Cott, his citrus cannery is making parts for merchant ships. So, the point is, we do our bit."

Mr. Lonzo stepped off the podium and the two men pushed themselves off the wall to draw alongside him.

"Who asked him," asked one of the hotel men after Mr. Lonzo had left. "I don't remember anyone asking him to speak."

"Mr. Lonzo is an important man," said Mr. Davis. "He has good counsel to give us."

4

Hilary felt a vibration, like humming in her bones. It was as if someone were shaking her mattress. She had felt it all night long. It was like the time they came to Miami on the Orange Blossom Special, riding for two days on the train sitting in a coach on reclining seats that faced in both directions, and eating meals in a dining car with immaculate white tablecloths where you printed your own order on the check.

The vibration was monotonous and soothing and she would not have woken except for the blasts coming from offshore. Freddie was still sleeping. Ilona and Frank talked in muffled tones behind the sheets.

"I don't know," said Frank, "maybe a backfire."

"It's too strong," said Ilona. "You know it's too strong. Oh, God, they can't be coming here."

"No one's coming here," he murmured. "They don't want Miami. They have other targets that are much more important, like the navy yard in Philadelphia, for instance, where my old man works, or the oil refineries in New Jersey. We got nothing they want."

"Don't you worry about your father?" she asked.

"No. If I know my old man, he'll be tanked up in some bar."

"I worry about the children. They're so young." She began to cry.

"Listen, no one's touching you and no one's touching them. You believe me?"

"I want to. I wanted to believe you before."

"That was before. You said you wouldn't bring that up again." His voice had an edge.

Hilary knew they were talking about the time Frank left carrying his suitcase and a box of his racing forms, and Ilona cried for weeks. Don't make him mad again, thought Hilary, please don't make him mad and make him pack up and leave and send me and Freddie to St. Augustine so you can find him.

"Well," he said, "what's it going to be?"

"All right."

"Well then, trust me. If I have to, I'll take you and the kids to Key West, and we'll take a fishing boat to Cuba."

"How can we get to Key West when you put the car on blocks?"

Frank remembered that the Reo, with two bald tires and no new tires to be found anywhere, was resting on cement blocks on the side street next to the hotel, for the duration, he had said, as everyone was saying when they made any sacrifice relating to the growing shortages. No one knew how long that meant, but the implication was that it was a finite time, something that would end, and when it did, successfully.

"We don't need a car. Marco's got a little boat. He'll take us to Key West."

"I heard them say on the radio that the war can last fifteen years if Sumatra is lost. Why? What is so special about Sumatra?"

"Oil, or rubber, something like that," said Frank.

"It's not getting any better, Frank. It's getting worse. Kaltenborn says the RAF is losing in the English Channel. I read that the Japs are committing suicide, but if things are so bad for them why do they say that if a tiny country is lost, the war could last for fifteen years? My mother is sixty. She may not live fifteen years."

Hilary wanted to speak, to push through the sheet and get into the shelter of their murmuring, but she did not. She waited for another blast. It never came, but morning did. She started to shiver, which was strange, because it was warm.

The sunlight at first only glowed through the blinds. Hilary dressed quickly and ran onto the dew-dampened beach, chasing gulls and terns ahead of her, and sending crabs to scuttle into the safety of their holes. One lone osprey building a nest of seaweed high on a palm remained unperturbed. On the horizon, over the softly rolling viridian waves, was a great towering column of smoke, climbing into the sky like a ladder.

Freddie ran behind her, skidding to a stop in the wet sand. "I knew you were here," he said.

A coastguardsman, one of a long string of sentries posted a hundred yards apart, stood looking out to sea. Hilary stared out to sea beside him, thinking that in fifteen years she would be twenty-five, older than Mickey was now, almost as old as Ilona. The column of smoke spewed and spiraled in the sky.

"Look at that," said Freddie. "I hope it comes here. It'll make everything black. Like night."

Hilary clutched his hand. He tried to pull away but she held it firmly.

"You're Jews, aren't you?" asked the coastguardsman.

Hilary turned to look at him. His blue eyes were frosted with pale blond lashes. "My mother is," she said.

"That makes you a Jew too," said the sailor, who had been told that the inhabitants of Miami Beach were Hebrews. "Let's see your heads."

Freddie donated his head to the inspecting hands of the sailor, who had stuck his bayonet in the sand. "What are you looking for?"

"Horns. But you don't have 'em yet. Must be you're too little."

Freddie put his hand on his head. "I don't feel any."

Hilary didn't like the sailor's hands on her brother's head. She yanked Freddie away out of his reach. "Don't touch his head again," she said. "Come on."

Hilary found Frank standing on the wooden decking of the kitchen with Winona at his side holding out a little paper bag into which he poured sugar.

"It isn't that I don't have the coupons," said Winona. "It's just that I never get to the store in time. When I do get there, they're sold out."

"Take it," said Frank. "We have plenty."

"I wouldn't bother you except I'm making Lionel a cake. We're giving him a little party."

"Is it his birthday?" asked Freddie.

"My boy Lionel got drafted, baby," she said.

"Maybe Lionel will be a guard on the beach."

"Colored and white don't mix in the Army," said Winona, "just like they don't mix in the bus, and all I ever seen on the beach is white boys. I thank you for the sugar." She turned to Hilary. "You look like someone's inside of you with a knife and fork."

"I have to see my father," said Hilary.

"Sounds like family talk to me," said Winona. She left clutching her bag of sugar.

Frank bent to check the pilot light, then stood and kicked the range.

"What are we?" demanded Hilary.

"Wait a minute," he said. The jets flared. "Okay. What is it?"

"What are we?"

"What kind of question is that?"

"Are we Jewish? Things are exploding in the ocean. We want to know."

The question had come up before, when his father told him that if he persisted in marrying his immigrant Jew his children would be mongrels. That was the last time the issue had arisen. It was also the last time he saw his mother or father except when he went to the shipyard to ask his father to lend him money.

Frank stood and wiped his hands on his apron. "Well, your mother is Jewish," he said. "I'm not."

"What are you?" asked Hilary.

"I used to be a Catholic. I'm not anymore. Your mother thinks the Scotch are one of the lost tribes of Israel, and since my mother is Scotch, I guess that makes me half-Jewish, like you."

"Which half of us is Jewish?" asked Freddie.

"He doesn't mean your body," said Hilary. "It's a concept. Well, what are you if you used to be Catholic and now you're not?"

"A not-Catholic."

"Is Ma not Jewish?"

"No, she's still Jewish."

"I don't understand."

"It has to do with sacraments," said Frank, "and other stuff like that. You can't be a Catholic if you don't do things right. The Jews aren't too particular about stuff like that. Your mother doesn't have to do anything and she's still Jewish. I could never explain it to you."

"But what does that make me and Freddie?"

The children will be half-breeds, said his father, *not here, not there, and you will have thrown your life away on someone who was not even born here.* The rebuttal in which Frank placed in evidence the fact that three of his grandparents had not been born in America either bore no weight.

"Why do you have to be anything?" asked Frank.

"People ask you what you are."

"What people?"

"The guy on the beach," said Freddie. "He wanted to feel my horns."

"Did he touch you?" asked Frank.

"He felt his head all over," said Hilary.

Frank pulled off his apron. "Son of a bitch!" He ran out of the kitchen, slamming the screen door behind him.

Frank's response did not assure Hilary. Rather it made her feel more unsettled, like Jell-O that had not molded, shapeless, without definition, vulnerable in her formlessness. If others did not know what and who she was, she surely did not. It was another difficult thing to add to bombing in the night, big ears, a war that could last until she was an old lady, friends who for no reason suddenly disliked her, loyal friends she was forbidden to have, and parents whose relationship was tenuous. No one told her that growing up was going to be so hard. A sudden flash of hot tears washed her eyes and choked her in the back of her throat.

They felt the vibrations again. Rows of glasses stacked in draining crates and silverware lying loose in aluminum pans began to rattle and clink.

"I'm scared," said Freddie. He began to tremble.

Gus put down his rolling pin. "I show you how to make a plane," he said. Gus took a grease pencil and peeled away a strip of string, revealing a black tip, then he unrolled brown paper used to drain shortening from croissants and placed it on his cooling shelf, brushing away excess flour with his naked arm.

"We're going to make a Messerschmitt," he said. "I show you how. First you make a cigar like your father smokes, like so, you put the wings, here, and the tail, here, then you make a flap over the tail. I forgot what they call it. Now you make the place where the pilot sits, so, the black cross here, and the swastika here. You try it."

Freddie clutched the grease pencil and copied the Messerschmitt while Gus rolled his strudel dough thinner and thinner until it became transparent. Hilary watched as the spreading dough threatened to cover the entire table, and thought it must surely tear before it could do so.

"Don't forget the wheels," called Gus. "You can't make a Messerschmitt without wheels."

Freddie finished his plane. It had no wheels. He went on to the next.

Gus shook his head. "Your brother doesn't listen," he said. "You can't learn anything when you don't listen."

5

Miss Wallace was passing out servicemen. You got one by sticking your hand in a World War I helmet, a souvenir of the teacher's father, and picking a piece of folded paper with the name and address of a pen pal in the service. The idea was that the fighting man who ordinarily did not get much mail was assured of something, if only a letter from a schoolchild he never met, who knew how to write in cursive script. It was a question of morale, and the patriotic thing to do, and Hilary waited her turn while Billy Connaught walked between the aisles with the helmet. Some people seemed very pleased with their names, especially Liz Bonnier, who drew a major, and Sorrell Myers, who got a paratrooper. Most people, however, drew enlisted men with no extraordinary military occupation. It seemed most officers and paratroopers had plenty of people to write to them and did not need pen pals.

When it was Hilary's turn, she closed her eyes tight, in her experience, a more fortuitous way to deal with chance, since a blind pick involved a limited personal responsibility in which one could never blame oneself for a poor choice. She plunged her fist into the helmet hoping she would draw someone who cracked codes.

"Be careful," said Billy. "You're knocking all the papers out."

"Then hold it tighter," she replied. "I have to do this in a certain way. I don't want to get the wrong one."

Billy Connaught sighed. "Hilary, will you stop being such a creep and just pick?"

Hilary plucked a folded piece of paper out of the helmet and opened it up. It read Private First Class Sylvan Farber and gave his address as Fort Meade, Georgia.

"What should we write to our pen pals?" asked Jackie Snyder. "I don't know what to say to mine."

Miss Wallace told them to write about themselves and include what they were doing to help the war effort. "Don't say anything unpleasant," she added. "Remember, they are far away from home and lonely. They need to be cheered up. Not down."

Hilary thought about cheering someone down, then began to make a list about things she could say in her letter. She concluded that, unembellished, there was not much to tell and so she decided to invent.

"Dear Mr. Farber," she wrote, scratching this out to write, "Dear Private First Class Mr. Farber, I am twenty-two years old and have blond hair. My sister got your name from her teacher and she is only ten years old. I am not ten. I am twenty-two. I like to swim in the ocean and make drip castles. If you hold your hand steady you can make a pretty good drip. The trick is to do it slowly. My brother and I have a ball of string eighty feet long. I know this because my father measured it. I also like to read Captain Midnight. Tell me what your favorite book is to read. Yours very truly, Miss Hilary MacIntyre."

When she was satisfied that her letter looked right, she copied it upon a sheet of V-mail, a tissue-thin piece of paper that folded to become its own envelope and from which a photostat would be made to save valuable cargo space that would be taken up with ordinary mail.

Hilary was among the first to finish. She decided to spend the time memorizing her poem. It was by Rudyard Kipling and it talked about how to be a man. "If you can keep your head when all about you are losing theirs"—she peeked inside her book and closed it—"and blaming it on you."

"Silently," said Miss Wallace. "Memorize your poem to yourself."

When the scent from the warmed oleander bushes had sifted through the screens and the monitors began to wash the blackboards, Miss Wallace clapped her hands. "Put your servicemen away," she said. "We're going to learn the new way to salute the flag."

Hilary sat on the steps of the third-grade shack waiting for Freddie, plucking blades of St. Augustine grass which she curled into whistles, and watching Shirley Leone and Jackie Snyder walk with their arms around each other in the manner of best friends.

Freddie did not come out, even after Miss Carmichael began to close the awnings. A lizard almost the color of the grass darted through Hilary's fingers and raced for the large curving roots of the banyan tree which clutched the ground like claws. Hilary chased the lizard to the tree, watching the pouch in his neck swell and turn red, then reached for the smooth, paper-thin bark over which it had made its saurian skitter, and began to peel it in strips.

Rudy ran back into the shack to get his pencil case. More or less a permanent resident since his mother decided they would live in Miami Beach for the duration, he swaggered like a native, even adopting, as did some children newly arrived from the North, a southern accent of sorts.

"Y'all's brother is in trouble for drawing German planes on the blackboard with swastikas. Miss Carmichael called the principal and he took him to his office."

"You better be telling the truth," said Hilary. "If I get over there and find you made this up, you're gonna get it right in y'all's face."

Hilary ran to the principal's office, remembering to pull up her socks as she entered. Miss Wackenhut, the office clerk, peered over her desk. "Walk, don't run," she said.

"Is my brother here?"

Miss Wackenhut paused as if she were making change and wanted to be sure she didn't cheat herself. "Yes, he is with Mr. Detwiler."

"What's the matter?" asked Hilary. "Why did he have to see Mr. Detwiler?"

"I'm not at liberty to say at this moment."

"Can I go in?"

"*May* I go in. No. You may wait here for your brother." Miss Wackenhut turned to make copies of an announcement, pressing sheets of paper, one at a time, onto a pan full of dark blue gelatin.

"My brother gets scared easy," said Hilary. "I want to go in with him."

Miss Wackenhut did not reply, but continued to press the papers onto the gelatin, gingerly lifting them by their corners when the transfer had been made.

Ace-card time. "Sometimes he makes in his pants when he gets really scared."

Miss Wackenhut pursed her lips as if screwing shut a jar, then turned on her heel and went into Mr. Detwiler's office. She returned within moments. Without looking at Hilary, she went back to her gelatin.

"Mr. Detwiler says you may go in."

Mr. Detwiler sat behind his desk making a tent out of his fingers. A man in a glen plaid suit stood behind him holding some papers. The man was immediately marked as a stranger, since Hilary had never seen anyone wearing a suit in Miami Beach, except for Mr. Lonzo, and his had been navy, not plaid.

"This is his sister," said Mr. Detwiler.

Freddie sat dwarfed in a chair, his face tearstained, his hands folded in his lap. Hilary grabbed the seat next to him and sat beside him, flicking off pieces of grass from his sneakers. He knocked her hand away.

"Perhaps she can shed a little light on this matter."

The man in the plaid suit looked over his papers at Hilary. "Your brother tells me that he learned to draw planes from a German named Gus. He said Gus is a baker and that he doesn't know his last name or where he lives."

As far as Hilary was concerned, Gus lived in the bakery. The idea that he had a separate life from his rolls and strudel had never occurred to her. It was very clear that Mr. Detwiler and this man were angry and frightened about something.

"Do you know his last name, young lady?"

"I don't know," said Hilary. "But my father would know. Gus works with my father."

"How long have you known him?"

All her life, it seemed. "A long time," said Hilary.

"Does this Gus person go off at night, does he leave for periods of time?"

"Sometimes he takes a bottle of beer into the lifeguard shack," said Freddie.

"Does he go away and no one knows where he has been?" asked Mr. Detwiler.

"I don't know," said Hilary. "But I don't think so. He has to bake. Why do you want to know about Gus?"

"There's a war on, young lady, we cannot be too careful. The problem with a democracy such as ours is that there are a lot of people walking around who shouldn't be. Potential saboteurs, people who could poison the water you drink, or blow up our electric plants, foreign agents, spies. You see, Americans, patriotic citizens don't draw swastikas. Now, your brother here, is a little boy, but he reflects the sympathies of another. It is clear in this case he reflects the sympathies of this Gus person. Can you give me a description?"

"He wears an undershirt," said Freddie, "and he has whiskers on his face."

"How old is he?"

The question of age applied to any adult was abstruse. Gus could have been thirty, forty, fifty, or sixty. There was no way to tell.

"I don't know," said Hilary. "He's old."

"How old? Is he as old as me?"

Hilary judged the gray-haired man before her. "No."

"He is younger than me?"

She nodded.

"Is he younger than your principal, Mr. Detwiler?"

He was not younger, he was hairier. Hilary decided not to give that information.

"I don't know," she said.

"You like this Gus person, Freddie?"

"Yes," said Freddie.

"And you wouldn't want to say anything that would hurt him?"

The question was one of those that you could fall into, like a pit. "Can we go now?" asked Hilary. "My mother will worry about us."

The agent nodded to Mr. Detwiler.

"That will be all," said Mr. Detwiler. "You may leave. But you are not to speak of this to Gus."

When Hilary and Freddie left the building, the stragglers on the sidewalk who had been kept in after school or who were not in a hurry to get home, shouted after Freddie. "You had to see the principal," in a monotonous, wailing singsong.

Their taunts did not seem to bother him, but Hilary wheeled and shook her clenched fist. "You better quit it," she shouted. "You'll be sorry if I decide to cross the street and get ahold of you."

Whether they heeded her admonition or not depended on what grade they were in.

Hilary and Freddie crossed the footbridge over Indian Creek. Before them lay Collins Avenue, lined with hotels standing smartly at attention, and beyond that by one short block, the beach, where the ocean was trilling neat little even rows of waves.

"Should we tell him?" asked Hilary.

"The man said not to tell," said Freddie.

"I think maybe we should tell him."

"Why?" asked Freddie.

"I don't know. I guess it's because it's about him. If people talked about me, I'd want to know what they were saying."

"I think we should tell Ma," said Freddie.

"No, Ma would get mad at him. If we don't tell him, we shouldn't tell her or Daddy either."

Freddie was satisfied. "What do you want to play?" he asked. "You want to do stuffing? I got a lot of papers."

"Not today," she said.

"You never want to play with me anymore." He kicked the stanchion with his toe.

"That's not true. Didn't we build a drip castle last week?"

"Yeah, but it washed away."

"Your sneaker is untied," she said.

"Leave it alone. I know how to tie my own shoes. I like it that way."

When they reached the familiar pagoda-shaped roof of their driveway, they noticed that all the guests in the Lord Feldman next door were leaving, streaming out the front door, most of them carrying their own luggage. They seemed very angry. One lady, who had booked a fourteen-day all-expenses-paid vacation for eighty-nine dollars and fifty cents, swung her makeup case at the manager who stood in the doorway with clasped hands.

"You could at least have given us some notice," yelled one of the men.

"I didn't know," said the beleaguered manager. "Believe me, I was just as much in the dark as you."

A flock of northbound robins, stopping after their flight across the Gulf of Mexico to feed on the berries of a holly bush next to the front entrance, fluttered from their perches with each departing guest while soldiers carried mirrors and furniture through the receiving dock to waiting trucks.

Freddie and Hilary would have stayed to watch, except that Freddie saw Mack inside the lobby, trim and handsome in his navy uniform, posturing in tight trousers and jumper that fit his spare body nicely. He had never looked better and he knew it.

Mr. Samuelson was shaking his hand. "After what happened to the *Normandie,*" he said, clucking his tongue, "you might have to go in the Army."

"Why?" asked Mack. He turned to ruffle Freddie's hair. "Hey, buddy."

"No ships," said Mr. Samuelson. "You need ships to be in the Navy. I don't know what this country is coming to when ships can be sabotaged right in a New York dock. A big loss for us, I'll tell you that." He held onto Mack's hand and would not let it go. "A liner big enough to carry a whole division, fifteen thousand men at one time, laying on its side with its funnels submerged. You tell me how a ship like that catches fire."

Mack yanked his hand free. "It beats me, Mr. Samuelson."

"Why do you tell him that for?" asked Mrs. Portman. "Don't fill his head with problems. He's going to fight for us."

"I have it on good authority," said Mr. Samuelson, who had now lowered his voice, "that there are enemy agents with instructions to sink every one of our ships. They're doing a good job so far. You got to admit that."

Mrs. Portman, smaller than Mack, reached up and kissed him on his cheek. "Has your mother seen you?" she asked.

"My mother died," said Mack, "a few years ago."

"Then you write to me," she said. "Just like I was your mother. I got my own son in the service, in the Marine Corps, and I know what it's like. You write to me, I'll send you socks and cakes, like I send to him, you'll see. His name is Elliott. If you ever meet him."

"Thank you, Mrs. Portman," said Mack. "If I ever meet Elliott, I'll say hello."

In the kitchen, Marco was peeling potatoes and telling Ilona that he saw them carry the body of Cornelius Vanderbilt off his yacht and that the Coast Guard had ordered all private boat owners to stay in port. The coastguardsman who spoke to him gave him no reason. He just called to him through his megaphone as Marco picked his way over the splintered dock to caulk the seams of his eighteen-foot runabout, not to cast off its lines. Marco was puzzled. He and Ilona were speculating as to why, when the children entered the kitchen.

"Where were you so long?" asked Ilona, in the nervous, quick-tempered way she had lately, which made Hilary and Freddie stand apart from her. "And why is his shoelace untied?" She bent to tie Freddie's sneaker.

They decided they did not want to get Gus in trouble any more than he already was. "Freddie drew German planes on the blackboard," said Hilary. "We had to wash the board."

Ilona's solution was quick. "Leave the blackboard alone," she said. "Draw somewhere else, and take your brother for a haircut."

"I don't need one," said Freddie.

"A person can't see when they need a haircut," she replied.

That's when Hilary noticed that Ilona was wearing lipstick. Her mouth glistened like a cherry.

"You look pretty, Ma," she said.

Ilona smiled. "Thank you," she said.

Gus was icing a cake, carefully squeezing out sugar-creme lilies with his cheesecloth bag. "Your mother is always pretty," he said.

Hilary felt guilty about not telling him that she and Freddie had spent almost an hour talking about him to strangers.

"Gus," she said, "did you hear that there are spies around who want to put poison in the water?"

"Yes," he said, "that's what spies do. They also steal secrets. Look at this lily," he said. "Did you ever see such a flower?"

"It's beautiful," said Hilary.

"Thank you," said Gus. "I make lilies the best."

"Leave Gus alone," said Ilona. "He has to work. Why don't you bring Shirley Leone home anymore to play?"

"I don't know," said Hilary.

"If you want a friend, you have to be one. I like you to have friends like that. You can learn something from her. Invite her for a swim."

"I don't think she wants to come."

"Of course she wants to come. Everyone likes to swim in the ocean, and how do you know if you don't ask her?"

It didn't matter that Hilary had no friends at school. She had Mickey. It was like having a movie star for a buddy. Hilary sat on a twin bed while Mickey hung up a mink stole that Mr. Radner bought her before he returned to Philadelphia to register for the draft and attend to his business. The lining had been ripped and the label snipped off, for sanitary reasons, he said, since the furrier wanted to be sure no insects were hiding behind the lining, as they frequently did in Florida.

Mickey reached over the stole to the shelf and tossed out a pink-and-white dotted turban. "Try this on," she said, "you should look cute in it. Be sure to pull it down over your ears."

Hilary slipped on the turban while Mickey stacked shoeboxes. The polka-dotted casque slipped down over her forehead.

"Push it back, baby," said Mickey. "It's supposed to cover your ears, not your eyes."

"Mickey," said Hilary, "you know when Dr. Gordon cut off Ronald Reagan's legs and he said to Ann Sheridan, 'Randy, where's the rest of me?' "

"That's a hard part to forget," said Mickey. She tossed an empty shoe carton on the floor of the closet.

"Well, why did they say that Randy was from the wrong side of town?"

"Every town has a wrong side and a right side."

"Miami Beach doesn't."

"Sure it does."

"Where do I live?"

Mickey turned and stared at her. "You're like me. You're on the wrong side."

The idea was sobering. "Why?" asked Hilary. "What makes it wrong?"

"It just is, that's all. There's nothing you can do about it, except to hope you get pretty, and get yourself out as soon as you can."

Hilary went to the mirror. "Do you think I'll get pretty?"

"Let's find out," said Mickey. She took some pink lipstick and smeared it on Hilary's lips. She didn't use her pinky. "Maybe," she said. "It's possible."

The telephone rang. Mickey answered it. "Yes I will," she said. "Charge it to the room. Momma, why did you call me? I said I'd write."

Hilary continued to study her turbaned face in the mirror, turning from one side to the other, knowing her future was bound up in some final judgment.

Mickey crossed her legs, twining them around one another like flower stalks. "I told you to tell him the Navy." She pulled off her earring. "Daddy closed his gas station? Well, I figured that was going to happen sooner or later. What's he doing? That's good. He can make a lot of money in a defense plant." Mickey clutched the receiver very hard. "Why did you tell Earl where I am? But why, Momma? I asked you not to tell him."

She hung up the telephone. "Damn."

"What's wrong?" asked Hilary.

"My momma told my ex where I am."

"Who's your ex?" asked Hilary.

"The guy I used to be married to. My momma told him, and she knows I never want to see him again."

"What do you want to do?" asked Hilary, pulling off the turban. "I have seeds for a victory garden. My father said I could make one on the roof. You want to?"

"Why not?" asked Mickey. "I'm so bored, I'm going to die if I don't do something. You and I have seen every movie in town. Sol won't let me dance, although I'm taking lessons to stay in practice, at a real studio, with mirrors, and everything. And a practice barre. Maybe I'll let you come with me once and you can take a lesson yourself. You'd be all right, I think, if you weren't so awkward. On the other hand, it might be better if you waited for everything to catch up with the rest of you."

Mickey smiled into the mirror to check her teeth and lipstick. Hilary had stopped trying to spread her teeth apart after the toothpick got stuck and made her gum bleed. She decided that a person was born with a space between their teeth like Mickey, and there was nothing else to do but accept the fact that her own teeth overlapped.

The ledge of the hotel roof was covered with cheeseboxes filled with dirt in which Hilary dug holes with a teaspoon. Below her,

Lenny stood on a ladder, trying to knock down an overripe cluster of coconuts from a palm tree.

"You're going to get an awful lot of lima beans," said Mickey, watching Lenny whack at the coconuts with a baseball bat. "Why don't we plant something else?"

Hilary poked a bean into a small, thumb-sized depression in the sandy soil. "Lima beans make good seeds. My father said. They grow fast, and they don't cost anything. I can get all the lima beans I want. For free."

"But they taste lousy," said Mickey. "Who wants to eat all those lima beans? I'd be willing to pay for some tomatoes."

A gauzy dragonfly, zigzagging in its transparent double set of wings, hovered about Hilary's face. She brushed it away with her teaspoon.

"Listen," said Mickey, "if you see anyone around and he's asking for me, don't tell him I'm here."

"Who?"

"My ex. Okay? Don't say anything."

"Why not?" Hilary watered her buried beans from a jar.

"I wish to hell you were a little older. It's really getting tough having to explain every damn thing to you."

"I'm sorry, Mickey," said Hilary. "I'll be eleven next week."

"That doesn't help."

When the dirt in all the cheeseboxes had been tamped down and watered, Hilary asked Mickey if they should put up a little sign on a stick to say what they were.

"There won't be any doubt," said Mickey. The sound of singing drew them back to the edge of the roof.

"What is it?" asked Mickey. "It sounds like a parade."

Down the street as far as they could see were open khaki-colored trucks, some with the piebald brindlings of camouflage, filled with men in khaki uniforms. The men were singing in unison, and the words, roaring and raucous, reached to the rooftop and bounced off the exhaust chimney. "*Around her neck, she wore a yellow ribbon, she wore it in the springtime, and in the month of May, hey hey, and if you ask her why the hell she wore it, she wore it for a soldier who was far far away!*"

"Soldiers," said Hilary.

"*Far away, far away, she wore it for a soldier who is far far away!*"

"I think it's the Air Corps," said Mickey. "I read about it in the paper."

Trucks, one after another, pulled up to the curbs, discharging squadrons of soldiers on both sides of the street, who threw down their barracks bags and jumped after them, most of them young former soda jerks, lawyers, farm boys, plumbers, artists, writers, and grocery clerks, now officer candidates of the Army Air Corps.

Some of the men sat on their barracks bags while they waited for the order to enter their hotels; some ran the half block to the ocean, gazing at the sand and the blue-green water; others just stood and gaped at the dazzling hotels about them. The soldiers waved to the gaping civilians, some holding up their fingers in a V. Most of the civilians also waved. "Keep 'em flying," someone yelled.

More trucks came roaring up Collins Avenue, spewing out men and barracks bags onto the sidewalks. When the last of the empty trucks had roared away, whistles blew up and down the street and a second lieutenant strode out from the hotel next door to stand on the top step and address his squadron.

"Here comes our butter bars," one of the soldiers said.

The second lieutenant turned his round, full baby cheeks into a frown. "Look to the right of you," he shouted, "and look to the left. Only one of you will be here to finish this training. Now, at the signal, I want you to pick up your bags, and prepare to enter the hotel, remembering at all times military bearing, remembering also that you are being closely observed, by not only our civilian population; we are a military post in the middle of a city, but you are also being closely watched by your superior officers every minute of your waking day. Each of you will have a running score, a tally of points; you will receive points for the right things you do, and you will receive gigs for the fuckups, like forgetting to keep your belt buckle shined. The schedule of points will be explained to you later, right now, keep your nose and your room clean. The sergeant inside has your bunk assignments."

When the men stood up, the robins flew away suddenly, swooping into the sky in a single body, leaving the holly bush stripped of every berry and its leaves shivering in the sunlight.

The second lieutenant blew his whistle and the men entered the hotel. Within minutes they could be seen at every window, lowering blinds, closing blinds, poking their heads out, hanging up their uniforms, and putting away their things. One came up to the roof, looked around, and spotted Mickey.

"Hey," he called down the stairs, "come up here and see what I found."

Two more soldiers raced up to the roof, with their ties tucked between their second and third shirt buttons, their faces clean-shaven, and their hair pomaded back.

"Hi, toots," said the first one.

"Don't pay any attention to them," said Mickey.

"Is that your sister or your daughter?"

"What difference does it make to you, flyboy?"

"None, sweetface, and I never thought you'd notice. Hey, I didn't catch your name."

"I didn't throw it," said Mickey.

"I didn't throw mine either," said Hilary.

"What's going on up there?"

They looked down to see Frank below, standing over a coconut, with a cleaver in his hand, and Freddie at his side. "You," he shouted, "I'm talking to you."

"I'm planting my victory garden," said Hilary.

"Come down here. I want to talk to you right away."

"Man with an ax, I'd do whatever he said," said one of the soldiers.

Mickey wiped off Hilary's lipstick with the heel of her hand then let her loose to run downstairs to the patio.

Frank had drilled a hole on either end of the coconut and had sliced through it, husk and all, with the cleaver. Freddie was kneeling on the cement picking out the meat.

Frank signaled for Hilary to come closer as he bent to help Freddie pry off the remaining husk.

"Don't make your mother any more nervous than she already is. I don't want you to give her anything else to worry about."

"What is she so nervous about? Her family?"

"Wouldn't you feel bad if you thought you wouldn't ever see me or your mother or Freddie again?"

"I thought so when I was little," said Hilary. "I thought I'd never see you again." She was immediately sorry. It was one of those things better left unsaid.

"That was different. I was coming back. Your mother is worried because it's dangerous in Europe. People are being taken away and nobody knows where. Do you understand that? She may never see her family again."

"You never see *your* family," said Hilary, thinking of the other grandmother and grandfather she also had never met, who lived somewhere in a place called Kensington.

"You're my family," said Frank. "Now listen, I have something very important to tell you. You see all these soldiers?"

"Yes."

"I don't want you to have anything to do with any of them, you understand?"

Hilary nodded.

"What about Freddie?"

"It's different for Freddie. He's a boy. Sometimes men do bad things to little girls. Remember those dogs Marco threw water on? Don't ever go with any of them, for anything. I don't even want you talking to them. Now go play with Freddie. He hasn't had anyone to play with all day long."

Hilary remembered a pair of dogs, locked back to back, one of them dragging the other down Collins Avenue. There was no way to relate the soldiers to the screaming dog. She looked at her brother. He looked at her. "When are we going to move to the right side of town?" she asked.

"Where did you get that idea? Who told you we lived on the wrong side of town?" He looked to the roof, which was now empty. "Her?"

"I thought it up myself."

"I'll bet," he said, then walked to the kitchen carrying the cleaver.

"Okay," said Hilary, "what do you want to play?"

Freddie figured out a new game. It was based on a minor flaw in the elevator which brought the carriage up and down, never allowing it to alight, at the command of a button on another floor. Properly stationed, they could, with the right timing and a good solid yell through the mail chute, keep an unsuspecting person trapped in the elevator, going up and down, for as long as they wanted or until they got caught.

They finally released Mrs. Portman after a half-hour ride, only because Hilary got frightened when she stopped screaming, and they ran downstairs in time to see her stumble into the lobby panting, "My heart is attacking me," then collapse into a brocaded Morris chair.

"I don't think that's a good idea," said Hilary, who hadn't liked the way Mrs. Portman gasped for breath. It reminded her of a fish Frank once caught that had lain on its side, its glassy eye staring at them as it feebly fluttered its gills.

"That's just because you didn't think of it," said Freddie.

She hustled him past Mr. Davis, who stood thinking, his arms folded, his bald head pointed in their direction.

They sat in their room, with "Blondie" on the radio, Freddie with a towel around his neck, and Hilary with nail scissors and a comb, snipping at his hair, the way she had seen the barbers do it. The wall began to bang again.

"I'm too busy to be bothered trying to decode that," she said. "This doesn't look right to me."

The sound of singing came through the window. *"I've got sixpence, jolly jolly sixpence, I've got sixpence, to last me all my life."*

Freddie's head looked lopsided. "Maybe you didn't hold your head straight," she said, continuing to snip. "Tilt it over so I can even it up."

"I've got sixpence to lend and sixpence to spend, and sixpence to send home to my wife, poor wife."

"When I grow up," said Freddie, "I'm going to be a soldier."

"There won't be any war then," she replied.

"Oh yes, there will," he said. "Winona says we're going to be in this war forever."

6

The decision to invite Jack Suga to the hotel was based partly on Ilona's ultimatum that Hilary bring a school friend home to swim, partly because of Freddie's lopsided haircut that was still growing out, and partly because Mr. Radner had returned and quickly claimed 100 percent of Mickey's time, including, as Mickey related, an accounting, when she went to the bathroom, of where she had been.

Jack, Hilary, and Freddie stood on the water's edge, their feet sinking into the swale of soft mud, watching a tug bring in a torpedoed freighter. Jack wore a shiny yellow bathing suit that bunched up his private parts like a sackful of grapes beneath its lustrous clasp. Most men that Hilary had ever seen wore loose-fitting boxer shorts. Form-fitting bathing suits were something foreigners wore and new to her experience. Hilary tried not to look but could not help it. She was lured to his bathing suit like a sailor to the lodestar. She had seen Freddie naked once, a long time ago, but that did not count, since he was her little brother. It would be especially interesting to know if Jack's private parts matched more accurately the faucetlike pictures of the male in *Growing Up* than her own matched the sacculate tunnel of the female.

The beach behind them was covered with people in little half chairs that let them sit upright on the sand. The fact that everyone was on the beach and not on the patio was because the pool, emerald green with algae, was on the fritz, the result of a double event—Lenny getting drafted and chlorine becoming impossible to get. Some of the guests discreetly left food under a palm tree for the sentry they were forbidden to talk to; the sentry would look over the water and say to no one in particular, "I wish I knew the name of what I just ate," and someone would respond with equal indirection, "Chopped liver," or "Potato kugel," or, "Come back tomorrow, I'll get you a nice piece stuffed derma." It was like an opera.

There were a few new guests on the beach, people that Hilary had never seen before. There were Mr. Samuelson's daughter and his grandson, a little baby with fat legs, who stumbled whenever he tried to walk on the sand; a married couple from Passaic, New Jersey; and Elliott Portman, Mrs. Portman's marine son on a weekend pass, lying on his side next to his mother, with his dog tags hanging from his neck.

"Hello, Mrs. Portman," said Hilary.

"This is my son," said Mrs. Portman, gazing at her crew-cut son with the diffidence of a Raphael madonna. "This is my Elliott."

Hilary had never seen dog tags before, a double set of metal identification tags strung on a chain. "What is that for?" she asked.

"That's so I don't get lost."

They reminded Hilary of the time she was sent to St. Augustine on the train to visit her father's sister, with her name and address hanging from a paper sign around her neck. "Yes, but you're not a little child," she said. "You couldn't get lost."

Elliott Portman decided not to explain that the real function of dog tags was to identify a body. He didn't have to tell this to his mother. She already knew it and clutched his hand.

"What does the H stand for?"

"That's for Hebrew," said Elliott. "The rest is my serial number, my service branch, and my blood type."

Mr. Samuelson lay in a lounge beside him talking to the couple from Passaic and telling them that he didn't think they would get enough gas to return North.

"Why don't you sell your car?" he suggested. "Take the train."

"What would I use to get around?" asked the husband.

"One thing at a time," said Mr. Samuelson, spreading suntan oil on his withered flanks. "Don't borrow trouble."

Behind Mr. Samuelson, Rudy's mother was crouched on the sand, changing Rudy's trunks the way one did on a baby, underneath a towel that she had wrapped around his waist. The only thing that prevented Hilary from laughing out loud was Rudy's mother's fierce, forbidding glance.

The children turned their attention back to the ocean. The tug had towed the freighter almost to government cut. A sandbar lay several yards out, covered with a few inches of shallow warm water, and stretching for almost a city block out to sea. To get there, they had to swim across a narrow section between shoreline and sandbar, a dark blue channel in which strong currents surged and tugged.

The sandbar was like a shelf. They walked across its breadth as far as they could, almost to its end while mild currents swept sand and wrack about their feet and a school of little yellow-striped sergeant majors, fleeing from a barracuda that waited in the deeper water, spun about their legs.

The only shade on the beach was the palm tree near the seawall under which the guests put treats for the sentry. By the time they swam back from the sandbar, the treats were gone. Only a slate-gray mockingbird with white feathers in its tail was there, singing "Figaro" and building a clumsy nest of thorny twigs and coarse grass which it dropped into the crotch between fronds and trunk.

A conch shell, with a shiny pink projection like an underlip, lay nearby. Freddie poked a stick into the chamber of the shell, past the desiccated, leathery trapdoor of the mollusk's foot, deep into the shell's penetralia.

"I think he's still alive," he said.

"I don't think so," said Jack.

Mrs. Steinfeld suddenly strode over, the flesh on her dimpled thighs quivering as she walked. "Who are you?" she asked Jack.

"Jack Suga."

"You mean like sugar?"

"No. Suga."

"What kind of name is that?"

"Japanese."

"How did you get here?"

"He's my friend," said Hilary.

"You're not a guest," said Mrs. Steinfeld. "Your parents work here. I'm going to speak to Mr. Davis about this. I didn't come here to spend good money to see Japs on the beach of my hotel."

Elliott Portman disengaged his mother's arm from around his shoulder and sprang up. His body was taut and well-muscled, like someone who could take off bottle caps with his teeth, or kick sand in someone's face and get away with it. His mother had never seen him, or any other male member of her family, ever looking so fit, except her Uncle Shlomo, who had a bicycle store, and who, in his youth, had been pressed into service hammering railroad ties for the Czar.

"I think these kids should be left to play," he said, "in peace."

Mrs. Steinfeld looked over the handsome young man who stood before her. She bent one of her legs at the knee, turned out the toe of the other, and thrust her pelvis forward as if she were pushing a dirt plow. "I'll bet you're Elliott. Your mother has told me a lot about you. I'm Mildred Steinfeld. Let me explain my position, Elliott, so you don't think I'm being unreasonable. I don't think it's right for him to be here. We're at war. I'd be with my husband right now, I wouldn't be all alone, night after night, with nothing to do if it wasn't for the Japs. Actually, and I know you're probably not going to believe this, I'm thinking of him. He'd be very uncomfortable if he stayed."

"You don't have to tell me we're at war," said Elliott. "I know it better than you do. I'd be finishing college this semester and applying to med school if we weren't at war, and I wouldn't have these around my neck. But these are kids. They're playing and they're not bothering anyone. So be a good sport, Mrs. Steinfeld, and leave them alone."

"What's the matter, Elliott?" called Mrs. Portman.

"Nothing, Mom."

"I can see you're going to be very emotional about this," said Mrs. Steinfeld. She straightened both legs and led Rudy off the beach.

"California was shelled by a sub," said Hilary. "I heard it on the radio."

"My grandparents live in California," said Jack. "My grandfather had to sell his nursery. They're moving to a camp. My grandfather says he doesn't mind. The milkman wouldn't deliver milk to them anymore, and the grocer wouldn't sell them food."

"What kind of camp?" asked Hilary.

"I don't know," said Jack. "He doesn't either. Right now he's at Santa Anita race track. He and my grandmother and some other people are sleeping in the stalls until they tell them where the camp is."

"I never saw any of my grandparents," said Hilary. "Not a single one."

"Are they dead?" asked Jack.

"No, I just never saw them, that's all."

"I did," said Freddie. "I saw my grandmother."

"No you didn't," said Hilary. "He means the one in Denmark. We've got one in Denmark, who's supposed to be in Lisbon, and one in Philadelphia. You saw a picture. That's not the same."

"I know you asked me to come today because you couldn't get anyone else," said Jack. Hilary stared at the sand, tracing patterns with the stick that Freddie had used to poke the conch. "I can tell you why the other kids don't like you."

"Who cares anyhow?" she asked.

A single-engine plane droned overhead. They shaded their eyes to look up.

"That's a Curtiss o-52," she said. "They call it an Owl. It's an observation plane. See the windows? They take pictures from it."

Hilary jumped up and ran to the center of the beach waving her arms and shouting. "Look at me, yoo hoo, look down here and take my picture!"

"Watch it," yelled Mr. Samuelson, brushing off the sand that adhered to his suntan oil. "What person in their right mind kicks sand all over the beach?"

"Sorry," said Hilary.

"In case you want to know," said Jack. "I figured it out and I'll tell you if you stop acting like a little kid."

Hilary trudged back and sat beside him.

"Two things," he said. "You want to hear them or don't you?"

"Okay," she replied. "Shoot."

"First, you fight too much. Ease up. Stop going after everyone who looks at you the wrong way. Second, stop telling everyone when they made a mistake. People don't like to know when they make mistakes."

They heard singing from the street. "*No cares have I to grieve me, no pretty little girls to deceive me, I'm happy as a king, believe me, as I go rolling rolling home."*

"I don't care about any of those dopey kids," said Hilary. "I got a best friend. She's twenty-two and she's the prettiest girl in the whole world. She's even prettier than Betty Grable. And I can tell her all I want when she makes mistakes."

The singing grew louder. "*Rolling home, rolling home, by the light of the silvery moon happy is the day when the air corps gets its pay and I go rolling rolling home.*"

"Hilary's not supposed to play with her," said Freddie. "But she does it anyhow."

"Shut up," Hilary said. "She knows how to do everything, and we go to movies and we planted a victory garden together. So there. Who wants any of those silly people when I have the best friend in the world?"

"If she knows how to do everything, how come you have to tell her when she makes mistakes?" asked Jack.

"How come?" she asked. "How come? It's because she does so many things she gets them mixed up."

Jack looked doubtful. Shouts came from the hotel next door.

"Let's see what they're doing," she said. Freddie sat where he was, looking injured, and pouring sand over his toes from the cup of his hand.

"I'm sorry I said shut up."

Mollified, Freddie followed them as they ran to the wall that separated the hotels, then leaped to rest on their bellies and peer over the edge. There on the upper beach of the hotel next door, 150 sweating and sunburned officer candidates in olive drab shorts and undershirts were preparing to do calisthenics.

"We're gonna do pushups by the numbers," shouted an instructor who stood with his back to the surf. "From a prone position, up on one, down on two, ready, one two, one two, don't touch your body to the ground, one two, one two, suck in your gut, keester level with your head . . ."

Every once in a while, a man would collapse, then get up again, brushing sand from his mouth to continue while the instructor switched the exhausted and groaning men to knee bends. One man was not sweating. Instead, his skin was dry and his face deeply flushed. Suddenly he crumpled.

"Get that man in the shade," yelled the instructor, able to distinguish a heat-stroke collapse from that of someone who simply could not get his overworked and undertrained muscles to cooperate.

They carried him under a striped awning to the patio where they stripped off his shirt, his sneakers, and his socks, and loosened his shorts. Someone brought cold water and wet towels and someone else ran up with ice cubes in a towel to put on his head, while the man who first carried him began to strip off the fallen man's shorts.

"You better not watch," said Jack.

"I could if I want to," said Hilary.

"I'll tell if you do," said Freddie.

One of the men saw the children peering over the wall. "Look at that," he shouted. "Someone get that Buddha-loving Jap out of here."

All the men turned and everyone started shouting. Hilary, Jack, and Freddie jumped down from the wall. Some of the soldiers broke ranks and ran to yell over it hurling invectives like rocks. Elliott Portman stood up.

"Elliott," said Mrs. Portman, "don't start."

"Leave the kids alone," he said.

"You and who else is gonna make us?" yelled another.

"Elliott, don't fight," said Mrs. Portman.

When he came closer, they were able to read his dog tags. "It's a gyrene," one shouted to the others behind him. "A pussy-mouth seagoing bellhop."

Mr. Davis came out, mopping his head with his handkerchief. "What seems to be the trouble?" he asked. "Sergeant, why are these men yelling at my guests?"

The sergeant indicated Jack with a thrust of his chin.

"Are you a Buddha lover?" asked Hilary, as they ran toward the kitchen.

"No, I'm Catholic."

"So is my father," she said, "a used-to-be Catholic."

"How did he get out of it?" he asked. "I thought it was for life."

Mr. Davis moved to the wall and stood face to face with the sergeant. "I still see no reason for your men not comporting themselves as gentlemen. I have guests. I run a hotel. You get my point, I'm sure."

A major with gold maple leaves on the epaulets of his shirt strode onto the sand. "What seems to be the problem, Sergeant?" he asked.

"It seems there was a small ruckus, sir, over a Jap kid."

"It was most unpleasant, Major," said Mr. Davis. "I hope it won't occur again, for any reason."

"Look here," said the major, "you hotel people are making things very difficult for us, demanding higher rates than you originally agreed upon. At this moment we may have to abandon plans to expand our program here, a serious setback to the war effort. So you will understand," he knocked sand out of his shoes, "that I am in no mood to be threatened."

When Hilary entered the kitchen, everything was in an uproar. Frank was shouting, Ilona was crying, and everyone was crowding around two FBI agents as they patted down Gus's body, and handcuffed his wrists behind his back.

"What did he do?" asked Ilona.

"You just can't arrest a man like that," said Frank.

"Please, Mr. MacIntyre," said one of the agents, "let us do our job, just as we would not interfere with yours."

Ilona reached over and took off Gus's baking cap, then smoothed back his hair. "We'll watch everything for you," she said.

"Thanks, missus."

The agents, one on either of Gus's hairy arms, hustled him past his dough-filled bundt pans that lay in a row on a wooden plank. Frank ran after them. "I'll get you out, Gus," he shouted. "They made some kind of mistake. It happens all the time."

Gus wasn't so sure. His face had a grim look. It was this expression that made Hilary feel sick, as if she would like to throw up. She should have told him.

"Where are you taking him?" asked Frank.

"To the Orange Bowl," said an agent.

"You don't have to be a wise guy," said Frank.

"Who would have figured Gus for a spy?" asked Vicky Sue.

"No one said he was a spy," said Ilona. "That's how rumors start. They made a mistake. It could happen to anyone. It could happen to you."

"Not me," said Vicky Sue. "I was born here."

Frank and Ilona turned to see Jack Suga standing behind Hilary.

"Who's that?" asked Ilona.

"This is my friend Jack," said Hilary.

"Hi," said Jack. "Thank you for letting me swim here."

"The ocean is free," said Ilona.

Frank just stared. Finally he said, "Don't you need glasses?"

"No," said Jack, who knew that there was nothing left to say except good-bye, which he said, carrying his bathing suit wrapped in a towel.

"What's his nationality?" asked Frank. "I hope his father has a laundry."

"His father plants flowers on the parkway," said Hilary. "He's Japanese."

"Two hundred children in the school and you have to pick the one that's Japanese," said Ilona. "What do you do, go out of your way to aggravate me?"

Hilary began to cry. "I'm not trying to aggravate you. He's just the only one who will come home with me. You told me to bring a friend home, and I did. Everyone else I asked couldn't come. I can't help it if he's Japanese."

"Forget about him," said Ilona. "I have too much in my head to worry about a Japanese." She turned to Frank who had lit a cigar. "What about Gus? What did they want with him? What did he do?"

Frank took the paper cigar band and put it on Hilary's finger. "You used to like when I gave you these."

"It was the swastikas," said Freddie.

"What swastikas?" asked Frank. He turned to Hilary. "Do you know anything about this?"

Hilary nodded. Tears fell again. "They called Freddie to the principal's office. A man and Mr. Detwiler asked about the planes. And Gus."

"What planes are you talking about?" asked Frank.

"The planes Gus taught Freddie to draw."

"And you didn't tell us? What about Gus? Don't you think he deserved to know that somebody questioned you about him? So he could defend himself?"

Hilary began to cry again. "I can't do anything right," she said.

"It's because you don't think," said Ilona. "You do things first. Then think about them later when it's too late."

Ilona sent them both to have supper in the dining room. Hilary walked with her head down, her chin almost to her chest. She took off the cigar band and tossed it in the wastebasket.

"What will happen? With Gus?" asked Ilona.

"I'll get him out. Davis will hire a lawyer. I'll talk to Mr. Lonzo if I have to." He nodded his head in the direction of the departing Hilary. "I think you better leave her alone. I think we both better leave her alone. If you want my opinion, I think you're too hard on both the kids, especially Hilary."

"I worry that she has no friends."

"I don't know what we can do about that," he said.

"She has no social graces. She's like some wild animal."

"Where do you get social graces? I wouldn't know one if I stepped on one."

Ilona laughed, a light little laugh that made her throw her head back.

Frank kissed her on her throat. "I made you smile," he murmured, "and I just thought of something. There is someone, right here in the hotel who knows all about that stuff."

Ilona pulled back. "Gomez?" she asked.

"Not Gomez. Gomez doesn't know how to do anything except thirty-two rhumba breaks and how to sniff in the air like she's smelling something. No, Mrs. Templeton."

"What about Mrs. Templeton?"

"Mrs. Templeton has class. She could teach it to Hilary."

"Why would she want to do that?"

"Everyone is ripe for a deal, baby, even Mrs. Templeton. I'll find out what her deal is, maybe an extra lamb chop now and then, I don't want to give more away than I have to. Dinner on the house for a friend, something in exchange for social-graces lessons."

"Do you think she'll do it?"

"Watch me," he said. "Consider it done." He drew her to him and kissed her. "Stop worrying about everything. It makes lines on your forehead."

Ilona found Hilary and Freddie in the receiving room, sitting on a board suspended over the giant scale of the loading dock.

"What are you doing?" she asked.

"We're practicing rolls and loops," said Hilary, "to be a pilot."

"Girls can't be pilots," said Ilona.

"What about Amelia Earhart?"

"She crashed. That should answer your question. How about a nurse? You used to want to be a nurse."

"She pulls off Band-Aids too fast," said Freddie.

"If I can't be a pilot," said Hilary, "I don't want to be a nurse."

Social-graces lessons, not a moment too soon for Ilona, started that evening for Hilary right after Frank struck the deal, for cooking privileges to be executed before the kitchen got busy, and the prerogative of modest food storage in the refrigerator.

The lessons were conducted in Mrs. Templeton's hotel room. Hilary came in after supper. The room, dim from the sixty-watt bulb people were encouraged to use, smelled of rose and lavender toilet water and mildew.

"Good evening, Hilary," said Mrs. Templeton. "You're here to study deportment with me, and we will begin immediately, as I have a bingo game to conduct in half an hour. We will start with the correct way to sit." Mrs. Templeton pulled out a chair. "Sit on it," she said.

Hilary sat.

"All wrong. You led with your derriere, and you looked. That is not how one sits. One drops down with one's back straight, one feels the chair with the back of one's calves. The Queen of England would never never look to make sure the chair is there. She knows it will be there."

"How do I know?" asked Hilary.

"You will feel it with your calves," she said. "Like so." Mrs. Templeton sat ramrod straight without once looking back.

Hilary sat again.

"Now, when you are seated," said Mrs. Templeton, "never cross your legs. Keep your knees pressed tightly together, and make sure your skirt is over your knees, and if you must, absolutely must, cross your legs, cross your ankles. Never, never your legs. Let me see corrected seated posture."

Hilary decided on an ankle cross.

"Your hands, Hilary, fold them in your lap. Not clench, Hilary, fold, as if you were putting them away for the night. What's the matter?" asked Mrs. Templeton. "You're twisting your hands as though you were wringing out wash. You're not concentrating."

"They took Gus away. I just feel bad about him, that's all," said Hilary.

"So do I, dear, but a lady does not wear her feelings on her sleeve. She forbears."

"What is forbear?"

"It means she takes it in her stride and keeps it to herself. She carries on. Let us continue." Mrs. Templeton assembled her bingo paraphernalia while Hilary concentrated on sitting down, learning to drop straight-backed into a chair guided only by her calves, sitting with her ankles crossed demurely, with her hands lying limp in her lap as if they were put away for the night, and suffering the misery of guilt.

When she returned to their room that night, Ilona told her that Mr. Davis had said that Jack Suga was not to come back. "Play with your brother," she said. "You'll keep each other out of trouble."

Someone was shouting from the hotel next door. "Do it over, dammit, do it right. Get this place clean. I mean clean. I'll be back in an hour." Then the sounds of grumbling men.

Someone was always telling someone what to do. Hilary had thought it stopped for grown-ups. Apparently it didn't.

7

With a little help from Mr. Lonzo, Frank found out that when the FBI agent told him he was taking Gus to the Orange Bowl, he wasn't kidding. After an anxious two-week wait marked by fruitless calls to the police, the FBI, and the city desk of the Miami *Herald*, and a sickening round of coconut cream pie and bread pudding, the only desserts Marco knew how to make, Frank learned that Gus was interned beneath the bleachers of the four-year-old stadium, along with 158 other suspicious aliens rounded up in Dade County.

Since the FBI could find out nothing more serious about Gus than the fact that he had never applied for American citizenship and did not like the Andrews sisters, they were willing to release him in Frank's custody.

Ilona had an appointment that morning with the Red Cross to list the names and last known whereabouts of her missing relatives, while Frank, through default, took Hilary and Freddie with him on the long bus ride to the Orange Bowl. After three transfers and one stop for Freddie to go to the bathroom in a Howard Johnson's, followed by some trial and error before they reached the right turnstile of the circular stadium, they finally found the ground floor headquarters of the makeshift jail.

Gus was led down a ramp with green crepe paper stuck to his soles, blinking in the light, and angry because he had to share his windowless cement-block cell with a dismantled orange and green parade float, and an Italian who spoke no English and who kept reaching for his shoes.

While Frank signed for him, a man with the straightest mouth Hilary had ever seen gave Gus back his watch, his wallet, some desiccated lemons, a postcard photo of the *Graf Spee,* upon which his machinist father had worked, and a photograph of his mother.

They walked to the bus stop in silence, Freddie walking backward in order to keep the Orange Bowl in his sight and Hilary wondering what the man with the straight mouth looked like when he smiled. On the bus, Frank and Gus sat on one perforated cane seat, and Freddie and Hilary kneeled on the seat in front so they could lean over the back and keep up with what was happening. Nothing was happening. Gus remained grim-faced and silent. Every window was open, some propped with little sticks and the air rushed in like a blast from an oven.

"I'm sorry about all this," said Frank.

"I don't like America no more," said Gus, rattling his "r's" like the maracas brandished by the ruffle-shirted bandleader at the hotel. "It's a terrible place."

"They made a mistake," said Frank. "It happens. Not that it's any of my business, Gus, but why haven't you ever applied for citizenship?"

"I don't know," said Gus. "I forgot."

It was as if she were holding her breath under water. Suddenly Hilary had to let it out. "I forgot something too. I knew they were looking for you. Me and Freddie. We both knew. They told us not to tell."

Gus looked at her with sorrowful eyes, shrugged, and looked out the window as they crossed the long causeway that would take them back to Miami Beach. Pelicans sat on pilings that marked a new island to be, one bird with a fish stuck sideways in his throat.

Hilary leaned over the back of her seat, coming so close to Gus she could see one whisker growing sideways under his skin.

"I'm sorry, Gus," she whispered.

Gus continued to look out the window.

"You sure can teach people to make good planes," said Freddie. Hilary punched him in his side. They rode for a while in silence.

Frank broke it. "I finished your bundt cakes for you," he said. "In case you were wondering."

"Bundt küchen," said Gus. "You don't say bundt cakes. It's one or the other."

"They tasted awful," said Freddie. "Mr. Carpathy sent his back."

"Of course," said Gus. "I betcha nobody put lemon rind in the batter." He took the shriveled lemons out of his pocket and threw them out the window. One landed in the bay with a little slap, the other rolled on the roadway to be squashed by an army truck behind them.

They returned to find a squad of officer candidates standing in the street in front of the hotel next door, facing their drill sergeant, and trying to learn how to march. Gus took one look at the clumsy recruits, shook his head, and went to see to his bakery, but Hilary and Freddie, with Frank behind them, stayed to watch.

The drill sergeant, regarding the collection of men before him in obvious disgust, aimed his voice over their heads, as if looking directly at their faces was too much to ask.

"In the position of attention," he shouted to the sky. "The body is held erect but not tense, hands curled naturally at the side, thumbs next to the trouser seams, right face, left face, about face, forward harch, by your left, your left, your left, detail, halt. Your left, Winslow, it's the hand you hold your dick with."

"Don't you see these kids standing here?" shouted Frank.

The drill sergeant glanced in his direction once, then turned his attention to his men. "Forward, harch, by your left, left, left, hup, two, hreep, po, hup, two, hreep, po."

"Let's go." Frank hustled the children into the hotel.

"I hold mine with my right hand," said Freddie.

"Who taught you that?" asked Frank.

The soldiers marched away, bumping into one another, stepping on each other's toes, and turning in the wrong direction, only to be yanked back into conformity by the restraining hand of their drill sergeant.

Hilary didn't wait for the elevator. She flung her braids over her shoulder and took the stairs two at a time all the way to the third floor, and knocked on Mickey's door. First there was no answer, which was strange because a moment before she had heard sounds coming from the room. Then Mr. Radner's voice, "She's busy, kid, go away."

Hilary thought she heard sobbing. "Can't I talk to her for just a minute?"

"What's the matter? You don't hear so good? I said scram."

Winona appeared, pushing her cleanup cart loaded with a stack of towels that threatened to topple. "I'd stay away from there, if I was you, honey, they're having an argument."

"What about?"

"Whatever it is menfolks don't like about womenfolks."

"Like what?"

"Depends on the man. Some men like to have their dinner on time. Piping hot. Served with the steam rising in your face. Never give that man anything cold unless it's beer. Some men don't like to see their women talk to other men. Some men don't like to have to explain things to their woman—where they go and what they do—and then there's men who just like to whomp whenever they've a mind to."

They heard the sound of a thud, a splintering crash, then a loud cry, followed by a shout and muffled whimpering.

Winona took Hilary by the arm. "Come on, baby. Time to move. Now how about helping me carry those towels. Grab them off the cart and follow me; 217 has been complaining all day. Towels and more towels. I sure don't know what they want with all those towels."

Hilary looked worried.

"It ain't none of our business," said Winona, gently pushing her down the hall with one hand, and pulling the cart with the other.

Hilary sat on the rumpled unmade bed of a guest room, holding a package of soap bars, while Winona scoured the bathroom.

"Winona," she called, "do you ride in the back of the bus?"

Winona came out holding a can of cleanser which she placed in the cart. "Unless they changed their minds," she said.

"Does it make you sick?"

"What do you mean?" Winona narrowed her eyes.

"Shirley Leone gets sick when she rides in the back, especially on the last seat."

"You might say that," said Winona. "Although I don't get sick about that kind of thing anymore. My Lionel, he does. He gets hisself all het up about it, but I don't. Like that coconut palm in the patio. If that thing gets upset in a hurricane, if it stiffens and says, can't do that to me, hurricane, what happens?"

"I don't know, what?"

"It breaks, that's what. But if the tree says, you can do whatever you like with me, wind, I'll still be me, no matter what."

"Then what?"

"It bends, honey. And lives to stand up straight when the storm is over."

Winona was clearly not talking about carsickness. The conversation had taken a more serious turn to mean something obscured in allegory. Then Hilary understood, quickly, like when she suddenly realized raisins were grapes or pickles were cucumbers. What was taken for granted by Frank was something to be patiently borne by Winona but not by Lionel. Why not? Was that because he was younger, or was it because he was a man? Were men less patient than women, or more angry?

She didn't have long to wait. By the time she had picked a scab off her elbow, Mr. Radner came out, slamming the door behind him. "I don't want you with me," he shouted. "Get a load of what you look like. I go out with a broad, she looks good. You got to clean up first."

He didn't see Hilary crouched on the steps, and he walked directly to the elevator, pulling out the collar of his shirt over his jacket and smoothing flat the sparse hairs on the top of his head. When the elevator doors closed, Hilary ran to Mickey's door and knocked.

"It's me, Hilary."

"Go away." Mickey's voice was faint as if she were far away.

"Are you sick?"

"Please, Hilary, some other time."

Hilary knocked again. Then the door opened slowly. Mickey stood in the frame, holding her upper arm, her eyes discolored, the corner of her swollen mouth bleeding. Her hair was in disarray, her face puffed and distorted. "I told you to go away," she said.

"Did he hit you?"

Mickey nodded her head and started to cry.

"I'm going to tell my father."

"No, don't tell anybody."

"What happened?"

"I went to this party with some kids from the Pago Pago, some soldiers, a few civilians. He heard about it. I had me this idea to paste defense stamps all over, I was wearing panties, fifty cents a pull. It wasn't really a strip tease. I did it for the war effort. I thought it was a way to sell bonds. I don't know how he found out, but he did."

"Why is he so mad?" asked Hilary.

"Because he doesn't want anyone else to see me without my clothes on."

"My mother doesn't want anyone to see me either, except for Dr. Hershbaum."

Through Mickey's window came the singing of a marching platoon. "Sound off, one two, sound off, three four, sound off, one two three four, sound off!"

"I don't think I can listen to any of that." Mickey closed the window with her good arm and fell on the bed. "You better not be here when he gets back," she said.

"Does it hurt?"

"Real bad."

"Why didn't you hit him back?"

"Because it's my fault. I brought it on myself. I should have stayed by myself at night, like Sol wanted. He doesn't ask very much of me. I deserved it."

"I think you should have hit him back. It's easy. You keep your guard up. Pow. You dance on your toes. Whap."

"I wouldn't do that."

"Why not?"

"Because I'm going to do like he says, whatever he wants, whenever he wants. He pays my way, he's good to me. That's the way things are. If you're good to men, they're good to you and if you're bad, like I was, you take the consequences. It's their game, honey. They hold all the cards. You got to play by their rules, nothing up your sleeve, no turned-down corners. You'd better go now. I want to close my eyes. I'm tired."

"If you're not going to hit him back, maybe you should try to forbear."

"What are you talking about?"

"Forbear. It's a word Mrs. Templeton taught me, about being a lady. It means you keep on going, no matter what. Like Mrs. Miniver."

"Being a lady has nothing to do with being with men. Mrs. Templeton don't know anything about men. I'm not interested in being a dried-up old prune without a man, and I sure don't know how the hell forbear can get you anything worthwhile. By the way, two letters came to you in care of me. One from a soldier. Who are you writing to?"

"A pen pal I got in school."

"Those guys are pretty lonely. You have to be careful what you say to them. The other one's an advertisement."

Mickey closed her eyes. She looked vulnerable and frail. Hilary felt a great rush of pity. She wanted to stay by her side and protect her from Mr. Radner.

"Go on now," said Mickey.

On the way downstairs, Hilary opened the letter from Private Farber. It read:

Dear Miss MacIntyre,

Thank you for your letter. I'm writing this to you from my cot in my barracks. It is the only building I ever saw that could leak through the floor and the roof at the same time. My feet hurt me real bad because my boot size is wrong. I have to go back and try on another pair. You do this by holding a bucket of sand in each hand. My sergeant thinks they didn't fill the buckets all the way the last time, that's how come I got the wrong size. You sound pretty. Why don't you send me a picture of you in your long blond hair so I can tack it up. That way I can look at you when I write to you and it will be just like we were talking face to face. This might sound personal, but when you go to sleep at night, is your hair spread out all over the pillow? Don't think I think that would be a bad thing if it were true. Very truly yours, Pvt. Sylvan Farber.

Hilary wondered what kind of man Private Farber was. Did he like to whomp people? Then she thought of Mr. Radner, who had whomped Mickey so badly she didn't recognize her.

Freddie was in the kitchen, eating a mango that Ilona had sliced into a bowl of sour cream.

"You want to do See You Next Fall?" she whispered.

"What did you say?" asked Freddie.

"I said, you want to do See You Next Fall."

"Sure. Who do you want to do it to?"

"Mr. Radner."

"We don't have any wire," said Freddie. "Daddy took it to tie up his car."

"What about string?" she asked.

"It doesn't work so good," said Freddie. "People can see string."

She sat beside him at the salad bar, dipping into his sour cream with a finger. Marco was telling Frank how he had been anchored offshore, lubricating the steering knuckles of his boat, when a German submarine surfaced, asked him for fuel, then took his fish and left.

"That sounds like a fishy story to me," said Frank.

Marco didn't laugh. "Fifteen jack," he said. "The bastards took a whole morning's catch."

Hilary licked her finger clean. "Do you have any line here?" she asked.

"You want to see a U-boat too, Hilary, eh?" Marco laughed.

"Maybe."

"I have some line in my locker. I'll get it for you as soon as I finish these grapefruit."

They rigged the fishing line ankle high from one side of the hall to another with thumb tacks pushed into the moldings.

"What if Mickey comes out?" asked Freddie.

"She's not coming out," said Hilary. "She's sick in bed."

Hilary wrote out the note in longhand, deciding that printing would automatically make them suspect. It said, "Have a nice trip, see you next fall," and she placed it on the floor.

After Freddie checked to make sure the line was securely fastened, Hilary ran with him to the beach, the only place where she was guaranteed privacy from Ilona, who did not like the sand, to open her Zonite letter. Freddie insisted she bury him first, which she did, heaping sand up to his neck, even folding her towel like a pillow which she slipped beneath his head so she could read the pamphlet in peace.

When she lifted her head she saw a line of ships on the horizon.

"Watch the convoy," she said. "Maybe it'll blow up."

Freddie settled beneath the mound of sand to watch the ships seemingly stand still, and Hilary flopped beside him to open the envelope.

The Zonite pamphlet was a small one. It talked about feminine daintiness and feeling confident. It also said that Zonite was a safe douche and medically recommended.

"Stay here," she said. "I'll be right back." She ran to their room to look up the word *douche* and found that it was "a jet of water directed at a body cavity." It had to do with teeth. Why didn't they say so in the first place? Another blind alley.

Hilary returned in disgust to sit at the water's edge. What an awful day. A black skimmer, flying along the top of the water, its long red bill cutting through the surface like a knife, came within a few feet of where she was sitting. "Watch it!" she yelled.

Her thoughts lapped at her mind like the sunlight dappled surf rushed at her legs. First she thought of Mickey, wondering how long it would take for the bruises to go away. Then she wondered how the men on the beach next door who were learning to hold their rifles fit into Winona's categories.

A drill sergeant barked to one of his men.

"Wright! Describe your rifle!"

"Sir, it is a breech-loaded, magazine-fed, bolt-operated shoulder weapon, United States rifle, caliber .30, model 1903. It holds five rounds in a clip and the weight is 8.69 pounds without bayonet, sir."

"Is that all, Wright?"

"Yes, sir."

"You forgot the serial number."

"Yes, sir, serial number is 7682678332, sir."

"Take one hour extra duty policing the beach, one mile in each direction."

"Yes, sir."

"And sing out the proper description of your rifle while you're doing it."

"Yes, sir."

The drill sergeant was probably a whomper.

The tide sucked the surf out to sea, leaving her legs bare, then the water paused and rushed back, as if it could stand the suspense no longer, and covered them over.

Her eleventh birthday had come and gone. Except for a pair of perforated white calf sandals from her mother and father, a barrette with seashells pasted on it from Freddie, and an anniversary issue of *Sheena, Queen of the Jungle* from Mel (Mickey forgot and said that she owed her one), there was nothing to mark it as special from any other day. When you were eleven, everything was supposed to start, like the school orchestra tuning up to play. A few girls in her class were getting their periods, whispering about bleeding between their legs in gym and congratulating each other on the achievement. Shirley Leone and Jackie Snyder wore Maidenform brassieres, and that wasn't just once in a while, it was every day. The whole world, it seemed, was softening like ripe fruit and leaking from its nether parts, everyone except her.

Hilary looked down at her body and squeezed her eyes shut very hard. "Start!" she commanded. Then she opened her eyes and looked down. Nothing swirled in the water except coquina shells and the egg case of a skate. She pushed and waited. Nothing. A soldier in gym shorts and white shirt, singing out a rifle description, came behind her to pick up a gum wrapper which he tossed into a sack.

"Are you the one who forgot the serial number?" she asked.

The soldier's light brown curly hair was almost the same color as the khaki cap from beneath which it poked. His hazel eyes were large and when he smiled at her, they shined. Hilary thought he was handsome.

"Yours truly, Corporal Bill Wright," he said. "Whose little girl are you?"

"Very truly yours, you mean," she said. "And I'm too old for that question. I'm eleven."

"Sorry." He bent to pick up a cigarette butt.

Freddie jumped up from his sandy tomb, damp sand plastered to his chest and back, and skid to a stop beside them. "Don't pick up any man-of-war," he said. "They sting like crazy. But if you touch one, come to see my mother. She'll put vinegar on it."

"I'll be careful," said Corporal Wright. "What do these man-of-war look like?"

"Purple, like ink," said Freddie. "With spectacles and everything."

"He means tentacles."

"Don't worry," said Corporal Wright, "I wouldn't have picked up anything that had either one."

"Where are you from?" asked Hilary. "You don't sound like you're from New York, or Chicago either. I can tell the difference."

"I'm from Iowa."

"They grow corn in Iowa."

"We sure do. We're the golden buckle of the corn belt. We also brag about Buffalo Bill and Glenn Miller."

"My teacher says Iowa is as flat as a table."

"She's wrong. The land rolls, softly, in little swells like that ocean in front of you."

"She probably said that because she's never been there," said Hilary.

"You're smart for eleven."

"I'm smart for fifteen. That's what Mickey says."

"Who's Mickey?"

"My friend."

"I can't hear that rifle description!" shouted a voice over the wall.

Corporal Wright winked at Hilary and Freddie and continued down the beach. ". . . breech-loaded, magazine-fed, bolt-operated shoulder weapon . . ."

A wave rushed over Hilary, splashing her face. She wiped away the salty water with her arm. "The ocean is all the tears of the world," she said.

"That's stupid," said Freddie. "People don't stand in the water and cry."

"Sometimes they do," said Hilary. "Remember Mr. Carpathy?"

"Smoke is coming from the convoy."

"Where?" Hilary asked. "You're making it up."

"No I'm not. Look there."

On the horizon, black spiraling smoke curled in and out of the line of tiny ships. She made it happen. She said it to keep Freddie quiet and it happened.

"I'm telling Daddy!" Freddie jumped up and ran to the kitchen shouting for Frank.

"What's going on?" called Mel from the tote board of his bookie cabana.

"A ship blew up," shouted Freddie. "Right in front of us."

Mel grabbed his arm and whispered to him. "Don't go spreading that around. Don't give the enemy information."

"I'm not, Mel, I'm just telling it to my father."

Gus had remained in the bakery all afternoon, not talking to anyone, just mixing and baking in a fever of activity, and carrying trays of pastries to cool on the racks. When Freddie ran in with his news, dripping water on the wooden deck, Gus seemed particularly offended.

"Why tell me?" he asked. "I'm a spy. Nobody tells spies nothing."

Frank stopped Freddie in the middle of the kitchen. "We're getting ready for dinner," he said. "What's up?"

"A ship. It blew up, right in the middle of a convoy."

"Get away from the beach," said Ilona. "Go to the east wing. Mrs. Templeton is having a bingo game."

"I can't hear the numbers. She talks too low."

"Then tell Hilary to come and play with you inside." Freddie looked disappointed. "And get out of that wet suit."

Frank wiped his hands on his apron and watched Freddie leave. His face became pensive.

"What is it?" asked Ilona.

"There's a war on," he said.

"Don't you think I know it? It's because of the war that my mother and sister are running God knows where all over Europe."

"I forgot you went to the Red Cross today. What did they say?"

"They told me it was too bad my family didn't make it to the Riviera. They said Nice was a safety zone for Jews because the French are under Italian jurisdiction and Italians leave Jewish refugees alone."

"Here I am, an able-bodied man, with eyes like an eagle, and I'm not doing a goddamned thing to help."

"You're 3-A, Frank. You're supporting me and the children."

"You could get along without me for a little while. Other women do."

"On a soldier's pay? They make twenty-one dollars a month. How could we live on twenty-one dollars a month? That's *bupkiss*."

"It would be just for a little while. When I get into OCS, the pay gets better."

"What are you saying? How do you know it's going to be for a little while? The Axis is cutting us up like a pair of scissors. Thousands of people are starving to death every day in Leningrad. You heard Kaltenborn. MacArthur had to escape from the Philippines."

"He said he'd return."

"Of course he said he'd return. What else could he say?"

"I don't want to hear any more," said Frank.

Ilona began to cry. "It's very bad, Frank. Everyone is saying so."

"All the more reason for me to join in. It's like this for me, baby. I see those guys training and getting ready to fight. It's my fight too, and I feel left out. Today I let Gus down some way, don't ask me how, I don't know. I see Freddie running in here with so much trust in me, and Hilary, well, even though she's older, she looks up to me too. They think I can do things and change things, and I feel like I'm letting them down. And you. I want to go over there and find your mother and sister for you. And bring them home. A present. I open the door and I say surprise and there they are. I know the odds are against me actually finding them, but still I think about it."

"You just like to fight. I know you. You think you'll put on a uniform, and they'll give you a gun and a bayonet, and you can *tummle* all you please, and dodge bullets, and be a hero, and people will throw confetti on your head."

"I admit I like a fight, but a good fight. I'm always ready for a good fight."

"What about your job? It took a long time to get such a good job. Now you're going to throw it away, just like that?"

"If the Air Corps takes over this hotel, there won't be any job. At least not here. And it stands to reason they're gonna take it. How can they take every hotel on this block and leave this one out?" He took off his apron and flung it over the salad counter. A string landed in the lettuce.

"Where are you going?"

"To see what's what."

It was almost six o'clock when Frank walked into the enlistment office of the Army and stood before the sergeant at the desk.

"Yes, sir, what can I do for you?" asked the grinning sergeant.

"I came to enlist," said Frank.

"That's very patriotic of you. What is your present status?"

"3-A."

"That means you have dependents. You realize that under the Selective Service Act you are deferred. You can't be drafted."

"I know all about that," said Frank, "that's why I'm enlisting."

"Have you thought about support to your dependents in that event?"

"I want to get into OCS. If I make second lieutenant, they'll have plenty to get by. My wife can live for the duration with my sister in St. Augustine."

"There's no guarantee that you'll be sent to OCS."

"I'll take my chances," said Frank.

"Does your wife know of your intention?"

"Why? Do I need a note?"

The sergeant laughed. "Just asking, buddy. Don't get sore. Fill out these forms, wait on that bench, and the doc will see you."

"What for?"

"To find out if you're fit."

"Jesus," said Frank, "all you have to do is look at me to know that. I can pick up a one-hundred-pound sack of potatoes with one hand. Straight out. Doesn't that tell you something?"

"It tells me you're pretty strong, but you could also have a dozen hernias. The doc needs to know other things, like your eyesight, your heart, your feet, things like that."

The wait on the bench was short. The wait in the examining room was longer. Stripped to his boxer shorts, Frank sat on the edge of a metal slab while a doctor in a white jacket prodded and poked him, thumped and sounded his chest and back, stuck a tongue depressor down his throat, felt his testicles, then asked him a lot of questions like if he wet the bed, had headaches or sudden blackouts, and if he liked girls. The doctor put a cuff on Frank's upper arm, squeezed a bulb that tightened the cuff, pressed a flat metal disk to the inside of his elbow, and listened through earphones. Then the same thing to his other arm. "Stand up," he said.

Frank stood and the doctor repeated the procedure.

"Your blood pressure is a little high."

"What do you mean?"

"I mean it's not low enough to get into the armed forces."

"That's crazy. I'm only thirty-three years old."

"Age doesn't have very much to do with it."

"Wait a minute. There's nothing wrong with me. I'm as healthy as a horse. If my blood pressure is high, it's because I'm excited, about getting in and all. I guess that would make someone's pressure go a little haywire."

The doctor folded his sphygmomanometer and laid it on an instrument table. "I'm sorry," he said. "I really am. I can see you're raring to go, but I have specific guidelines that I have to follow. If I were you, I'd see my own physician, have it taken care of."

"If I come back and my pressure is down, do I get in?"

"Not if you're on medication."

"You don't get it. Suppose I come back, just like that, and it turns out this was a mistake. Then what? Do you take it off my record?"

"I not only take it off your record, I personally pronounce you fit for military service, and then I hang up my stethoscope."

Hilary and Freddie heard him when he came in. Ilona's restless movements had kept them awake.

"Where were you?" asked Ilona. "I've been worried out of my mind."

Frank's voice was lower than Hilary had ever heard it. "I'm 4-F, baby," he said.

"That's wonderful."

"It stinks. It means I'm an old man. It means I can't do my duty by my country. I'm no better than Lipschutz, or any other slacker."

"Maybe the doctor can inject you," said Freddie.

"Be quiet, honey. Go to sleep," said Ilona.

"That's what they did to Captain America," said Freddie. "He was 4-F and they wouldn't let him in the Army, then the doctor gave him something that made his body and his brain swell up and he became a super agent."

Ilona came behind the sheet. "I told you to go to sleep," she said. "Your father doesn't want to talk."

"But it happened," said Freddie.

"It's a comic," said Hilary. "It doesn't mean it happened. Someone made it up."

"It happened," said Freddie. He went to sleep as he always did, quickly, without tossing, seraphic, with damp curls plastered to his forehead and heavy lashes lying on his cheek.

"It did not," said Hilary. It was impossible to argue when one's opponent fell asleep in the middle of the dispute. Hilary tried to sleep but found herself tossing and punching her pillow. She concluded that it was one of those things that happened to you as you got older. Since some light came through the hanging sheet, she decided to write to Private Farber. In bed, she scribbled: "Dear Private Farber, My hair spreads out over two pillows. It looks like spokes." She scratched this out. "It looks like the rays of the sun." That sounded better. "I have an important question for you. What kind of man are you? Do you like to whomp people? Also, did you ever make anything happen by saying it first? My friend said a convoy would blow up and it did. What do you think of that? Very truly yours, Hilary MacIntyre." She would ask Mickey for a picture tomorrow.

"I don't care what the doctor said"—Ilona's voice, soft and trailing, like the moonvine behind the diving board—"to me you are perfect."

Frank remained quiet.

"My wonderful husband."

"Not *vonderful*. Wonderful. Okay. Name one thing about me that's wonderful."

"That's easy. Your hands. I love your hands, Frank. They're strong hands. Good hands. Loving hands."

Silence.

The light went out. Hilary heard murmuring, then more restless movements, tossing and turning, sighing. They too were having trouble falling asleep. Was it possible they were doing it, the enigmatic act of copulation alluded to in *Growing Up* in which a man somehow stuffed his peepee into the body of a woman? Not likely. Frank, yes, but not Ilona. She was too dainty to be involved in anything like that unless it was specifically to make a baby, which she already had, so what was the purpose of doing it again?

8

Hilary crossed the lobby on her way to school just after the bell captain had hustled Mr. Samuelson, his luggage, and a sackful of Indian River grapefruit into the bus that would take him to the Silver Meteor. What sent Mr. Samuelson back to New York was shortages. Mr. Samuelson could no longer get batteries, and since they were indispensable to his hearing aid, decided it was better shouting at family than at strangers.

The bell captain pocketed his fifty cents and stood behind his desk singing "I'll Never Smile Again." He made no move in the direction of the man who walked into the lobby, primarily because he had no luggage.

The man was as old as Frank, maybe older, dressed in cotton pants and shirt, his belly pulvinate and drooping over his belt, his face and neck deeply sunburned and creased. He held a little boy of about four by the hand and approached the bell captain. He seemed hesitant.

"Do you know Maryann Slade?" he asked, pulling a photograph out of his back pocket. The bell captain studied it.

"Hey, Eleanor," he called. "Doesn't this look like your friend, Mickey?"

Hilary put down her books and walked over to look at the picture. It showed a woman standing with a baby in her arms. It looked something like Mickey, but Mickey in a printed cotton dress and white anklets. The sun was shining in her face and she squinted.

After what had happened to Gus, Hilary needed no more lessons. Friendship came first, before anything else, even, what appeared to be, truth. She remembered what Mickey had made her promise if a strange man came looking for her.

"No," she said. "This isn't Mickey."

"Are you sure?" asked the man. "I heard she was staying here. We came all the way from Georgia to see her."

He was making it tougher. "I'm sure," said Hilary.

The man turned to the bell captain. "Do you mind if we set awhile? It's pretty hot outside. Me and Sonny here could use some cooling off."

"Sit all you like," said the bell captain. "Eleanor, I could swear that was your friend Mickey."

"Tell Freddie to wait for me," Hilary said, running toward the east wing where the house phones were kept.

Mr. Radner answered the phone first. His voice was gruff. "She's sleeping."

"Please, I have to talk to her," said Hilary.

"You're getting to be a pest," said Mr. Radner. "I'm gonna talk to your old man about this."

Mickey came on the phone. "What's up? What time is it?"

"He's here," whispered Hilary. "That man is here and he's asking for you."

"What did you tell him?"

"I told him the woman in the picture wasn't you."

"It's all right, Sol, I'll be off in a minute."

"Is your name really Maryann Slade?" asked Hilary.

"Used to be. What else did you tell him?"

"Nothing."

"That's good."

"Mickey, he has a little boy with him."

There was a pause. "I can't do him any good," she said.

"Who is he? The little boy."

"I can't talk anymore." Mickey hung up the phone.

When Hilary ran back into the lobby, the man was still sitting on a sofa, the little boy beside him sunken into the cushions. "Do you know where me and my son can get some breakfast?" he asked.

"Dining room's right there," said the bell captain. "Your money's as good as anyone else's."

Hilary watched as the man set the pale blond little boy on the carpet. The child's eyes were big and solemn and he followed the man quietly into the dining room without a word. Hilary wondered if anything would make him smile. She crossed her eyes, the way she did when Freddie was little but that only made him burrow his face into the leg of the man.

"Quit that!" said the man. "Don't go acting foolish."

Miss Wallace was checking off who was memorizing what. There were two choices, both of them Tennyson. The first was *The Charge of the Light Brigade,* which all the boys chose because of the part that said, "Cannon to right of them, Cannon to left of them"; the second, *The Lady of Shalott,* about a woman who was weaving a magic web.

Hilary didn't like either one, but she did find a poet that she liked in the back of the book. Her name was Emily Dickinson and she wrote about trees that swung like tassels. Hilary asked Miss Wallace if she could substitute Emily Dickinson for Tennyson, adding that, to be fair, she would make it two poems, since Tennyson's poems were longer. Miss Wallace said no, that Emily Dickinson was scheduled for the sixth grade.

"But why?" asked Hilary. "If I do the same amount?"

"Because Emily Dickinson is difficult to understand."

"I understand her."

"No, dear. You think you do, but you don't. Look here." She took the book and flipped until she found what she was looking for. "'There's something quieter than sleep, within this inner room, it wears a sprig upon its breast and will not tell its name.' Apart from its being rather morbid, I would like you to tell me its meaning."

"I think it's about spooks, or maybe it means when you're thinking to yourself. Sometimes I do that and I forget where I am. I don't know exactly but I like it."

Miss Wallace closed the book. "Emily Dickinson dressed in white and talked to people through closed doors. There was much much to that woman. Believe me when I tell you it will be better if you wait. I'll tell you what, how about Walt Whitman? Why don't you look through the book again and see if you can find one of his that you like. I don't mind making an exception for Walt Whitman."

She said it, but she didn't mean it. When Hilary returned with her choice, which began, "I sing the body electric," Miss Wallace reneged on her offer. Hilary then chose *The Charge of the Light Brigade,* which Jackie Snyder said was disgusting.

"Freddie was called to the principal's office again," said Frances Simmons. "They ought to put his desk in there."

Hilary reached over and flicked her finger hard at Frances' funny bone.

"Miss Wallace!" shrieked Frances. "Hilary gave me pins and needles."

Miss Wallace made a sucking sound, as if she was kissing the air through her teeth. "This silly feud between you girls must come to a stop. Hilary is school spelling champion, Frances. Accept it graciously."

Frances continued to nurse her tingling elbow, shooting malevolent scowls at Hilary, who smirked from behind her geography book.

"For our lesson today," said Miss Wallace, "we're going to study the Philippines. I want you children to understand the desperate situation of the men on Bataan. They have no quinine and they get malaria, they're weak from dysentery," her voice broke, "and they have no planes. Going after a Japanese Zero in a P-40, well, those of you who know planes know how futile that is."

Everyone looked down at the floor. The whole class knew Miss Wallace had a brother in the Philippines. Only a few of the boys knew what a P-40 was, but that only related to its design, not its performance capabilities. The somber mood was broken by Mr. Detwiler, who came in with his arm around the shoulder of a new boy. The boy had a shock of red hair that fell over his forehead and freckles sprinkled over his face and arms in constellations worthy of an entire galaxy, more than Hilary had ever seen before on any one person. Mr. Detwiler told Miss Wallace he was the son of an army air corps major who had been assigned to Miami Beach and that his tuition had been waived.

"Has he been tested?" asked Miss Wallace, the Philippines for the moment forgotten in her zeal for standards.

"He has been tested, and not found wanting," said Mr. Detwiler. "I would be surprised if this young man didn't turn out to be one of your better students."

Miss Wallace searched for a place for the new boy to sit and decided to place him next to Sorrell Myers, who would be the least likely to do the things one did to newcomers like shoving garter snakes and sneezeweed into the back corners of his desk.

His name was T. H. Dallas, and he had been born in Tillamook, Oregon. Since Liz Bonnier was the only one who had ever lived away from the eastern seaboard, having spent a year as far inland as Hartford, Connecticut, it was the same as if he had said he came from Pluto.

It had been a very dry March. The fire began with a flare amid the cattails that lined the green-slimed river bank, then grew to include airy little explosions as the brittle weeds caught. The fire puffed up, orange and sudden in a little whirl of sky-blown ash, causing heat to beat across the muddy water, driving the key deer and their buzzing flies before it. The blooming goldenrod wavered and flashed and fell into soot, cabbage palms and saw palmettos caught and blazed, and the dwarf cypress, alive and green at their tops, became a glowing mass of embers below. Saw-grass prairies blackened into spiky stumps as the fire spread, becoming in its wake a thousand-acre cinder bed, spinning dust as the wind carried the ash and smoke eastward.

When recess came, no one wanted to play in the grayish-blue smog. Sorrell Myers said that he was allergic and was sent back to the classroom. Miss Daly said the blaze in the Everglades had a clearing effect and that its purpose was to thin the brush, but Jack Suga whispered to Hilary that he would like to know how something that burned your eyes and scratched your throat would be good for anything that lived.

Hilary had more important worries on her mind, mainly if Freddie had come back yet from Mr. Detwiler, and what the problem was. The third grade was out on the playground, but no Freddie.

She found his teacher standing next to the swings, facing in all directions like a weathervane.

"Miss Carmichael, I can't find my brother."

At first Miss Carmichael stared at her, as if she were memorizing her face. "You know, Hilary, this is one of those times when I find no pleasure in saying I told you so. Didn't I ask you months ago for an appointment with your mother?"

"Yes, ma'am." Hilary stubbed her sneakered toe into the dirt.

"And didn't your mother say she was too busy to come?"

Miss Carmichael already knew the answers. This was a game. "Yes," again.

"I rest my case. Rudy Steinfeld, no standing on the swings, dear. Your brother has gotten into one scrape after another. He cannot read. He will not listen; consequently, he has fallen far behind the other youngsters. There is no question that he will not be promoted with his other schoolmates. Now that is something that might have been avoided had your mother shown the slightest interest."

"That's not fair," said Hilary. "My mother is very interested." Her voice cracked like splintering glass.

"Watch your tone," said Miss Carmichael.

Rudy pumped his legs, then tipped his heels high into the air, swinging up and back, each time forcing his swing higher. The support frame shuddered and one end threatened to lift out of the ground. Miss Carmichael reached over her hand to steady it.

"My mother works. I told you that before. And Freddie can read."

"I know. You told me. Racing forms, or something like that."

"And comics. He reads *Captain America*."

"This is pointless. Do you know why I sent him to Mr. Detwiler? I sent him to Mr. Detwiler because he has been defacing school property. In a time of the most serious shortages, you know how scarce paper has become, your brother has been making planes, not one, not two, but hundreds; they are all over, littering the classroom, the lavatory, even the cafeteria. Of course, I'm not surprised he has such little regard for property."

Rudy swung by, smiling. That did it. Hilary was angry. There was nothing more to say. She quickly weighed the consequences and decided that the worst that could happen to her would be that she would have to stay for detention, in which case she could pretend to be Emily Dickinson, a deliberate anchorite, instead of an unwilling detainee. She turned on her heel and walked away.

"Just a moment, young lady. I haven't dismissed you."

Hilary kept walking, stopping to pick up her socks and flip her braids over her shoulders. Rudy Steinfeld's interest in banging sideways into the swing beside him was the only thing that prevented Miss Carmichael from going after her.

T. H. Dallas stood near the gumbo limbo tree in a knot of children which included Shirley Leone and Jackie Snyder who giggled and poked one another when Hilary approached. Hilary refused to look at any of them, especially this dumb boy who thought he was special just because his father was a major in the Air Corps. T.H. turned to watch her strut across the dusty playground. Some of his freckles shifted. Hilary didn't know if it was a smile or not but she refused to smile back.

"She thinks she's smart," said Jackie.

"Everyone hates her," said Shirley.

"Does your father fly the Flying Fortress?" asked Billy Connaught.

"No, he's a finance officer. He negotiates leases," said T.H.

"What kind of leases?"

"Hotel leases. He's renting them for barracks, but he's running into snafus. He has to negotiate them one at a time and they keep asking for more money for the next one."

"You bring any baseball cards with you?"

"No."

"Bring them next time," said Billy. "In a rubber band." Billy and the other boys ducked behind the gumbo tree to spin out their cards, flipping them like missiles between thumb and middle finger, while the girls stood behind them to watch.

Hilary sat on the steps of the third-grade bungalow, making whistles out of grass blades while she waited for Freddie, thinking it would be nice to talk to people only through the doors of the lifeguard shack. It was difficult to make the blades whistle. Hilary blamed it on the smoke, which had gotten worse. When T. H. Dallas came by, wheeling his bike, she narrowed her eyes and looked through him as if he had been made of cellophane.

"How come you're still hanging around?" he asked.

"None of your business," said Hilary, cupping her hand over the grass blade.

"Okay." He threw his leg over the bar and started to pedal away.

Something about the way he carried his head made her feel

sorry for him. "I'm waiting for my brother," she said. "He's got detention."

T.H. wheeled back and knocked out the kickstand with his heel. "Why didn't you say so?"

"I just did."

"What are you so mad about?"

"Teachers. I hate them," said Hilary.

"They're all the same. I've been in twelve schools and I ought to know."

Hilary shaded her eyes against the hazy sun. "Really?"

"Honest. They say the same things and they do the same things. All over the country. Teachers are the only ones who ever say lavatory. Think about it. Your mother never says lavatory. But teachers do. Another thing is, teachers stand sideways. Watch one at the blackboard. They never turn all the way around. When your father paints a room, he never stands sideways. He faces the wall. See what I mean?"

"My father doesn't paint anything," said Hilary. "Maintenance does it."

T.H. bent down to tie a shoelace. "I'm going to the municipal golf course to watch the soldiers parade. You want to come?"

"I have to wait for my brother."

"That's okay. I'll wait with you."

"I don't have a bike."

"I'll ride you on mine." He sat down on the step beside her and Hilary turned to give him her first good look. Some of his freckles melted into one another like batter on a cookie sheet.

"Yow! Something stung me!" he said.

"Those are red ants. They bite. They also steal babies from black ants and make slaves out of them."

"It stings like fire."

"You dumb bunny, you have your foot in their path."

Freddie came stomping out of the bungalow, his face, as always, dusty and tearstained. "I hate school," he said. "I'm going to blow it up."

"Is everyone in your family always so mad?" asked T.H.

Hilary didn't answer him but jumped up to run after her brother, catching him by his shoulder. "Hey, I waited for you. The least you could do is wait for me."

Freddie stopped and turned around. "Who's he?"

"He's taking us to the golf course."

It was difficult balancing with all three of them on the bike, but they managed, wobbling in and out of traffic, the front wheel wiggling from side to side, with Freddie perched on the handlebars, Hilary sitting on the seat, T.H. riding on his rear wheel, his arms stretched forward to the rubber grips, and all of them singing "Praise the Lord and Pass the Ammunition." A few grown-ups on the street yelled that they were going to kill themselves and one man said they could lose an eye like that. Even Freddie began to feel better about his detention and yelled, "Your mother wears army boots," to a woman who only had asked where the soldiers were going to march.

The municipal golf course swarmed with squadrons of officer candidates executing neat, precise drills past a reviewing stand where they snapped into punctilious salute while a military band played "Remember Pearl Harbor." Applauding them were officers and officials on the platform, and hundreds of civilians standing in the sand traps and on the sidelines. Overhead floated a blimp on its way to reconnoiter the ocean, a great lazy dollop, hovering for a moment, then drifting eastward in the overcast sky.

T.H. lifted Freddie piggyback in order to let him see better. Hilary sneaked a look at him as he juggled her brother into place, somewhat surprised at how nice a boy could be. Jack Suga was nice, but he didn't count. She remembered T.H. had his arms around her on the bike and that she liked the warm prickly sensation. She would have to talk to Mickey about that.

When Corporal Wright marched by, Hilary recognized him immediately, even though he was in uniform, his tie neatly placed into his shirt between his second and third button, and his cap sitting smartly on his head.

"That's my friend," she shouted. "I know that guy. He lives next door to us. Corporal Wright, it's me, Hilary!" His squadron marched by, followed by another. "He didn't turn."

"He's not supposed to," said T.H. "He would get gigged if he did."

"What's a gig?" asked Freddie.

"It's like detention."

"It's easy to get into trouble," said Freddie, "for everybody."

When T.H. deposited Hilary and Freddie on the sidewalk in

front of their hotel, Bill Wright had just jumped off a truck with a dozen other men. Freddie saluted him.

"Did you see us on the golf course?" asked Hilary.

"Sure did."

"Remember me?" asked Freddie.

"Your face but not your name, little buddy."

"It's Fred."

"Pleased to meet you, Fred." They stood for a while smiling at each other.

"We can't go to the beach," said Freddie.

"Why not?"

"The mockingbird has babies and it dive-bombs us."

"I'd stay away for a while, until they get a little bigger."

"Real dive bombers go right down the funnels of ships," said Freddie.

"He skips around a lot," said Hilary.

"I don't think that's really what dive bombers do, Fred. They dive at a pretty steep angle, though, so it looks like they do. Actually they ride that bomb down, come as close as they can to the target, but there's no way they can go down funnels. The plane wouldn't fit." He stopped explaining when he saw the men beside him polarized, all facing in the same direction.

"Here she comes," said one. "What a dish."

It was Mickey, wearing dark glasses, wedgies, and slacks, the newest fashion. She looked wonderful. Her hair was arranged in one roll at her neck and another on her forehead. Most of the bruises had faded but couldn't be seen very well anyway since her skin was the color of bronze, the result of days of careful tanning. Hilary had not seen her in over two weeks.

"That's my friend Mickey," she said.

"Why didn't you say so?" asked Bill Wright.

Mickey ignored the soldiers and took Hilary aside. "You didn't tell your mother or your father or anyone, did you? About what you called me about this morning?"

"I wouldn't do that," said Hilary.

"Good. I didn't think you would." Mickey rewarded her with a kiss on her cheek and a bright smile that showed the space between her front teeth. She smelled like jasmine. "Don't worry. He's gone. The bell captain called to tell me. Listen, Sol is leaving this week. We can see a movie Saturday if you like. Only I don't want to go with all those kids. I want to make the four o'clock."

"How about *Yankee Doodle Dandy* with Jimmy Cagney?" asked Hilary.

"I don't like that little shrimp," said Mickey. "He struts like a bantam rooster my daddy once owned. Pick a movie with a tall hero. I like a man to be tall."

"Mr. Radner isn't tall."

"That's different. I just stay with him," Mickey whispered. "I don't have to look at him big as life on some screen in a dark movie house."

"Introduce me," said Bill Wright, striding toward them. "You may not have noticed, but I'm tall."

"This is Corporal Wright," said Hilary. "He forgot his serial number."

"Hello," he said, his eyes taking Mickey in, in little sips like a connoisseur of brandy. "Hilary told me she had a friend named Mickey. I thought you would have braces on your teeth."

Mickey looked up at him in a practiced, sober way, in the manner of Frank checking a steak for marbling, and conceded that while he was tall, and maybe even handsome, he was nothing else. It was clear from his eagerness that he didn't have a dime.

"Mickey what?" he asked.

"You mean Mickey who," corrected Hilary.

"Mickey none of your business," said Mickey. "And you can get arrested for running around with little kids."

The other soldiers on the sidewalk began to laugh. "What's the matter, Bill?" yelled one. "You struck out and you didn't even pick up the bat!" This made some of the other men laugh even harder. One of them slapped his knees with his cap.

Bill Wright looked down at Mickey. She had the kind of heart-shaped face he liked to cup in his hands. "You on vacation?"

Mickey flicked her long thick lashes once, as if brushing him out of her sight, then turned deliberately and elaborately from him to address Hilary.

"I'm going to Lincoln Road to do a little shopping, maybe look for your birthday present, stuff like that." She moistened her fingertips and tucked up the stray wisps on her neck into the roll.

"That's okay," said Hilary. "You don't have to get me anything."

"Do that with your hand again, honey," called one of the men, a big smiling fellow with his thumbs hooked into his belt. "You know, raise it up over your head."

Bill Wright turned around. "Lay off," he said.

"It's my way of complimenting her. She knows it. Ask her."

"I told you to lay off, June Bug."

Bill reached the cluster of men in two lanky easy steps and began to speak in low and angry tones to the offender.

"Keep your guard up, Bill," yelled Freddie. "You're leaving yourself wide open."

Hilary had Mickey all to herself. She knocked her elbows together behind her back, forcing her shoulder blades to meet. "There's a new boy at school," she said.

"What's his name?"

"T. H. Dallas."

"He sounds like a cowboy. You like him?"

"He's okay." Hilary couldn't bring herself to tell Mickey how nice it felt when he put his arms around her to hold the handlebars. There was something funny about that, something that was better off keeping to yourself.

"Right on schedule," said Mickey.

"What is?"

"That ol' black magic." Mickey clumped away on her wooden-soled wedgies.

"Wait a minute," called Bill, breaking away from the cluster of men on the sidewalk, but she had already crossed the street and was flagging down a bus. He watched as the bus rumbled and backfired its way down Collins Avenue, even though the second lieutenant had already blown the whistle which signaled that it was time to line up to march to mess.

"Is she married?" he asked Hilary.

"No," said Hilary. Freddie started to say something about Mr. Radner, but Hilary shut him up with a look.

Bill Wright got into line with a leap and a whoop, and slapped one of his comrades on the back, then after another blast of the whistle, threw his chest out and marched toward the makeshift mess hall that had been converted from a card room, singing with his classmates "Someone's in the Kitchen with Dinah."

A rift over top billing developed between Gomez and her 4-F partner, Lipschutz. Although they continued to dance together, and even practice artful and elaborate routines by the pool, not a word was spoken. They did it all by touch and sight. It came to a head when Gomez found out that Mrs. Steinfeld was not paying for her lessons, having been alerted when Mrs. Steinfeld, something of a klutz, suddenly knew all the breaks, even some special flourishes that were ordinarily not taught to amateurs but considered the bailiwick of a true professional, like one in which he bent her over backward, supported only by a thumb on her coccyx. When Gomez began to investigate, she found no record, no chits, no stubs, no checks, no notes, nothing, which made it almost certain that Lipschutz was involved in another exchange. That did not bother her, as she had no interest in Lipschutz that way. What bothered her was the loss of revenue.

When the conga chain wove through the lobby that evening with Mrs. Steinfeld at the head and Lipschutz right behind her, his hands glued to her hips, Gomez knew.

"Gooey gooey, conga," said Mrs. Steinfeld.

"Stop," said Gomez.

"One, two, three, kick," said Lipschutz.

"We're going to have this out," said Gomez. "Where's the money for all the lessons she took?"

"I don't know what you're talking about," said Mrs. Steinfeld. "One, two, three, kick!"

"I don't either," said Lipschutz. "Excuse us."

"Excuse nothing. You've been giving her lessons on the sly, you flat-footed 4-F!"

"What makes you say that? How can you say such a thing?"

"Come on," yelled the other conga dancers. "Stop holding up the line."

"What makes me say that? Because of the way she snaps her head when she turns, and clicks her fingers when she walks, and stomps her feet, that's what makes me say that. She never used to be able to put one foot in front of the other. Now she thinks she's Rita Hayworth."

"You're just jealous that someone else can dance as well as you can," said Mrs. Steinfeld. "One, two, three," she kicked Gomez aside.

Gomez let out a terrible yell. "You chiseling bitch!"

Mr. Davis had been talking to Mr. Ornstein who came over from his own hotel to find out why Mr. Davis had so much meat on his own menu while he was forced to serve mullet. Mr. Ornstein wanted to know specifically where Davis was getting all the extra red stamps, which was the only way restaurants got extra meat and butter. He alluded to Davis' connections with Mr. Lonzo. Mr. Davis was getting ready to answer with his customary aplomb, but the word *bitch* arrested his attention. He would have heard it in his lobby if it had been said under water.

"Excuse me," he said to Mr. Ornstein, handing him the conversation as if it were a package. "This will not do," he said to Gomez. "Not do at all. Remember our guests."

"That's the problem," said Gomez. "This guest just chiseled me out of a lot of money."

"There has to be a rational explanation. You're excited. Why don't we all go and sit down together and talk it over."

The conga line without a leader was like a worm without a head. It wiggled its way aimlessly into the dining room as the combatants selected an empty sofa.

It was obvious to Mr. Davis that there was something between Lipschutz and Mrs. Steinfeld. He could tell by the way they sat at a discreet distance, Mrs. Steinfeld carefully smoothing her skirt over her knee, Lipschutz looking at the ceiling. Mr. Davis' view of the situation was both Continental and practical, and he concluded that moral judgment had no place in a relationship that kept Mrs. Steinfeld happy and a guest of the hotel.

"I'm a natural dancer," began Mrs. Steinfeld.

"Yes she is," said Lipschutz. "She's a natural."

"Miss Gomez," said Mr. Davis, "you're making some pretty scurrilous charges. You have to be prepared to back them up."

"I'll back them up, all right. With the heel of my shoes."

"Now, now." Secretly the thought was very exciting, but Mr. Davis was a businessman first. "We simply have nothing to go on. Further, this is a dispute which rightfully belongs to you and Mr. Lipschutz. Mrs. Steinfeld, as I see it, is not a party."

"I'm up to here with all of this," said Gomez. "And with you. Who needs this aggravation? I could get a job making twice, three times the money as a welder."

"Why don't you?" asked Lipschutz. There was silence.

Mr. Davis thought of half a dance team, added to his other problems, like no bellhops, no pool boy, and no gasoline, and said, "Now, now, let's not be hasty."

Lipschutz thought of freedom. "It's been coming, Mr. Davis. The handwriting has been on the wall."

"You schmuck!"

"It's amazing how we non-Jews pick up these expressions," said Mr. Davis.

Gomez turned to him. "Putz!" she said, and stormed away.

Mr. Davis mopped his forehead and the top of his head and stood up. Instantly Lipschutz and Mrs. Steinfeld snapped together. He turned back to continue his conversation with Ornstein who stood questioning his desk clerk for a count of the house. On his way to the front desk, he was consoled by the sight of Mrs. Portman, always a pleasant, comfortable lady, like cocoa with marshmallows.

"What do you hear from your son?" he asked, still mopping his forehead.

"He's in New Guinea, in the Coral Sea. He says he has a cueball haircut called the guinea clip, and that some of the natives are still in the Stone Age. He writes he can fish by putting his hand in the water and that he is very tanned. I also heard from Mack. He's putting in for submarine duty. Because of his height."

"Mack is a good man. We're all proud of him."

"I worry about my Elliott. I hear such bad things now."

"I wouldn't worry, Mrs. Portman. Bataan is where the problem is. It's nowhere near New Guinea. That's on the other side of the ocean. Why don't you go to the east wing? Mrs. Templeton is having a horse race."

"I'd rather bet on the real thing. Mel gives better odds."

Frank's depression was common knowledge. Everyone knew he was down. Ilona tried without success to talk him out of it, asking to compare himself with amputees or people on the other side who were running from the Nazis. The bartender thought a few shots of Jack Daniel's would do it. Marco tried some jokes. Gus, who had somewhat forgiven everyone for what happened to him, came to put a floury hand on his shoulder. Even Mr. Davis came to talk to him, telling him that Miami was an important part of the war effort, since it provided a vacation place for the nation, and hadn't President Roosevelt himself come out in favor of vacations, saying how much they helped the war effort? Mr. Davis added that even the Defense Council, mindful of the national importance of Miami Beach as a vacation place, promised no more blackout drills until after the season.

Nothing worked. When Frank burned himself, which he never did, they knew things were bad with him. Ilona called for Dr. Hershbaum, the house doctor, who usually treated nothing more serious than a bad case of sunburn, although once he had been called to help hoist a woman who had fallen in her bathtub and sprained an ankle, and would allow no one but a bona fide doctor to see her naked.

Dr. Hershbaum looked like Adolphe Menjou, complete with a thin mustache and a sneer. He wasn't really sneering. It was just the way his mouth and nose came together. Actually, he was a very pleasant person.

He treated Frank in the receiving room on top of a crate of tomatoes, sprinkling powder from a paper packet over the burn.

"Tell me," asked Frank, "I hear that if you take Bromo Seltzer, it makes your blood pressure go down."

"The major thing that Bromo is good for is heartburn. And as far as your blood pressure is concerned, I can give you things that will work a lot better than a Bromo Seltzer."

"Can't use them," said Frank. "Forget it."

"Keep this dressed. You look tired, Frank. Getting enough rest?"

"That's the problem. I'm getting too much rest."

Hilary helped Ilona take down their laundry from the line rigged beneath the pipes of the engineering room. It was her only domestic responsibility besides watching out for Freddie and she resented it because it interfered with "Blondie," one of her favorite programs for which she could not count on Freddie to give her a rundown on the evening's episode. They hurried because Ilona wanted to get back to Frank.

"Why do we have to fold everything when it only gets messed up anyway?" asked Hilary.

"Because we start off neat and clean. What happens after that is each person's responsibility."

"Is Daddy still sad about not getting in the Army? Vicky Sue said he was."

"He'll get over it. There's worse things."

"I get sad sometimes too," said Hilary. She voiced this admission looking over the top of a petticoat.

"Everyone gets sad," said Ilona. "There's sadness you can do something about, and there's sadness you can do nothing about. You have to know the difference. You work your way out of the sadness you can do something about with your hands and your back. It goes."

"What kind does Daddy have?"

"He has the kind that it's no good to leave him alone with. He broods when he's alone."

"Emily Dickinson was alone. She stayed in her room and wrote poetry. All day long."

"That's what I mean. People can go crazy when they stay alone. And fold, Hilary. Don't roll." Ilona noticed everything.

"Ma, I met this new boy at school. His father is a major. In the Air Corps."

"You're too young for boys. Get yourself a girlfriend. And I don't mean that one upstairs."

It was time to change the subject. "Freddie's teacher said he won't be promoted."

"Now what?"

"He's in trouble. All the time. I think you should go to school."

"What if I write a letter. You can take it in."

"A letter's no good. She wants to see you."

"If I have to go, I have to go. Tell her I'm coming as soon as the season is over. She'll understand."

They sorted socks, rolling them up to the toe, then turning them inside out, so that one fit into the other. "That's how you fit inside me," said Ilona. "Once upon a time."

It was the most Ilona had ever said about such matters. It brought them, for a moment, close. "Ma, could you ever leave me?"

"How could you ask such a question? Of course I could never leave you. What do you do, lie awake and think them up?" Ilona reached above her to unpin more clothes from the line. "Sometimes you remind me of my father, may he rest in peace."

"You never told me that." Hilary rested her elbows on the basket.

"I forgot. The man had a million questions."

"Who did he ask? The questions."

"Sometimes my mother, but mostly the rabbi. He should have been a rabbi himself."

"Can girls be rabbis?"

"Girls are rebbitzen. The wives of rabbis."

"I could never be that. Anyway. I'm not Jewish."

"Yes, you are."

Hilary looked up and saw that her mother was serious. "How come?"

"Because I am Jewish. It's a basic law. If the mother is Jewish, so is the child."

"But what if I didn't decide to be Jewish?"

"Decide has nothing to do with it. It just is."

Hilary needed a few minutes to digest that one. It meant that she and Frank were different. It meant that she was the same as Mrs. Steinfeld. They continued to fold and sort in silence. When the basket was full, Hilary picked it up.

"Ma, could a mother leave her child?"

"Impossible. No mother could do such a thing." Ilona caught her lower lip with her teeth and turned away.

Hilary was relieved. Mickey was not the mother of the little boy. It would have changed everything. Ilona held up one of Freddie's shirts, which still showed a gray stain. She rubbed it between her fingers and held it to the light.

"That's a little like leaving your arm. Leaving your own child." They turned to see Winona getting ready for the night. She wore white gloves and a little hat with a veil.

"You look very nice," said Ilona. "Where are you going?"

"My church is having a social. But I'd be going anyhow, to give thanks. Lionel has been assigned to loading docks at Gulfport, Mississippi, and it looks like it's a permanent assignment."

"Isn't that hard work?"

"Hard work never hurt nobody, you ought to know that. Mainly it means he won't go overseas."

"He won't have to fight those yellowbellies," said Hilary.

Winona pulled her veil down to her chin. Its black dots sparkled on her face. "Honey, look at my skin. What do you call me when I'm not around?"

"I don't call you anything," said Hilary.

"You just called some other folks you never saw an ugly name."

"But it's not the same. You're not the enemy."

"Not now I'm not," said Winona. "But things have a way of changing. What would you call me then?" She turned to Ilona. "I don't mean to be correcting your child for you. It just seemed like something that ought to be said. Try rubbing that stain with salt," she said. "It'll move for salt."

"I don't mind. If you don't mind that I show you how to tie that veil. May I? Twist it under your chin, like this."

"I never saw you wear a hat," said Hilary, after Winona left.

"There's lots of things you never saw me do."

"Like what?"

"If I told you, then I would have no surprises left."

9

In April the season had come to a close. It was time to head north. The birds knew it. Great flocks of migrating sparrows, swallows, little thrush with speckled underbellies, and hummingbirds passing through on their way from Mexico flew overhead guided by the sky. The snowbirds knew it, the hangers-on and drifters who hustled tentative livelihoods saw that the pickings were slim and it was time to leave, except, of course, for the card sharks and bamboozlers who regarded the naïve servicemen as an easy buck.

The tourists knew it too and left in droves, most of them going by train or bus because there was not enough gas to ensure a return trip any farther north than Pahokee, a tiny hamlet on the edge of Lake Okeechobee, which any seasoned traveler could tell you was in *yenemvelt,* clearly no place to get stuck without gas. Some of them left their cars in Miami, planning to return for them when things eased up. Others, taking advantage of the fact that there were no cars coming off the assembly lines, sold them at high prices. People didn't feel like vacations anyway. Things were very bad. The worst that they expected, that they didn't expect, the unthinkable, had happened. Japan and Germany were winning. Boys who had rushed off swaddled in patriotism, strong boys, American boys, were dying. There was not a family who did not have someone in service, and if not a relative, then a close friend, whose global destination and future were both uncertain.

The demand for dance lessons decreased, as did the number of guests, so Gomez was not missed, except by Mel. Lipschutz and Mrs. Steinfeld were still enamored of one another, casting heavy-lidded, soulful glances and clinging in vimineous entanglements. Sometimes Lipschutz even trembled, and could be seen vibrating on the dance floor. Gomez wrote to Lipschutz once a week telling him that leaving him was the best thing that ever happened to her since now she earned four times what she had earned as a dance instructor and what was more, she didn't have to associate with slackers like him. She said she wore leather jackets, overalls, hood, long gloves up to her elbow, and she could weld overhead because she was so practiced lifting up her arms. Most important, she was welding ships. She concluded by writing that she got quite a thrill out of knowing she was helping the war effort, which is more than she could say for him.

The only good news was that after weeks of anxious worry, the hotel staff began to breathe a sigh of relief when it was learned that the Air Corps did not want the Flamingo Arms because of a basic flaw in design. It seemed that the building was shaped in a U, with no way to take out garbage except through the beach or through the lobby. Since the hotel lacked the facilities considered basic in its sanitation course, the Air Corps made no move to acquire a lease.

Mr. Davis mopped his head and began to plan for the slack summer season. Perhaps they could attract the wives and parents of the servicemen with bargain package tours. The problem was how to do it. He could either advertise in the newspaper or, with permission, put up posters on the military bulletin boards. He favored the latter plan, since it would not indicate to the competition, such as it was, how bad things really were.

Rather than making Frank feel better, the news of the Army's decision made him feel worse. When Marco came in to ask if he had heard about the hotel, Frank turned away and continued to pound pepper into a lamb shoulder. Now he was trapped in a civilian job when men were fighting and dying and it was clear his country, losing on every front, needed every able-bodied man it could get. He slammed the meat with the flat of his butcher knife.

It was during this month that the issue of religious affiliation became a vital one. Hilary and Freddie had gone to the Purim festival weeks before with Ilona at a little synagogue on South

Beach, where they sat in a crowded auditorium and were given noisemakers to rattle away a bad guy named Haman. Everything was fine until it was time to introduce the little girl chosen as Queen Esther—Shirley Leone, of course. Freddie asked Ilona if Queen Esther was President Roosevelt's wife and everyone in the rows around them laughed. A man asked who said that and the woman beside him turned and pointed to Freddie. Hilary crossed her eyes and thrust out her chin like a bulldog when the man turned. Fortunately, Ilona could not see her face.

It was Frank's turn to show them what he had to offer, even though Ilona had said it would make no difference in the long run, since they were Jewish, and that was all there was to it.

Frank, somewhat dispirited since the bromide he had been taking daily had not been effective in bringing down his blood pressure, even after he gave up his cigars for Lent, took them to St. Patrick's church on Easter Sunday. Ilona said she wouldn't go, but dressed them up anyway, Hilary in a little straw hat with a ribbon around the band, a dress with a starched petticoat that wouldn't lie flat, and patent leather shoes that Hilary shined with spit, and Freddie in a jacket and bow tie that he said was choking him to death.

When they were dressed, Ilona even had Hilary go out into the hall and enter their room, as she had been taught to do by Mrs. Templeton, standing with her back to the door, changing the knob from one hand to the other, and closing it softly.

Frank was unimpressed with Hilary's door-entering skill. "Let's go," he said. "We won't get seats if we get there late."

The Catholic church presented a more thrilling scenario. The synagogue, with none of its arcanum, paled in comparison. For one thing, the synagogue was a tiny, musty place, with nothing special about it except a cupboard in front in which Ilona said they kept the Torah. The Catholic church on the other hand was magnificent, with stained-glass windows, vaulting ceilings, organ music, coloratura sopranos, and priests in white and fuchsia silk, who swung incense and chanted in Latin, mixed wine and water in a golden chalice, and put something in the mouth of everyone who lined up for it. Frank lined up but didn't swallow what was put in his mouth as he was supposed to but brought it back to them so they could see it.

"This is the Host," he said. "It's the body of Christ, but I don't expect you to understand that."

"It looks like a smooth matzoh," said Hilary.

Frank took it out of her hand and swallowed it, then sat like a grown-up who didn't want to be in a place, stiff and wooden, as if he'd checked all his body functions outside with his umbrella.

The only drawback was that they had to bob up and down and kneel on a cushioned bench, causing Hilary's petticoat and dress which it supported to flip up behind her as she knelt, and unless she was quick, expose her pants marked Sunday.

When they returned to the hotel, Ilona made everyone, including Frank, hang up their dress clothes. "Well," she said, "what did you think? Is it what you thought it was going to be?"

"Me and Freddie want to be Catholic," said Hilary.

"It's not as easy as that," said Ilona. "I told you that before."

"I think the kids should make up their own minds," said Frank. He smoothed his trousers and folded them over a hanger. "They're not making pants with pleats or cuffs anymore. You think you can do something with these?"

"What do you like so much about the Catholic church?" asked Ilona.

"You get to go to confession," said Hilary. "That's what Billy Connaught does. Every week."

"Confess to me," said Ilona. "I'll tell you what to do."

"You're our mother," said Freddie. "It's not the same. Catholic kids get to go into this little house and talk through a grating."

"That's no reason to choose a religion," said Ilona.

"We like the ceremony better," said Hilary. "I think God pays more attention to the Catholics."

Ilona decided that it was not a true test and that they had no way of knowing who God paid attention to. She would take them to the synagogue for regular services sometime when she was not so busy.

Corporal Wright had a fifteen-minute breather between his course in defense against chemicals and his course in map and photo interpretation. Now he climbed to the roof two steps at a time to get some sun in private and read his mail. Standing with his face to the ocean, he slit the envelope with his finger. His mother wrote that his father was working very hard now that he was feeding the nation, his sister had become a cheerleader, and she had sent him his favorite cake, which he could share with his bunkmates if he chose. She concluded by asking him if he was taking care of himself and making him promise to wear something on his feet at all times, since Miami, being in the tropics, had fungus, some of which she understood rotted one's feet.

Voices from the opposite roof drew his attention to Mickey, only a few feet away, working with Hilary on their victory garden. Mickey wore an off-the-shoulder blouse with ruffles, shorts, and high-heeled wedgies. She looked to him curvy and adorable, sculpted in glowing pinks and tans and about whom his mother would ask, usually with a frown, how serious he was. They were tying sallow, drooping lima-bean tendrils to Popsicle sticks.

"How are your beans coming?" he asked.

"You can see for yourself," said Hilary. "What do you think?"

"They look pale to me. They might be shy of a little nitrogen."

"We don't need your advice, farmerboy," said Mickey.

"Actually I'm not a farmer. My people raise hogs."

"That's even worse," said Mickey. "I'll bet you're real good at calling."

"I used to be, when I was her age."

"How come you don't do it now?" asked Hilary.

"I'm studying something else," he said.

"Like what?" asked Hilary.

"Don't encourage him," whispered Mickey, but it was too late.

"Agricultural engineering. I want to work for the soil-conservation service." Corporal Wright came close to the edge. "Listen, I think we got off on the wrong foot, when we first met. Every time I see you, you give me the cold shoulder, especially when you're with your father. Can't I do anything to make it up?" He smiled. "I'll even do a real good hog call if that will help."

"Let's hear it," said Mickey. She winked at Hilary.

Corporal Wright threw back his head. "Souweeee," he yelled. "Pig, pig, pig. How's that?"

Everyone sunning on the patio of the emerald green swimming pool looked up. One woman's shoulder straps flopped to her waist, uncovering her pendulous breasts. She grabbed her towel and looked about her to see if anyone had noticed. "What's going on up there?" shouted Mr. Carpathy, shielding his eyes against the sun. "What kind of a balagoola carries on like that?"

Then the door to the roof slammed open admitting the second lieutenant. He scanned the rooftop and quickly assessed the attraction next door. "Wright, that isn't appropriate military bearing. It is unbecoming an officer, especially on Easter Sunday. You're gigged. Get downstairs on the double."

"Yes, sir."

"He was chasing away the mockingbird," said Hilary. "It comes up here and gets our beans."

"Get yourself a scarecrow," said the second lieutenant, who grinned at Mickey in a half smile that curled up one corner of his mouth before he jumped down the stairwell.

"How do you think them up so fast?" asked Mickey. "You're better than I am."

"I don't know," said Hilary. "Sometimes I don't even try. Sometimes they're right there on my tongue and they come out. Like spit."

Bill Wright turned and stepped to the stairwell.

"Wait," said Mickey. "Look, I'm real sorry I got you into trouble. I didn't want that to happen."

He stood with his hand on the doorknob. "It was worth it if it got you to talk to me. I'm not a bad guy. Honest. All I want to do is talk to you. I promise I won't make a move on you."

"I've heard that before," she said.

"You have to trust someone sometime," he said.

"Why?"

"Because. You'll go through life missing everything that's good."

"Everything good," she said, "doesn't wear pants. Everything good is either green with black ink and pictures of presidents or blue skies and sunshine. Anything else, and that includes most people, stinks."

He looked sadly at her. "I'd like a chance to show you you're wrong. Look, I have open post next weekend. Can you go out with me Saturday night?"

"I'm busy."

"What about the Saturday after?"

"Same thing."

"Too bad. So long, Hilary."

He swung down the steps and disappeared.

"Is that true?" asked Hilary. "That most people stink?"

"You'll find it out sooner or later. Might as well be sooner."

"I think he's nice," said Hilary.

"That's because you're not experienced. He's like all the rest. He just looks sweeter, that's all. These beans are sure a funny color. I never saw white limas before."

"Maybe we made up something new."

"That and a nickel will get you a cup of coffee."

The conversation switched to religion. Mickey admitted reluctantly that she was a Baptist. She corrected this to say, used to be Baptist. She said she didn't know much about Jews and Catholics, except her father hated them both and she thought Mr. Radner was Jewish, although he had never come right out and told her.

"I'm trying to pick one," said Hilary. "I can't make up my mind."

"If I could pick," said Mickey, "I'd pick the Pentecostals. They do all sorts of things with snakes and jumping and people shouting and hollering, moaning on the floor, cripples throwing their crutches in the air. I'll tell you, you go to one of those, you really see something."

Everyone in school knew that T.H. was her boyfriend. The fact had changed her life. The road from Ishmael to Little Eva is marked with such simple signposts as having someone to sit next to in the cafeteria. When she came to a squatting circle shooting marbles, everyone made room for her, and Paul even showed her how to do a backspin for a close shot. People began to tell her jokes, like Liz Bonnier who asked, "Did you get my letter," and when Hilary answered no, stamped her on the foot and said, "I forgot to stamp it." Hilary was right in the middle of all her old games like Kick the Can and Ring-a-levio, and Frances Simmons told her to get an autograph book with colored pages, because they were all going to sign one another's books. Life was heaven.

The friendship, though, was not without cost and proved to be a trade-off in many ways. For example, one time when everyone stood by the gumbo limbo tree during recess to have another swinging and hanging contest, Hilary, who had been first in line, said, "Me first."

T.H. had looked strangely at her. "Girls shouldn't do this," he advised.

"Why not?" she had asked.

T.H. had shrugged. "Do it if you like. I think girls look dumb hanging upside down like bats."

Hilary decided not to hang and instead watched the boys slip their legs over the thick branches, pressing against them with the muscles of their calves. She could do better. She knew she could do better, but she didn't try. Instead, she stood there, basking in the glow of T.H.'s approbation and doing what the other girls were doing, which was nothing, unless you counted cheering for the boys doing something. Billy Connaught won, which surprised no one.

Another trade-off was in gym. Hilary took to climbing as easily as all other skills taught by Mr. Saunders, her arms and legs responding to the challenge, as soon as she had the rhythm, hand over hand, legs curling and climbing, pushing up with her ankles, faster, faster, exultantly reaching the top, hanging there and swinging, looking below, and pretending she was a spangled circus girl twirling her way to the top.

T.H. watched her from below, waiting his turn in line. He looked uncomfortable and disappointed, even from twenty feet up. Hilary slid down.

"What was it like up there?" he asked.

"Actually," she improvised, "it's kind of scary."

"I knew that," said T.H. "I could take one look at you and I knew you were scared."

The last trade-off had been in the classroom that morning. Mr. Detwiler had been wrong. T.H. was not one of the best students, he was one of the worst. Actually, arithmetic was his only good subject. He struggled in all the others, including geography, in which he said he had had the same text in another school.

Hilary usually knew the answers in arithmetic as she did all other subjects. She would put her hand up first, waving it, sometimes having to support her arm in her eagerness to be recognized. Miss Wallace put a particularly hard decimal problem on the board and asked if anybody knew the answer. It was tricky because of the zeroes. Hilary put her hand up but quickly brought it down when she saw that T.H. had done the same thing, reasoning that it was better to let him succeed in the one thing he did well. Hilary had to hold her hand to keep it down, the answer had been so simple.

"Hilary," said Miss Wallace, "I'm surprised you didn't know this one."

"It's too hard," she lied.

T.H. had his hand up. He was smiling, not smugly, but with genuine pleasure. Miss Wallace called on him to explain at the blackboard. When he returned to his seat he whispered to Hilary, "I'll show you how to do it later. It's easy."

T.H., for all his restrictions, could be very sweet. He said the magic words one afternoon the week before. He said, "I want you to be my girlfriend."

Hilary replied she thought she already was, but he was only firming things up, in the manner of his father negotiating leases. "I don't have any other girlfriends. Do you have any other boyfriends?"

"No."

"Well, then, this means we're going steady."

"Okay," said Hilary. A heady moment.

Going steady gave both of them prerogatives. Hilary already knew hers. Now T.H. took his. He led her around the maintenance shack. They ducked through the moldy wooden door.

"You said yes when I asked if we were going steady."

"Yes," said Hilary again, corroborating his assumption. "We are. We're definitely going steady."

He moved in for the kill. "If we are, then I'm supposed to kiss you. That's what everyone does when they go steady. They kiss."

Mickey was right. It cost something. Hilary, however, was willing. She had never kissed a boy before and she wanted to try it, since everyone in the movies did it and T.H. wanted to do it, and she never wanted to go back to the way things were before T.H.

They sat down together on a pile of grass clippings. T.H. positioned her shoulders. "Turn like this," he suggested, "and close your eyes."

"But yours are open," said Hilary.

"The girl is supposed to close hers. The boy has to keep his open, or else how is he going to know what to do?"

The logic was irrefutable. Hilary closed her eyes. "Don't scare me," she said.

He tried to put his lips on hers but their noses were an obstruction.

"It's not going to work," said Hilary. "I can't get my nose out of the way."

"I don't know," he said. "We must be doing something wrong. I think in the movies they tilt their faces sideways, like this."

Hilary let T.H. turn her head, then press his lips on hers a long time, making squirming sucking movements. Hilary's lips felt like rubber. She knew they were being pulled out of shape and hoped that when he was through they would return to their original design. His mouth was wet. When he pulled his head away, the saliva remained.

"Are you going to do any more?" she asked.

"Why?"

"Because if you're not, I'm going to wipe my mouth."

By the time the afternoon recess came, Hilary was still wiping her mouth with the back of her hand. If that was what kissing was all about, she didn't like it at all. Why they did it in the movies and looked like they were enjoying it was a mystery. It was also a mystery why they didn't take out handkerchiefs afterward and dry their mouths.

Everyone was on the playground. A few heavy rains had doused the fire of the Everglades, making the air heavy and sweet. The new moisture brought everything to life, transforming the playground into vermicular new growth that crept over the dirt and wiggled over worn spaces with green.

Sorrell Myers stood picking stickers off his socks, but most of the fifth grade were in circles, bouncing off each other like pinballs, most playing Territory, a game in which each person flipped a penknife into a circle. At the point where the knife struck, the players each drew a line, dissecting the circle into smaller and smaller parcels of territory, and teaching themselves, although they didn't know it, fractions and decimals.

"Hilary!" The shout came from the bungalows.

"It's your mother," said Shirley Leone.

"Hilary, over here."

Ilona came out of the third-grade bungalow, wearing a cotton print dress with puffed sleeves, her hair in a smooth and tidy upsweep. She hurried over to where Hilary stood. How could she have possibly learned about kissing T.H. in the maintenance shack? Hilary's heart began to race.

"I spoke to Miss Carmichael," said Ilona, "I think she understands. She said she would reconsider her decision very carefully, and that she would give Freddie another chance." Ilona looked at the children about her. "Hello, Shirley."

"Hello, Mrs. MacIntyre."

Ilona smiled a pretty smile in which one of her cheeks dimpled. "Are these your friends?" she asked.

Hilary nodded.

"Bring them home to swim," she said. She took a handkerchief out of her purse, wet it with her tongue, held Hilary's face in her hand, and wiped at something on her chin. Then she put the handkerchief back, clutched shut her purse, and walked away.

"I didn't know your mother was foreign," said Frances.

"I told you that before," said Shirley Leone.

"What is she?" asked Jackie.

"She's from Austria."

"That's German," said Billy Connaught. "She's a German."

"No she's not," said Hilary. "She's an American citizen."

"It doesn't matter. She wasn't born here. How come you don't talk like her?"

It was like being on a sandbar. You look away one minute, turn back, and suddenly, everything has shifted, water where there was sand, and sand where there was water.

"How do you mean?"

"With an accent. Your mother can't say swim. She says *svim*."

Hilary was ashamed. Why did Ilona have to come then, and why did she have to speak? She wouldn't have minded even the face washing if she hadn't spoken.

"She's taking lessons," offered Hilary, "in speaking better."

The votive was accepted. "That's a good idea," said Jackie Snyder. "I take elocution lessons and it's helped me a lot."

Hilary realized that she had forgotten to introduce her mother to T.H. Then her face grew hot. She had not forgotten. It was something that she did not want to do. She was a rotten person. Freddie had been telling her that lately and he was right.

T.H. meanwhile seemed to have something else on his mind. He was staring across the playground, his eyes squinted, his hands balled up in fists upon his hips.

"What is it?" asked a sixth-grade boy named Paul. "What do you see?"

"I'm thinking about what the Japs did on Bataan," said T.H.

Everyone knew what he meant. The death march was in the newspaper, on the radio, and all their parents talked about except for Doolittle's daring raid on Tokyo that did little strategically. And it plunged everyone into the gloom of stark reality, unvarnished truth where things are seen exactly as they are, like pores in a magnifying mirror, and into numbing awareness that the nation was in serious trouble.

"I think it's unpatriotic," said T.H., "to have anything to do with a Jap. Any Jap."

They turned to the object of his stare. Jack Suga was coming across the lawn, carrying his cigar box full of baseball cards. "Get lost, Tojo!" shouted T.H.

Jack slowed down, said nothing, and dropped his cigar box to his side.

"I don't think you listen good," said T.H. "I told you to get lost."

Jack stopped where he was and searched the faces of the ring of children, his eyes coming to rest on Hilary who held his for a moment, and then looked to the ground.

"I don't think you should say that to him," said Sorrell Myers. "He didn't do anything."

"Shut up, fatso," said Paul, shoving him backward into a croton bush. What happened next was a flurry of escalating events that ended somehow in Jack Suga's cigar box being knocked to the ground.

"Doolittle bombed Tokyo," shouted Jackie Snyder. "And they're all dead. How do you like that, you Jap creep?"

Jack Suga knelt to pick up the cards that had fluttered to the dirt. Sorrell Myers, scratched from the twigs and sweating from the unaccustomed effort, scrambled awkwardly to help him. Then Jack stood, tucked his box beneath his arm, and walked alone across the schoolyard.

"Get out of here!" yelled Frances Simmons at the slim retreating figure. Billy Connaught picked up a pebble and threw it. It landed near Jack's feet.

"That's enough," said T.H. "I think he's learned his lesson."

That was the moment when the subtle change in leadership from Billy Connaught to T. H. Dallas became apparent to everyone.

"What should we do now, T.H.?" asked Paul. "We have fifteen minutes before the bell."

Going steady was also a public matter. Hilary learned this when she was in the library trying to get Jack Suga's eyes and Ilona's retreating back out of her mind. Most of the girls in the class were in the Robins, which was the best reading group, the worst being the Pigeons. When they were sent to the library to discuss the books they were reading in free reading, they were all reading Nancy Drew, most of them passing around the same mystery about a lighthouse and a one-eyed lighthouse keeper, and there was no point in discussing it. No one wanted to talk about Hilary's book, which was *The Call of the Wild* and which Hilary said was about a dog. Frances Simmons spoke first.

"How many points do you have?" she asked.

Hilary didn't know what she was talking about.

"She doesn't know," giggled Jackie Snyder.

Frances Simmons explained that there was a printed sheet in circulation which she was surprised Hilary had not seen. She drew it out of her pocket.

"You see, everything you do gets points. Look." Hilary looked down the list. Kissing was five points. Kissing with tongues got you ten, touching above the waist, clothing on, got you fifteen, touching above the waist, clothing off, got you twenty-five.

"How come everything goes up five points but then here it goes up ten?"

"Because, silly," said Shirley Leone, "it's a big jump."

Hilary continued to read. Touching, this was ridiculous, below the waist was thirty-five, clothes off, fifty, unthinkable, touching a boy, below the waist, clothing on, seventy-five, clothing off, one hundred and two hundred points for going all the way, which probably meant the uniting of sacred organs as discussed in *Growing Up*, and who in their right mind would do that?

"Does anybody get more than five?" asked Hilary.

Everyone started to giggle. Frances Simmons, who was going steady with Billy Connaught, laughed. "Are you kidding?" she asked.

The librarian issued a big shush from her desk. It swept over the library and the shellacked shelves like a broom.

"Well, how many do you have?" whispered Hilary.

"I have fifteen," said Frances.

"For what? Did he touch you above the waist?"

Frances Simmons started to blush, which pinked up her babyfat cheeks like litmus paper sprinkled with lime juice. "Hilary, I thought you were mature. If I knew you were going to be such a baby, I never would have shown this to you."

"How many do you have, Hilary?" asked Jackie Snyder.

"Five," said Hilary. They all looked disgusted, as if she had said the doctor found out she had leprosy.

"Well, the minute you go from five to ten, you call us, you understand?"

She did. She also could not imagine in her wildest dreams ever wanting to touch anyone's tongue with her own. It was unsanitary, germy, and worse than using someone else's toothbrush. From the catalogue, it looked as though she would spend the rest of her life as a five.

Having a boyfriend was not only subject to sanction and scrutiny; it also meant her time was not her own. Now she not only had to give excuses to Ilona, she had to give them to T.H. as well.

"I have to talk to Miss Wallace about the spelling bee," she said to T.H. after her crossing-guard responsibilities were over. "About which lists to study."

T.H. left on his bike, following after Billy Connaught. "You should have told me before," he shouted. "I wouldn't have waited for you!"

Hilary returned to her classroom. The blackboards were unwashed, still filled with the day's work, including the complicated problem in decimals.

Miss Wallace was bent over her desk, cradling her head in her arms. Hilary thought she was probably taking a nap.

"Miss Wallace?"

Hilary's teacher lifted up her head as if the effort were too great. Her eyes had the tortured, twisted look of pain. She had been crying and her lids were swollen. "It's my brother, Hilary. He was on Bataan, captured by the Japanese and marched to his death. Twenty-five thousand died. They dropped from hunger and exhaustion, and the heat. And if they fell, they were beaten, kicked, shot if they couldn't get up. The Filipinos were not allowed to give them water. Then they were packed in boxcars. Some of the dead had no room to fall. They died standing up.

The Japanese took sick, starved, weakened men and they drove them to their deaths. They have no humanity. None at all."

Hilary had heard Marco say that some of the men and nurses escaped by swimming to the island of Corregidor two miles away.

"Maybe he's in Corregidor," she said.

Miss Wallace murmured through her arms, "He couldn't swim, Hilary. He never learned how."

She began to sob—deep, compulsive sobs that left her choking for air. Hilary didn't know what to do. She put out a tentative, grubby, nail-bitten hand to touch her shoulder. Miss Wallace uttered a cry like a cat and flung her arms around Hilary's waist.

"He was my baby brother," she said. "I took care of him when he was little. I was like his mother, don't you see, he was my baby."

Hilary thought of Freddie and she began to cry too, stroking Miss Wallace's salt-and-pepper hair while Miss Wallace wet her jumper with her tears. She would have to figure out herself what words to study. She didn't know how long she was supposed to stand there. It would be better to say nothing and let Miss Wallace decide.

April was also the time that Mickey began to realize that her arrangement with Mr. Radner was not what she thought it was going to be, but, because she was basically optimistic, she was looking for it to improve. Her reasoning was that now that the track was closed, he would have more time for her. She had expected expensive baubles in soft velvet boxes that other girls, if they were lucky, sometimes got, but they had not come. She did not count rhinestones and 14-carat gold. She knew better than that. It was true that Mr. Radner paid for her rent and meals, and gave her plenty of spending money, dollar bills rolled and bound with a rubber band, but it was only enough for shoes and clothing, and since shoes were rationed to only two pairs a year per person, there was a shortage of nylons and fabric, and Mickey didn't like hats, that didn't leave very much to buy.

It was true that she had a fur stole, but furs were hard to sell. They turned bad after one or two years, unless you had a refrigerator, which few people she knew owned. Most people had iceboxes. Her stole was already losing hair from its pelt, and looked like a dog of her brother's that had had mange. Jewelry on the other hand, good jewelry, was like money, an investment, and Mickey knew that this was the time when she had to make the best investments she could. She had hinted to Sol, commenting on how bare her arms, fingers, neck, and ears were. Now it was up to him.

Another difficulty with the arrangement was that she had too much time to think and she considered that a handicap, like walking with a limp. The only thing that thinking did for people was put them in the dumps. To counteract this tendency, she took Hilary to the movies, did her nails, filing them into long ovals and polishing everything but the moons, sat in the sun, which she could do all day long, turning over and basting her body into a deep, golden tan, and continued her dance lessons—keeping in shape, as she called it, but also keeping her means of legitimate support intact, in case this thing with Radner didn't work out. She also wrote to her mother from time to time, advising her to try Lydia Pinkham's Compound, which promised to help female weakness, told her that she had moved and that the post office sometimes had trouble finding her address, and not to be surprised if her letters came back. She stayed judiciously away from the kids at the Pago Pago, since that only got her into trouble, and Sol could be very mean when he was angry. There was just no stopping him. She had seen that kind of righteous fury with her own father, and she considered it part of the normal repertoire of male behavior.

Mickey knew she needed to keep busy, because when she didn't, she sometimes thought about Bill Wright. She was not impervious to his good looks. A man like him, though, just didn't figure in her plans. She had already imagined kissing him and she never wanted to melt with passion again for anyone. When that happened, something happened to her mind. It was okay at sixteen and at twenty to need a man so desperately she was willing to scrub his floors and sleep on a mattress without sheets. At twenty-two, one began to think of comforts. She needed her wits about her.

It was somewhat of a surprise when Mr. Radner told her his wife was coming for a week. Mrs. Radner hated Miami Beach, but still she came, hot, sticky, wearing a flowery handkerchief pinned to her bosom, her hair marceled in tight little waves that had gone out of style five years ago, and turning down the corners of her mouth when she spoke.

Mickey had to leave their room and move into another, being careful, at Mr. Radner's request, to remove all traces of her presence, including such giveaways as blond hairs, underwear hanging over the shower rod, and bobby pins. That presented no difficulty, since there were plenty of empty rooms; however, housekeeping had to move her things on a cleaning cart because there was only one bellhop, and he was busy checking people out. He was not interested in moving Mickey, as he called it, "sideways." Mickey didn't mind. The things she worried about she carried herself, including her tiny white ceramic poodle with even tinier curls, a picture of her family sitting together on a wooden porch, and her best tap shoes, white Capezio T-straps with double-action jingle taps.

After the last cartload of Mickey's things had been rolled down the hall and Mr. Radner combed their room for her spoor like a spaniel sniffing out a weasel, Mickey was given strict instructions not to talk to him, not to call him, not to smile at him, not to acknowledge in any way that they knew one another. She understood, of course, perfectly. That was not the problem. The problem was that he had forgotten to give her money. Mickey was left with two dollars and thirty-five cents in her purse. No matter how you sliced it, it wouldn't last a week.

Mickey positioned herself in the middle of the lobby, as conspicuous as a log jam in a delta, but when Mr. Radner came through with his wife on his arm, he looked right past her, even though he had dripped sweat on her all night long, trying to go one more time so she wouldn't miss him during the week, insisting that he needed just a few more minutes, ignoring her assurances that it was okay and not to worry. Now, when she stood in the lobby looking a little forlorn, he gave her no more attention than he gave the Morris chair.

Mickey signaled to him again, a timid little wave of the hand, not really caring if he did get mad. She had to eat, and she had expenses.

Mr. Radner led his wife in the dining room and stalked back into the lobby. He began to hiss like a steam radiator. "I told you not to talk to me. What's the matter with you? Are you so dumb you can't even do a simple thing like that?"

"I'm sorry, Sol," she said. "You forgot to give me money."

He reached for his wallet, glanced quickly into the dining room, peeled off a few bills, and stuffed them into her hand. "There, that should hold you for a while," he said, and went back into the dining room.

Mickey was stung, but she was used to such stings and blinked away her tears in the rapid fire way she had learned to do. She couldn't stay in the hotel. Everyone in the lobby was staring at her, especially Mrs. Templeton, who put her lips together in a jagged smile that looked as though she was straining at the toilet.

Mickey walked out the front door, holding her head up high as she did onstage, but not without first handing a five-dollar bill to the bell captain. It was cooler outside, with soft ocean breezes that played over her face and neck like a caress. The plate-shaped moon appeared ghostly and fragile, and a constellation of four small prominent stars could be seen over the horizon. Mickey never remembered seeing it before.

She picked out Corporal Wright from the other soldiers on the sidewalk at once, and thought as an omen it was bad, like seeing a black cat. He looked good in his uniform, no question about it. While he stood talking to his buddies, Mickey decided to walk in the other direction.

"Hold it," he called, issued a few warning remarks to his comrades, and ran after her. "What are you doing out here alone? All dressed up and no place to go?"

"That's not funny."

"Hey, I was only kidding. Iowa joke. No one could ever say that about you."

"I'm sorry, I'm just touchy."

"Yeh? You get touchy? What about?"

"Nothing. Certainly nothing that's any of your business."

"Whoa. I think I can do better if I keep my mouth shut." He folded his arms across his chest. His eyes traveled over her face and shoulders. "You sure look beautiful tonight. You're shining, do you know that? Sorry, I couldn't help it. It slipped out." Mickey laughed. "I knew I could get you to smile," he said.

"Keep talking," she said, "I just want to hear if you got anything to say I haven't heard before."

"Maybe you've heard it before, but I've never said it before."

The breeze continued to brush over her face and neck. She

would not imagine that it was his fingertips. "I have to go," she said.

"What's the hurry?"

"I have an appointment, with a friend."

"Lucky guy."

"What makes you think it's a guy?"

"Anything else would be a waste, like throwing away good Iowa land and rainfall on wheat."

"How did this change from me to farming?"

"Sorry. It kind of ran away from me."

"You did it. You said something to me I never heard before. Were you comparing me to wheat?"

"I would say you're closer to cornsilk."

"And I would say you're getting too fresh."

Mel, wearing a tie, with his hair neatly parted and combed back with hair tonic came out of the hotel entrance followed by Hilary. They were carrying a small case and a megaphone and they were heading for the Lord Feldman next door. Hilary wore her Easter outfit, except for the straw hat, complete with her starched petticoat and with new ribbons at the ends of her braids. She reached down to pull up her socks.

"What's up?" asked Bill.

"I'm giving a lecture on card sharks and flim-flam men. The kid is helping me demonstrate. You ought to see her palm high cards."

Hilary pressed down her petticoat. "You get your uniforms fixed yet?"

"Any day now. How'd you know about that?"

"I heard your Tack officer. We all hear him. He doesn't like the way yours fit."

Bill laughed. "What else do you know?"

"I'm not telling." Hilary hurried to catch up with Mel.

"She's quite a kid," said Bill.

"She's my friend," said Mickey. "Just like she was a grown-up."

"That's okay with me. Age has nothing to do with it. One of my best friends is Charlie Hand and he's seventy-four years old."

"Better than a grown-up, she doesn't have any of the prying, sneaky ways that grown-ups get, or the meanness, she's not jealous, and she thinks I'm wonderful."

"So do I."

Mickey turned away then turned back. "About Saturday. It's okay."

"You mean it?"

"Sure I mean it."

"You won't change your mind?"

"What makes you think I'll change my mind?"

"Because you're hard to figure. I don't know what you will or won't do. I guess before I shine my shoes I want some assurances."

"If I say yes, it's yes. And you have to shine your shoes anyway. We heard that too."

"How much time do I get?"

"I don't know. What's a usual date? Three, four hours?"

"I was hoping for all afternoon and all evening. Kind of an endurance contest."

Hilary emptied the sand from her socks into the wastebasket and realized that she still carried Mel's loaded dice in the arch of her shoe. Freddie was lying on his stomach staring at the taped windows.

"You want to see what happens when I drop these in a glass of water?" she asked. He continued to stare. "Why aren't you listening to the radio? 'The Lone Ranger' is on." Hilary walked around the bed. "Hey, I'm talking to you. What's the matter? Why didn't you answer me?"

"I was thinking of something."

"Well, how come you don't have the radio on?"

"It's busted. Daddy tried to fix it; he socked it and looked inside. It's busted all right, and we can't get another one. For the duration. Mr. Davis said there was no radio any place in the hotel. I'm going to grow up without one."

It was a sobering thought. "What do you want to do?"

"I don't know."

She hadn't spent as much time with him as she usually did. The realization nipped at her conscience like a sand flea. "You want to play secret agent and spy on the people in the patio? We can talk to each other on our phones. Where's the tin cans with the string?"

"Ma gave them to the scrap drive."

Hilary flopped down on the bed beside him. "I saw her on the playground today. What happened?"

"Miss Carmichael doesn't like me."

"Sure she likes you. She's just bossy, that's all. That's how teachers act."

"They made me promise to pay attention. I do pay attention. I can't help it if I don't know what they're doing."

"Do you want me to help you with your homework?"

"What homework?"

Hilary sighed. "I'm going to read my book. Why don't you read *Captain America?*"

Freddie continued to stare out the window. "I hate school like poison," he said. "I hate it worse than the Japs."

Hilary thought of Miss Wallace's brother. She reached over and began to tickle him.

"Quit it!" he shouted.

"Not till I make you laugh."

"Shut up in there," called a voice from the next room.

"Let's go swimming."

"We're not allowed."

"Who said?"

"Ma and the sentry. They both said."

"We can do it. We just have to be quiet. But we can't splash. We have to slip into the water, the way you spoon into ice cream."

"I don't know."

"Are you scared?"

They put on their bathing suits and crept down the hall, out into the dimmed patio where Mrs. Steinfeld and Lipschutz stood locked together in the shadowed edge.

"What are they doing? Are they kissing?" asked Freddie.

"Who cares. Come on."

They crept over the sand, then dropped to their bellies, inching their way along on their elbows like Randolph Scott, the sentry only yards away. Hilary took a piece of coral rock and threw it like a grenade in the direction of Mrs. Steinfeld and Lipschutz. It landed on the patio with a clink.

"Who goes there?" called the sentry. "Come out where I can see you."

Mrs. Steinfeld and Lipschutz came out of the shadows and

stood hand in hand in the glare of the flashlight, Mrs. Steinfeld's hair in her eye, and Lipschutz's face smeared with red.

"Oh, Christ, no," said the sentry, "you ought to be ashamed of yourselves. You're old enough to be my mother, lady. I hate to think my mother's doing stuff like that. You're not allowed out here. Now both of you get inside."

Hilary and Freddie stayed submerged up to their necks, letting the warm currents swirl them around and carry them like drifting flotsam, first this way, then that. The water sparkled in the moonlight and each little wave, scarcely more than a ripple, broke into a fine white thread. When the sentry went farther down the beach, they crawled out of the water and inched their way back across the sand, Gary Cooper in *Sergeant York*, coming in to save everyone in the trench at great personal risk and with great courage.

10

Hilary lost the spelling bee, partly because she had spent so much time with T.H., and partly because after Miss Wallace cried against her jumper, she never went back for the lists, expecting that somehow, she could figure out any words she didn't know.

When they got to the auditorium, Miss Wallace, looking very sad, was already there, seated in the second row next to Mr. Detwiler, who had clapped Hilary on the back and said, "We're counting on you." Her name was announced, and she was led to the stage by a boy she didn't know, a Sherpa in short pants who helped her up each step as if she were a cripple. Then she sat down the way Mrs. Templeton had taught her, wearing her Easter dress with the petticoat, limp and unstarched, as she had refused to go unless the starch was taken out, and flipping her braids behind her, although she had asked to wear her hair tied with a ribbon and had been refused by Ilona, who said that loose hair would interfere with her ability to think straight.

When it was her turn, she got up, stared over the faceless crowd, pronounced the word, spelled it, was applauded, and sat down. The contestants were narrowed down to four, three girls and one boy. Then it was her turn again. The announcer said the word *recidivist*. Hilary had never heard the word before. He said it meant one who backslides. Hilary tried to decide between an "a" and an "e," hesitated for one moment, and opted for the "a."

There was a groan from the announcer. Hilary stood up and pressed down her petticoat, forgetting that Ilona had taken out the starch, and stepped down the stage.

Afterward Ilona was very matter-of-fact. "You did the best you could," she said. But Hilary knew better, and so did Miss Wallace, who only nodded and said, "That's too bad, Hilary. It was on the list." Mr. Detwiler was busy chatting with a squad of other principals and while she never got a chance to speak to him, she could tell by the way he looked at her that she had let him down too.

Hilary tried to discuss her ruin with Mickey, but Mickey was involved in a juggling act which took all her skill and know-how to pull off. Mr. Radner could not find out about Bill Wright, and Bill, for some reason, could not believe that Mr. Radner was anything but her father. Fortunately, Wright only had a pass from Saturday noon to Sunday noon, which limited his request for her time to one day out of seven. Sol, on the other hand, was only in Miami one week out of three, sometimes four. Logistically, both circumstances helped to make everything workable, if not strained.

Mickey and Bill were falling more in love, the kind of weightless fall, where one's arms and legs spin out, and the fallers don't want to help themselves, can't help themselves, any more than they can help the color of their eyes.

Sol didn't notice the difference in Mickey, but Hilary did. Mickey was softer, like butter that had been left on the counter. She disliked fewer things, spoke less spitefully about other people, and she was even more beautiful, if that was possible, shining with the radiance of a scoured cake pan. Most of all, she laughed more, although Hilary thought that was the direct result of Mr. Radner having to go to Philadelphia because price controls were making his business a losing proposition.

Bill was new to Mickey's experience, unlike other men who, since the time she was in junior high, took every opportunity to put their arms around her shoulders so they could, unannounced, rest their hands on her neck, then dive like cormorants for her breasts; or the man who she married, who pulled down the shades and pushed her back on the bed as soon as he parked his rig, but who never said more than a dozen words to her in a week. True to his promise, Bill so far had not made a move on her.

She wondered if he was a fairy. She had known one in the Pago Pago, a fellow who had been the stage manager and had wonderful ideas for lighting, sometimes spending all afternoon adjusting the kleigs and the spots, changing filters, topping one hue with another, until he got the effect he wanted. He was the one who came up with the idea of dressing the ponies as fireflies in mosquito netting wired with tiny Christmas lights, then dousing all the house lights while they danced around giant lanterns.

Despite his lack of ardor, the major way that Bill was different from all other men she had known, with the exception of her stage manager, who had been very sympathetic, especially when her firefly costume caught fire, was that he listened to her. He encouraged her to talk and really paid attention to her when she spoke. She could tell he wasn't just being polite by the questions he asked, which were always right on target with what she was saying and which helped her explain more clearly what she meant. She could tell him anything, about how she was afraid of her uncle when she was nine, something she had never told anyone, of how she hung by her knees every night from the rail fence so that she would be tall when she grew up. He didn't mind when she cried after she called home and her father told her her mother had died; he just sat with her on the bus stop bench near the phone booth and held her hand. He even nodded with sympathy when she told him how her father had been fined by the county because he didn't give her mother's ration book back within ten days of her death. And he was not afraid to tell her that she was beautiful to him, golden, shining, everything about her luminous, her skin, her hair, especially her eyes, and was, when she let her guard down, very sweet. He told her so a thousand times.

Freddie sat in the portico, his knees drawn up, his arms around them, holding a baseball that Mr. Lonzo had given him.

"Where's your sister?" asked Mickey.

"She's with T.H."

"Well, she'll be back before you know it and you'll have someone to play ball with."

"It's okay," he said. "It's her fault that I throw like a girl. I don't care if she comes back or not."

Bill stepped out of his hotel carrying a box under his arm, and Mickey waved her hand wildly, even though he was only thirty feet away. A week was a long time to wait to be together, especially when they couldn't really talk during that time, or see one another except for brief moments in passing. He brushed back his glistening pomaded hair, which he had just plastered with Brylcreem and worked with a comb until his arms ached, pressing it even flatter than it was.

"You waiting long?" he asked.

"Not so very."

He took her arm and they walked away; then Mickey turned back. "Let's take him," she whispered, "just for the afternoon. He looks so lost."

"Whatever you say," he replied.

Mickey bent down to Freddie. "You want to come?"

"Maybe. What are you going to do?"

Bill pointed to the box he was carrying. "Get my uniforms fixed. Come on. I'll buy you a soda."

Freddie jumped up and followed them to the bus stop. "T.H. told Hilary that Clark Gable is coming to Officer Candidate School."

"That's what they tell us," said Bill.

"I think he's real handsome," said Mickey. "In a foreign way."

"I'm glad you added that," said Bill. "I was getting jealous."

"Who says I think you're handsome any kind of way?" asked Mickey.

"Hilary," said Freddie. "Don't you remember, you told her?"

Within a half hour they were in the men's department at Saks, where Bill had originally bought his uniforms, paying six dollars for the trousers, three and a half for the shirts, and eighty-five cents for a flight cap lined with the leather sweatband.

The salesman said that because the uniforms had been purchased two months before, they could not make good on the tailoring, since it was obvious that military training had changed the contours of his body.

"This happens all the time," said the salesman. "The Army really shapes you guys up. I know one fellow dropped fifty pounds, another fellow put them on. Not the same pounds, you understand."

No one laughed and the salesman continued, setting his face in a more serious mien. "Of course, we would be happy to alter your uniforms, at a slight charge."

Bill, who had always been in good physical shape, and more or less the same dimensions for the last five years of his life, looked down at the salesman. "Don't give me that malarkey. They didn't fit right in the first place is the problem."

"You from Chicago?"

"I'm from Iowa."

"Oh yeah? I have a sister in Columbus."

"That's Ohio."

"Son, I wish I could help you. Put yourself in my place. We'd go out of business if we had unlimited alterations. You yourself told me these uniforms were purchased two months ago. My hands are tied."

"I know another place," said Mickey. "Saks isn't the only place to buy uniforms."

They walked out, stopping to pick up Freddie, who was squirting testers at the perfume counter. "But what difference will another place make?" asked Bill. "I'll still have to pay for alterations."

Mickey, a smiling and silent Lorelei, put on her sunglasses so she wouldn't be recognized and led him to Washington Avenue where Sol bought his slacks. The street was lined with little one-story shops, most of them closed. The name of the place they sought was Levin's, and they found it, tucked between a kosher meat market and a ladies' shoe store, with a sign that read UNIFORMS displayed prominently in the window. It was open.

Levin was in the back. "What can I do for you folks?" he called.

"His uniforms don't fit right," said Mickey.

Levin walked to the front of the store, carrying a boxload of shirts. "Did you buy them here?"

"Don't doubt his word," said Mickey. "He's in the United States Air Corps."

"I can see that," said Levin.

Bill was ready to walk out. He wanted no part of chicanery and started toward the door, but Mickey pulled him back by the arm. "I know how to do this," she whispered.

Levin had his doubts about where the uniforms were purchased, but he didn't want to argue. The boy was so young, and he reminded him of his own son in service, not so much in the way he looked but in the way he was so obviously crazy about his girl.

"He'll tell everyone to shop here," said Mickey.

"Let's see what's what," sighed Levin. He indicated a changing booth. "Go in there and put them on."

Bill went into the dressing room, then came out to stand on the little podium, while Levin, with chalk and tape, clutched at the seat of his pants.

"Here," he said, "the problem is here."

Mickey turned away while Levin chalked and pinned. "When I finish," continued Levin, "you're going to look like a poster."

Then Bill came out of the changing room for the last time and handed Levin the box. Freddie was trying on flight caps, most of them falling to his nose. "How much?" he asked.

"For the little boy? God forbid he'll grow up to have to wear it. Half a buck."

They walked out together, Freddie happy with his flight cap, Mickey on Bill's arm, Bill feeling very guilty. "You didn't do anything wrong," said Mickey. "He wanted to do it. I can tell."

It was a lovely afternoon, warm, breezy, and fragrant with caraway, pine needles, gardenia, and sea. They went to a drugstore where Bill bought a soda for everyone and a Whitman Sampler for Mickey. Then they strolled to Flamingo Park, Freddie with chocolate smeared on his face, and Mickey and Bill leaning heavily on each other like road workers on their shovels.

Mickey sat on a bench and turned her face to the sun while Bill showed Freddie how to pitch a curve. A poinciana tree nearby was shooting out tiny red blooms that later in the summer would make the tree look as though it were on fire.

Bill came to sit beside Mickey while Freddie practiced throwing curve balls at the poinciana. They looked at each other with the obvious pleasure of being near someone you're crazy about, their bodies taut and yearning. They had never exchanged more than a quick kiss, simply because there was no place to go: no car, no apartment, no desolate alley way or beach without a sentry, no living room; and hotel rooms were becoming scarce—not that Bill would have asked her to go to a hotel room anyway.

"You want to kiss me?" asked Mickey.

"That's the general idea. You must be a mind reader. Snap your wrist, Fred."

"I thought I didn't interest you that way," she said.

"Listen, you interest me every way. If I could, I would kiss you silly. The problem is, you need a quiet private place to kiss your girl." He touched her arm and his hand trembled. "I think about you all the time."

"You better not," she said. "You won't make flight school if you do."

The sudden cast gloom was a tangible thing and struck his shoulders, forcing him to slump and lean his elbows on his knees. "I'll be leaving next month," he said.

Mickey turned. "So soon? I can't believe that. You just got here."

"That's how it feels to me too. As soon as I finish preflight training, I get my commission with my class, and then—off to flight school. The Army needs pilots. Fast."

"I didn't realize it would be so soon," said Mickey. "I mean, we're just starting to know each other."

Bill looked miserable. He stared ahead. "Let the ball roll off the tips of your fingers, Fred. Don't throw it. A natural forward break of the wrist." He stood up. "I better go help him. That kid does better when you show him how."

When he returned, Mickey was frowning. "You know about the war and everything?" she asked.

Bill smiled. "I don't know any military secrets, if that's what's on your mind."

"I don't want to know secrets. I just want to know something about it."

"I don't think anyone knows all about it, not even the top brass."

"It isn't going to be over soon, is it?" asked Mickey. "They sunk the *Lexington* in the Coral Sea. That was a big carrier. It sounds like such a pretty place, doesn't it? So many men went down."

"That's true, sweetface, but you have to look at it another way. We stopped them. You see the Japs may have damaged the *Hornet* and scuttled the *Lexington*, but when we knocked out one of their carriers, it made the score even. Japan needs to isolate Australia from the U.S. and the first step was control of the Coral Sea, which they don't have."

"All I want to know is, how long—a year, five years?"

"Nobody knows that. June Bug would like it to last forever. He's got this kind of fever to fight. He wants to drop tons of bombs all over Europe and he will too. I'm betting on him."

"What do you want?"

"To be two people, so I can do my duty, and be with you at the same time."

They brought Freddie home on the bus and deposited him at the entrance of the Flamingo Arms with his flight cap askew on his head, then turned around to go out again, back to Washington Avenue where they had supper at Feldstein's cafeteria, cheap and good, and you didn't have to spend money tipping waiters. Then they went to a movie theater on Lincoln Road to see Alan Ladd and Veronica Lake in *This Gun for Hire,* where Bill held her hand in the dark, once apologizing for clutching it too hard.

"You look like her," he said when they came out, "only you're softer-looking, and much prettier."

"I didn't like the way he strong-armed her," she said, "making her go with him into that drainpipe."

"I promise I'll never drag you into a drainpipe, although that may be the only place I'll ever get you all to myself."

"I thought you said you weren't going to make a move on me."

"When did I say that? I must have been crazy."

When they returned to Collins Avenue, the street and most of the sidewalk were covered with land crabs—great, clawing horseshoes, the large females carrying the smaller males on their backs, crawling ashore at high tide on their yearly spring trek to lay their eggs in the sand, where the waves would wash the sperm of the males over the eggs to fertilize them. Many of the crabs left the overcrowded beach and continued west, surfacing Collins Avenue, making it impossible for vehicles to avoid them, and causing trucks and autos which crackled over them, splintering their carapaces into shards, to cut their tires to ribbons.

"Oh, God," said Mickey, with her hands over her ears, "I can't stand to listen to them. Somebody do something. They're making my skin crawl."

Bill picked her up and carried her across the street, treading carefully to avoid the crabs that scuttled to the opposite sidewalk looking for a place to lay their eggs.

The couple stood together in the shadows under the portico,

swaying toward one another like taffy threads, stretching, yet connected, about to part, neither wanting to do so, especially since it would be another week before they would see each other again. A car went crunching by. Mickey shuddered.

"Don't look at them," he said. "Forget about them." He cupped her chin in his hand.

Mickey put her fingers in her ears. "I know a place," she said, "where we can be alone. Follow me through the hotel, but stay behind me, I don't want people to see us together. Go to the patio. There's a lifeguard shack on the seawall. No one will bother us there. I'll be inside."

He followed her through the lobby and out into the patio. The lifeguard shack was musty and mildewed, with torn photos and magazine pictures tacked to the walls, and in the corners a pair of Lenny's swim trunks, a pile of stacked beach mats, moldy blackened towels, empty bottles of chlorine, and a stray crab which Bill flung through the door by its claw.

"Mickey, this is no place for us."

"It's the only place. I can't think of another."

He looked around doubtfully. "I don't know."

"I do. It's okay. But you have to be quiet. The sentry will hear you."

Mickey moved toward him. He put his arms around her and bent his head to kiss her, but because she was so much smaller, lifted her off the ground, her toes dangling on the wooden floor, holding her tighter than he had ever held her before, and kissing her lips in a long, fevered salute as if trying to melt into her mouth.

Mickey was released gently and her feet allowed to settle to the ground, then, feeling her way with her hand, she lay back on top of the lounge pads. Bill stood staring down at her.

"It's okay," she said. "Honest."

He closed the door but it would not seal shut. A sliver of moonlight filtered in.

Like all first-time lovers, they were hesitant and slow at first, holding their breath and spending time accommodating one body to the other on the narrow pallet. Then, as they gained passion and confidence, their movements were less hesitant and became direct, purposeful, insistent, forceful, even selfish.

Those times that Mickey opened her eyes through languid lids she saw him looking down at her with a combination of tenderness and desire that she had never seen before in any man. Something else happened that was new to Mickey's experience. He talked to her afterward, and when they made love again, he talked to her again, asking questions, wanting to know about her mother, who he said must have been a wonderful lady, and her father and brother.

"My momma was tired all the time, and she used to wrap my hair in rags to make it curly. My brother, well, he's my brother, and there's not much to say about him except he hogs the bathroom. My daddy's pretty strict and he's usually mad about something. He says 'tarnation' a lot."

"That's a country word," said Bill. "It missed the cities, but all country folk know it, Iowa, Georgia, it doesn't matter, it's all the same. 'Tarnation' is the only thing you can say when you step on a rake and it kicks you in the face."

"I know something to say a lot better than that."

He smiled and put his finger on her lips. "Did you have a lot of fairs to go to?" he asked.

"Not so much that I can remember."

"After Decoration Day," he mused, trailing his fingers down the curves of her supple back, "it's one fair after another, all summer long. We used to go to a county fair every weekend; of course, the big one is the state fair. It's held in August in Des Moines. My kid sister's ambition is to win a prize for her piglets." He touched a faded bruise on her thigh that was almost invisible in the moonlight. "How did you get this?" he asked.

"It's a birthmark," she said.

"And what's this on my hands? It looks like makeup."

Mickey chuckled, soft and low in her throat. "It is. It's leg makeup. You can't get nylons for love or money, so I paint them on with this kit I have."

"But I remember seeing seams."

"I paint them too. It's easy. A lot of women can't make them straight, but I can, just like they were the real thing."

"You're the real thing," he said, leaning over to kiss her again.

11

"The Aleutians are the weather factory of the world, gentlemen. That's no exaggeration. Many of the weather disturbances of the northern hemisphere start right here. What controls the weather is this great semipermanent vortex in the earth's atmospheric circulation known as the Aleutian low, which results from the meeting of cold arctic air from the polar regions and warm, moist, northward-moving air from the Pacific subtropics and the warm air over the warm Japanese current."

The instructor stood in front of a chart on a tripod faced with thirty soldiers who took notes as he spoke. It was hot, and the back of his shirt was stained with sweat. His tie off, and the cuffs of his shirt turned back, he pointed to the chart with his stick.

June Bug leaned over his seat. "I'm telling you, the guy we see her with isn't her father."

"You're nuts," said Bill Wright.

"Bill, you got blinders on. All the signs are there for you to see but you won't look at them. Watch them sometimes when they walk together. Christ, not only do they not look alike, they don't even sound alike. She has that southern twang you like so much, and he sounds like he's in Times Square selling ties that light up."

"The meeting of cold and warm air creates storms of near hurricane intensity that rush across the cold Bering Sea into Alaska, or bank up against the western North American coast; eventually they may sweep down through Canada, across the East Coast, the Atlantic, even into Europe. With these high winds comes thick fog and drizzle making this weather tricky and dangerous."

June Bug leaned over again. "Okay," he hissed, "answer me this. Now how come she never took you to meet him? I know he's only here once a month, but in three months now you mean to say she doesn't want her daddy to meet a guy she's supposed to be crazy about?"

"Well, that's the thing. I don't know for sure Mickey's crazy about me. I know she likes me a lot, but the other, it's a line you cross, where you can't stop thinking about a person. I don't know if she's crossed it. I know I have. I just don't know about her."

"She's shacking up with you, isn't she? What do you call that?"

"I don't know. Most girls like you to tell them how you feel, especially if you're going all the way with them. Tell me you love me. That's all they want to hear, and you do it. You do it because you know it makes them feel good. Some want you to tell them you love them forever, or that you never felt about anyone the way you do about them. They tell you exactly what they want to hear. Sometimes you cross your fingers behind your back, but you say it, whatever they're asking for. And it satisfies them. Sometimes they want you to lie to them outright, like that Charlene you've been seeing. Mickey lets me tell her how I feel about her, but when I ask her, she jokes or changes the subject. The other night, we were, you know, and I told her I loved her, and I said, how about you sweetheart, that go for you, too? And she said, you're not going to believe what she said. She said, 'Next week I'd like to go to the Parrot Jungle.' "

"Chadwick, Wright, listen up," said the instructor. "You may have trouble returning to your home base someday because of a sudden onset of fog, that is, if you make it into flight school. What I'm teaching you here today is necessary to your survival. It's going to make the difference between getting your hair parted by a Jap or gliding home with a margin of endurance because you've compensated for weather conditions."

"Sorry, sir," said June Bug.

"How many of you have ever seen a weather balloon at your own weather station?"

Bill Wright had, but he kept his hand down. One man raised

his hand. His name was Duff and the other men called him Hotshot.

"The balloon carries a small box about ten miles into the stratosphere. This box is known as a Rayob, and sends out the relative humidity, pressure, and temperature to a receiver. Another balloon is released at intervals to determine the direction and velocity of the wind at different levels above the earth's surface. It travels with a constant vertical velocity and can be observed through a theodolite, which is simply a telescope with attached scales for the simultaneous recording of the azimuth and elevation angles. At night a small light is attached to the balloon."

"Another thing is, he doesn't like servicemen," muttered Bill through the corner of his mouth. "A lot of civilians are like that. She says he would worry too much about her when he was in Philadelphia if he thought she was running around with a soldier, but that when things ease up with the war and all, you know, when we have a clear edge situation going, which it looks like we may have soon, she'll introduce me."

"And you bought it?"

"There was nothing else for sale. What could I do?"

"Wright!"

"Sir!"

"The observer follows the free balloon by keeping it continuously in the field of his telescope. Every minute on the second, the observer gives his readings over an intercom to the plotter at a plotting board. After the pattern is made on the plotting board, conversion tables based on what would you guess, give the direction and velocity of the wind?"

"Was that a question, sir?"

"It was a question."

"Trig, I guess."

"Lucky guess, Wright. I'd pay attention if I were you. You might wind up having to stick your finger in the air for weather information, instead of in your ass." Everyone laughed. The man they called Hotshot laid his head back and roared. The instructor continued. "Japan lost its bid this month for Midway because our long-range bombers were able to disperse their fleet. Japan really needed that island, and they pulled out all stops for it, but the weather cooperated with us, even the fog. And, gentlemen, we had that weather information in advance. We knew when it would lift and when we could count on air strikes."

"We also broke the slant-eyes' code," said June Bug. "That's Q.T. material. I got it from my cousin Leroy who's a Pigeon Officer."

"If he isn't her father, who is he?" asked Bill.

"Beats me. That's for me to puzzle over, and you to find out."

Hilary and Freddie slept in their new room in separate beds. Now that it was June, there were plenty of empty rooms in the hotel, even more than usual for off season, and Mr. Davis told Frank and Ilona they could have it for the summer provided they tacked nothing up on the walls, didn't stuff up the toilets, and Freddie didn't wet the bed. Ilona was offended, for Freddie had not done the latter since he was three years old, but she promised anyway. A room was a room.

It smelled of strong pine disinfectant and the carpet had a scorch hole the size of a penny. A can of talcum powder stood on the nightstand between the beds. Freddie's ball, tin sand chute, and flight cap, Hilary's dial typewriter, all their comics, and a Nancy Drew mystery that was overdue at the library, lay in boxes stacked against the wall. Because it was hot, Ilona allowed them to leave the window open provided they were careful to turn off the light. The breeze that blew through was warm and moist, perfumed with the saline, piscine scent of the sea.

Roaring blasts had come from the ocean all night. Noises like thunderclaps, only more rending and shrill, which kept rousing Hilary from the strange dream in which she was trying to run but could not move her legs. She woke up in a sweat and sprinkled on powder, Ilona's remedy against the heat, then put her fingers in her ears so she wouldn't have to listen to the din.

"Don't let them come here, God," she prayed, not particularly sure which God she prayed to, or that there was a difference between the Jewish and the Catholic God. The God she imagined was something like Mr. Detwiler, only invisible and much, much bigger. She started to shiver as she had done before that last time she heard explosions in the ocean. The shivering would not stop, even after she pulled the covers all the way up to her neck.

Freddie continued to sleep, although fitfully, throwing his arms and legs about and thrashing from side to side, his translucent, blue-veined eyelids fluttering like moths. Hilary had fallen asleep again, and was still trying to run away from the demonic something behind her that was gaining on her, her arms and legs bogged down in molasses, when shouting woke her up.

"Halt, who goes there?" And again, "Halt, or I shoot."

"They're coming." She reached over to shake Freddie. "Wake up," she said, then rolled up her pajama legs and pulled her shorts on over them. Freddie rubbed his eyes with his fists, while she stuffed the protruding pajama legs back underneath her shorts.

"What's the matter?" he asked.

"I don't know. Wake up."

"Where are you going?"

"The beach."

"Wait for me." Freddie did not bother to change. He ran after her in his pajamas, down the hall, through the gardenia-scented patio, and over the seawall, where they came to a stop in the shadows, hiding behind the fan-shaped leaves of a sea grape tree. Far out to sea, a fire skewered the horizon with orange and yellow spikes, spiraled with curls of billowing smoke. The fire raged more savagely than anything Hilary had ever seen before. It looked as though the sun was rising. Before it, the waves were dappled with bronze and silver flashings, making the water seem metallic. The tide was very high, a late spring tide in which the level of the water rose higher and fell lower than usual; now, as the water rose, the young larvae that had been deposited as eggs by the land crabs, weeks earlier, were flushed into the ocean.

Hilary pulled her brother close to her side as the fire's flames licked the night sky higher, when the sentry suddenly bolted to something at the water's edge, his bayonet fixed and ready.

"You think it's a Jap?" whispered Freddie.

"Get ready to run," Hilary said.

The sentry bent to look at something lying half in and half out of the water, surrounded by a tangle of seaweed, which he poked at with his bayonet. It looked like a log. He knelt beside it, his leggings crusting with wet sand, lifted something up, then let it drop. It was an arm. The sentry blew three sharp blasts on his whistle.

"Look," said Freddie. "Out in the water."

Several yards from the beach, swimmers bobbed in the argent moonlight, most of them hanging onto pieces of flotsam and palm trees. Some had discarded their floats and had begun the labored trudge to shore, slogging, groaning, flopping, exhausted, into the water where they sputtered and gasped and got up to stand and try again. A few staggered to the shore where they crawled and collapsed full length on the sand, their faces in the soft mud where they lay.

Hilary clutched Freddie tighter. "Quit it," he said.

Behind them, shadowy figures began running down the steps and climbing over the seawall onto the beach—MPs, guests from the hotel with bathrobes over their nightgowns and pajamas, women in curlers, and servicemen in skivvies from the hotel next door. The MPs shouted at the civilians to get off the beach, but no one listened. Instead, everyone ran back to their rooms for blankets and towels with which to wrap the exhausted survivors, until they could be put in the ambulance, which could be heard shrieking down Collins Avenue.

"No lights!" shouted the sentry to someone who had run out with a flashlight. It wasn't needed anyway. There was enough illumination in the chalky white light of the full moon to see that the men who had drifted to shore were glistening with oil. Some floating to the beach were already dead or dying. Many were badly burned, their skin charred and coagulated, split by immersion in the salt water, revealing raw red tissue beneath.

Frank had pulled on a pair of trousers and ran out carrying coffee in a gallon jug, with Ilona barefoot and in her bathrobe, following close behind. Her hair hung loose about her neck, making her look very young in the moonlight, almost as young as Mickey.

Even Mr. Davis was there, completely dressed in short-sleeved white shirt and bow tie, helping to carry the survivors to the patio, and wondering privately how they were going to get the oil out of the blankets. People were wading into the water in their pajamas to help bring out survivors who were unable to walk. A man with pieces of bone protruding through the flesh of his leg cried like a kitten, his piteous mewing drowned out by the wailing siren of the ambulance that had just pulled up the side street.

Within minutes, the narrow beach was jammed. Just a few yards from where Hilary and Freddie hid behind the sea grape, Frank laid down the coffee and cups to drag a sailor out of the water, bending to cradle him in his arms.

"You're all right, fella," he said. "I got you."

"Lift his head, Frank," said Ilona, wading after him to touch the man's cold, clammy hand. "His ears are still in the water."

"Would you get the oil out of my eyes, lady?" asked the sailor.

"Of course." Ilona wiped his face with the sleeve of her bathrobe, then wiped his eyes gently with her fingers. They came back clean. There was no oil. She looked at Frank, then cradled the man's head in her arms. "We're right here," she said.

"You didn't wipe my eyes good, I still can't see," the sailor said. Frank carried him off the beach as the dawn began to ribbon the sky in mauves and purples, and squawking shorebirds skittered over the far reaches of the beach, picking up crab larvae that had not been flushed to sea.

Suddenly someone shouted, "Get those children off the beach. This is no place for kids!" and a few people turned to stare at Hilary and Freddie angrily, as if they had no right to be there and somehow were the cause. Hilary's pajama legs had spilled out of both sides of her shorts and hung below her knees. She had stopped stuffing them back.

"Scram," said one of the sentries. "You kids get inside."

Freddie followed the lead of the grown-ups, who didn't listen to the sentry either. "We don't have to," he said.

Hilary had nothing to say. She had watched what was happening around her keenly, straining to comprehend. After a while it was as if her eyes were not wide enough to take it all in. She saw it in bits and pieces that she could not sort out or add together. Overwhelmed, she turned and walked toward the hotel behind her, her feet itching and bitten by sand fleas.

Freddie ran after her. "Why don't you want to stay? The ambulance is here and everything."

Hilary kept walking. "I don't want to stay," she said. Her eyes were wet.

"Well, I'm going to stay," he said. "I'm not going just when it's getting good."

"Don't," she replied, continuing to walk, past a pair of stretcher-bearers carrying a wounded man off the beach, and past Mrs. Templeton who held the hand of a blanket-wrapped man on a stretcher, smiling at him in a benign, motherly way and asking, "Your first time in Miami?" By the time Hilary reached the back entrance, the sun hung red on the horizon, gravid and globular, waiting for something to push it up in the sky.

Hilary tried in succeeding days to relate some of the events of the scene she had witnessed, but no one wanted to talk about it. Frank and Ilona were very angry that she had run out into the night, taking Freddie with her onto the beach without telling them that she was leaving the room. They predicted all sorts of dire consequences for the repetition of such a reckless act, while remaining nonspecific about what form they might take. Mr. Davis never talked to her anyway, preferring the mediation of her parents, so he was unlikely to want to discuss it. Mickey had slept through it, although she said she heard shouting, adding that in any case it did no good to dwell upon a thing. Winona missed it all. Freddie had nightmares about it, so she didn't want to discuss it with him, and T.H., after hearing some of the details, said that it was a military secret, and that she should not repeat anything of what she saw to anyone. She was all alone with her thoughts of a black night, vivid orange sky, white full moon, and burned and drowning sailors coming ashore onto her beach.

She thought about it so much in the next few days, T.H. began to complain that she was no fun anymore. Hilary resolved to be fun. The alternative was to be left out in the cold again with no one but Jack Suga and Freddie to play with, and while she had Mickey, her beautiful friend was too preoccupied with her double life to have much time left over.

Hilary tried to put the night's events out of her mind, the way one erases a blackboard, and was able to thrust out most of her thoughts, all except the picture of the man who had asked Ilona to take the oil out of his eyes. Hilary thought about him, wondering what happened to him after the ambulance took him away, particularly if he put his hands out in front of him when he walked. She decided she would rather be deaf than blind. That way, if someone were to sneak up on her, she could see them. On the other hand, she would more likely hear someone sneaking up on her. The choice was a horrible one.

It was especially difficult now that school was over and every day was free, with a surfeit of time as unstructured and prodigious as a double scoop of ice cream lopping and melting over a sugar cone. The only features were bright sunny days, a town full of marching soldiers, and a tepid ocean where one always came up with tar someplace on one's body, usually one's feet.

At the end of the same week, Hilary, T.H., Billy Connaught, Frances Simmons, Jackie Snyder, and Shirley Leone, traveling in a pack, were riding their loaded bicycles to the scrap depot. Sometimes the pack membership varied, but its nucleus was always more or less the same. Jack Suga, of course, was never included, Sorrell Myers was too fat to keep up with them, and Liz Bonnier was away at camp in North Carolina, where she sat around campfires and told ghost stories at night, and short-sheeted her bunkmates' beds so that they couldn't stretch their knees past their ears.

Today T.H. had come for Hilary with his bike laden with a basket and two scrap-filled saddlebags hanging over the bar. Hilary smiled when she saw him although she didn't feel like it, a perky smile she had seen Shirley Leone make, which pushed up her cheeks under her eyes. She only did it because smiling was synonymous with being fun. She continued to lift her lips off her teeth even after the muscles of her cheeks began to hurt.

"Freddie has no one to play with," she said, after T.H. had arranged the saddlebags beneath her legs. "Can we take him?"

"We're already loaded down with stuff," he replied. "I can't fit him on the bike. And we spend too much time with him anyway."

They zigzagged down the sidewalk, passing trucks and marching platoons in the street beside them. Although she had to hold her legs out to avoid the saddlebags, Hilary was at least able to relax her smile, allowing her mouth to droop in the sad and comfortable way of someone with a worry.

The scrap depot was stationed behind the movie theater in an empty warehouse. Today's drive for metal was under the auspices of the Boy Scouts who had erected a sign that read, JUNK THE AXIS. They all got off their bikes to empty the contents of their packs and baskets onto a big heap of gleaming trash—razors, rusty scissors, tin cans, and empty toothpaste tubes, culled and scoured from back alleys, empty lots, apartments and houses, hotels, and strained and sifted from the richest source of all, the beach. Frances Simmons, whose father owned a Ford dealership, threw in a box of old license plates.

Members of the American Legion stood behind the Boy Scouts. Hilary recognized one of them, a veteran of the Spanish-American

War. Veins could be seen through the fragile, parchmentlike skin of his hands, which were spattered with brown dots the size of dimes. He had marched in the Decoration Day parade next to an even older veteran in a wheelchair, who someone said was ninety-five and a former member of the Confederate Army.

"I saw you in the parade," she said.

"Only metal," he replied.

Hilary cupped her hands around her mouth. "Decoration Day!" she shouted, "I saw you march!" The man leaned away from her like a twig in the wind.

The Boy Scouts praised Frances' contribution, and gave her a tiny pin. Frances went back to her bike, singing "Chattanooga Choo-Choo" and thrusting out her chest like a pigeon.

"I hope that pin sticks her," said Shirley, "right in the bazoom."

When Hilary jumped off the bike, she saw that she had somehow scraped her leg. She spit on her hand to wipe away the blood and only half heard T.H. when he said, "I can't play with you tomorrow. I have to help my mother stuff envelopes for the Red Cross."

Hilary felt a pang of fear that made her want to throw up, but she masked her face and swallowed hard. "That's okay," she said. "I have to help Mel get ready for a demonstration." When she went to her room to wash the scrape and put on a Band-Aid, she found Ilona sitting on a bed, her hands folded in her lap, waiting for her.

"I want to talk to you," she said. Trouble. Hilary sat on the other bed. "What happened to your legs?"

"I scraped them."

"I can see that. First go wash them off and put on Band-Aids." Hilary did so then returned to the bed. "Now listen to me. Your brother is outside by himself. He has no one to play with. Hilary, I count on you. I can't take care of him and work at the same time. You have to help. You're the older sister. He's your responsibility too."

"Other kids don't have to take care of their baby brothers and sisters."

"I'm not interested in other kids. I'm interested in my kids. I only have two, and one needs a playmate. You have to spend more time with him. Not so much running all over town, especially with this boy, this T.H. What kind of boy has initials for a name?"

"His real name is Thomas Henry."

"Is he a shvartzer?"

"No."

"Never mind. Freddie has been promoted on condition. He's supposed to fill in all those workbooks. You have to help him. You know what they want in the spaces."

"It's not fair."

"How can you talk of fair? I have a sister who gave me most of her savings so I could have the fare for America. I don't know if I'll ever see her again, now when I have a chance to help her, to pay her back, to take care of her here. Is that fair? I got a letter from England. The same man. He had no letter from them, only a message. They're going to try to get to Sweden with the help of the Danish underground, to Elsinore. That's very dangerous. They could get caught."

"I saw a movie like that. They changed the books in the window of this book store. That's how the people knew it was safe to come in or not. From the titles of the books."

Ilona sighed. "Why do you think of movies? My mother is afraid to see a doctor because he might report her. Can't you understand how sick I am with worry? Why do you give me extra grief? Don't I have enough?"

Hilary hung her head. Tears dropped on her Band-Aids.

"You're a selfish girl. You only think of yourself. Don't turn into a selfish woman. Please. I couldn't stand to look at you if you did."

Hilary swung her legs, banging her heels into the frame of the bed. "Don't be mad at me, Ma."

"Mrs. Templeton didn't teach you to swing your legs like that," said Ilona. "I know that much about social graces." She left the room. She was not as tall as Mrs. Templeton, nor as straight, but daintier, more like a tiny china teacup that someone had given Hilary for Christmas.

Hilary found Freddie on the beach, sifting through the sand and pouring it from the funnel of his hand into his tin sand chute. Hilary dropped in the sand beside him.

"Why don't you bring a kid home from your class?"

"School's over. You know school's over."

"You ought to think about it next year. Say to yourself, I'm gonna bring a kid home to play. Find a kid you like and ask him."

"I don't want to play with other kids. I'd rather play with you."

"But I'm your sister."

"Mickey gave me something to give you," he said. Freddie reached into his pocket and handed Hilary a piece of V-mail, a thin sheet of folded microfilm. She opened it and read it on the sand.

> Dear Hilary, Thank you for the picture. You're a real knockout, although I guess you heard that before. I hope you don't mind about me not calling you Miss MacIntyre. I feel like I know you pretty well by now. I hope you feel that way about me. I'm writing this aboard a CENSORED. It's hard to see because there's only a few light bulbs. I'm laying in my bunk. The CENSORED has stopped, when I went on CENSORED I saw the lights of some city. There's nothing to do except lay here and listen to the whir of the ventilators or stand in line. I don't get CENSORED like some of the guys who throw up all the time and I don't play craps or poker, so I just think about you. I hope I can see you when I get leave. I think about taking you out and showing you a good time. Put your lips to a mirror. That's me kissing you. Put your arms around your shoulders and squeeze hard. That's me too. Your friend, Sylvan.

Hilary stuffed the letter deep into her pocket on the way inside. It wasn't that she wasn't allowed to have a pen pal. It was that she knew the turn the contents were taking would not be approved and almost certainly Ilona, with an undeveloped sense of privacy, would ask to read it.

When Hilary got to the kitchen, it was clear that it didn't matter where she put the letter. No one was interested in her. She could have walked in wearing high heels and lipstick. The kitchen was in an uproar, with a policeman who stood near the dishwasher taking notes, and everyone yelling, the people from the front office including the bookkeeper and the telephone operator, the lobby staff, and Frank yelling the loudest. Hilary thought Gus was in trouble again, and so did Gus, who had retreated, glowering, to a corner of the bakery, his arms, coated with confectioner's sugar, crossed over his chest.

It was easy to piece together what happened from the shouts. Two drums of lard and a side of beef were missing from the storage locker. There was no question about it. Frank knew his inventory and so did Ilona. To be sure, they double-checked carbon copies of order slips, shipments, deliveries, which was unnecessary. The breach created by the missing goods was large enough to accommodate a squad of men.

Gus was high on the list of suspects, since he had recently been in trouble with the FBI, but Frank vouched for him and he was free to glower over his macaroons. Being an enemy alien was one thing, stealing supplies another. It was just something Frank didn't think Gus could ever do.

Since it was a theft of some magnitude, the policeman asked Frank and Ilona questions like who had the keys, and where the keys were kept. If it was known who had access to the storage locker, the field of suspects could be narrowed to a manageable size.

Marco suggested perhaps someone from the outside had done it, a very strong burglar, or a pair of burglars; then the policeman took his name down and asked him to account for his whereabouts for the previous day and night. After that, no one else made a suggestion except for Mrs. Templeton, who said, "*Cherchez la femme.*" The policeman dusted the doors and shelves for fingerprints, but there were so many, including those of half the people who worked there, that there was no way to sort them out.

Frank let it be known that if he caught the guy who did it, he would personally send him to the hospital. It was a great loss, and one that was not made up easily. It wasn't a question of money so much as it was availability. There were great shortages of meat and of fat. Mr. Davis was very upset, standing bent over in his thinking position, with his head facing out, reflecting the harsh overhead lights of the kitchen. He told Frank to make out as best he could, adding that now that the season was slower, he wouldn't feel the pinch as much.

The bell captain suggested to Frank that he could find what he needed on the black market. There was an active and prosperous one in Miami, and one had only to know where to go and whom to ask for. The bell captain then offered, for a slight commission, to put Frank in touch with the right people. Frank was furious. There was no way he could deal in the covert, unpatriotic channels through which one could buy nylon and steak, gasoline and extra ration coupons, even electric motor bearings, which were perhaps the scarcest commodity of all. He threatened the bell captain, coming right up to his face and standing toe to toe. Marco stepped between them. "You got to quit flying off the handle at every little thing, Frank. Remember your pressure."

Frank's pressure was something he could not forget. There it was, something he couldn't see or feel, pumping too high like a generator out of control and keeping him home dealing with a theft of a side of beef when he could be tossing grenades, and just at the time the government, hoping to enlist married men, upped the base pay, adding another twenty-eight dollars a month.

For some reason, the disturbance in the kitchen brought tears to Hilary's eyes and she retreated to the sanctuary of the lobby. It was almost empty. The bell captain, still smarting from his altercation with Frank, was hiding behind a newspaper. Mr. Davis, too, was back, handling the front desk, from behind which he stepped every now and then to stretch his legs, leaving a bell on the counter just in case someone came to check in.

The season was not only over but it had suffered a serious crimp. There was no way to get to Miami. Cars were nonexistent, as were tires. Gas was severely rationed. Planes were largely for military use; bus and train stations were jammed with servicemen, who had priority; and newer stricter travel regulations left civilians standing with luggage in the station.

Those few guests still in the hotel had heard about the theft. It was impossible not to. News traveled through the lobby and hallways as fast as the palmetto bugs that zipped in and out of the drains.

Mrs. Portman was rereading the letters from her son. "It's a terrible thing," she said. "I hope they catch him."

"How do you know it's a him?" asked Hilary.

"Women don't do those kinds of things," said Mrs. Portman.

Lipschutz was in the lobby, treading in the wraithlike manner he had adopted in the past few days. There was no demand for dance lessons, on top of which Mrs. Steinfeld, upset by what she had witnessed on the beach, had taken Rudy home to New York for the summer. It had been a particularly trying departure because Lipschutz, a loyal man, waited two days in the train station with his beloved, trying to get seats for her on the train, putting her and Rudy in their seats, only to have them bumped by some serviceman, and having to carry their luggage on and off by himself, although to be fair, the servicemen, swinging duffel bags overhead, usually offered to help.

The loss devastated Lipschutz, especially after it was learned that eight people had died when another Silver Meteor was wrecked by a freight train in North Carolina. While it wasn't Mrs. Steinfeld's train, it could have been. Lipschutz told everyone he was an empty pecan shell. Hilary was glad, not for Lipschutz's loss, but because Rudy Steinfeld was gone for the summer.

Resticking a Band-Aid that had flopped loose, she walked over to him. "Did you get a letter from Miss Gomez?" she asked.

Lipschutz shook his head. Hilary wondered if he could have robbed the storage room. She didn't think so. He was so skinny it was inconceivable that he could have carried anything as heavy as a side of beef.

"What about Mrs. Steinfeld?"

"She's okay," he replied. "That lovely lady is back in New York. I'm an empty pecan shell."

Hilary sat beside him on the sofa. It had a rip on the seat that no one had bothered to repair and she poked back the stuffing. "You're a great dancer," she said.

"You think so?"

"Sure. I used to watch you twirl around the pool. You're as good as Fred Astaire."

Lipschutz smiled, his teeth yellowed from tobacco. "You should have seen me with Gloria Russo, my first partner. A great dancer. She knew how to follow. She really had class."

"Like Mrs. Templeton?"

"No one with blue hair has class, sweetheart. Gloria Russo, though, that little girl had class. She knew how to finish on a dime. That's the secret of a good dancer. The finish. Once she tripped on a floor some janitor had put too much wax on. She went sprawling, but she didn't miss a beat. She got up, still smiling, and made her finish. That's what I call class."

There was a lull in the conversation. Hilary plunged. "A lot of sailors washed up on the beach last week. Did you see it?"

"I heard about it."

"I saw it. Me and Freddie did."

Lipschutz lit a cigarette. "You did? Why did your mother let you stay?"

"She didn't know we were there."

The bell captain yelled across the lobby, "Hey, twinkletoes, that's jailbait in case you don't know."

"What's jailbait?" she asked.

Lipschutz didn't answer. Instead he turned to the bell captain. "Watch your mouth," he called, then turned back to Hilary. "Put it out of your mind. It's not for you to think about. You're just a little girl. Little girls shouldn't think about gruesome things like that. It's not right. You should be thinking about ice cream sodas and organdy pinafores."

"What's that? A pinafore?

"Like an apron, very ruffly and little-girly."

The thing that Becky Thatcher wore. Hilary doubted that anything like a ruffly apron could be something she would want.

"How do you put something out of your mind? All of it."

"I don't know," he said, and stubbed out a cigarette.

When he left, she sat down at the big mahogany desk and took out a few sheets of hotel stationery. Then she picked up the scratchy pen and dipped it into the inkwell.

Dear Sylvan, Poker is easy. Mel taught me how to play. The main thing you got to remember is that you always fold with jacks, unless you can beat openers, or you only need one card for a flush or straight. I don't know about craps except you have to watch for loaded dice which you can test in a glass of water. If the same sides turn up, you better play with another pair.

Things are fine here. Where are you? There were a lot of places on your letter that were blacked out. Why did you do that? How do you expect a person to read it that way? I saw Clark Gable marching on the golf course. He looks like any other soldier, except he doesn't march so good. I know others who march a lot better, including my friend Corporal Bill Wright who has almost finished his training.

I took metal to the scrap drive. Frances Simmons got a pin for all her license plates. The other night a lot of sailors floated to the beach behind my hotel. You could see in the darkness. They came from a torpedoed ship. Some of them were dead bodies. When a body is in the water, it gets swollen.

Did you ever see a dead body? It's not like in the movies. It's messy and some of them smell bad. I can't decide if I'm afraid of a dead body or of being dead. I think both. Anyhow, I can't get it out of my mind. It's like it's stuck or something. How do you get bad things out of your mind? And don't tell me to forget it. That's what I've been trying to do all week. Your friend, Hilary.

"I'd worry that Florida would slip down somehow," said Charlene, fluffing up her curly red bangs with her swizzle stick. "Drift away from the mainland if they cut a canal through it."

"That's not possible," said Bill. "The land is anchored to the rocks beneath."

"The point is," said June Bug, who wore a fez with a tassel, "we can use a quick way for tankers to get through to the gulf, and a few senators of this stupid state don't want to do it."

"But why do it at all?" asked Charlene. "Isn't the war coming to an end any day? I read that when the RAF bombed Cologne, twenty thousand people died. That's a lot of Germans to kill."

"It's a wash," said Bill. "When Tobruk fell, the Germans took twenty-five thousand British prisoners. The numbers are almost the same. Only the teams change."

"I don't want to talk about the war," said Mickey. "Everything we see and hear is war. I want to forget about it."

"She's right," said June Bug. "Why are we talking about the war when we got these two gorgeous tomatoes." He signaled to the waitress for another round, then turned to Charlene who was reapplying her lipstick. "You gonna miss me, baby, when I shove off?"

"I'm gonna miss you like crazy," she replied, pursing her lips at the mirror of her compact.

"Until you latch onto the next sucker," said June Bug.

Charlene put down her lipstick. "Now that's not nice. That's not nice at all." She began to unpin her corsage.

"Don't you know when I'm kidding?" June Bug pinned it back, trailing his hand across her breast as he did so.

"Watch out you don't get stuck," she said.

Bill stared across the table at Mickey.

"When are you leaving?" she asked.

"Two weeks. I thought you understood that. I've been telling you that for weeks."

Then she turned away, her blue eyes misted. "There you go again," she said. "Another wet blanket."

"My folks write that they're having a bad drought. It's so dry and hot, the corn tassels are scorching just as they're pollinating. No pollination, no kernels, no kernels, no corn crop."

"The only colonels I'm interested in," said Charlene, "wear eagles on their shoulders. What about you, Mickey?"

Bill put his hand under the table and took Mickey's. "What about you?" he asked.

"I don't lead with my right and I don't telegraph my poker hand."

Bill laughed. "That sounds like Hilary."

"Who's Hilary?" asked Charlene.

"A friend of mine," said Mickey.

"How come you didn't invite her?"

"She's only a kid," said Bill.

"What do you want with a kid for?" asked Charlene. "Unless she's got a great-looking father or brother. Am I right?"

"That's a stupid thing to say," said Mickey. "Just because you don't understand it, don't make something nasty out of it."

"Pardon me for living," said Charlene.

June Bug whispered something into Charlene's ear. Bill took the moment to drop his hand to Mickey's leg and brush her thigh. She squirmed. The movement was not lost on June Bug, who prided himself on being an expert on women. "You're gonna get yourself barred from the Clover Club for life if you go any higher," he said.

Embarrassed, Bill withdrew his hand, bringing it to the top of the table where he wrapped it around his glass. "Skip it."

June Bug put his hand up and leaned back in his chair. "Whoa, back. It was only a joke."

"It wasn't funny," said Bill. He led Mickey out onto the dance floor.

The music, fast and syncopated jazz, was meant for a jitterbug, but they clung to one another on the corner of the floor, the crowd pushing against them, their bodies so used to one another anyway, there were no spaces between them.

"Mickey, I love you," he whispered into her hair. His breath was hot on her ear. Mickey felt weak in the knees, her body melting and opening. "Let's leave," she said.

"What about them?"

"I don't care about them."

"You love me?" he asked. "Tell me if you do. I need to hear it, baby. I need to hear it now."

"Let's leave," she whispered. "I want you. Isn't that enough?"

"Do you love me?" He stopped dancing and pulled her face up, cradling her heart-shaped chin in the palm of his hand.

Mickey wasn't sure what was love. If it was that she had to lie beside this man at this moment and feel his hands and lips on her, if love was a desire so strong she couldn't stand, then this was love.

"Yes."

"I knew it. I knew it." He lifted her up and swung her around.

"Watch it, buddy," said a sailor beside them. "If you want to dance like that, go over there where there's room."

"Sorry, pal." He led her to the edge of the floor, beside a table of people banging their swizzle sticks. "Mickey, I want to marry you."

"I can't," she said. "Not now."

"Why not?" He brushed his hair from his eyes.

"Because I can't. Stop pushing me. You're pushing me too hard."

"I'm sorry, baby. I don't mean to rush you, except we're running out of time. Is it your father?"

Mickey ran off the dance floor, pushing her way through the crowded room to the table where she picked up her purse.

"Where are you going?" he shouted. "Wait a minute."

"Now what did you do?" asked June Bug. "Didn't I tell you not to make a move without checking first with me?"

"Why did you have to spoil things?" she asked.

"What did I spoil?" Bill followed after her.

"Watch it, buddy," said the naval officer from the next table.

"Sorry, sir."

"She forgot her compact," said Charlene. "I was using her compact and she forgot to take it."

Bill chased Mickey to the door where she had hailed a cab and was climbing into the back seat. "He's not my father!" she shouted from the opened window. "And you can tell that to your friend too. He's not my father."

The cab driver leaned backward, nodded his head, and drove away.

Hilary stayed off the beach, which was darkened now by iridescent arabesques of oil cabled through the sand, even though she had gotten over much of the horror of the night the sailors had drifted ashore, to the extent that she could think of other things, like reading her new Nancy Drew mystery without losing her concentration.

Tonight, she and Freddie were in Frank and Ilona's room, an inner room in which they were allowed to have lights, filling out a coupon for a Whoopee Cushion, an inflated pillow that made a flatulent blast when sat on, which they planned to sneak into the lobby.

Mel had come to visit Frank and stood in the doorway, talking about Whirlaway, who had beaten Seabiscuit at Suffolk Downs. "The greatest stretch runner of all time, Frank. Like a streak of lightning. He set fire to that track."

Frank was reading a newspaper and came to something that said, "Wake up your liver bile," which he clipped out. Perhaps what was bothering him was somehow connected to his liver. He would send for it anyhow. "Do you know," he said, "the draft is taking men with three fingers missing, as long as they have a thumb, IB they call them, for limited clerical work, and they won't take me. Can you beat that?"

"But you don't want to do limited clerical work, Frank."

"I know, but if a guy missing three fingers can pound a typewriter, why can't I man a gun? Answer me that!"

Winona came behind Mel with a note for Hilary. "Some soldier gave this to the bell captain," she said.

"Who's sending you notes?" asked Frank. "Let's see it."

He read the note aloud: " 'Hilary, I need to see Mickey. She won't see me. Please go and talk to her. I can't get her to come out. I'm leaving in a few days, and I must see her. Bill.' What the hell is this? Who is this guy? Who is Bill?" yelled Frank.

"He's the soldier who taught me how to pitch a fast ball," said Freddie.

"Well, why is he sending this to Hilary?"

"Don't ask me," said Winona. "I don't know about such doings. I just delivered the note."

"I'm gonna have to have a talk with this guy." Frank put down his paper and went to the door.

Hilary jumped up. "He's nice," she said. "Don't hit him."

"Who said I'm going to hit him? I'm going to talk to him. You know"—he turned to Mel—"some of this is your fault. I shouldn't have let her go with you to those demonstrations you put on."

"Why not?" asked Mel. "What does one thing have to do with another?"

"Because she gets ideas that she's grown-up." He turned to Hilary. "You're not grown-up. You're just a kid, and don't forget it. Stay out of business that belongs to grown-ups. Didn't I tell you I didn't want you to have anything to do with her?"

"Who?"

"You know who. It still goes." Frank walked out to the sidewalk, chomping on a corona corona. He saw Bill Wright standing in front of the hotel, alone and waiting.

"You Wright?" he asked. Bill nodded. "I'm Frank MacIntyre. Hilary's father." They shook hands. "I understand you taught my son how to throw a fast ball."

"That's right. I did. He's a good little guy."

"I guess you got kids of your own?"

"Not yet."

"I don't have the time to do that kind of thing, play ball and all. I could do it, you understand, I just don't have the time. Now what do you want with my girl? What's going on?"

"Hilary knows someone I know. I was hoping she could talk to that person for me."

"You mean Mickey Biscayne. I read your note. Why can't you do it?"

Bill Wright turned his flight cap around in his fingers. "She won't talk to me."

"Then that's that. What do you need the kid for anyway? That's not a kid's business, soldier."

"I know, Mr. MacIntyre. Look, it's like this. I'll be leaving in a few days. She means a lot to me. I need to say good-bye to her."

"Well, that makes a difference." Frank knocked off a heavy ash onto the sidewalk with the heel of his hand. "I wouldn't do it, though, unless you knew for sure old man Radner was gone."

"Who is old man Radner?"

"You don't know?"

"I don't know."

"He's the guy keeping her."

Bill Wright looked stricken. He put his cap on his head.

"Look," said Frank, "I'm sorry. I don't like to tell that kind of thing to a guy who's got the hots for a dame, but that's where things stand."

"It's not like that, Mr. MacIntyre."

"Like what?"

"The hots. She really means something to me."

"You kids are so sappy. Take it from someone who's been there. You'll learn someday it's all the hots. Look, I'll tell her. Better yet, I'll send a woman to talk to her, less suspicious that way. Not my kid, though, she's just a little girl. You were wrong to pull her into the middle of this."

"I'm sorry," said Bill.

Frank spoke to Vicky Sue, who was complaining about a party of five that neglected to leave her a tip. "They stiffed me," she said. "The sons of bitches stiffed me."

"Do me a favor," he said, "and I'll take care of it."

"Anything, Frank."

"Go upstairs to 311 and ask to talk to Mickey. You know, the blonde that's shacking up with Radner. Make sure he can't hear, and tell her someone's waiting for her in the lifeguard shack, and that she better go and see what it's all about, or else, make sure she gets this part, or else Radner is going to find out about the soldier. You got it?"

"Got it, Frank."

When Mickey entered the lifeguard shack, she was furious. She saw him in the shadows, leaning against the wall, smoking a cigarette in the dark. She stood where she was, making no move toward him, her fists clenched, her hands down at her side. "I think blackmail is nasty."

"I don't know what you're talking about."

"That waitress, she threatened me."

"Mickey, I don't know what she told you. I was pretty desperate. I sent a note to Hilary. Her father saw it and he arranged for you to get the message."

"What is this? Is the whole hotel in on this?"

"Tell me something," he said, stepping off from the wall. "Were you really willing to let me go like this, never see me again maybe, just so I wouldn't find out?"

"Find out what?"

"Find out what you were hinting at from the cab. I know, Mickey. Hilary's father told me. I know about you and this old guy. Why didn't you tell me? You saw I was falling crazy in love with you. You saw, you knew, and you didn't tell me. Why?"

"Because, just because of what you're doing now. I didn't want you yelling and screaming at me."

"I'll bet the ballet is bullshit, too."

"No it's not. I can do an arabesque on pointe if I have a partner that can lift."

"Does he know? About me?"

"No, and I'm not going to tell him either."

"God damn it. You're not going to tell him. And then what? You keep us both on a string? Like two yoyos?"

"And you're not going to spoil it for me either. He's got money, and he takes good care of me. What do you have? Nothing. I've been on a farm. I know all about scratching for a living. I don't want to scratch anymore."

"But he's not offering you anything, Mickey. Does he want to marry you?"

"He's already married."

"Sure, he's using you. He gets tired of you, drops you, then what do you have? Nothing. You're right back where you started, only a little older, and maybe a little bitter. I'm not offering you that. I'm offering myself on a permanent basis."

"You're going off to war. You can't offer me anything on a permanent basis. You're going off to war and you're gonna get shot, and killed . . ."

Mickey began to cry, deep sobs that racked her shoulders, and made her shudder where she stood. Bill reached for her, and held her to his chest.

"I don't want to love you," she said. "I don't want to love you."

"But you do."

"But I do."

"Isn't that terrible?" he said. "And I love you, too. I'm so crazy in love with you I can't see straight. It's the worst thing I ever heard of."

He led her to the stack of lounge mats upon which someone had put a clean sheet. A pitcher of water stood on the floor nearby. Bill didn't ask questions. He wouldn't have wanted to spoil the mood for anything. He peeled her clothes off, the way one takes off chewing-gum wrappers, crumpling them in his hand and throwing them into the corner, then falling beside her and covering her with kisses.

"You're so beautiful," he whispered. "I have never seen anyone so beautiful."

"Yes," she said, "yes."

Winona had a smile on her face that Frank hadn't seen in a long time. "I took care of things," she said. "Everything's going to be all right."

"What things?" asked Frank.

"Never you mind. Things. I never liked that man anyway. He has never left me a tip, been coming here for months, taking all my towels off the cart, and hair all over that bathtub. It's like they keep a bear in there. I took care of things."

Mr. Radner came storming into the lobby, looking for Mickey. His first stop was the front desk. "Did you see her?" he asked Mr. Davis. Mr. Davis shook his head with the discretion of a hotel manager who knew, of course, who *her* was.

"Where the hell could she have run off to? When I want her, she's not there. When I don't want her, she's all over me." He crossed the lobby and headed for the east wing, where Lipschutz sat staring with his fingers made into a tent.

"Radner," called Frank. "You ever taste Gus's Rumpelmayer?"

Mr. Radner stopped. "What's that?"

"It's a strawberry cream cake, layers of strawberries, custard, whipped cream; the baker makes it. Sugar, cream, eggs, the real goods. You've never had anything like it. I can promise you that. Why don't you come into the kitchen? I'll personally see that you get a piece on the house."

"He use margarine?" Mr. Radner asked, thinking of the white lard with the little red dot his wife kneaded until it turned yellow.

"Butter," said Frank.

"Well, all right. I don't mind trying a piece."

Frank put his arm around him and led him into the kitchen. "I knew you appreciated good food," he said. "I can tell by looking at this." He patted Mr. Radner's abdomen.

"That's my glands," said Mr. Radner.

"I thought a person's glands were in their neck," said Frank.

12

The telegram came in August, a week after Mrs. Portman's letter from her son Elliott which she read to everyone in the lobby. The return address was an A.P.O. number and he wrote that he left New Guinea on a transport from which he made a hair-raising climb down a debarkation net with a rifle, a pack on his back, and wearing his boondocks, saying that each time the ship rolled, he slammed into the side, but because he was in such good shape, he didn't feel a thing.

"Can you imagine?" Mrs. Portman had commented to her audience. "I used to keep a gate at the top of the steps so he wouldn't fall down."

Then she related more of his letter, of his landing craft getting stuck on a coral reef, and his having to wade to shore with his rifle over his head, and of the beach jammed to the shoreline with mounds of supplies that reminded him of when his mother made an excursion to Schmulke's delicatessen. Mrs. Portman smiled at this, everyone else did too. When she read of the whining mosquitoes and how he had to hack his way through a mile of jungle, everyone frowned in sympathy, but smiled again when Mrs. Portman said he and his buddies found white orchids growing wild, and abandoned supplies, including a case of sake which he said tasted like the schnapps that Uncle Phil liked.

Mr. Davis had leaned over the sofa, nodding in polite appreciation, his arms folded across his chest, the only one who had figured out that Elliott Portman was probably on Guadalcanal, although he didn't say anything. The newspapers had been full of grisly reports of what was happening to the marines who had landed on that barren knoll—dysentery, malaria, foot rot, nightly bombardments that left them without sleep, muddy foxholes, and one especially gruesome story of hundreds of wounded men who died floating in the water, some of them pulled down by sharks. The last thing he wanted to do was increase Mrs. Portman's anxiety.

When the telegram came the week after the letter, the word circulated quickly. Telegrams were infrequent, and the sight of a messenger on a bike was enough to arouse even the most slothful sunworshiper. Everyone said they weren't surprised, that the letter somehow had been a portent. Hindsighted Cassandras, they drifted to the lobby, some still shining with suntan oil, where Mrs. Portman sat with Mrs. Templeton discussing a certain way to twist wool when making argyle socks. It was like waiting in a darkened theater for the curtain to go up. Mr. Carpathy, his wife, Mr. Samuelson (back after an unsuccessful few months with his daughter-in-law who claimed a chronic sore throat from yelling loud enough for him to hear), two schoolteachers who were visiting Miami Beach for the month of August, and some of the staff, waited in the background like potted ferns, neither moving nor speaking.

Hilary sat under the portico with Freddie, killing time until the arrival of T.H. They watched as Mr. Davis spoke to the messenger, took the telegram, then came to sit beside Mrs. Portman, delivering it to her personally, and wiping his head with his handkerchief. Everyone held their breath. Even the bell captain, who these days spent most of his time reading the newspaper, observed the episode with interest.

Mrs. Portman dropped her purse. It rolled off her lap along with her needles and her knitting to the floor. She let it lie where it had fallen. Mrs. Templeton picked it up for her and Mr. Davis handed her the telegram. She held it for a moment, her hands trembling.

"Do you want me to open it?" he asked.

"No," she replied. "I'll do it."

She ripped it open, read the message, and let out a lonely wail, low and agonized. It surprised Hilary to learn what the message contained, for Mrs. Portman didn't cry *Elliott,* or *my son.* Instead she said, *Mama,* like a little girl.

Mrs. Templeton tried to help her to a sitting position, so did Mr. Davis, but neither was successful. She remained slumped like a half-filled sack of oranges against the damask cushions.

"Why is she crying?" asked Freddie.

"I'm not sure. I think it's her son," said Hilary. "You remember him, the tall guy, Elliott. I think he's dead."

Freddie was less concerned about the death of someone far away than he was about the fire the week before in the Big Top of Ringling Brothers in Cleveland in which many animals that got burned had to be destroyed. Because he had seen a circus, he could imagine such a thing. He could not imagine the tall man with the dog tags dead, certainly not dead enough for everyone to be crying over it.

This was the second time Hilary had seen grief close up. She still didn't know what to do about it. She went for Frank. Frank would know what to do. He was in the kitchen with Ilona, supervising the local locksmith as he replaced the third lock in two months on the storeroom door. The thefts of meat from the storage locker continued, as did the theft of butter, sugar, and, this morning, two dozen lobsters. Frank was going to have to carry all the keys on his person, especially after Mr. Davis had admonished him by saying that Frank bore some responsibility for this latest rash of thefts, that he held him personally accountable, and that he had to be more careful where he kept his keys and who had access to them.

Ilona, who was planning a meatless menu for the whole week, instead of just Tuesday and Friday as the government had suggested all restaurants do, saw Hilary first.

"We're busy," she said.

"Mrs. Portman got a telegram."

Ilona's pencil poised in midair. "What kind?"

"The War Department."

Frank handed the locksmith a tumbler. "That's too bad," he said.

"Oh, my God." Ilona wasted no time. She was out of her apron in a flash, and running into the lobby where she shoved everyone else aside and enveloped Mrs. Portman in her arms, crooning to her in a way that Hilary only dimly remembered, and rocking her on the couch.

It was too intense, too private, like seeing someone in their underwear, something to avoid as if it were contagious. Everyone left except Lipschutz, who stood pallid and grave, silently weeping.

Hilary watched her mother stroke Mrs. Portman's hair. Instead of being soothed, Mrs. Portman cried even harder, and more surprising, instead of telling her not to cry, as Ilona had done with Hilary when she was little, Ilona said things like, "Let it out," and "I know, it's terrible."

Later that night, when Frank and Ilona were conjecturing who the thief could be, with Frank laying odds on the bell captain, who he said he was now watching like a hawk, Ilona suddenly said, "That's the worst. What happened to Mrs. Portman. God forbid we should ever know from it."

Hilary, who was reading on the floor, asked what was the worst, but no one answered her. Frank just leaned down and gave her a hug, so hard it hurt her shoulder. She didn't say anything, just relished the smell of his shaving lotion and the warm protection of his great big arm. He couldn't help it if he was strong.

Ilona organized the *shiva.* There was no question that Mrs. Portman would return to New York. There was no body to bury, nor would there be. Elliott Portman had been dismembered by a grenade so completely that the only thing the government was returning was his dog tags. The funeral service would be in South Beach, at Ilona's shul, and the shiva would be at the hotel afterward, with Ilona personally seeing to it that there was plenty of food and drinks for everyone, primarily food.

"This is not a wake," she said to Frank. "Forget the liquor. They want to eat."

"That is the basic difference," said Frank to Hilary, "between your mother and me. My family likes to drink a man down, and her people like to eat them to rest."

Mrs. Portman sat shiva in the east wing. Her brother, Phil, who looked just like her, came down from New York on the train and he sat by her side holding her hand. No one talked about Elliott except Ilona, who came dressed in a pretty navy and white printed cotton dress that Hilary had never seen before, and sitting next to Mrs. Portman, said, "Tell me about your son. My children say they knew him."

"He was going to medical school," said Mrs. Portman.

"He wanted to be a doctor," said her brother Phil.

"He must have been very smart," said Ilona.

"The best grades. Always," said Mrs. Portman, then she began a silent weeping, tears streaming down from her eyes, as she made little choking sounds, to Hilary more terrible than the loud wailing she had heard before.

There were not enough Jewish males for a minyan, and so the rabbi, in the interests of fulfilling the spirit of the Law, if not the letter, allowed the three missing places to be filled by gentiles, which in this case included Frank, Mr. Davis, and Marco, all wearing yarmulkes, in deference to Mrs. Portman and her deceased son, using the logic that their ancestors were all Jews originally anyhow.

"I don't know what to say to her," whispered Hilary, who had been dressed by Ilona in her Easter outfit.

"Say something about her son. Tell her how sorry you are."

Hilary approached Mrs. Portman tentatively, hanging back until one of the grown-ups made room. One of her braids had come undone and she stood winding the ends together as she spoke.

"I'm sorry that Elliott died, Mrs. Portman."

Mrs. Portman held a handkerchief to her eyes. "Thank you," she replied.

"Mr. Davis said a beachhead on Guadalcanal is very important."

Ilona pinched her upper arm and yanked her away. "Did I ask for a newscast? I said something nice. That's all. Don't add."

Conversation was awkward and strained. Everyone sat around, trying not to smile, speak too loudly, or God forbid, laugh. Mr. Carpathy said that the war would be over in six months. His wife added that would be a good thing because then all the boys would come home. Mrs. Templeton put her fingers to her lips and nodded in the direction of Mrs. Portman, and when she could, leaned over to Mrs. Portman to whisper, "Keep a stiff upper lip." Hilary wondered if that was the same as forbearing.

They talked of the shortages, particularly of rubber, and then of zippers. Everyone hated the new plastic zippers that jammed and never worked. Mickey said that she had a friend who was a dancer and had a breakaway costume, and that she went back to snaps which were much more reliable. Mrs. Carpathy asked what a breakaway costume was, and Mr. Radner told Mickey to shut up.

"You'll get a gold star," said Freddie. "That's what they give you." Mrs. Portman grabbed him and held him, sobbing great shudders against his small body and knocking off his flight cap.

When the air raid siren warbled, everyone was startled. Some had not heard it since the first test in January, several months before. The singsong wailing was raucous and insistent, and it sounded to Hilary like the day before when Mrs. Portman got the telegram. Freddie came to stand beside his father, reaching for his hand.

"It's a practice," said Frank, after the wailing stopped, "otherwise it would have lasted longer."

"Lights out," said Mel, his Civil Defense band appearing from nowhere to cinch his arm with authority, his World War I helmet painted white and on his head. "It's a brownout and it's for real. Only the red hall lights to see where you're going. All other lights out. No cigarettes. Everyone stay inside."

He ran through the halls, knocking on doors, giving orders to the rest of the hotel. The lights went out one after another, and they sat with Mrs. Portman in the shadowed east wing of the lobby, the only light a yahrzeit candle glowing softly on a table.

"Elliott," she suddenly shouted in the semidarkness. "Elliott!" Hilary shivered. Then worse, "my baby," then "Mama," a piercing shriek. Hilary started to cry, then remembered the day she had been with Miss Wallace when she had stood there and allowed Miss Wallace to cry into her dress while she put her arm around her. That was really all there was. That was what you were supposed to do. How easy it was and how hard.

Mickey whispered to her in the semidarkness, "Hilary, come over here. Sit with me."

Glancing quickly at the silhouettes of Ilona and Frank who were occupied in conversation, Hilary wiped her eyes and went to sit beside her friend. Mickey smelled wonderful, as she always did, and she was alone. Mr. Radner, who had come only to make a minyan, had left, telling Mickey he wanted her upstairs in twenty minutes.

"You got taller, baby," she said, "you're stringing out like a bean. Sol bought me a pair of earrings. I'd show them to you, but I'm afraid they'll get lost in the dark. They're pearls. Real ones."

"They irritated some oyster."

"What are you talking about?"

"That's how pearls get made. A piece of sand gets in the shell and irritates an oyster and he covers it with some gummy stuff. I learned it in science."

"You make my pearls sound ugly. I don't want to hear all that about oysters. Anyhow, I have to have my ears pierced, because they're very valuable."

"How could you do that?" asked Hilary. "It's like getting vaccinated in the ears."

"No it's not. I have a friend who did it. They put an ice cube behind your ear lobe to deaden the pain, then they just stick it, put in the earring, you never feel it."

They were silent for a moment. Hilary decided not to add that oysters were mollusks. If Mickey was not interested in how pearls were made, she surely wouldn't care about phylum. Mickey bent closer. "I got a letter from Bill," she whispered.

Hilary knew that Bill was in primary flight school with June Bug at Ocala, a town primarily devoted to the raising of thoroughbred horses, now also a training center for the Army Air Corps. She was there the day his class slung their duffel bags over their shoulders and jumped onto the dozens of waiting trucks.

"How did you get it?"

"Winona gave it to me. I miss him so much," she said. "It's just awful."

"Are you going to marry him?"

"Not you too. I'm crazy about the guy, but I can't make plans like that. I sure do miss him though. I think about him every day, all day long."

Hilary thought about T.H. a lot too, but somehow it was different. She wondered what she had done to make him come around less often to see her. Somehow she was at fault, and she was trying to figure out why.

"He wrote me that his very first day they strapped him into a plane with an instructor, and the plane tore across the field, the wheels bouncing and banging so bad he thought they were going to smash up, when suddenly it lifted right off the ground. They're very strict. He has to keep his sneakers laced, even when he's not wearing them, and have every button buttoned in his closet, and every day after lunch he marches to his flying line and puts on his flying suit and his goggles, and his parachute and everything. Now he's learning turns, and rolls, and what to do if the plane stalls. A cannon goes off at five-thirty and rattles all the windows, and there's a neon sign that tells them what to wear every day. I wouldn't mind that myself. 'Put on a sweater Mickey, and your red sandals.'" She didn't mention Bill's questions about Mr. Radner or that he was crazy with worry that she would forget him.

"Why do boys not like you so much all of a sudden?"

"Shshsh," someone said.

"Why did you ask about boys not liking you? Is T.H. acting funny?"

"Not exactly. He just doesn't seem to like me so much anymore."

"Did you have a fight?"

"No."

"I don't know, sugar. Guys are strange, even when they're kids. Sometimes there's no figuring them."

"Why can't things stay the same?"

"I don't know about that either. I only know things heat up, or they cool down. There's no in between. I also know there's plenty of fish in the sea. That means, there's plenty of other boys."

Hilary doubted it. "What could I do? If I want to keep the one I got?"

"If you were older, I could tell you the answer to that. Right now, I don't know. Go along with what he wants. Be sweet. That always helps."

This looked like as good a time as any. "Mickey, do you like kissing?"

"Are you kidding? No, I guess you're not. Don't you?"

"Not very much."

"That's too bad. You're probably too young. Not too much longer though. I remember I liked it a lot when I was about twelve. The right boy, and you'll like it just fine."

"How do you know when you like it? What does it feel like?"

"You'll know."

"I hope I'll be able to tell."

Mickey fingered one of Hilary's braids. "Get your mother to cut these," she said. "You'd look a whole lot prettier if you fluffed out that hair around your face. It would cover your ears, you know."

Ilona who was in the opposite corner of the east wing, heard the last remark. "What's wrong with the way she looks?" she asked.

"It was just a suggestion," said Mickey.

Hilary poked her in the side and they began to giggle. Ilona came over to suggest that they both leave, adding to Hilary that she would speak to her later, and to Mickey privately that it was ridiculous for a grown woman to make a friend of a little girl.

They ran down the hallway, taking advantage of the fact that Ilona was again preoccupied with Mrs. Portman. Mickey was still giggling, when suddenly she stopped, leaned against the wall, curled her fists under her chin, and began to cry great tears, pearlescent, shimmering drops that rolled down her face.

"What's wrong?" asked Hilary. "Are you crying about Elliott? I didn't know you knew him."

"I'm crying about Bill. I may never see him again," she sobbed. "We just got to know each other. It's not fair. I just met him. And he's gone. To Ocala. It isn't like you can just get on a bus. Ocala is six hours from here. He has to wait until he gets a pass, then he has to wait until he can hitch a ride, and then, before we know it, one, two weekend passes, and he'll be shipped overseas. He likes his eggs over easy and I never got a chance to fix it for him. Oh, Lord."

Hilary, who wondered what eggs had to do with anything, made a move to touch her when almost as quickly as it started, it was over, and Mickey dried her eyes and smiled as if it had never happened, turning to Hilary and saying, "When I get my new earrings in, I'll give you the training studs. You can use them someday."

Hilary, who doubted that she would ever do anything to call attention to her ears, said, "Thanks."

Mickey kissed her on the cheek, then ran off to the elevator in her clopping wedgies, leaving Hilary in a haze of White Shoulders perfume while Freddie, who had followed them into the hallway, came out of the shadows.

"It's getting sad around here," he said.

"That's because we used to be little kids." She bent over to fix his flight cap, which hung skewed over one eye. "It has to do with growing up. Kids are happy. Grown-ups are sad. The bigger you get, the sadder you get."

"How come little babies always cry?"

"I don't know. You can't count little babies. You have to start counting when people get out of a crib to walk around by themselves."

"Are you happy?" asked Freddie.

"Not exactly."

"I don't want to grow up," he said.

"You have to," she said.

"Who says?" he asked.

"It's like dying," she replied. "You never met anybody who wants to die. Well, no one wants to grow up either."

"Lipschutz wants to die."

"Who told you that?"

"Lipschutz."

A few days after Mrs. Portman's brother Phil returned to New York, T.H. and all the kids came riding their bikes on their way to see the new prisoner-of-war camp being built in Baker's Haulover. T.H. stopped to say that since the watchtower and the electrified fence were over ten miles away, it was too far to take her on his bike, but that he would tell her all about it when he came back. He also came to bring a bagful of comics. "My mother doesn't want me to read these anymore. She wants me to concentrate on books."

"I read books," she said. "But I read comics on the weekend."

Hilary was about to ask him if he wanted to go fishing for mullet, using the little round balls of dough for bait that Marco gave her when he knocked away his kickstand, and left with the group, which was almost the same except for Liz Bonnier, still at sleepaway camp, and Jackie Snyder.

Jackie had caught polio and now lay in an iron lung in a hospital in Miami. Everyone whispered about it. It had been in the newspaper and Hilary saved the clipping. Ilona said it was probably because she ate a piece of fruit that a fly had walked on, a common cause of the dread disease. Frank said what difference did it make, the kid's life was now over. After the first time they heard that Jackie had been stricken, none of the other kids mentioned her. She was a pariah, washed out of their existence.

Hilary didn't think of her much longer after the article appeared in the newspaper either, until the next night, when she saw Winona bringing fresh linens to Mrs. Portman's room, and a small bouquet of flowers that looked suspiciously like those on the parkway.

"How come you're making up the beds again?"

"It's better to do for the living," she said, "while they're still alive. It doesn't do much good for them when they're gone. That poor woman's pillow is wringing wet from all the crying. I got a chance to do for someone I like, I do it. Same way if I got a friend who's doing poorly, I make sure to visit them. I might never get a second chance. Especially if they go to the hospital. I never knew anyone to come home from the hospital."

Hilary decided to visit Jackie. It took three buses and two lies for Hilary to visit her school friend. The first lie was to Ilona, who never would have permitted it had she known. Hilary said she was going to the library since her book was overdue, and Ilona said she would not pay her fine, that it was her responsibility. The second lie was to the lady in front of the information desk, who asked Hilary how old she was. Hilary's braids were pinned on top of her head and she said, with a bold, defiant look, fourteen, the age you were supposed to be for admittance. The woman looked doubtful, but let her in anyway.

It was the first time Hilary had ever been in a hospital. She didn't like the smell. It was pervasive and antiseptic, something like the soap Ilona used, only stronger, less forgiving. Hilary didn't look to the left or to the right. When she got off the elevator, she went to the nurses' station, a small counter behind which stood women wearing starched high white caps. One of the nurse's aides pointed her to the end of the hall.

Hilary found the ward. There was no way to miss it. It was a huge room, in which were several children and young people, most of them in iron lungs, huge metal vaults through which only their cushioned heads protruded, with an overhead mirror that allowed them to look behind them. Nothing moved, only their eyelashes and, on occasion, their mouths. At first Hilary was sorry she had come and wanted to bolt and run away. Then she noticed a peculiar sound in the room, a serpentine tocsin like someone saying shush, and then realized it was the movement of the lungs, doing something to the bodies of the people trapped inside.

Hilary started to run out. A nurse stopped her. "Are you looking for someone?" she asked.

"I came to see my friend Jackie."

The nurse turned and pointed to an iron lung. "You have a visitor, Jackie."

In the mirror, Hilary saw the face of someone who looked like Jackie, only thinner and paler. Hilary came closer. "Jackie? It's me, Hilary."

"Hello, Hilary." Jackie could speak only in rhythm with the mechanical bellows.

"How are you?" asked Hilary.

"I'm paralyzed."

Hilary looked out the window at the sidewalk three stories below, which was where she wanted to be, back at the bus stop and on her way home.

"I read that they put hot packs on you and give you braces, and pretty soon you can walk again."

"Sure."

"The kids went to see the new prisoner-of-war camp. I didn't go. I'm waiting for them to tell me about it."

"Who cares?"

"I know. That's what I said."

"That's different. You're gonna. Walk out of here."

Hilary bit her lip. She had no rejoinder for true fact. She shifted her weight to the other foot and put her hands behind her back. She didn't want to tell her to forbear. Jackie looked as though she had done a lot of forbearing. "You want me to do anything?"

"No."

"Okay. Look, maybe I ought to go now."

"Comb my hair."

"Sure." Hilary picked up the comb from Jackie's nightstand and hesitated, then bit her lip and ran the comb through the lank strands that lay spread over the towel.

"I wish. I was dead," said Jackie. Tears hung suspended in her eyes.

There was no escape. It was all around her. On the beach. In the lobby. Here with a friend from school the same age as she. Hilary was sorry she had come. She put her hands in her pockets and felt the studs. "You want earrings?" she asked.

"What for?"

"I have earrings. For pierced ears. They're training studs. I got them from a friend."

"My ears. Don't have holes."

"I could make them," said Hilary, with a double helix of the cocksure rodomontade of Frank, and the enterprise of Ilona.

Jackie's eyes shifted to the side, regarding Hilary who stood over her head with suspicion. "Really?"

Hilary crossed her fingers behind her back. "Definitely."

"When?"

"Now."

"How?"

"I don't know yet." Hilary began to rummage through the ward, improvising, the keynote to survival, surreptitiously going from one nightstand to the other, arranging flowers, seeing a pitcher of ice cubes, that much was easy, and searching for something with which to pierce Jackie's ears. Mickey said her friend did it with a needle. Something like a needle. Hilary found what she was looking for, but she could not pick it up right away, she had to hang around another iron lung for a few minutes, while its occupant's eyes followed her every movement. When none of the nurses were looking, Hilary smiled, picked up the lancet, and carried the things she needed back to the table beside Jackie's lung. The first thing she did was to hold an ice cube to Jackie's ear.

"What are you doing, dear?" asked a nurse with a cheerful voice.

"Her ears are hot," replied Hilary, smiling an adorable smile that crushed her cheeks under her eyes. The nurse walked away, toward another iron lung whose occupant wanted a sip of water from a straw.

"Tell me when your ears are numb," said Hilary.

"Now," said Jackie.

"This part is going to hurt," said Hilary.

"Show me. The earrings. First," said Jackie.

Hilary took the studs out of her pocket and held them up. "They're fourteen-karat gold."

"Do it," said Jackie.

Hilary hesitated, then made a quick thrust through the gristled lobe. She became frightened when it began to bleed copiously, but was reassured when she was able to staunch the flow with a tissue; then, pursing her lips, she thrust in the golden studs as she had seen Mickey do, and fastened their posts from behind with their nuts. They looked pretty, sparkling against the white, blood-stained toweling beneath Jackie's head.

"There," said Hilary. "What do you think?"

The entire operation had taken only fifteen minutes. Jackie smiled, a wan, fleeting smile that disappeared as if someone had brushed it off her face. "When they ask you. How many points. Don't tell them."

The overdue notice didn't spill the beans. The telephone call did. Ilona received it in the kitchen. By the looks she continually cast in the direction of Hilary and Freddie, who were having their supper sitting at the salad counter, they knew it was trouble.

At first Frank didn't notice. He was having his own problems with Margie, who was shouting, in a tear-edged voice, "I've been hustling trays a long time, Frank, and I don't need you to yell 'pick up' at me at the top of your lungs. What do you think I'm standing here for?" And Frank, hot and tired, yelled right back at her to keep her female problems out of the kitchen. Ilona squelched the whole affair by banging down the receiver.

"She's crazy," she said. "That's the only answer for it."

"What's wrong?" asked Frank.

"I'll tell you about it in the room."

"I can't leave now."

"Get Gus."

No one finished supper. Ilona swept them up like a cyclone pulling in tumbleweeds, hustling Hilary and Freddie in the middle of eating a mushroom omelet that neither one liked, and pushing them down the hall.

"She takes after your brother," said Ilona. "That much I can tell you."

"Why do you have to bring my family into it? You never met my brother."

"That's true. But you told me enough about him. Anyone who goes into bars and arm wrestles for money is crazy."

"This isn't getting us anywhere. What did she do?"

"She knows. Ask her."

They entered the room and closed the door behind them, then turned to Hilary, who sat on the bed, the prisoner at the dock. Freddie sat on the opposite bed, staring at her in wide-eyed wonder. This was going to be good.

As far as Hilary was concerned, it could have been any number of things. She ticked them off, discarding them one by one. Private Sylvan Farber, no—Mickey had all the letters. Mickey, no—

nothing with Mickey could have generated anything like this. *See you next fall* which they rigged again for Mr. Radner, no—Mr. Radner had not tripped. From Ilona's anger, it could only be one thing.

"Did you go to the hospital? To the polio ward?" asked Ilona.

"She did what?" asked Frank.

Hilary nodded.

"Oh my God," said Ilona. "When?"

"Yesterday."

Ilona felt Hilary's forehead. "She feels cool, but you can never tell. I'm going to call Dr. Hershbaum." Ilona stood, shaking her head. "And then, if it isn't enough that you endanger your own life, you stick holes in a poor sick girl's ears."

"It wasn't like that. I pierced them. For earrings."

"She's a maniac," said Ilona. "It's all this hotel living. That's what it does to children."

"Why would you do something like that?" asked Frank.

"She could only see her face. I wanted to do something nice for her face."

"It makes sense," said Frank.

"Oh, fine. Encourage her," said Ilona. "Her mother says her ears don't match. The holes are lopsided."

"Like when she cuts my hair," said Freddie.

"Keep quiet." She turned back to Hilary. "What possessed you?" Hilary could only shake her head, beginning to wonder as she had months before if there really wasn't something wrong with her, some out of control demon that had entered her brain.

"Get in the tub, miss, I want you to scrub every inch. I'll bring the soap. Use it. All over. Then you're going to gargle with salt water."

"But I don't feel sick."

Frank only stood there, looking troubled, his brows knit; then he shook his head and left.

When Hilary was in her pajamas, pink from the hot water and the scrub brush and the laundry soap with the Hebrew lettering on it that Ilona said would kill anything on contact, Freddie came to the door. He was not allowed to sleep in the same room for the next week while she was in incubation, a period determined by Ilona, and he spoke to her from the doorway.

"Did you really stick her in the ears?" he asked.

"Yes."

"Why? Because she couldn't fight you back?"

"No. She wanted me to."

"Boy." Freddie turned to someone in the corridor. "Hello, Dr. Hershbaum, it's not for me. It's my sister. She went to the polio ward."

Dr. Hershbaum came in, looking as he always did, like Adolphe Menjou, and carrying in his hand the major tool he worked with, a tongue depressor. Hilary started to gag even before he reached the bed.

Frank went back into the kitchen to secure it for the night, and to get a shot of Jack Daniel's, giving special attention to the lock on the storage room which he shook several times. "When I catch that bastard," he said, "his face is gonna be hamburger."

Marco was putting his things away, fastidious as always, hanging up his bowls and his utensils, hosing down the wooden decking.

"I'll tell you," said Frank, "there's something to be said for the single life. Not that I can ever remember being single, you understand."

"I don't know that being single is all that it's cracked up to be," said Marco. "It gets lonely."

"I could do with a little lonely. I don't know what's worse, the kids or the wife."

"You're lucky you got 'em, Frank."

"I know, it just gets to be too much sometimes."

Marco put away his mop and folded all his towels. "Hey, Frank, I'd like to talk, but I gotta run."

"Where are you going?"

"I belong to this flotilla."

"What's that?"

"The Coast Guard organized all us private boat owners. We're kind of a reserve unit. We go out at night to pick up the torpedoed sailors. They give us gas, and we're glad to do our bit."

"No kidding? That sounds pretty risky, out there with all those subs around."

"We'd pay them to do it. That's how all the guys feel."

"How come you never told me about it before?"

"We're not supposed to talk about what we see."

"You going tonight?"

Marco folded his apron and nodded his head.

"Take me?"

"I don't know, Frank. You ever been out before? It's tough at night. You really have to know your way around a boat, even a small one. The water gets pretty choppy. If you get seasick, well, to be honest, you'll be more trouble than help. Then I have to take care of you instead of doing what I'm out there for."

"I won't get sick," said Frank.

"How do you know?"

"I know. That's all. You can bet your last dollar on it."

When Frank went to talk to Ilona, she was composing a letter to her family in Denmark, addressed to the man in England, who perhaps could get it through. She told them of how worried she was for their safety, and how lonely it was, and how hard, that a husband could not help you with a child. Such things required a mother or a sister, and how wonderful it would be when they were all together, and how she was sure they would love Frank, a good, steady provider, and a kind man. She did not tell them that he was not Jewish, figuring they had reasoned that one out themselves by his name.

"I'm going for a little cruise in the bay with Marco," he said.

"At night? Are you crazy too? What for? You're going to leave me alone with the problem?"

"What problem?"

Ilona pointed to the other room with its closed door, behind which Hilary sat in purdah. "In there."

"She means Hilary," said Freddie.

"She's not a problem child," said Frank. "She just gets these ideas, that's all. The main thing is, we got to stop her from getting ideas. Otherwise, she's a good kid. Look, sweetheart, I got to get out. I'm feeling restless, nervous, you know?"

"Now I have to worry about you, too."

"I'll be careful."

"Don't do anything foolish."

He stroked her hair. "You sure are a worry wart."

Ilona listened until she could no longer hear his footsteps, then blotted the letter, folded it, and placed it in an envelope along with a snapshot of Hilary and Freddie smiling from the seawall.

13

"You two-bit tramp, what goes on when I'm gone? And you better tell me the truth."

"Nothing, Sol, honest. Let go my hair. I had it done today."

Mr. Radner pulled Mickey's face up to his. "You think I'm dumb?"

"My hair! You're hurting me."

"Answer me."

"No, Sol, I don't think you're dumb."

"Well, I think you're dumb. Very dumb." He slapped her, casually, as if he were chasing a fly. Mickey started to cry. "Don't, Sol, please don't."

"Why shouldn't I?" He slapped her again, then shoved her into the corner of the room where she stayed, curled into a little ball. The straps of her sunsuit had fallen over both her shoulders.

"I treat you right, and then I come back and find maybe you been running around behind my back with these soldiers. What's to stop you? You're free and easy with your favors, that's for sure, otherwise why did you come here with me so fast, I didn't have to twist your arm, so don't try to tell me you wouldn't think of it."

"No," she whimpered, "please, Sol. I haven't been running around on you."

He hit her again, his signet ring catching her lip and splitting it.

"I find out everything sooner or later so you might as well come clean. What's the bell captain got on you?"

"Nothing. So help me God, nothing."

"Nothing? Nothing? What kind of idiot do you take me for?" He kicked at her. Mickey pulled her face into her chest. "I hear you give him ten bucks a month, sometimes twenty. That's a lot of money."

"That's a lie. Who told you that?"

"Is it? You little bitch. You little tramp. Don't try to lie to me. You're not smart enough to get away with it."

"Who told you I gave him money?"

"Never mind. I'm just going to have to watch you better, that's all. I thought I could trust you here by yourself, but I see I can't. What else goes on when I'm gone, that's what I want to know, and why do you have to give the bell captain money? It sounds to me like he knows something. What does he have on you? It's got to be something. Ten bucks buys a lot of lipstick."

Mickey lifted her face out of the cradle of her arm, gingerly. "He sent money home for me. To my mother."

"Oh, so now you admit you gave him money. Don't try to weasel out of it. Your mother's been dead for four months."

"There was expenses. For the funeral and everything. I couldn't pay for it all at once."

"You couldn't send it home yourself? You don't know how to mail a letter?"

"He said he'd take care of it. Honest, Sol. Please believe me."

"The day I do that I sell my business and kiss my ass goodbye."

She crumpled up and cried, the pearl earrings glowing in the shadowed light of the cloudy day.

"I don't know why I put up with you. I give you a first-class place to live, spending money, I keep you happy in bed; true, I'm not here all the time, but you got it good. You got no appreciation. None at all. You're worse than a dog. A dog's got appreciation."

"I appreciate you. I do."

There was a knock at the door. "Who is it?" he asked.

"Will you be wanting towels?"

"Yeah. Just a minute." He reached over to lift Mickey's arm. "Get up."

"Don't hit me again, Sol."

"I will if you don't get up. Go sit on the bed. Move."

Mickey got up, protecting her face in the cradle of her shoulder, and sat on the bed, her head bowed, her hands in her lap, while Radner opened the door to let in Winona, who carried a sack of towels in her arms.

Winona looked directly into Mr. Radner's eyes, then glanced at Mickey, cringing on the bed.

"Well, go on, what are you standing there for? Put them in the bathroom and get out of here."

"Folks don't talk to me like that," she said. "No kind of folks."

"All right. All right. Just hurry up, will you? There's a draft coming through the door."

Winona took her time placing the towels, folding them carefully over one another, washcloths over hand towels, hand towels over bath towels. Then she came out and put a candle and a book of matches on the nightstand.

"What's that for?" asked Mr. Radner.

"I got to put these in all the rooms. In case there's a hurricane."

"It's all the way out in the ocean."

"Just the same, Mr. Davis wants everyone prepared." She looked once more at Mickey with a bland expression, then straight into Mr. Radner's eyes as if she were trying to bore holes into his skull. "They don't make these hotels like they used to," she said. "Walls so thin I could knock them in with my hand." She closed the inner louvered door behind her leaving the outer one ajar.

"You got to keep them in their place," he said, "otherwise they run all over you. I'm going to talk to Davis about that one."

Mickey resumed weeping. Her hair was now disarranged from the careful coiffure of the morning, and strands crisscrossed her face. He went over to the bed and sat beside her, smoothing his own sparse hair over his scalp to cover as much of his pate as possible. "I'm sorry baby. Look, I fly off the handle. That's my personality. You make me so mad. I mean, you got the power to aggravate me. I can't help myself. You make me lose control of myself. Let's see your face."

Mickey turned her face up carefully. Her lip had stopped bleeding, with the blood coagulated in a little jagged line. He ran his hands down the length of her body.

"Still got the best ass in town. How about a kiss for your old man? Come on, baby, show me you appreciate me."

Mickey turned her face to his slowly, carefully. He bent over to kiss her, careful of her lip, sticking his tongue into her mouth, and running it over her gums. Mickey's eyes were wide open. He forced her back on the bed and she lay there, impassive, immobile, staring at the crack in the ceiling that was running into spiderlike traceries in the plaster. He pulled off her clothes, then took off his slacks. Still wearing his sport shirt and his socks, he fell on top of her.

"You're really something, hot little number, turn me into a kid, you know that? I asked you, you know that?"

"No, Sol."

"How about a little life? You're like a dead body, come on, baby, no grudges, no grudges, sweet baby."

He groped over her body, as if he were checking a carburetor. "Are you ready?"

Mickey tried to keep from crying. She smiled. "Almost."

"Hurry up," he said, "I can't wait much longer."

The ceiling crack extended all the way to the door. Mickey kept her eyes on it, wondering if it would ever crack enough for the floor above to fall in, then cried out in pain.

"That's it, baby," he said, "that's it, express yourself. Tell me how much you want it," he whispered hoarsely.

"I want it, Sol."

Ilona had a letter from Sweden from her sister Margit. When she first saw the postmark, she was jubilant, thinking that they had reached safety, but then found it had only been posted from Sweden from someone else who had escaped from Denmark. Still, it was in her sister's hand, and that was something. The letter said that they had had to postpone their plans to flee because their mother was ill. She had some type of lung congestion that made it impossible for them to keep up with the small group with whom they were scheduled to travel the furtive itinerary that would lead them over the Kattegat, the tiny strait off the Baltic Sea, to Sweden. The letter continued with the hope that if everything went as planned, they could be smuggled soon from Denmark to Sweden, that a new way to do it was to get admitted to the hospital in Copenhagen which had just begun to cooperate with the underground in smuggling out Jewish patients, usually in the backs of hearses. They were waiting to get admitted, which would not be too difficult because of their mother's condition, and Margit would go as her nurse, which was all right, since there was always a shortage of nursing staff. She added that Ilona was not to worry about their mother's condition. With a minimum of obstacles, which one could always expect, they would be in Sweden within two months. From there, it was a matter of obtaining visas, perhaps to Cuba, which they understood was very near Miami, or to South America, or at the very least, waiting in safety until the war was over, which could not be too long now, for the Germans, it was said, were getting a trouncing from the Russians.

Margit closed by telling Ilona that she hoped when they came, they would not be too much of a burden, or cause too much distress in her household, that they could hardly wait to meet the children and Frank, who did indeed sound like a good man, and that they longed, as they knew she did, to be once more a united family.

Ilona closed the letter and put it in her purse, along with the others, brushed the tears from her eyes, then looked over the two rooms that were her home, slowly shaking her head. There was no place to put in two more women and a little child. They could put Frank, Freddie, and Dieter in one room, and the three women and Hilary in the other, but that meant that she and Frank would have to sleep apart, which was out of the question. She could not imagine not being able to snuggle up against his broad back, lying together like spoons in a drawer.

She looked out the window of the children's room. The wind had freshened and the waves rose higher and more angrily against the little beach. Huge hunks of driftwood covered the sand. A pink and gray sea butterfly and a swarm of gnats, responding to the dropping barometric pressure, flew low to the ground, as if they were reconnoitering the beach. The radio said that there was a hurricane one thousand miles away. Her mother and sister were over three thousand miles away, over the same ocean, both distances impossible and non-negotiable, making either eventuality remote.

Yet Ilona, cautiously optimistic, guardedly confident, fed on hope. One did the best one could, improvised when possible, did not whine or cry, and waited. If things were very bad, they could only get better, the converse being true as well. It was an axiom with which she governed her life.

She picked up Hilary's pajamas from the floor, hung them up, and tossed Freddie's baseball glove into the box. Then she went into her own room where she changed, taking off her work dress to put on her navy and white dotted dress with the white pumps, even a pair of hose that she had been carefully saving. She would not go like a shlepper. Then she took a new tube of lipstick, and with her pinky, carefully applied it, taking an extra bit to smooth over her cheeks.

She went into the kitchen and found Gus in his bakery, checking his yeast culture, which, because of the excessive humidity, had turned bad.

"Would you cover for me?" she asked.

"Sure."

"Just see that everything goes okay at lunch."

"I know what to do, missus. Leave everything to me."

It had rained all morning, heavy drops that dimpled the beach and washed the oleander clean. No one went out except the soldiers who marched in the street in their khaki ponchos, singing "She Wore a Yellow Ribbon" and sloshing through the water. The gutters were overflowing and the streets beginning to flood. Mickey watched through her window as the water rose almost to the sidewalk and the men splashed up to their ankles in swirling current.

She had been able to wash away the blood and cover her bruises with a little pancake makeup and sunglasses. When Mr. Radner had finished dressing, she followed him downstairs to lunch. There was only a dozen or so people scattered throughout the dining room. Lipschutz was there, pleading with Mrs. Steinfeld, leaning forward, his face set in earnest entreaty, while she dabbed at her mouth from time to time with her napkin. Since her return she had a new coiffure, her hair parted in the middle, caught with two barrettes, and fluffed out around her face.

Mr. Radner ordered what he always did, pickled herring for an appetizer, a club sandwich, hold the tomatoes, and a glass of seltzer. Mickey wasn't hungry. She sipped a Coca-Cola.

"You don't have to worry about your figure," he said. "Remember I don't like skinny women."

"I'm not worried, Sol. I'm just not hungry."

"Listen. You want to come North? How about it? Hon, just you and me. We'll go to Atlantic City for a weekend. Then you'll come back here, and I'll go back to Philadelphia."

"I don't think so, Sol."

"Why not?"

Vicky Sue brought his sandwich, which he took apart, pointing to tomato slivers. "I said no tomatoes." Vicky Sue made a face and picked up the plate, which she promptly carried away.

"I asked you why not?"

"I don't think I like the North."

"You never been there. How do you know about a place you never saw?"

"I just know. It's cold there."

"Not yet it isn't. It doesn't get cold until November. Okay, I'm not gonna beg you. Don't say I didn't ask."

After lunch, Sol went to the bookie cabana to place his bets for the day, including the World Series in which he put fifty dollars on the Cardinals over the Yankees, and to ask Mel (who said taking such a bet was like taking candy from a baby), if it was true that the Firestone estate, a few blocks away, was really a secret listening post for the Signal Corps.

Mickey went outside and stood under the awning, watching the marching soldiers slosh through the water, and wondering about Bill, if he was wet or dry, and what he was doing. Someone had written KILROY WAS HERE on the front portico of the hotel, but the rain had smeared it, and the letters ran down in long streaks. She went back inside. The man stood in the lobby, waiting.

"Maryann."

She turned around. He was soaking wet, the water dripping from his hair and running down his sunburnt face. "Is that any way to greet your man?"

"No more, you're not. You're not my husband no more. I got the paper to prove it. What do you want?"

"To talk to you, honey. Just to talk to you."

Mickey glanced around the lobby. Mr. Davis, at the front desk, was watching her over the register.

"You're not messing up my life again, Earl. You're not."

"Sweetheart, when you left, the sunshine just went out of my life. I'm no good without you. I miss you. Sonny misses you."

"How could he miss me? He doesn't even know me. He thinks your sister is his mama."

"Honey."

"Don't honey me. I don't ever want to see you again. Why can't you understand that? I told you before. Now get out of here. And don't come back. Ever."

"How can you say that to me when you know it does my heart so good just to see you? You know that. You come back, things'll be different. I can promise you that."

"Please, Earl. Go away. I don't want to come back. Ever. If you stay, you'll ruin everything for me."

"And I wouldn't treat you like that, mark you up that way, like some other fella did."

"Go away!"

Mr. Davis was out from behind his desk, gliding over the carpet as fast as a skimmer whisking over the ocean. "What's the trouble?" he asked.

"Nothing, Mr. Davis," she said.

He took her arm very gently. "May I speak with you a moment please, Miss Biscayne?" and led her into another corner. "I don't want anything like this going on in my lobby, you understand?"

"Yes," she nodded.

"Then take care of it, please. Make sure it doesn't happen again." He glided back to the desk where he continued to watch them over the top of the register.

"Earl, please," she whispered, "I don't want to come back home. Not ever. Not now, especially with my mama gone. Not later either. Forget about me. Leave me alone. Don't mess up my life. If you don't leave me alone, I'll call the police."

He laughed, a deep, throaty laugh. "Somehow, I don't think you're ready to do that little thing. That's all she wrote," he said. "I'm on my way, but when I get another load to truck in this direction, I'll be back."

He turned his collar up and left the lobby, going out into the pouring rain. Mickey turned in every direction, like a bird trapped in a house, then went to the pay phone booth, closed the glass doors behind her, and dropped in the coins.

"I'd like to speak to Second Lieutenant Wright, please."

"Is this a family emergency?" asked the voice on the other end.

"Not exactly, I'd just like to speak to him. It's real important."

"Is this his mother or his wife?"

"No, just a good friend."

"I'm sorry, miss. I can't put you through."

"But he has a phone. I know he does. All you have to do is transfer the call. Please."

"I can't put you through. He can't take outside calls unless it's a family emergency. I can give him a message though. I do that all the time."

"No, I don't think so."

She hung up the phone and sobbed. Soon the glass was fogged. When a hand rapped on the door, she waved it away.

She stayed in the phone booth for a long time. When she came out, the bell captain had just sold two free passes to the dog track and he was smiling.

"Why did you let him in?" she whispered.

"Anybody can walk in the lobby. I can't stop that. It's a free country, at least so far it is. He saw you. That's all there is to it."

"I want my money back."

He laughed. "That wasn't the deal. The deal was I wouldn't tell Radner about him, and I wouldn't tell that poor slob who followed you here that the woman in that pathetic picture he's been carrying around is you."

"You're a rotten bastard," she said.

"Careful, sweetheart. I got too much on you. You don't want to make me mad."

Damp, cooler winds and lots of rain marked the first few weeks of school. Everyone was kept indoors, but no one minded. There was a feeling when you were outdoors, even if it wasn't raining, of heaviness. It entered your body, you felt it in your head and in your blood, and it made you feel tired, as if you needed to take a nap.

Freddie was still getting used to his new fourth-grade classroom. The teacher, Mrs. Goddard, was very heavy, her legs like tree trunks, and when she walked, she swayed from side to side, her whole body rumbling and shaking, like a sand castle that was getting ready to slough.

He didn't like her very much mainly because she wouldn't permit him to wear his flight cap to school. Some of the kids were new, but most were from last year, including Rudy Steinfeld, who was back, buying more war stamps and bonds from the stamp-bond monitor on Fridays than any other kid in the class.

Most of the time Freddie explored his new classroom, or tried to. He left his seat to inspect the globe, the huge, round, shiny thing, touching it, spinning and feeling it smooth and slick beneath his hand, in some places, then rough and raised over others. He wasn't quite sure what the globe meant. Hilary had told him it was the world, but the concept was vague as yet. Understanding tantalized him, eluding his mind like someone playing hide and seek, getting ready to jump out of the closet door.

Suddenly, just as he was about to make a connection between the blue of the represented ocean and the real water he knew, which was not exactly that color but was water nonetheless, the teacher's heavy hand was on his shoulder. Then he saw her angry face, and knew that he had done wrong.

"Go back to your seat and sit down. I didn't give anyone permission to get up."

Freddie turned and shuffled back to his seat. The other kids snickered behind their hands. Rudy turned and said something about him to the little girl behind him. Mrs. Goddard, bloated and quaking, followed him to his desk.

"Where's your long-division work?" Freddie shrugged his shoulder. "You're supposed to be working on your long-division work. I'll tell you right now, you might have gotten away with this kind of thing with Miss Carmichael, but I won't stand for it. You're here on condition and you better measure up."

Freddie turned over his long-division sheets in his mind. The problems were on the papers. The other children were solving them, putting numbers under lines, making columns, putting numbers on top of the lines, but he didn't know what to do. He rolled his pencil in his hand, twirled it back and forth. Hilary had once told him that's how the Indians made fire. He wondered if he could start a fire by twirling his pencil. After a while he got tired of twirling, and chewed on the rubber nub, wondering when he would see Bill Wright again. He had seen him two weeks before and Bill said he didn't have time to take him to the movies, but when he came back he would help him with batting. Freddie didn't tell him he didn't have a bat. He didn't want to say anything that would make Bill not come back. The nub came off in his mouth and he spit it on the floor. It had begun to rain again. He smelled and felt it before he saw it, and was watching it turn the dust of the playground into puffs when his teacher was at his elbow again, yanking him off his seat, then leading him down the hall. They headed in the direction of Mr. Detwiler.

Mr. Detwiler was very sad. He listened to Mrs. Goddard explain how she had done her best, even worked extra time with him, but it was hopeless, and that it was highly unprofessional of Miss Carmichael to recommend him, even conditionally, for the fourth grade when it was clear that he was not ready. He was not up to fourth-grade work. Mr. Detwiler thanked Mrs. Goddard then led Freddie himself to Miss Carmichael. When Freddie saw Miss Carmichael and knew he would be back in third grade, he began to cry.

"Men don't cry," said Mr. Detwiler. "Dry your tears. You want Miss Carmichael to see you crying and think you're a little baby?"

Freddie kept on crying. It was too much.

He came home without Hilary, who was busy with T.H. and made out Mickey's blond head in the telephone booth in the lobby. When he rapped on the foggy glass door, she made a sign for him to go away. He went to his room, where Ilona found him much later, kicking at his box of toys, especially the tin chute, which was mangled and twisted, and which he had punted into the corner.

Ilona came to school the next day, asking Gus to cover for her again despite the protests of Vicky Sue and Margie, who said Gus ordered them around like a storm trooper. Mr. Detwiler was polite but firm, and made it clear that there was no chance for reconsideration. They had done their best. It was clear that the boy could not handle fourth-grade work. He had to be made to pay attention. It was a behavior problem. And that, he pointed out, was the responsibility of both school and parent. It was kinder, he added, to leave him back, where he had a fresh start, and a new opportunity to learn the work and to acquire better work habits.

Ilona said she was taking him home with her because there was only an hour before school was out. The way she said it made it clear that it was not negotiable. Mr. Detwiler may have been the principal with the power to move her son back and forth as he chose, but she was his mother, and if she wanted to take him home earlier, she would do it.

"I have something to show you," she said, when they came out of the third-grade bungalow, where he had left his sweater. It had stopped raining, and everything was shimmering and still very wet. By the time they cleared the schoolyard, both their shoes were soaked.

She led him six blocks away, to a little pale green house with circles cut into the stucco trim, portholes to nowhere.

"How would you like to live here?" She turned to him. "Answer me when I ask you a question. I said, how would you like to live here?"

Freddie looked at the house before him in disbelief. He had never been in a private house in his life, except once, and that was to visit his aunt in St. Augustine, which he didn't remember very well, except for lacy things on the arms of the sofas. He had seen houses on the way to school. There were pictures of them in schoolbooks, usually in a rural setting, with long white picket fences, and grazing horses, and of course, there were houses in the movies. Andy Hardy lived in one and so did Dagwood. So he knew all about houses. He had just never lived in one.

"You fooling?"

Ilona, who had found the house on a rainy afternoon with the classified section tucked into her purse to guide her, examined her soul. The question was one of basic honesty and it could be answered yes and no. If one stretched it, as one always did where hope and probability were concerned, she could answer yes.

"Do I look like I'm fooling?"

"Can we go inside?"

"I don't have the key, but we can look in the window."

They crawled through the shrubbery which snapped drops of water at them as they passed and peeked inside. The house was empty and waiting.

"Look over there," said Ilona. "Can you see down the hall?"

Freddie shaded his eyes. "Uh huh."

"That's where your room is."

"Where's Hilary's?"

"Right next to you."

"And where's Daddy's?"

"With me, close by."

They walked around to the back garden. Everything had grown higher than Freddie's head, and Ilona pulled back the branches so that he could see. A concrete statue, fallen from its pedestal, lay on its side. Ilona set it upright. Then she picked up a chip from the patio stone and put it in his hand. "This is to remind you of what is waiting here for us, and when you're feeling sad, you take this stone and you say, someday I'm going to live in a house with a beautiful backyard."

They walked back to the hotel. Freddie skipped beside Ilona, clutching the stone in his pocket. It started to drizzle again and Ilona took out a newspaper which she unfolded over their heads. "Don't tell anyone about the house," she said. "It's a secret."

"Does Daddy know?"

"Not yet."

"What about Hilary?"

"We'll tell her when we get the key."

Offshore gusts, only mildly affected by the tropical depression that hovered three hundred miles offshore, began to whip the rain about. Meandering and formless, almost stationary, the winds of the tropical depression, not yet a storm, spiraled inward.

It had an eye, a balmy center where everything was soft and gentle, but the winds in its outer circle were picking up, and transporting vast amounts of warm, moist air, redistributing it within the troposphere. It was being watched, as it had been for a week, by aircraft reconnaissance that kept it under surveillance, especially now that it was moving toward the beach where sandpipers, able to hear the infrasonic sounds of its winds over the ocean waves, flew inland.

If it wasn't enough that Mr. Radner was going to be in Miami for the next two weeks, there was a storm watch, a state of affairs in which those with radios listened for the next sporadic advisory which would tell them whether or not to stay indoors and wait for the hurricane, or whatever it was going to be, or to be merely cautious, boarding up store windows, as many people were now doing, and bringing in garbage cans which became, in a good wind, projectiles. It was not that the weather bureau was cavalier. The mystery of the storm's whereabouts was the result of the limited information that had to come from ships at sea, most of whom did not want to give away their position. Unless the storm hit the Bahamas or Cuba, they had little way of knowing exactly where it was.

Both conditions, Mr. Radner's ubiquity and the meandering storm, aggravated and complicated Bill's expected arrival for the weekend. Mickey worried about it so much that she had rearranged her hair three times that morning, finally brushing it loose, and securing it on both sides with matching barrettes. Mr. Radner had offered to take her shopping on Lincoln Road, always a flamboyant excursion in which he peeled off bills like Kleenex, and he became suspicious when she turned him down. Mickey was prepared. She drank a cup of hot coffee, took her temperature, and showed him the elevated thermometer, a trick she learned from the Pago Pago from those who wanted to get out of the late show. Since he had an aversion to illness, it was a sure way to get rid of him temporarily. He told her to take two aspirins and to sleep in the extra bed, as he didn't want to catch whatever it was she was getting. There was no need to call the hotel doctor, he added. The two aspirins would do it.

When he left, Mickey waited long enough for him to catch a bus, then took the next one herself to South Beach to the drugstore with the penny scale in front where she and Bill had spent so much time. There she waited for two hours, sitting at the counter slowly sipping an ice cream soda which she asked the counter girl to fill with extra seltzer to make it last longer. A soldier on the seat beside her offered to buy her another, but she cut him off with a disdainful flick of her lashes. When the counter girl asked her to give her seat to someone else, she slid off the stool and went to the newsstand where she flipped through the magazines, looking up from time to time to check the door.

The weather was bad, the wind picking up, the sky to the west blacked as if by shoe polish. It was not the same system as the tropical storm somewhere in the Caribbean, but part of the normal fall rain squalls spawn over the Everglades. The rain began with a spatter on the sidewalk, then came smashing in oblique and angry slashes against the plate-glass window which the store owner was trying to batten down with boards.

Mickey began to be afraid that he wasn't coming, especially after she passed the second hour. Maybe the rain made it hard to get a ride. Maybe the tropical storm had turned into a hurricane and was finally coming to Florida and everyone on the post had to stay put. She couldn't stand it if she wasn't going to see him. She missed him so much, it was as if part of herself were gone along with him, especially the part that helps you get up and get going. She began to thumb through a *Saturday Evening Post* with a Norman Rockwell picture on the cover of a sailor writing to his mother.

"You can buy it for a nickel," said the man behind the counter.

"I don't want it," said Mickey.

"Then put it back."

A hand was on her shoulder. "Mickey."

She turned and there he was, water dripping from his chin, his visor, his raincoat, trickling down his shoes to puddle on the floor.

She embraced him with a little cry, soaking her dress all the way through her slip beneath it.

"Hey," he held her off. "I'm sorry, baby, I got you all wet."

"I don't care."

"Well, I do. I don't want you to catch cold on my account, not when I haven't seen you in three weeks. Did you miss me, sweetheart?"

"It was awful."

"Me too. I can't get you out of my mind. Sometimes my instructor's voice gets mixed up with yours, then I have to shake you out of my head and ask stupid questions to catch up. I live to see you, Mickey. The rest of the time, I'm just putting in hours. God, you look great. What happened to your lip?"

"I fell."

"How? On what?"

"The hall was dark. Because of the brownout. I didn't see the hole in the carpet. I tripped."

His face darkened. "Is he here? In Miami?"

"Yes."

"Damn." He turned away, took off his cap and shook it away from him.

"We said we wouldn't talk about him," she said. "We said we would only talk about us."

"We can't talk about us unless we discuss him. He's there. Between us. Like a wart with a hair in it. It's hard to ignore. I can't pretend he doesn't exist."

"I can."

They moved to the counter.

"What'll you have?" asked the waitress behind it.

"I don't want anything," said Mickey. "I already had a soda."

"Then you'll have to give your seat to someone else."

"No she doesn't," said Bill.

Mickey convinced him not to make a fuss. They gave up their seats to two soldiers, and stood near the entrance, while the drugstore grew darker.

"I think I got a room," he whispered. "For the weekend."

"I won't be able to spend much time with you," she said.

He pulled her close. "Don't tell me that. Don't tell me that after I waited for three weeks and nearly lost my mind thinking about you and him, and after I busted my ass to get a pass for the weekend. Mickey, it's almost impossible to get away during this part of training, I'm on rocky ground as it is. I had to pull a few strings, and step on a few toes, not that I wouldn't do it again, but don't tell me you can't see me. Tell him you have to go home for the weekend. To Georgia."

"He wouldn't believe that. He'd know it wasn't true."

"Think about what to tell him after we get there. The room will have a phone. You can call him. I'll help you think something up. I've been good at that lately. Did you know you're my kid sister who got stuck in Miami and who I had to come down and help get back home?"

The room was in a small hotel off Collins Avenue called the Palms, an art deco building from the twenties, with rounded corners, a thin blue stripe on the cream facade, and glass bricks. It stood between similarly designed hotels now occupied by the military.

First pushing through a press of milling soldiers who all saluted at Bill's approach, they entered the mirrored lobby where Bill signed the register as Mr. and Mrs. Wright, explaining that their luggage was coming in a taxi. The desk clerk didn't need the fiction. The girl wore no wedding band, but more important, she didn't have the cheerful forced expression of visiting wives who were grimly determined to show their men a worry-free and pleasant time.

The room was stuffy and damp, the window shut because of the rain, the carpet faintly moist from the humidity. Mickey checked the bathroom for hot running water. When she was assured of its continuous flow, she fell on the bed beside him.

"I like to take a bath afterward," she added.

"I didn't know that," he said.

"You could have figured it out." She began to unbutton his shirt. "I like your chest," she said. "It's so smooth."

"I'm not good in bathtubs. I don't know what to do with my legs and my knees get cold." He began to kiss her shoulders, especially the base of her neck and the hollow of her throat. "Besides, how do you expect me to know that? We've never been in a real room before. You could just as easily been a shower girl."

"Never. A shower is over too fast," she murmured. "I like to fill the tub as high as it can go, keep the water running, throw in perfume, get it smelling sweet and steamy, and then just lay there and soak as long as I want."

He kissed her eyelids and licked her lashes.

"Hurry," she said.

They made love all afternoon. When the early evening cast the sky with silver, the rain stopped. Mickey got up to open the window. Soldiers could be heard marching in the street below and singing about spurs that jingle jangle jingled.

"They sing the same songs you did," she said.

Bill lay back, staring at the ceiling. "I don't believe your story about the way you hurt your lip. You know I can't believe your story. It's too much to ask that I do."

"You said you wouldn't bring it up."

"Mickey, I want to kill him. Do you understand that? I want to kill the guy. So don't ask me to go along and pretend that he's not taking shots at you like a punching bag. Why are you staying with that bastard? I'll pay your hotel bill if that's what you want. Just say the word. I'll take care of all your expenses."

"With what? You gonna sell off some hogs? Look, I don't want to go into this again. You promised you wouldn't bring it up. The only people I see in this room are you and me. I don't see anyone else. Why can't we keep it that way? Please, Bill, I waited for weeks to see you. Now you're spoiling it. All we've done since you came is fight."

"That's not exactly true." He reached for her, but she pulled away, wrapped herself in the sheet, and walked back to the window.

"That settles it," he said. "I didn't want to do this, but I think it's the only way. You got to make a choice. I can't take this."

She turned to face him, her jaw jutting forward, but her lower lip pendant and trembling.

"I mean it. I can't go back to knowing you're with him. No man would put up with that. I know you love me, and you know I'll do everything to make you happy . . . I'll move to Miami after the war, as soon as I finish at the university, if that's what you want."

"That's the stupidest thing I ever heard of. Who needs an agricultural engineer in Miami?"

"That's beside the point. I could always find something. Look, I got a job to do now. They're going to send me someplace, against the Japs, against the Germans, where I don't know, but I do know this, when I come back, I want to think I'm coming back to you. I want us to have a little house with a yard, and a couple of kids that look like you, and you waiting for me at the end of the day, and me, walking in with my hands in my pockets. The last is very important because it means I'm a civilian. The Army won't let you put your hands in your pockets. And I could make you happy, Mickey. I would spend my life making you happy."

"I'll think about it."

"That's not good enough. I want you to make a decision. Now. Today."

"I can't." She put down the sheet and began to dress, pulling on her slip first, then searching on her knees for her panties which had somehow gotten lost among the bedclothes.

"Why can't you?"

"I want to be somebody."

"But you would be somebody. You would be my wife. And I don't see living with him making you somebody."

She buckled her shoes and pulled her dress over her head. "Why did you have to spoil it?" When she picked up her purse and went for the door, he leaped out of bed.

"Come back," he said. "Come back. We'll work it out. I'm sorry I pressed you. It's just driving me crazy. You're driving me crazy." He hugged her, lifting her onto her toes as he did the first time they kissed.

"I love you so," she said. "I never loved anyone before you."

"I can't breathe without you," he said, then began to take off her clothes again.

"I got to go. He'll be waiting and wondering where I am."

"Tell him anything, call him if you like, only stay. Stay."

Mickey reached for the phone and called Mr. Radner, telling him, while squeezing her nostrils shut, that she was at the doctor's office waiting to be seen. She also told him not to wait for dinner and to have it without her.

The major thing that kept Sol Radner mollified when she returned was the menthol smell of Smith Brothers cough drops on her breath, and the sight of a bottle of Listerine, props which corroborated the illusion of illness. Even her face, reddened from Bill's beard, contributed to the deception.

"I don't know why you had to go to a clinic. I told you to take two aspirins and stay in bed. I bet that's what the doc told you."

Mickey was so confident in the dissemblance that she became emboldened. "You want a little action?" she asked.

"Stay away. We got time when you feel better."

The next day was windy and wet. Mickey and Bill only had an hour together. Whether she brought it on herself by her outrageous lie to Sol, or whether it was because she got soaked to the skin three days in a row, Mickey caught a cold, one of those awful stuffy things that made her feel cranky and miserable, and certainly not like making love. It was okay with Bill, who was content to hold her in his arms, give her his handkerchief to blow with, and assure her that she wasn't ugly just because her nose was red. When she had to leave, he held her close at the door, not wanting to let her go.

"Mickey, they're teaching me to throttle by sound, fly by the horizon, in case I'm up there at twenty thousand feet and my instrument panel is shot away. I can still fly the plane. I'm telling you this because I think it has something to do with getting married. You don't need all the fancy extras you think you have to have. We may not have as much money at first, or ever, but we can still fly the plane. You understand? We'll be okay."

When they left the hotel room, the rain had stopped. Neither spoke, they just held hands tightly, walking side by side, leaning against each other in the windy, humid afternoon. The sewer was jammed with debris and water swirled to the curbs. A jeep splashed by, the new half-track military vehicle, neither car nor truck, which they turned to watch along with everyone else on the sidewalk, as it sloshed its way up the street.

One of the hotels they passed was a recuperation station, a place for wounded and convalescing servicemen in pajamas and robes, some of whom were in wheelchairs on the sidewalk. Many of them were bandaged, some were missing arms and legs. Mickey turned her face away.

"I can't look," she said. "Why do they have them on the sidewalk in plain sight?"

"What if one of them was me?" he asked.

The thought had never occurred to her, or if it had, she pushed it down into her subconscious as she shoved and stored all the other unpleasant things of her life, like her mother's death, or the men who had disappointed her. "It couldn't be you. You wouldn't let it happen."

That night Mr. Radner went to the movies to see Brian Donlevy in *Wake Island*, and Mickey lay in bed alone. Her cold had gotten worse and nothing helped. If she had had a teakettle she would have put her head over the steam as she had seen her mother do, but hot plates were not allowed in the rooms. The only thing to do was read the paper, something she seldom did. She scanned the headlines which told of the Nazis tightening their grip on Denmark, Himmler's announcement that there would be no Jews in Germany by the end of the year, and a major general's warning that defense preparations be urged for New England, where the Nazis would most likely strike first. The editorial page was no better. One columnist called for an American air assault on Germany, the other asking what the United States was waiting for. She also came across an article in the women's section, a plea for volunteer nurse's aides who would be trained in an 80-hour course at a number of convenient places, including two on Miami Beach. All that was needed from a candidate was a high school education, good physical condition, and a pledge to serve for 150 hours following training. At first Mickey was uninterested and turned the page in order to get to the comics. Then she turned back: 80 hours plus 150 made 230, laid end to end, almost ten days, if you wanted to look at it that way. If she volunteered and had something to show for it, like a pin or a hat, she had just bought ten days of alibi.

The storm hit the eastern tip of the Bahamas, and was now spinning itself north in the vicinity of the Carolinas. No one talked about it. As a subject, it was as obsolete as Hilary and T.H. Once safe within the ring of those who belonged, Hilary now sat in the cafeteria between Sorrell Myers and Jack Suga, expatriated to the bad end of the long table. All the good kids, the ones who counted, were at the other end, T.H. next to Shirley Leone who continued to twinkle like a sequin, Frances Simmons, who it was rumored had begun to wear Tangee Natural, Billy Connaught, Paul, and some new kids who knew enough to wear their saddle shoes dirty. They were laughing and having fun, and everyone else strained toward them like leaves toward the sun. It was worse for Hilary. She had been there and she knew how good it was. The other outcasts just guessed. Some of the girls were wearing their cardigan sweaters backward, like the kids in junior high, and all the girls at the good end were wearing saddle shoes, or, newer still, loafers with pennies in them. Hilary was one of the few still in perforated sandals, Buster Brown terribles through which her toes were beginning to protrude. Even the teacher, Miss Daly, directed her comments to the kids on the good end, and when the other kids spoke, she never looked in their direction. It was as if they were invisible. The only time she turned was when little Pinky Weiselmann, coming down with the flu, threw up.

Hilary couldn't eat. Besides the fact that she had lost her appetite, her hand was cramped from penmanship, the only subject in which she did not shine, where she spent an hour trying to make perfect ovals, whole lines of overlapping rolling curves that looked like unwinding barbed wire.

Everyone had heard how Hilary had visited Jackie Snyder and stuck her in the ears. The story was whispered about, even printed in detail in a slam book, a covert dog-eared volume passed from hand to hand in which kids could anonymously slander one another in any way they chose. It was Hilary's second mention in the slam book. Her first was under the heading, Girls Who Wear Sweaters Just to Keep Themselves Warm, which dubious honor she shared with a new girl, Tracey Hollister, the tallest girl in the sixth grade by a head.

Hilary could not finish her ten-cent lunch, and pushed the picked-over tray aside to wait for the teacher to announce that it was time to return to their room. Sorrell, who had finished his twenty-cent lunch in thirty seconds flat, including slugging down two cartons of milk, leaned over to ask in a whisper if he could finish hers, which was fine with Hilary, because Miss Daly was sure to say something about wasting food in wartime and Hilary did not want to be an object lesson. They quickly switched trays, since it was forbidden, for sanitary reasons, to eat from someone else's plate.

The unprecedented wave of juvenile delinquency sweeping the nation, with boys openly smoking cigarettes and thirteen-year-old V-girls offering themselves to servicemen as going-away presents, resulted in frantic Miami's thinning out the bushes in Bayfront Park, and new school controls which regulated behavior everywhere, even extending to the books in the library.

Huckleberry Finn was off the list. It had appeared one day and was now mysteriously struck, a big line crossed through it, on the list of free reading which included *Alice in Wonderland* and *Treasure Island*. Hilary, who had liked *Tom Sawyer*, and wanted to read another book by Mark Twain, asked Miss Daly why *Huckleberry Finn* was off the list and was told that it was no longer suitable. Then Miss Daly sealed off all discussion by clamping her lips shut. There was only one thing to do. Hilary went to the public library on Twenty-first Street and took it out.

It turned out to be an exciting, colorful story of Huck Finn running from his drunken father, and the Negro Jim escaping from slavery in Missouri, riding together on a raft down the Mississippi. More important than the unfolding story, Hilary understood Huck. He came alive for her. She liked him even better than she did in *Tom Sawyer*, or even Tom Sawyer. He was just like her, somehow apart from everyone else, like when Gus separated egg yolks from their whites and put each in a separate bowl. This was how she too felt, isolated and separate.

When it came time to write the report, Hilary didn't have time to read a book on the approved list. She wrote the report anyway, hoping the teacher would forget that *Huckleberry Finn* was off the list. No such luck. Miss Daly called her to her desk.

"What is this?" she asked.

"My report."

"This book is not on the list. I told you that before. Still, you went ahead and did it anyway."

Hilary plunged. "I thought free reading meant we could read anything we liked."

"Don't get smart with me," said Miss Daly. "I remember when last year you tried to make me think that Rudy Steinfeld had thrown rocks at you. I'm on to you, Hilary. You're not going to get away with that kind of nonsense in my classroom. Now, I want you to write, 'I will read only what is on the list' five hundred times, in good penmanship."

Hilary sat down and began to write. She was already beginning to get a nub on her middle finger, the part against which the pencil pressed. She wondered what it would look like by the time she finished junior high.

Ideas were getting her into trouble again. Ilona, who was still closely watching her after the episode with Jackie Snyder, said she was crazy, like her father's brother. Maybe it was so. Why had she read the book after the teacher told her not to, and what were you supposed to do with ideas that seemed good at the time? How did you know when they were going to turn out bad, and what did you do with them after you got them? It was like sitting in shul with Ilona, trying to keep her arms and legs still. How do you keep your mind still? How do you get it to sit quietly? Liz Bonnier and Billy Connaught didn't seem to have that problem. What was wrong with her?

Hilary wrote during recess, which was okay, since no one would play with her anyway. It solved the problem of what to do. Jack Suga came back into the room just as Hilary was on line number 378.

"Hey," she called, "you want to come to the hotel after school? Me and Freddie are playing paratrooper."

"I don't think so," he said, sliding into his seat.

"We got an old umbrella that we fixed up with a shower curtain, and a ladder. It works real good, except you have to jump over the sand."

"I have to help my father," he said.

Sorrell Myers turned to her with a big, friendly smile on his face, waiting, expectant. Hilary could not ask him. He would surely break either the parachute or the ladder. Out of kindness she did not tell him this. At that moment it was announced on the P.A. that Rudy Steinfeld from Miss Goddard's fourth grade won the war-bond contest, having purchased the equivalent of

$250.00 worth of bonds and stamps. Mr. Detwiler was going to give him a special certificate, and they were all told to watch for the story in the Miami *Herald*.

When Hilary came home from school, Mr. Lonzo's light blue Cadillac was parked on the side street, a prominent X sticker—intended for telephone linemen and doctors to guarantee all the gas they needed—on its windshield. A driver sat behind the wheel. Hilary smiled at him, but his eye was on the rearview mirror.

Mr. Lonzo, with another one of his men at his side, was in the rear of the receiving dock, standing and talking to Frank. "I don't know," he said, "why we don't go in and bomb the hell out of them now that we got the stuff to do it. I don't know what we're waiting for. The P-47 Thunderbolt is as heavily gunned as any fighter in the world, the Mustang is faster than any fighter in the air, and the Flying Fortress has a thirty-five thousand-foot ceiling. The krauts with their Heinkel can't approach it."

"Beats me," said Frank. "It seems like the faster we go in, the faster we clean up. The longer we wait, the worse things seem to get."

"On the other matter, I'm glad you called me, Frank. You did good to call me. We'll see what we can find out. I'll put my boys on it. Look who's here. The typewriter still work, sweetheart?"

Hilary didn't tell him that the dial typewriter he had given her for Christmas had been broken the day Freddie kicked the box into the corner. "Uh huh," she lied.

"That's fine. A nice kid you got here, Frank. A little sweetheart. She's going to make someone a fine secretary some day, learning to type and all."

Hilary did not want to be a secretary. The only secretaries she knew, one in the school office, the other behind the front desk of the hotel, both wore glasses and had furrows between their eyes, but she didn't mention that either. It was part of her new policy of keeping her mouth shut and her mind still.

Mr. Davis came into the receiving dock. He shook hands with Mr. Lonzo.

"Gotta move," said Mr. Lonzo.

"I had no idea you were here," said Mr. Davis. "Can't I interest you in a drink before you go?"

"I can't touch the stuff," said Mr. Lonzo. "Doctor's orders."

Mr. Lonzo's bodyguard helped him down the steep cement

steps of the receiving dock and opened the door of his car for him. When the car pulled away Mr. Davis turned to Frank.

"What was that all about?"

"He came about the heists. You know, in the storage locker."

"Why must he be involved?"

"I didn't want to bother you again," said Frank. "And he told me that if I ever needed help to call him."

"Don't take it on yourself again to go over my head, Frank, because that's what you just did. I don't like it."

"Sorry," said Frank. "I didn't mean it that way." Hilary waited for Frank to say something else but he didn't.

"Don't do it again," said Mr. Davis.

Hilary put on her bathing suit and went down to the beach, yanking up her top even though she had tied it so tight it felt like a chest cold. The sand was wet through, damp from days of rain with no time to dry out. Next door, a different group of soldiers was drilling behind their hotel, and farther down the beach she could see a coastguardsman on horseback.

A cloud of sandhoppers fed on a clump of seaweed, broad flat ribbons of turtle grass that waved with each swell of the ocean, tangled in a morass at the water's edge. Hilary pushed her way through the oil and driftwood. Some of the seaweed clung, and once she scraped her foot on something sharp, but finally she got beyond it and stood in pale green water.

Although it was only October, the water was cold in spots and warm in others. There was no one else in the surf. She sought the warmth and stood motionless up to her waist, shivering each time the waves splashed against her chest, then braced herself, taking each one as it came, sometimes diving beneath the crest. Gray and white plovers, newly arrived from Maine, flew overhead, checking out the temporary feeding ground that would support them until they would once more take to the sky and head south.

Hilary did not want to be a secretary. She did not know what she wanted to be, only what she did not want. She no longer wanted to be a test pilot, after Bill told her something of what was involved in learning how to fly, nor did she want to be a nurse, unless she could be Sister Kenny, and there was already a Sister Kenny. She did not want to be a teacher, which was Shirley Leone's dearest dream. The future yawned wide and uncertain.

The waves came in stronger, enveloping her, sustaining her,

bringing in sea beans from the Caribbean, jellyfish, and a violet snail riding on a bubble float. She tried to catch the snail, but it zipped by leaving her with a handful of sea beans. A plank came flashing by and lightly grazed her side, tagged the shoreline like a running back making a touchdown, then was sucked back quickly to bob in the swell. The water glistened with paillettes of sunlight, while currents at her feet brushed her legs with sand. The sun was in the water. The sand was in the water. On the beach, the water was in the sand. She no longer felt chilled, and it was hard to know where her skin ended and the water began. It was as if somehow she was the same as the water, the violet snail, the sand, and the distant aloof white sun above.

When she came out, she was chilled, and dried herself quickly, then wrapped herself in the beach towel. Freddie was standing on the seawall, opening the folds of the shower curtain that was attached to the old umbrella.

"How come you were swimming?" he asked. "I been waiting for you." Then he stood on the seawall, pulled the ladder up, opened it, climbed to the top, held the umbrella over his head, and jumped, yelling, "Geronimo!

"Now you try it," he said, brushing off sand from his face and hair.

Hilary tried it. She climbed the ladder. It seemed unsteady. She jumped, holding the umbrella over her head and yelling Geronimo as he had. It was fun two weeks ago. What had happened to make her see it as a silly broken umbrella and a mildewed shower curtain?

14

As soon as Mickey's cold was better, at least enough for her to breathe through her nose, she went to the address listed in the newspaper. It was a private women's club on Collins Avenue, north of the hotel, with potted palms and old group photographs on the walls, and ladies sitting in the upholstered wicker furniture smiling and chatting with one another. They looked up when Mickey walked in, all registering the same wary recognition of a stranger.

"I'd like to sign up for the nurse's aide course," she said.

One of the ladies, a short, plump woman, got up to take her place behind the desk. She wore a strand of pearls around her chubby neck, some of the pearls sunken into the creases and folds of her flesh. "Well, aren't you darling," she said. "Are you a high school graduate?"

Mickey nodded her head. Nobody had to know that she dropped out at fifteen. "Yes, ma'am," she replied.

"That's fine, dear. We will have to see the transcript, of course, but we can get that later. You have to be in good physical condition to become a nurse's aide."

"I'm real healthy," said Mickey.

"We take your word for it, naturally, but we need a doctor's signature. On this form." She handed Mickey a piece of paper. "You might tell your friends and your mother too, dear. We can use all the help we can get."

"My mother died," said Mickey.

The woman lifted her pearls out of a crease, and resettled them on her neck. "Now that's too bad. Well," she smiled brightly, "as soon as you come back, we'll find a place for you in one of our courses. Oh my, you give your address as the Flamingo Arms. Will you be in Miami long enough to finish the course? We don't like to start people who drop out to go back North, you understand how that is."

"I live there," said Mickey.

"Lucky you." She turned to one of the ladies seated on the wicker sofa. "Isn't that where Mattie works? I had heard that she had some position there."

"I don't know," said the woman on the sofa. "I haven't seen Mattie Templeton in years, especially after she dropped her membership in the Surf Club. Poor thing. I did hear she lived in some rented apartment, or hotel room. When I think of all the money her daddy made and the way that family used to live. They owned almost all of Fort Dallas Park, you know. Choice land. Right at the mouth of the Miami River."

"That's why it's important," said another, "to know all about the person your children intend to marry. You can't know enough about a person. Never."

Mickey's entrance into the hotel was heralded by wolf whistles and catcalls from the soldiers at the Lord Feldman next door. She stepped inside, took off her sunglasses, and shook her hair back from her face, then handed a bill to the bell captain. It was only when she got close did she notice Hilary reading a book on the damask sofa, the stuffing of which had now been pulled out like an intestine.

"Why aren't you outside playing with T.H.?" she asked.

Hilary put the book on her knee. The title was *For Whom the Bell Tolls* and it had been left by a guest. "He dumped me. For Shirley Leone."

"That rat. That's too bad." Mickey sat beside her. "To tell you the truth, he didn't sound like much to me anyhow. You're better off without him."

That was as difficult for Hilary to believe as that the character

Maria wanted her hair to grow. Hair as short as a beaver pelt sounded good to her, certainly the wearer suffered none of the yanking, pulling, combing, and sitting still required in the daily maintenance of braids.

"Shirley's cute. I'm not. I trip all over myself. A girlfriend is supposed to walk straight."

Mickey flashed a smile that showed the tiny space between her front teeth. "Shirley Leone is going to grow up to be fat."

"How do you know?"

"I saw her. That type is cute until about eighteen. Then they get pudgy fast."

"I wish she'd hurry up and get pudgy. I wish I was going to be fat. Then I'd be cute now. Instead of all skinny and knobby. I'd give anything to be cute."

"It's easy to be cute," said Mickey. "It's called winning ways. Let's see if I can give you a few winning ways. Can you cock your head over like this?"

Hilary dropped her head to the side.

"Not like that, honey. You look like something is wrong with you. Cocked, not hanging, sort of like a little bird. Say a boy says, 'What's the homework assignment?' You cock your head and smile and say, 'Would you like for me to write it down for you?' "

"Then I have to write it down for him."

"Well, sure you do. If you say you're going to do it, then you have to do it. Let's see if I can think of any other one. Drinking an ice cream soda is a possibility. Go in the dining room and get a glass of water and a straw."

Hilary did as she was told and returned with both items.

"Now put your head down," said Mickey, "and sip, but lift your eyes up. Look up through your lashes. Up. Up. Keep sipping. That's it. Don't suck air, Hilary. It's not a winning way."

"It feels dumb," said Hilary.

"I can't help you," said Mickey, "if you're not going to co-operate."

Hilary tried it again.

"Now flutter them. Like a butterfly."

Hilary fluttered her lashes. "I feel nervous when I do that. It's like blinking too much."

Mickey sighed. "Okay. Let's see if we can do something else." She drummed her red, white, and blue enameled fingernails over her lips, a winning way for sure. "Can you stand with your toes in, the idea is to be a little pigeon-toed, not a lot. It makes men think you're delicate and helpless. They like that."

Hilary stood and turned her toes in, then stumbled, and tried it again.

"Not so far in," said Mickey. "Just a little. And bend your knee. Not both knees. One."

Finally after about fifteen minutes of instructions Mickey conceded defeat. "I don't know, sugar," she said. "Maybe it's something that you're born with. I wouldn't worry about it, though. There are other qualities about you that some boy will like someday."

"Such as?"

"Such as, we'll have to wait and watch you grow up. They're sure to be there. We just have to be patient."

"But they're not there now," said Hilary.

"No," said Mickey, as softly and as gently as she could. She left to go upstairs and announce to Mr. Radner that she had signed up for a nurse's aide course, that it would take hundreds of hours for which she had already committed her signature, and that they were very happy to have her because of the terrible shortage of nurses.

That afternoon, Hilary and Freddie went to a Three Stooges movie to see Larry, Moe, and Curly jab two fingers at each others' eyes and bang each other on the head with their fists. Mickey, who wouldn't have gone anyway because it was only shown at two o'clock, the noisiest, rowdiest show of the day, was busy helping Mr. Radner pack. When she returned to their room, he announced that he was on his way to Washington to get a contract from the government. All he had to do was demonstrate his factory's capability to change production from mechanical pencils to bomb parts. After a year of continuous problems obtaining parts and labor who kept leaving him for better-paying jobs in defense work, despite a scheme to import cheap unskilled colored help from Alabama on the Greyhound bus, a plan worked out on a per person basis with an alderman and a dispatcher from Selma, he decided that the only answer was to switch to defense work. The government agreed. He could not believe his good fortune. Mickey could not believe hers.

The next day, after waiting an interminable hour following Mr.

Radner's departure in which she skinned back all her cuticles, Mickey ran to the telephone booth in the lobby and called Bill at the air base, telling the soldier who answered that she was Bill's mother.

"Forgive me for having to say this, ma'am," said the soldier, "but you don't sound like his mother."

"I can't help how I sound," she replied, "and you'd better hurry up, this is a family emergency."

Bill was breathless when he got to the phone.

"Mom?" he gasped.

"It's me," said Mickey, "and don't give me away, or else he won't let us talk."

Bill recovered quickly. "Mom, how the hell are you? Is everything okay? How's Dad?"

"Dad is going away for three weeks, maybe a month. First to Washington, and then back to Philadelphia. Can you believe it? It's too good to be true. Come down next weekend. You can stay in my room."

"How can I do that, Mom? I don't know if I can get a pass. Anyhow, I don't think it would work out."

"I don't care. I want you with me. We can sneak you in and out the side door. I want to spend the whole night with you on a mattress with sheets, and not have to get up and get dressed till morning, or noon if I feel like it." She dropped her voice to a whisper. "I want to curl up against you and feel safe in your arms. I want to wake up and see your ugly beard."

"I'll have to think about that, Mom. It doesn't sound like a good idea to me. The dinner sounds great. It's just that I don't like where you're planning to serve it." There came a muffled voice, then Bill's. "This is an emergency, sir. My mother is a very nervous woman."

"I love you," she said. "I love you to so many pieces I could feed you to the sharks."

"Don't do that, Mom."

Hilary spent the next Saturday afternoon on the beach, watching the waves roll in like steps. The school week had been like all the others, except for the Thanksgiving pageant, which they rehearsed three times, and in which she, even though she had real braids, had been given the part of a pilgrim, while Shirley Leone took the prize part of Pocahontas. It was a serious blow since she read better than Shirley and was even able to say with great emotion, "Wait! Don't kill the man I love!" while Shirley kept misreading, "Wait. Don. Kill the man I love." It helped to lose herself in her reading, and she was finishing *For Whom the Bell Tolls,* her first grown-up novel not set in the nineteenth century.

Mrs. Templeton was also on the beach, fully dressed, a big floppy straw hat tied under her chin. She was gathering seashells which she tossed into a net bag. Mrs. Templeton seemed to have difficulty bending over. Hilary could see that she was tightly corseted beneath her dress. Ilona, whose body was lithe and trim, didn't wear corsets, but Hilary had seen enough pictures of girdle stays in advertisements to know that they were responsible for the extra ribs showing beneath the dampened sharkskin dress.

"Is your name Mattie?" asked Hilary.

"My first name is Madelaine," said Mrs. Templeton. "Why do you ask?"

"Mickey told me."

Mrs. Templeton wrinkled her nose as if she were closing down a valve. "What else did she tell you?"

"That you probably used to be very rich. Is that true?"

Mrs. Templeton picked up a striped turkey-wing seashell which she tucked into her purse. "We were fortunate," she said.

"Did you used to live around here?"

"We lived over in Miami, very close to the Miami River. When I was your age, ladies used to carry parasols, even in January, and the Seminoles would come from the Big Cypress, poling in their dugouts to trade their otter skins and their egret plumes. They were very polite. The men would always ask permission to tie up to our seawall. They had no other way to get there, you see. All the land to the west was very dense hammock in those days, even the land next to our property was filled with beautiful hardwood trees, great oaks draped with air plants."

"How come you don't still live there?"

"How come is ungrammatical, Hilary. One asks, why, or how is it that such and such a thing has come to be." Mrs. Templeton turned and left the beach, holding up her skirts as she climbed the coral rock steps, although they were not long enough to touch anything, not even the sand. It was hard to imagine her as a young girl. She had already crossed the patio before Hilary realized that she never answered her question.

Hilary was so arrested by the departing corseted figure and the net bag dangling from an outstretched hand, she didn't notice Freddie, who came tearing over the seawall, until he grabbed her hand and began to yank her away. "Come on," he shouted. "He's here!"

Mickey's attempt to keep Bill's arrival secret was doomed at the start by the very same network that spread any information, including impending storms and who won the Preakness, through all the ductwork and wiring of the hotel. The only reason Mr. Davis did not find out was that he was away when Bill came in through the receiving dock carrying a coconut carved into an ugly mask, a shaving kit, and a small package with a bow on it. It was a point of entry which immediately got Frank's attention since Frank had posted as a lookout a busboy who dropped trays, his job to report who was carrying what either in or out. Then Bill took a wrong turn which brought him to the attention of Mrs. Steinfeld who kindled at the sight of the handsome young man in uniform trying to find his way. When he gave her a decoy room number, hoping it would take her and her arching breasts out of his path, she replied sympathetically, "We don't have a fourth floor. You probably have the wrong hotel. Are you new in town?" and he replied, "No ma'am. I spent a few months here in OCS."

Ordinarily she would have countered that that made him practically a native, but the ma'am clamped shut her lips and creased her nasolabial folds into runways. Couldn't he see that she was still young and attractive, a woman who definitely was not ready to be called *ma'am?*

By the time he reached the third floor, he had passed Mel, who was filling boxes with sand and pails with water, standard air-raid equipment for hotel corridors, all Mel said was, "Keep 'em flying, kid," and Winona, who smiled at him through an open hotel room in which she was stripping the beds.

He was partially down the hall when she called from the doorway, "I have a boy in the service."

"In what branch?"

"He's in the Army. Stationed at Gulfport, Mississippi. I expect him home for Thanksgiving. He's not sure he can come, but he's gonna try."

"That's great," he said. "Give him lots of turkey. I dream of all that turkey and stuffing, and I know he's doing the same thing."

By the time he reached 311, Hilary and Freddie were running up the steps, always faster transit than the fickle elevator, to greet him. Freddie, wearing his flight cap, reached him first.

"Bill!" he shouted.

"Hi there, Fred." He picked him up in the air and spun him around. Hilary stood behind her whirling brother, flipping her braids over her shoulder. Bill could not do the same to her, nor could he kiss her. She was getting too big for a swing, and yet was not big enough for the sisterly embrace he might have given to another girl closer in age to Mickey. Instead, he put his hands on his hips. "Hilary, I'm sure glad to see you."

Without thinking, Hilary put out her hand as she had seen Mrs. Templeton do many times. "Hi," she said. It seemed to help. He took it, somewhat surprised, and shook it gently, almost by her fingers.

"Bill! Bill! Bill!" chanted Freddie.

Mickey opened the door, looked out in both directions, then yanked him inside by the sleeve of his jacket, and Hilary and Freddie followed after.

"Who's the coconut face for?" asked Freddie.

Mickey took one look at it, grabbed the rope that held it from Bill's hand, and swung it over to Freddie. "You," she said.

"It's not for you, Hilary, it's for me," said Freddie. Hilary pursed her lips into her *who cares* face.

"I was afraid you weren't coming," said Mickey.

There were no chairs. Everyone stood in front of the dresser, awkwardly shifting from foot to foot, until Freddie plopped on one of the beds, which helped settle matters immediately. Hilary curled up beside him, her legs tucked beneath her, Bill sat on the other bed, and Mickey sat perched and isolated on the other end.

"Are you thirsty?" she asked. "I have a couple of Cokes in a bucket of ice."

"Not right now."

Bill and Mickey smiled at one another and then looked at the children. "So," said Bill, "how was your week?"

"It was okay," said Mickey. "How was yours?"

"Terrible," said Bill, leaning sideways as far as he could.

"Why?" asked Freddie. "Why was it terrible? Did they make you do sit-ups?"

"No," said Bill. "There are other things that make a week terrible."

"Like what?"

"Like missing someone."

"Tell us about flight school," said Freddie. "Tell us about how you learn to fly. Hilary doesn't want to be a test pilot anymore but I do. Can you fly the Flying Fortress? That plane is as big as the whole world."

"Well," said Bill, with his hand stretched toward Mickey's. "Big bombers are okay, but the ace of air combat is still the fighter plane—it's really a gun with wings. To score a hit, the pilot has to aim his plane at the enemy, the problem is that your visibility is poor, and you have to rely on formation flying. I won't learn that until advanced training."

"When will that be?" asked Hilary.

"As soon as I make it out of primary and basic." Bill and Mickey's fingers connected and curled around one another. He pulled her to his side.

"You need a haircut," she said, running her fingers over the back of his neck.

He turned to look into her eyes. "I haven't been able to get to a barber."

"Can you fly the plane low?" asked Freddie. "One plane came over the beach almost to the ground."

"You're not supposed to fly low," said Bill, loosening his tie. "Most guys do that so they can show off for some girl. He probably wanted Mickey to see what he looked like." He took off his jacket, Mickey helping him by pulling on one of his sleeves. "Sometimes a guy does it because it seems faster to fly closer to the earth. It's the main cause of accidents, though. The only low flying that makes any sense is strafing, and that's another matter." He folded his jacket and lay it behind him on the bed.

"I got a hot plate," said Mickey.

"What for?" Bill asked.

"You'll see."

Freddie twirled the coconut head. There was a knock at the

door. Mickey and Bill jumped off the bed, Mickey reached for her shoes which she had kicked off, and put them on.

"Oh God," said Mickey. "Didn't you come in through the receiving dock like I told you?"

The knock came again, this time more insistent. Mickey opened the door a crack to see Frank standing in the hallway, with Winona behind him.

"Are my kids in there?" he asked.

Mickey turned behind her as if she were seeing Hilary and Freddie for the first time. "I think so," she said.

He stuck his head in the crack and yelled, "Get out of there! Now!" Then he brought from behind his back a bottle of wine wrapped in a napkin. "It's a bad year, but it's chilled."

Dangling the painted coconut, Freddie came out from behind Mickey. "We weren't doing anything," he said.

"I know," said Frank. "I just want you to leave them alone."

Hilary came after him grudgingly. "Why do we have to leave? He just got here."

"They have things they want to talk over."

"You need towels?" called Winona from the hall.

"I think we're fixed real fine," said Mickey. Bill thrust his hand through the narrow crack and shook Frank's hand. "Thanks, Frank, for the wine, it was a nice thing to do."

Frank led Hilary and Freddie away, and Mickey closed the door behind her.

"This is crazy," said Bill.

She put her arms around him and laid her head on his chest.

"I didn't give you your present yet," he said.

"That's because I gave it away to Freddie before you had a chance."

"I don't mean the coconut head. I mean this." He handed her the small package. She opened it and took the lid off the cardboard box. On a piece of cotton batting lay a rhinestone V-for-Victory pin. Mickey knew it was rhinestone even before she turned it over to check the coating behind each stone. Diamonds would have come on velvet. It didn't matter. She lifted it out of the box and pinned it on her dress.

"Do you like it?" he asked.

"It's patriotic," she replied. "Are you hungry?"

"That's a bad question to ask me."

"I mean for food."

"Don't tell me we have to go out and sneak around again."

"No," she said. "I'm going to cook. Right here in this room. And later I'll go out and bring us corned beef sandwiches."

"What's that?"

"It's on rye bread and it comes with a pickle. They make it here in Miami Beach. It's sort of a native specialty like Key Lime pie and stone crabs." She cooked his eggs the way he liked them, over both ways, on the hot plate while he went to the bathroom to empty the contents of his shaving kit on the edge of the sink.

"Is this his razor?" he called.

"It's for my legs."

"Don't dodge the question. Is it his?"

"Probably," she replied.

"I hope he cuts his throat. I can still smell his aftershave."

"Forget it," she said. "Try this." She handed him a gold-rimmed plate that she had held back from room service on which his eggs lay shivering.

"It's hard to forget Aqua Velva," he said, "it lines your nostrils."

Bill lay with his hands folded beneath his head.

"I had my final check ride yesterday," he said.

"How did you do?"

"It's hard to say. I had to do a power-on stall. It's an important safety maneuver. You have to recognize the exact second you go into a stall so you can recover before you go into a spin. You recover by dropping your nose below the horizon to pick up more air speed and increase the engine power. Anyway, I set the throttle at cruising, and then went into a steep climb."

She snuggled up next to him, holding him as tightly as she could while he continued to stare at the ceiling. "The plane began to shudder, I kept the stick back, then the controls began to mush, I jerked the stick forward and shoved the throttle full forward, and pressed the right rudder in one motion. The nose pitched down, and I held it below the horizon in a glide, but I veered too far to the left. I didn't use enough right rudder. I just couldn't seem to coordinate stick, throttle, and rudder."

"It sounds pretty good to me."

"It's got to be better than pretty good, baby. It's got to be perfect."

"Well, you must have landed. Otherwise you wouldn't be here. How did that go?"

"Awful. I got into the pattern at five hundred feet, I established a straight glide down, no crosswinds, the ground was fifty feet below, but like an idiot I looked down at the ground, instead of to another point where the ground doesn't blur. I lost my reference point. I got confused, I didn't know how high up I was, I pulled the stick back to take the plane out of glide, but I had too much air speed left and the plane zoomed, then my wheels hit the ground and the plane bounced hard enough to rattle any loose teeth if I had any, right out of my head. It leaped ten feet off the ground, then bang, down again. I managed to avoid a wing scraping, but it was clumsy."

"Well, nobody's perfect," she said.

"In flight school you are." He stood up and walked to the window to crank it open. The night was brilliantly lit with stars that twinkled as brightly as the rhinestones on Mickey's new pin.

"I used to mess up on the line all the time. My friend Trixie, she was almost the same height as me, that's why we stood together, anyhow, she used to yank me around the right way if I didn't keep up, or if I turned the wrong way. What I'm saying is, she covered for me."

"Nobody can cover for you in the air."

"Well, when will you find out?" she asked.

"I won't know until the end of this week whether I go on to advanced training."

"What happens if you don't?"

"If I wash out? I try not to think about it. Bombardier school, I guess, or navigator school, that's usually what happens."

"Come back to bed," she said.

He turned from the window. "First pull off the covers. I want to see you in the moonlight."

"I'm going to be a nurse's aide," she said. "I start this week."

"How about an aide to a second lieutenant?"

That night Hilary punched her mattress and her pillow, as if she were trying to dig her way into sleep. She wondered about Mickey and Bill in the hotel room. It looked like Bill was going to sleep there. If he was, to what degree would there be intimacies? Were they doing more than kissing, how far on the schedule of intimacies would they go? They were not married, so it could not be all the way. Could it be touching above the waist?

Probably it was like Robert Jordan and Maria. They were holding each other naked, which was the sense she made out of a passage about smoothness, and coolness, closely holding and closely held, hollow making, happy making, hollowing chest aching tight held loneliness. Which made infinite more sense than another passage which spoke of the filling, the possessing, the having, or a really obscure reference to something which led to nowhere, then to nowhere, and again to nowhere. Who in the world could make sense of that? It was strange, because all the other parts of the book were clear and simple to understand. She would have liked to ask the person who read the book before her what they thought of it.

15

Ilona's vigil began at midnight. When Frank did not return from his third foray with Marco, she began to waken every few minutes, listening for the sound of his footsteps, the key in the lock, the doorknob turning. By two, she was fully awake, roused into nighttime anxiety in which one hears one's pulse, and had wrapped herself in her robe to sit at the window, although there was nothing to see. Her heart continued to beat quickly, thudding harder against her chest with every passing minute. Mainly, she felt her dread as an ache that would not go away.

Without Frank, she would surely die. Frank was her life. She loved the children, yes, but that was not the same bond as the terrible love which can attach man to woman beyond reason, beyond cause, beyond hope. She felt that way about Frank when she first saw him, handsome and competent, standing behind the counter of the luncheonette.

The question of marriage did not arise at first. Ilona was too busy learning the language of the noisy new country to which she had come, headstrong and independent, leaving her father, mother, and sister behind, none touched by the gripping obsession which caused her to sell the earrings her grandmother had given her in order to purchase passage to America.

The question of marriage was only incidental to the question of whether or not she could live without him. When she decided that she could not, all other issues, such as differences in religion or national origin flew out the window. She would stay with Frank and love him forever. There was simply no choice. Her friends at the millinery shop where she made baby caps, ruffled lace bonnets with trailing ribbons, told her that he would not make a good husband, that he did not cherish the same values as she. It wasn't just that Frank was not Jewish. He had no prospects. Ilona passed their warnings off with a wave of her hand, as she did all matters with which she did not agree.

By the time morning came, Ilona was already dressed, and had gone, hollow-eyed and tight-lipped to see Mr. Davis.

"When did they leave?" he asked, composed as always, and ready to handle any situation. Ilona told him that Frank and Marco had left the night before. The Coast Guard was called and it was confirmed that one of the little boats attached to the flotilla had not come back with the others. There was as yet no cause for alarm, assured the coastguardsman. A number of things could have happened to detain them. The boat could have run out of fuel, they could have docked somewhere else, and were at this moment waiting for transportation back to Miami. The Coast Guard promised a search. Even now, he added, ships had instructions to look for them.

"Ask them about planes," said Ilona.

Mr. Davis relayed her suggestion and was told that the Navy had certain priorities for its blimps and other aircraft, adding that it was still precipitous for serious concern, and that they were sure, since there was no sighting of wreckage, that all was well and that the missing men would soon be home, probably sunburnt, and to have plenty of vinegar on hand.

"You see," said Mr. Davis, hanging the receiver on the hook, "they're probably on their way home right this minute."

"I don't think so," said Ilona.

"Now, Ilona," said Mr. Davis, "you must look on the bright side."

"I cannot see only one side of a thing," she said, pulling her sweater more tightly about her, "and say I know it. I must see it totally, even if it takes a long time to get to the other side."

Gus took over the kitchen with his customary Teutonic efficiency, which had the waitresses storming in and out of the swinging doors and one of the busboys dropping trays again. Ilona tried to do her customary work, but she was not able to concentrate and twice cut herself with a paring knife.

Hilary and Freddie had no idea that anything was wrong when they woke up. It was an ordinary Sunday. They both assumed that their father had done what he always had, gone to bed after they did, and then got up before them to open the dining room, and they read the comics in their pajamas, trading one completed section for another and nibbling out of a forbidden box of Cracker Jacks.

It was not until they went for breakfast, sitting at the high stools before the salad counter, pouring syrup over pecan waffles that they began to get the first inkling.

Freddie noticed it first. "Something is funny with Ma," he said.

Hilary was waiting for her syrup to soak in so that she could pour some more. "Like what?"

"I don't know. She looks funny."

"You're supposed to put your knife down after you cut," said Hilary. She looked at her mother. Ilona was gathering breath in her small chest as if she were storing it. Further, she did not look either of them in the eye, but gazed instead at the ceiling fan, the wooden decking, or a bowl of radish roses near her fingers. It was clear that she was not angry. Ilona was direct and open with anger. It was something else.

"Ma," called Hilary, "what's the matter?"

Ilona took another breath and turned, her face as blanched as an almond, her eyes twisted with worry. "Your father didn't come back last night." Her voice was flat and matter of fact.

"Maybe they found a whole lot of sailors and they're still fishing them out," said Hilary.

"No," said Ilona. "The other boats have come back."

Hilary put down her fork. Her stomach had turned in some manner and was now upside down. She was no longer hungry. "Are they looking for him?"

"The Coast Guard says that there are lots of reasons why they could be late. Eat your breakfast."

"I can't, Ma," said Freddie. "I'm worried."

Ilona pushed his hair out of his eyes. "Be a good boy and try."

Hilary remembered when Frank tried to give her his cigar band and she threw it away. She would be sure to ask him for another when he came home, and she would never talk fresh to him again.

She made a promise to the Mr. Detwiler God that if he brought Frank back safely, she would do everything just right and then some, including anything else this God had in mind.

Neither finished breakfast. Freddie stuffed two pieces of bacon into the pocket of his shirt and they ran to the only place to be at that moment, the beach. They took off their shoes, which they left on the seawall in order to stand as close to the shoreline as they could. The sand, blackened again with tar, swirled like streusel batter. Next door, some of the soldiers were doing pushups, coating their nostrils with sand as their instructor called them dodoes, while others, working in small teams, were practicing with sticks how to cut off blood to an enemy's brain by pressing a bayonet hilt to his neck.

There were only a few people in the water, most of them just standing and picking off seaweed from their bodies or pushing away debris. Mel was paddling back and forth, doing his laps as he called them, although they were just ferocious splashings, the kind a dog makes when you throw him in. Hilary and Freddie had no interest in going into the water, just in gazing out to sea on which waves somewhere their father rode. It made them feel closer to him.

"He's not in that direction," said Hilary, pointing. "He's farther south. That way."

The ocean looked troubled, one of many typical October day oceans, with nervous, erratic waves, the waters cooling down and graying, coursing with chill southward-driven waters of the Labrador Current. Hilary tried to visualize Frank. If she saw him in her mind, it might make him appear faster. Fathers and mothers were as much a part of the landscape as the sun or the sand she stood on. There was no room in her conceptualization for a father who became lost.

Freddie's shirt pocket was shiny with grease. "I'm going to wait for him. All day," he said.

"So am I."

The children moved to the seawall, where they sat shading their eyes, looking out to sea, watching for anything that moved, and seeing only strings of ships on the horizon, convoys like beads moving south.

Something was turning Hilary's stomach to water. She jumped

down from the seawall. "I have to go to the bathroom," she said. "Wait for me."

"I'm not going anywhere," he replied.

By later afternoon the entire hotel knew that Frank was missing. Many people had come to the beach, both guests and staff, even the telephone operator, Tessie, who plugged in her entire switchboard so that no calls could go in or out, all thinking that somehow they too would be the first to sight Frank and Marco skimming over the horizon in the little motorboat.

The seriousness of the problem was enough to flush Bill Wright and Mickey out of their hotel room. Mickey and Bill heard the news from Winona. Their instinct at first was to remain where they were, sheltered in the cover of their room safe behind the door on which a tariff schedule was posted. It began to bother Bill first.

"I should go down," he said as they lay on their sides, redesigning each other's bodies with molding, smoothing fingers.

"What for?" she asked.

"To see if I can do anything."

"What can you do?" asked Mickey. Her palms were on his chest, gently rotating, her fingers bent backward so that she would not scratch him with her nails. "You can't go out and look for him."

"I don't know." Suddenly he held her hands. "There must be something. When a friend is in trouble, you don't ask if you can do something. You just do it. Once my father's barn had burned. All the way to the ground. Our neighbor came by anyway, even though the fire was already out, and the ashes cleared away. He asked if there was something he could do. My father told him he could drive us to Sunday school. Maybe Mrs. MacIntyre needs something. Maybe the kids do. I don't know. It's your friend's father."

"If you go downstairs," said Mickey, "everyone will know for sure you stayed overnight."

"I'm getting dressed." He put on his pinks, his pale shrimp-cast pants, his shirt, his tie which he knotted and stuck between his second and third buttons of his shirt, his jacket, and his flight cap. "I won't be long."

"I'm going too," she said.

"Now you don't have to do that, honey. It's enough if I go.

You stay here, take one of those soaking baths you like so much. I'll be back in a few minutes."

"I want to come with you."

He took both her arms and held them. "You know what will happen if you do. They'll talk. And the talk will be nasty. That's exactly what I didn't want to happen. That's why I didn't want to come here in the first place. At least if I go alone, they might guess what I'm doing here. But if you come down with me, they'll know. They only have to take a look at us to know. A person would have to be blind not to figure it out."

"I don't care. People have talked nasty about me before."

He stared hard into her eyes. "It will get back to him."

Mickey wrenched herself from his grasp and sat on the bed to put on her shoes. "Let it."

When they emerged together, side by side, her arm linked with his and her head held high, the V-for-Victory pin twinkling on her blouse, everyone in the lobby began to whisper and stare, all except Mr. Samuelson, who had cornered the bell captain and was jabbing him in the lapel explaining that now that Rommel's Afrika Korps had been pushed out of Egypt by the British Commander Montgomery, it was clear that the Allies were on the offensive. The bell captain countered that it didn't amount to a hill of beans because the only thing Egypt had was the pyramids, which were too old to do anybody any good, and that the only thing that meant anything was when the United States Army got into Germany and strung up Hitler by the short ones.

The whispering concerned Mickey, not Bill, his hegira predicated on a basic law. Men, particularly those in uniform, could do what they pleased. After all, men were men, especially those who were fighting for their country. Mickey, on the other hand, had violated the code. A tramp to begin with, a judgment that was obvious from her glossy good looks, her boldness, and her state of being kept, tolerated only because of her association with a man they all knew and respected, now she turned her back on that man by whose grace she was able to enjoy the benefits and luxury of the Flamingo Arms and showed up with a soldier—an officer, true—but a soldier, which lent her defiance a dimension of inconstancy, sullying it further into the worst thing in the world, a one-nighter.

It was too much. Mrs. Templeton angrily stared at her, as if the stare alone could expunge her from their sight. Mr. Carpathy just shook his head and clicked his tongue, while his wife whispered behind her hand to Mrs. Portman. The bell captain, who saw the move only as a loss of revenue, was trying to get rid of Mr. Samuelson. Only Mr. Davis took it upon himself to speak to her.

"This is a family hotel, Miss Biscayne."

"What is that supposed to mean?" asked Bill.

"I think she knows."

"*I* don't know. Spell it out."

Mr. Davis conducted them to a secluded corner behind a ficus tree that was losing its leaves. "I was hoping to be able to handle this quietly. I was certain you would both want the same thing. Please don't force me to do otherwise."

"No dice," said Bill. "I want you to come out and say what you mean."

"Miss Biscayne is not officially registered at this hotel. Mr. Radner is. Is that explicit enough?"

"No. You got something else on your mind?"

"You are not registered at this hotel, Lieutenant."

"Then register me, right now. And don't tell me you don't have any rooms. This place is a morgue."

Mr. Davis, not one to make a scene when none was warranted, led Bill to the front desk and snapped his fingers at Tessie who was unraveling her switchboard.

After he had registered, Bill and Mickey went to the beach and found Hilary and Freddie where they had been all morning, sitting on the seawall watching for Frank, their legs dangling, their noses and kneecaps beginning to burn, with a pitcher of lemonade at their side.

"Hi," said Bill.

Hilary had been crying. "My father went out in a boat with Marco last night to pick up sailors. He's awful late."

Freddie was sniffling into the hem of his shirt.

"Where's your mother?" asked Bill.

"In the room. She doesn't want to stand here on the beach," said Freddie. "But we do. She wants to be near the phone."

"I'll go to see her. You stay here with the kids," said Bill to Mickey.

Mickey sat beside Hilary. "You're gonna be pretty sunburnt if you don't cover up with something."

"I don't care," said Hilary.

"Well, I do. I don't want a friend of mine all peeling like some kind of potato. Here. This came for you. I forgot to give it to you." She handed her a piece of V-mail.

"I don't want to see it," said Hilary.

"Sure you do. Open it. See what he has to say." She opened it and handed it to Hilary. "Well, come on, you don't want me to read it. It's your letter."

Hilary grudgingly read the letter. It said:

Dearest Hilary,

I am in England sitting around and waiting. The Limeys are o.k. You have to keep a few things in mind, though like not flashing your money around, don't show off, and keep out of fights. Also they have different words for things like lorrie for truck and wireless for radio, and they like warm beer and drive on the wrong side of the road, but otherwise, it's not bad. Pretty soon we will *censored* and then let's see what *censored* can do.

The first thing I do when I get back to the good old U.S. of A. is come straight to see you, sweetheart. You are the only thing that has kept me going. I already told that to my folks and they understand. Love forever, Syl.

Hilary crumpled it up and threw it on the sand. Mickey picked it up and read it, then put it in her pocket. "Does this guy know you're a kid?" she asked. Hilary shrugged her shoulders. "You better tell him." They all sat silently, their hands shielding their eyes, staring out to sea. Hilary picked out a wave, one special rill of water that she pretended had been where Frank was, and she was following it to the beach, united through time and space in one rolling motion with her father.

A blimp circled overhead, lurching and staggering in the turbulent autumn air currents, looking for U-boats. The blimp released a great yellow ball to mark the spot where an observer on board had sighted one hiding in the shallow yellow-green waters. The ball drifted slowly through the air, tossed skyward again by updrafts, then plunged to the sea.

"Tomorrow," said Mickey, "we can ride the bus into Miami. Sabu the Elephant Boy and Sonja Henie are going to parade down Flagler Street to sell war bonds."

No one answered her. Mickey took out her sunglasses and put them on, then took them off and slipped them over Hilary's ears. The sunglasses fell down Hilary's nose, as her wave splashed into the morass at the water's edge.

Bill found Ilona in her room sitting on one of the beds with a glass of iced tea in her hand. Vicky Sue stood beside her, holding a small tray and trying to get her to take a sip. Ilona had been crying and her eyes were swollen. Vicky Sue remained close at her side with the authority of one whose own husband was missing in action somewhere in the Pacific, who understood what it was to wait with uncertainty for the phone to ring, for the knock on the door, confident that when she told Ilona things like no news is good news, and where there's life there's hope, it was the correct and only thing to say.

Bill came in hesitantly, since the door was unlocked and no one had told him to enter. With his cap in his hands, he introduced himself as a friend of Mickey's. Vicky Sue gave him a knowing look which required one eyebrow to dip, but Ilona didn't seem to care whose friend he was. He told her that he knew the children and that he also knew Frank who had been very kind to him.

"He's not dead yet," she said.

"I didn't mean that, ma'am."

"Well then," said Ilona, "don't start telling me good things about him like he was."

"Is there anything I can do to help?" he asked.

"Do you have a boat?" asked Ilona.

"No, ma'am."

"That's the only thing we need now. A boat, or a plane."

"Maybe I can put in a word to someone. About the plane. I would sure like to."

"Go ahead if you like," said Ilona.

Bill put his cap back on his head and walked out of the room, closing the door softly behind him. Ilona called to him before it closed. "Thank you for coming to see me," she said. "Where is your mother?"

"In Iowa."

"Do you write to her?"

"Not as often as I'd like."

"You should write to her every day. She worries."

Bill went next door to the Lord Feldman to find his former commanding officer. Men lounged in the lobby in fatigues and gym shorts; some were lined up to use the telephone and were sniping at the man who held on to the receiver, his other ear closed off with his fist. A sign above the front desk said, "What you see, what you hear, when you leave it, leave it here."

Bill located the major sunning himself on the patio. The major asked him how his flight training was going, and Bill gave a sketchy, optimistic recounting of the past few months. The major thanked him for coming to see him as he always liked to hear from his men and find out what they were doing. Almost as an afterthought, the major had a question.

"You know that girl Charlene your friend June Bug used to take out?" he asked.

"Yes, sir," replied Bill.

"She still live in Miami?"

"I'm not sure. I think June Bug still sees her."

"That means you're not giving out her number," said the major.

"It means I don't know it, sir."

Then Bill said he had come for his help. The major sat upright, his hands on his knees, while Bill told him about Frank's efforts on behalf of the Coast Guard and how he came to be missing. The major asked him what his interest was in this man, and Bill said he was a very good friend. The major lay back on his lounge, closed his eyes, and promised that if there was no word by Monday, he would ask the blimp people to provide an extra watch. "It's not easy," he added, "to get those guys to do what we want them to do. But I'll do what I can."

Bill made no move to leave. "If you please, sir," he said, "could you also find out what the Coast Guard is doing?"

The major said "shit," glanced at the sun, which was now moving behind a cloud, and stood up. "You were told to get along with the civilian population on the beach, mister, not to get so involved you forget your purpose here." He grabbed an outside phone and called the Coast Guard while Bill stood before him. Apparently there was a search, but a limited one, because of all the possible places that the boat could have been disabled and the occupants forced to seek shelter. They would do what they could. In addition Bill was told, which information he did not pass on to

Ilona, that these were the casualties of war, just as were the men on the front line. Something could not be done for everyone who was lost or missing; there were not enough men to spare, or time. The major concluded by telling Bill that he better get his ass back to his base, as Sunday was rapidly coming to a close.

Day turned into evening. Mickey had left the beach hours before to walk Bill to the corner where he would get his first ride in a series of jeeps, trucks, and one private car that would get him back to Ocala before curfew.

Hilary and Freddie sat shivering in the chill night air in the same spot where they had been all day, on the ledge of the seawall. They were now sunburnt and tired, Freddie leaning against his sister with his head on her shoulder, while a band in ruffled shirts played "Begin the Beguine" on the shadowed patio. A few couples danced despite the chill, Mel with a young soldier's wife who had come down to Miami and was waiting for her husband to get a pass, Mrs. Steinfeld with an older widower from Scarsdale, a dapper gentleman, who, although thatched with white hair, wore an ascot around his crepy neck, and into whose hairy ear she whispered the lyrics. The women wore filmy dresses that clung to their bodies. Some of the men, wearing gold-buttoned blazers and white pants, dipped as they danced, forcing their stiffened legs between the legs of the women. Sometimes a couple poised in midflight, arrested in motion, three legs intertwined for the count of an entire measure, before they dipped to the ground.

One man was so tall that when he dipped, he lifted his partner off the ground and onto his thigh. From the back, it looked as though he was dancing by himself.

Ilona came to the seawall, bringing sweaters. She looked thinner and much older. Hilary and Freddie did not make their usual fuss about sweaters, but put them on, grateful for their warmth.

"I hope Daddy isn't cold," said Freddie.

"Your father is very strong," said Ilona, "and very smart. He will know how to stay warm."

"How?" asked Hilary.

"I don't know," said Ilona. "If I knew, I would be as strong and as smart as your father."

Water, sky, and beach coalesced into an inky opacity. A horse and rider appeared out of the blackness of the beach, like something materializing out of velvet. The rider shined a flashlight at the seawall.

"You have to get off the beach," he said.

"We are watching for my husband," said Ilona.

"He shouldn't be swimming now, anyway," said the sentry.

"He's in a boat," said Freddie.

"Well he can't dock here, that's for sure, and you still have to get off the beach. And that means the seawall you're sitting on."

Ilona led them off the wall and onto the patio. Hilary let herself be helped down, as if she were a little girl. Mel saw them first, all with their heads down, Ilona in the middle. He excused himself from his shivering partner, telling her to wait for him, then took Ilona's arm.

"Any news?" he asked.

"Not yet," she answered. "We were watching on the beach. It was something to do, you understand. It made the children feel closer to Frank. The sentry made us leave."

"Well, wait a minute," said Mel. "The beach isn't the only place to look. I'll take you up to the roof. The plane spotter has all kinds of field glasses and a clear view with nothing to block it. You can stand with him and look to your heart's content, although you won't be able to see very much."

The plane spotter was a sixteen-year-old high school student named Bernie Schulman, a tall, skinny boy with a bony neck and an Adam's apple that bobbed when he swallowed. Mel made the introductions, lending to their visit an official imprimatur, then ran downstairs back to his dancing partner while Bernie Schulman handed an extra pair of glasses to Ilona.

"You have to focus them," he said. "Everyone's eyes are different."

Ilona had trouble focusing her glasses, primarily because the night was so dark, there was little against which to make reference other than an endless pitch.

"You expect to see someone on the water?" he asked. "I'll tell you what to look for. Look for a break in the foam, or too much foam in one spot, and turn away from time to time. Otherwise the ocean makes no sense."

Then he trained his own eyes upward, scanning the heavens for the silhouettes of enemy aircraft of which he knew dozens, both German and Japanese, and standing next to a telephone into which he could relay his information instantly, one of dozens like him all over the city doing exactly the same thing.

"Listen," he said, "I forgot to warn you. If you see a full front view of a plane, throw yourself flat on the ground in case of machine-gun fire, and if you see its undersides, try to get underneath something, anything. A bomb may hit you any second."

"Don't scare them," said Ilona. "They're scared enough."

"I'm sorry. But it's something everyone should know. I'm surprised they didn't put it in the newspaper."

When Mel swung down the staircase onto the patio, the band was packing up its instruments and unhooking the microphone, one ruffled musician catching sheet music flying off a music stand. The evening had grown windy and chilly, with little suggestion of tropical splendor, and the other dancers including Mel's partner had fled indoors to comfort. The only things that remained were their glasses half filled with rum and Coke, with little paper umbrellas blowing out of them onto the patio.

16

Ilona wrote to Frank's parents and to his sister that he was missing, feeling it was both her duty and her responsibility to let them know. His father sent back an envelope containing twenty-five dollars, nothing else, not even a piece of paper to wrap the money with, which is what you were supposed to do if you sent money through the mails. His sister Hazel wrote that she was coming to Miami, as soon as she could make arrangements for her son Roy and her husband Harry.

After Hazel had prepared ten pounds of fried chicken, two quarts each of cole slaw and potato salad, and a big pot of corned beef and cabbage, she came to Miami on the Greyhound bus. Hazel was ten years older than Frank, a stocky woman with Frank's face, only hers was swollen, as if it had been inflated. She wore a dark green rayon dress with a matching jacket, her hair permanented into dry russet curls, her lipstick starting to seep into tiny grooves over her upper lip. She carried her purse over her abdomen and leaned backward when she walked.

Hilary and Freddie had seen her once before, when Frank took them all to St. Augustine. The only thing they remembered about the visit was the trip to the Indian burial grounds that scared them both, especially when her son, their older cousin Roy, came up behind them and yelled, "Yah!" near a pile of old bones lying in a shallow grave, and the fact that they could touch nothing in the house. Hilary remembered wondering how people could walk around in a house where you had to be careful not to touch anything. Probably you became skillful with practice and could do it blindfolded if you had to.

Hazel embraced Ilona first, then Hilary and Freddie, folding them into her capacious body the way a cook folds egg whites into a batter. She handed each child a foil-wrapped chocolate kiss, told them to wait outside, then led Ilona into her room.

"Now then," she said. "What about the insurance? What did he leave you?"

"He's not dead," said Ilona, sitting on one of the beds. "Please don't act as if he's dead."

"That means there's no insurance."

"We don't have the money for that kind of thing," said Ilona. "This year is the first time we're able to put anything aside. Not much. But there are other things we need money for."

"You have any money in the bank then?"

"A little."

"How much?"

Ilona folded her hands in her lap. "That is between Frank and me."

Hazel reached for her purse, took out a handkerchief with which she daubed under her armpits, then returned to the problem. "Look, this is as hard for me as it is for you. Frank was my brother. But he is probably passed on. You might as well face it, and face it fast. As soon as you do, we can decide what to do about you and the children."

"What do you mean, what to do? What is there to do?" asked Ilona.

"Ilona, we are not people of means, none of us, even with the overtime at the plant, Harry and I still have a mortgage, and we still owe on the furniture. But you're Frank's wife, and those are his children out there, and we want to help you. That's why I'm here. I know there's bad feelings between my folks and you, but we still want to help. Harry and me. I know Frank would want to do the same for us if things were switched around."

Ilona thought of Frank's nephew, Roy, a gangling oaf for whom she would not want the responsibility under any circumstances.

"We don't need help," she said. "And there are no bad feelings between me and your mother and father. We don't even know each other."

"My folks are set in their ways," said Hazel. "You can't change them now; besides, I had nothing to do with that. I know a few Jews myself, and they're good people, same as everyone else. The place where we bought our dining room suite is owned by one, so the fact that you're Jewish means nothing to me. Let's get on another subject. How long do you think the hotel will allow you to stay here without Frank? You help Frank, Ilona, but you're not Frank. It's time you start planning what you're going to do."

"I will do what I always have. I will continue to work until Frank returns, and then I will work at his side."

"Harry and I talked it over. We can fix up the garage and make it into a comfortable little apartment for you. There won't be a kitchen, but you can share mine, and you can come in to use our basement bathroom. That way, at least, you have a roof over your heads."

Hilary had been listening with a glass held to the wall and relaying the message to Freddie. She heard everything except some of Ilona's low tones. Neither wanted to go to St. Augustine. They hoped that Ilona felt the same way and held their fingers crossed behind their backs. St. Augustine meant hands at your sides and Indian burial grounds with chilling echoes that bounced off the stones, and no Frank. St. Augustine was the loss of hope.

"You came a long way to help," said Ilona. "And I am grateful. But Frank is not dead. I know it. I feel it here. Don't you think I would know it if he were?"

"You can't fool yourself forever," said Hazel. "I'm just telling you that you have to make plans. For you and for the children. You and the girl could help me in the house, if you're worrying about charity. I asked you before how much money you have."

"I don't want to discuss it," said Ilona.

"Well, I hope you won't be so foolish that you won't take what I'm offering you." She took an envelope out of her purse and handed it to Ilona.

"I can't take that," said Ilona. "It's not that I don't appreciate it, but I can't take your money."

"I think you ought to talk to a priest. Is there one on Miami Beach? I imagine you'll probably have to go into Miami to find one."

"We have one near Forty-first Street," said Ilona. "At St. Patrick's Cathedral. But why should I talk to a priest?"

"Because I wouldn't want you to do anything Jewish for Frank. Frank wouldn't have wanted it either. Go to the priest. He'll say a requiem mass for Frank. It's for his soul. I don't know if you people believe in it or not, but we do. You can't put a man down with a proper mass for him. It's bad enough Frank didn't have last rites, which is sometimes all right if you trust in God's mercy and in the dead person's good intentions, but at least arrange for a requiem mass for Frank. The priest will know what to do. If you like, I'll go talk to him."

"He's not dead," said Ilona, weeping into her lap. "He's not. Not now. Not when we have everything."

Hilary and Freddie, who had been standing outside the door deciding when to make a move, broke into the room. Freddie ran to his mother and lay his head on her shoulder. Hilary spoke first. "My father's not dead!" she shouted. "My mother told you so! Why don't you listen to her?"

Hazel looked down at Hilary, who could see into her nostrils. Hilary heard that if a fly got in there, it went all the way into your brain and killed you.

"You have a sharp tongue for a little girl," said Hazel. "It seems everyone is too lenient with you. I'd correct that if I were you, Ilona. That leads to other bad ways. Worse ones. Much worse. I heard of girls not much older than her, doing all sorts of things with the sailors behind the bushes, girls who probably started out with sassy tongues just like hers."

Ilona stood up. It seemed an effort. She swayed once, but steadied herself. "Hazel, you're Frank's sister. I respect you as a member of his family, but you cannot talk about my children that way. Not now. Not ever. You cannot." Ilona put her arm around Hilary. "This child has been sitting for days on a seawall watching for her father. She has squint marks burned around her eyes. I could not manage without her."

Hilary was stunned. It was the first time Ilona had ever said anything like that about her. She put her arm tentatively around her mother's tiny waist.

Hazel picked up her purse which she rested once more upon her shelflike abdomen. "I came to help you. I can't do any more. I'm going to put this money here, on the dresser. When you come to your senses, as I'm sure you will, you will change your mind. The offer is still good. If you need a place to stay, you can come to Harry and me in St. Augustine. Roy will help the children get acquainted with a new school. There is money enough here for your bus fares. No pets, though. Roy is allergic."

They had never had a pet other than a turtle with a palm tree painted on its back which had died in the little bowl in which it was purchased, lying stretched out over a tiny rock, with its arms and legs and head dangling in the slimy water. The idea of pets was silly, especially that they would transport one to St. Augustine.

When Hazel left, the first thing Hilary asked was if they were going to St. Augustine. "Not if I have to scrub Collins Avenue on my hands and knees," replied Ilona.

"What do the girls do with the sailors behind the bushes?" asked Freddie.

"Never mind," said Ilona.

Hilary said nothing but bent to rub dirt off her sandals.

"How come you don't want to know too?" asked Ilona.

"I just don't," said Hilary.

"You know something?"

"About what?" Hilary stood up.

"You know about what. What girls do with sailors behind bushes."

"Ma," said Hilary. "Come on. I'm not a little kid any more."

"That's what worries me."

"What?" asked Freddie. "What do they do? It's not fair if she knows and I don't. Tell me too, and I won't tell anyone."

It came as a surprise when Ilona then asked Freddie and Hilary if they would like her to take them to the movies. She had never before taken them to the movies and neither had Frank. They were used to going by themselves on Saturday afternoons, and had been going, ever since Hilary was eight and could demonstrate that she could take Freddie, then six, without incident on the bus and return home safely.

"Sure," said Hilary. "What do you want to see?"

They selected *George Washington Slept Here* because they missed listening to Jack Benny and he would make them laugh. By catching a Jitney, an eight-seater taxi rigged with strings and ropes to open and close the doors, they made the afternoon show with time to spare. Ilona asked for one adult and two children's tickets and was somewhat surprised when the cashier asked, "How old is the girl?"

"Eleven," she replied.

The cashier continued to regard them with suspicion but Ilona gunned her down with a look of her own.

"This is where we get candy," said Freddie, leading his mother to the glass counter. Ilona took the hint and bought them each a package of candy, Jujubes for Hilary, Good and Plentys for Freddie, and a box of popcorn for all three to share.

When they went inside the darkened theater, Ilona could not get used to the noise. "Is it always like this?" she asked.

"Like what?" asked Hilary.

It took a while to select seats, not too close, Freddie explained, because that hurts your neck, but not too far back either, because then you couldn't see. On the way down the aisle to three promising seats in the middle, they passed Billy Connaught and Paul with some kids Hilary didn't know. She slunk past, hoping that they wouldn't see her, or if they did, not notice that she was with her mother.

Once settled in their seats, they watched three cartoons, a newsreel about a big fire in a nightclub in Boston in which four hundred people had died in a panicked scramble to escape, and then the movie about fixing up an old house. Hilary and Freddie became hysterical when seventeen-year locusts stripped Benny and Pa Kettle to their underwear, the kind of wild laughing that makes you fall from your seat and clutch your stomach. It was during this hilarious scene when Ilona began to weep silently in the dark. Hilary reached over to tap Freddie's shoulder behind Ilona's back. They both turned to look in the other direction, leaning away from their mother as if they had no connection with her.

During all of this, pieces of popcorn continued to hit them all on the shoulders and on their heads. Once Hilary turned around to find out where it was coming from and saw a group of big, smirking youths who looked like high school boys, sitting with their feet up on the seats in front of them. She knew that it was not a group to start up with and continued to pick popcorn out of her braids. Ilona at first did not notice.

It was when the sequence of the missiles accelerated into a barrage and Freddie yelled "Ouch," that Ilona suddenly stood, took a half-finished box of popcorn, and hurled it at the big boys. "You like to throw so much?" she asked. "You like to throw? I like to throw too." She followed the popcorn with a half finished container of soda she found sitting on the concrete floor that had belonged to someone else, splashing it over the seats in front of the big boys even before it hit them.

"What's that for, lady?" one of them asked. "We weren't doing anything."

"And don't bother us again," she shouted, "or I'll call the usher."

Then the other people around the big boys, also tormented popcorn victims, began to yell and throw things, and soon everyone around them was throwing something at them, whether they had been victims or not. A whistle blew and the ushers came running down the aisle, isolated the four big boys, and hustled them, complaining bitterly, out of the theater.

Hilary and Freddie and Ilona continued to watch the movie, Ilona taking note of how one could fix up a house with rotting timbers, even one two hundred years old, and Freddie and Hilary each leaning against a shoulder.

Later that evening, after Ilona went to the kitchen to make sure that the restaurant gave no more than one cup of coffee per customer, because of the shortage, Winona stopped by their room on her way home. She looked upset.

She told them that her son Lionel had been injured on the loading dock in Gulfport when a shipping crate slipped from its cargo net and fell on his leg and that he was in a military hospital in Tuscaloosa.

"They say he has a broken leg bone," said Winona. "And that it got infected, and they got him in traction."

"I'm very sorry to hear that," said Ilona.

Winona seemed to be waiting for something. She stood there, pulling on her little white cotton gloves, then spoke.

"I wouldn't ask this, I know things aren't good for you either, but there's only a few places I can go. I want to visit my son, but I don't have the fare. I'll pay you back, just as soon as I can, but I'm gonna have to borrow some money. I don't want to strap you. But I sure would be grateful."

The envelope from Hazel lay on the dresser. Hilary noticed it the same moment as her mother did. Ilona picked up the envelope. "How much do you need?" she asked.

Winona ran it through her mind, making an inventory of facts that she ticked off her gloved fingers. "I have folks I can stay with, kin folks of my dead husband. The fare is about forty dollars round trip and I have about twenty. I guess I need about twenty-five more."

Ilona peeled off twenty-five dollars. "Take it," she said.

"Thank you, honey," said Winona, "that's real generous of you. I'll pay you back. I been worried sick about that boy. They wrote me something about they have to go in again and clean out the infection. They didn't explain it."

"He's alive," said Ilona. "That's what counts and at least, you know where he is."

"I forgot," said Winona. "I sure forgot about your man." She went to Ilona and they embraced, bolstering each other with their own frayed courage.

Winona stepped back. "I hear you had a visitor today. Someone said it was Frank's sister."

"Hazel came to give us money," said Freddie. "She's fatter than a house."

"Aunt Hazel," corrected Ilona. "She came all the way from St. Augustine. She didn't stay."

Winona shook her head. "When they thinks folks is gone, they come out of the woodwork. How come I never see her around when Frank is here?"

"Don't wish that on me," said Ilona.

"You lucky," said Winona. "My husband's sister lives across the street. She's all the time coming over for this thing and that thing, in my kitchen, under my feet. She's worse than any cockroach I ever saw." Winona took a look at Hilary. "Hilary favors you," she said. "I never noticed it before."

Hilary didn't think so. Couldn't Winona see that she looked exactly like Frank? She stood with her legs apart and her hands on her hips.

"She looks more like my father," said Ilona, "may he rest in peace, and she acts like him too."

There had been a brief mention of Frank and Marco's disappearance in the newspaper. Frank's age was given, as was Marco's and their occupations listed as restaurant workers. Hilary read the notice. That wasn't Frank. It didn't tell anything about him, nothing of his expansiveness, his handsome face, his laugh that you could hear all the way down the hall, or that he could pick up one hundred pound sacks of potatoes with his arm extended. She decided that you could never tell about a person from just a few words. You needed a whole lot of words.

All the kids in school and all the teachers knew about Frank being missing. For a while everyone was kind, Miss Daly forgiving, and friendly, even Freddie's teacher, Miss Carmichael, who was struggling through a second year of trying to get Freddie to learn anything new. When Mr. Detwiler saw them in the hall, he nodded gravely to them, which was a step up for anyone. The other kids were nice, no one did or said anything bad. They moved aside for her in the cafeteria so that she could squeeze in at the good end of the table, they suffered her presence on the playground, although she didn't feel much like playing, and when they practiced the Thanksgiving pageant, everyone became quiet when Hilary spoke her lines instead of their usual nonstop shrieking and hooting which left Miss Daly with a conditioned reflex, an instant headache at the sight of a stage. When Hilary held up an ear of corn, now dried and shriveled from days of practice, and gave her short speech, which was, "The Indians gave me this. They call it maize. I think we should try it," people shuffled their feet and looked down at the ground—all except T.H. He disengaged himself from Shirley and all her feathers and from Shirley's new best friend, Liz Bonnier, to tell Hilary that he was sorry that her father was drowned, and that it was too bad there were no medals for guys like him because they deserved it just like the guys who died fighting on the front lines.

Something funny was happening when he spoke that made her not hear his words. The first was she felt a terrible urge to hit him on the head with her ear of corn. The second was she was taller than T.H. How did that happen? She hadn't noticed it before. It must have been all of a sudden. It must have happened when she followed the advice of Mickey and hung from her legs on the railing, trying to stretch herself. She wondered if he noticed it too.

Hilary was playing hopscotch alone on the sidewalk in front of the hotel, her braids flipping in the air with every jump, as a squadron of soldiers marched beside her in the street singing "Sixpence." She was as used to them as she was to the seagulls flying overhead, and paid them no more attention.

Lipschutz was beside her on the sidewalk, balanced on his haunches, while he helped to chalk more boxes. He had been a hit at the USO his first time out when he reluctantly agreed to Mel to pinch-hit for the regular MC. At first, nobody laughed when the tall, lean, sad-faced man in the tux took the microphone, he was so deadpan, so serious, his voice so flat, but by the time he got to "Fire at will, where's will?" they were doing what all comics want their audience to do—splitting their sides. He became so popular with the servicemen that the USO Committee asked him to alternate with the other MC, and there was talk that they wanted to give him the number-one spot. This added recognition and the knowledge that he was making a real contribution to the war effort by entertaining the men in uniform made Lipschutz expansive. It didn't change his basic personality, which was essentially depressive, but it made him forget that he wanted to kill himself, and he could, from time to time, laugh in a harsh, unaccustomed bark that made the hair stand up on everyone's arms. What was more, one of the young hostesses at the USO, a college student at the University of Miami, who thought he was the funniest man she had ever seen, was in love with him.

Because he had been depressed as long as he could remember, Lipschutz recognized the malady in others. "Your father is a good man," he said, "you know that, don't you?"

"I know it," said Hilary, on her way to threesies. The squadron in the street was given the order for dismissal and broke rank.

"He'll come back. If I know Frank, somehow he'll find a way."

"Hey, 4-F," yelled one of the soldiers on his way to the sidewalk. "What's wrong with you? No balls?"

"Is that any way to talk to an eighty-three-year-old man?" asked Lipschutz, with his characteristic ennui. The soldiers laughed. Hilary didn't think it was so funny. One of them looked at her in a peculiar way. She screwed her face up at him. Did he recognize her or something from when she went with Mel on demonstrations, and if he did, why didn't he say so?

Mickey watched them from her window—the tall, lean Lipschutz bending down to chalk boxes, the laughing, shouting soldiers on their way into their own hotel, and Hilary scissoring her way into sixies. She had just been on the telephone with Bill and felt that her life was out of control again, making the sights below and the people just scenery, backdrop like the blue and green cellophane waves hanging from the flies of the Pago Pago. What was important, what mattered, was what was happening between her and Bill.

He had given her something she had never had, an attention that had fleshed out her spirit, smoothing out the wrinkles of seldom used feelings, stretched her entire being. She was losing it, and without it she would shrivel to what she was before him, half living, half feeling. When he called, she had known by his voice that something was terribly wrong. He had washed out of flight school. He would never be a pilot. What was worse, he was going home for Thanksgiving.

Mickey desperately did not want him to go home, demanding for the first time in their relationship, at one time shrieking into the phone, that he spend Thanksgiving with her, especially since they never had more than one day and a half together, that Mr. Radner was definitely not expected, as she had checked that out with a letter, and, most important, the big question, who knew where Bill would be sent next? Bombardier school, navigator school, these were the usual options for someone who didn't finish flight school, and such facilities were all over the United States.

Bill became very quiet on the telephone, more subdued with each of her outraged cries. He asked that she try to understand, that he loved her more than anything in the world, that he wanted to marry her, but that he had not seen his parents for months, they worried about him, and this was a busy time for his father, who could use an extra hand, even if only for a few days. She became wildly jealous and asked if there was someone waiting for him at home. Bill reassured her, but she did not believe him. He offered a palliative, the way one pops a foaming sedative into a glass of water. He said that they probably would send him back to Miami for reassignment and he asked that she be patient, as women had to be all over the country, and not make things more difficult for him than they already were.

Mickey did not know how to be patient. It was one of the things she did not want to learn. Patient was what you had to be if you were plain and pimply and couldn't get a guy interested in you. Patient was what you were when your mother asked you to boil greens and the bubbles wouldn't come and you wanted to go outside and play. Patient was swelling with a pregnancy that made you so fat you had to ask someone you hated to turn you in the middle of the night.

Mickey paced her room, then found herself standing in the middle of the floor. She heard the soldiers below laugh with Lipschutz and forgot for a minute why. Then suddenly she reached into her closet. She had to keep busy. When you were busy you did not think. She bypassed her dresses and her blouses, and her molting fur, and found what she was looking for in the back, the pink and white uniform of a nurse's aide. She took it off the hanger and put it on, adjusting the bib critically in the round mirror over the dresser, then set the cap on her golden hair, tucking the ends under the band. A flamingo etched into a corner of the mirror obscured the cap and she stepped aside in order to see it better. It was, she thought, the dumbest thing she ever saw, but it was a ticket to forgetting.

She would go to the ladies' club where the second nurse's-aide class was to be given, having already taken a stupid orientation in which she was told that she would help replace the nurses of the nation so that they could go into combat zones. She would never do that, of course, replace the nurses of the nation. The sound alone, much less the tasks involved, was formidable, but she would sit and chatter with the other women of things she liked to talk about, like nail shapes, and fashions, and movie stars, and listen to them gossip about people who lived on Miami Beach that she did not know.

She would stop when the course was over. That old bitch could ask again about her high school diploma, and she would smile sweetly, as she had done in the line at the Pago Pago, focusing on the guys at the front row tables, the big tippers, the money boys, and say it was in the mail.

Mickey stepped into the sunshine, wearing her nurse's-aide uniform. The soldiers remaining on the sidewalk to banter with Lipschutz stopped in their conversation, and Hilary stopped on square number ten.

"I never saw you wear that before," said Hilary.

"You like it?" asked Mickey.

"Sort of. It makes you look different."

"Different how?" Mickey screwed tighter an earring that had loosened.

"Like a poster. Serious. Like Joan of Arc."

"Talk about people I know," said Mickey.

"Where are you going?" asked Hilary.

"To roll bandages, probably. Or to practice placing the open end of a pillow case away from the door."

"Can I come?"

"You're too young. You have to be eighteen." Mickey started to walk away, but stopped. "Any news?"

Lipschutz shot her a warning look. Mickey disregarded it. As a close friend, she had some privileges. One of these was information. Hilary just shook her head.

Three people stepped from the bus that was snorting its way up Collins Avenue and walked toward the hotel. The two women were members of the synagogue. Hilary recognized them from the small knot of people that had stopped to talk to Ilona the day she took them to shul and had told her about the people in Romania who had to dig their own graves, and of the son of a congregant who had been stationed in London and had been buried under the rubble of an air raid. She also recognized the rabbi, even out of his robes.

"That's her child," said one of the women, plump and soft, like bread dough. "You're playing in the street at a time like this?" asked the woman, taking out a handkerchief and wiping the perspiration from her face and neck.

"She's a child," said the rabbi. "A child cannot be expected to do more than a child's task, and we are not certain that this is such a time. Where is your mother?"

"Inside," said Hilary.

"I'll see you later," said Mickey, "and I'll tell you about it. Okay?"

The women nudged one another. The plump one said to the other, "With those nails the *shiksa vet helfen vi a toyten bankes.*" The other woman laughed, and the rabbi, with a look of annoyance, put both hands out palms down, as if pushing feathers into pillows.

"What did she say?" asked Hilary.

Lipschutz lit a cigarette. "She said, with those nails, the non-Jewish girl will help like cupping a corpse."

"What does it mean, cupping a corpse?"

"It means they didn't like her. It means they're giving her a dig.

It means they don't think she'll do much good with long fingernails."

"I'd better go," said Hilary. She ran up the steps into the lobby and followed after the trio who were at the front desk asking questions of Mr. Davis.

She led them to Ilona, who took them into the corner of the dining room and offered them coffee cake and tea. The plump woman took a napkin and continued to dab at her face and neck.

"We heard about your husband," said the rabbi. "Mrs. Fenster and Mrs. Weinstein, who you know, wanted to accompany me when I told them I was planning to visit you."

"You didn't have to come all the way from South Beach," said Ilona.

The rabbi shrugged. "This is fine tea," he said.

"Very refreshing," said Mrs. Fenster.

"Now," said the rabbi, "what is the Coast Guard doing?"

"Nothing now," said Ilona. "They stopped the search. They found some wreckage from the boat. There was an explosion."

It seemed to Hilary that her mother's accent was becoming thicker.

"Do you believe your husband is still alive?"

Ilona clutched at her throat, then shook her head. "I don't care what they think. I know he's alive."

"I must ask you some questions," said the rabbi. "They may seem harsh at such a time, but necessary." His voice was gentle. He lowered it. Hilary strained to hear. "Were you having marital problems?"

"What do you mean?" asked Ilona.

"The kind of problems between husbands and wives that creates ill feelings."

"No. Nothing like that. Why do you ask such a question?"

"Sometimes, when a man is missing, we have to find out if there was some reason that he would want to run away, to hide. For example, I know of such a case where a man owed a great deal of money. He left his wife, he left his job. One morning, he went to work and never returned. His wife thought he was dead but he was actually alive in another city, under another name."

Ilona stood up. "Frank is not like that. If owing money would make him leave, he would have left a long time ago. I don't want to hear any more of this."

Hilary wondered why her mother did not mention that Frank had left once before.

The rabbi took Ilona's hand. "Please. I am sorry I upset you. Sit. I must ask these questions. Did your husband have any enemies?"

"No," yelled Hilary. "Everyone loves my father! Everybody in the whole world."

"Why does the child shout so?" asked the rabbi.

"A *bren*," said Mrs. Weinstein.

The rabbi waved her down with his hand. "First, Mrs. MacIntyre, let's not jump to conclusions. You are not a widow until a determination is made. With a missing person such as your husband, not on a battlefield, there cannot be a presumption of death until the final facts are in. Perhaps something will be found that will tell us something else. One little straw leads to another until we find the bale of hay. Specifically, regarding your husband, there is mention of such a situation in the Talmud. It has to do with waters with end, and waters without end. It is easier to make a determination of death with a person missing in waters with end, such as a pond, or a lake, or a stream. But in waters that have no end, such as the Atlantic Ocean, it is more difficult. However, there is a bright side. It also gives us more room for hope."

Hilary thought of the words *waters without end* and ran them over her tongue. They sounded like something Emily Dickinson would say.

"What?" asked Ilona.

"I didn't say anything," said Hilary.

"Then don't talk to yourself," whispered Ilona. "I don't need anything crazy now."

The rabbi leaned over. He had something more to interpret and it wasn't good. "Now, if there is some final determination made, God forbid, under Jewish law, I can conduct a nondenominational service for your husband. I only tell you this to put your mind at ease."

"No," said Ilona. "Frank is Catholic. If I learn that he is dead, I will give him a Catholic burial."

Mrs. Fenster and Mrs. Weinstein exchanged looks.

The rabbi nodded. "You have your children at your side, that's good." He stood up to leave. "Where is the boy?"

"He had to stay after school," said Hilary.

"How old is he?"

"He's almost nine," said Ilona.

"It is time for the boy to be in Hebrew school learning his Aleph Bayz. He's a Jewish child, under the law, and I know you want to do what's right for him." The rabbi stood and everyone else did the same.

"He didn't make up his mind yet," said Hilary.

"Rabbi," asked Ilona, "do you hear anything? About the other side?"

"It's not good," said the rabbi. "Bits and pieces of an ugly puzzle. Where are your people again?"

"Denmark. They got to Denmark and they are hiding there, but they are trying to get to Sweden."

"That's good. So far. That's good. But who knows? We have to wait and see. One trouble at a time." He patted the top of her head. "One trouble at a time."

"Wait, please," said Ilona. She turned to Hilary. "Run and get my *pushke*. It's on the windowsill in my room."

Hilary returned with a tin can rolling with pennies and dimes earmarked for a special fund marked in pencil FOR MILK FOR JEWISH CHILDREN IN HOSPITALS IN THE OLD COUNTRY. Ilona emptied the contents and handed it to Mrs. Weinstein.

It looked like a lot of money to Hilary. Mrs. Weinstein counted it and put it in her pocketbook. "Thank you," she said. When they left, Hilary heard them say, "A nice looking woman. A good woman. As far as I'm concerned, married to that *shaygets* is *aroysgevorfeneh yoren*."

That evening, Ilona was in the kitchen, helping Gus get ready for Thanksgiving. Hilary sat at the salad counter with Freddie, picking at her supper. They had had the Thanksgiving pageant that day, and Hilary had begun to cry on stage in front of all the parents and the kids from the first five grades, for no reason, right on stage at the moment she was supposed to give her line. Freddie thought it was good acting because obviously something was wrong with the corn. But Hilary would never forget it as long as she lived and neither would anyone else in her class, except for Sorrell Myers who told her that she was probably nervous, and when you're nervous, you do funny things—like his father, for example, who when he was nervous, ate everything in sight.

Ilona held string in her hand with which she would sew up another turkey. "What are you thinking about?" she asked.

"I'm thinking," said Hilary, "that fat people sweat a lot."

"That's what you're thinking? I don't believe that's what you're thinking."

"Why are you so mad? I can't help what I'm thinking. How come you don't ask Freddie what he's thinking? He thinks about a lot of things. Ask him."

"Don't get fresh. I'll give you a *frask in punim* you won't forget, so don't get fresh. I was only trying to let you tell me what you were thinking. I thought maybe you wanted to talk about your father."

"What's *aroysgevorf* something *yoren*?"

"Wasted years. Where did you hear that?"

"I don't remember," Hilary lied. She heard a siren. "I hope it's not another air-raid drill," she said.

"What is?" asked Freddie.

"Don't you hear that siren?"

"Sure," he said.

"Well, it could be an air-raid drill."

"I hope not," said Freddie. "I didn't finish my chocolate pudding."

The siren stopped. Freddie finished his chocolate pudding, dipping his pinky into a chocolate-filled depression in the glass dish into which his spoon could not reach. It was probably a test. There was no Mel running in shouting orders and besides, the siren did not have its usual singsong wail.

"You look like Hitler," Hilary said.

"Take that back." Freddie punched her in her shoulder.

"See for yourself. You have a mustache." Hilary held up a knife blade for him to look into while Ilona carried the string to a row of turkeys, upended and ready to be laced up, purchased from Mrs. Fenster's husband, a butcher who, through incredibly good luck, had cornered the southern fowl market. Ilona was planning what to say to Mr. Davis, who was talking seriously about bringing in someone else to run the kitchen, her thin shoulders bent as she ran the skein into the pimply, pallid skin of the next bird.

The kitchen became silent, the usual noises of the steam table and the waitresses suspended, even Gus's hoarse directions halted. It was as if their ears had stopped up. Hilary swallowed once to check, then heard her mother give a cry. She turned around. A deeply sunburned bearded man stood smiling, barefoot on the wooden decking. He carried a small box under his arm. "Isn't anyone happy to see me?" he asked.

Frank. Ilona was in his arms first, sobbing against his chest, and Frank was kissing her hair and her neck, then Hilary and Freddie came flying off their stools, Freddie knocking his down in his rush, running to hug any part of their father they could get a hold of. Frank put his arms around all three, and suddenly, for no reason, Hilary began to cry—great, shuddering sobs that exploded in her chest.

Frank was thinner. In some strange way, he looked younger. "Get ready for a crowd on Thanksgiving, Gus," he shouted. "I just invited the whole squadron next door for a dinner on me!"

Marco stood in the background. "Marco," called Frank, "hey, everybody, Marco's here too." The greeting for Marco was subdued but genuine. Everyone came to shake his hand while some of the kitchen staff brought food and drinks to the two police officers who had brought the castaways home.

Hilary stood next to her father and held his hand. She would never let it go, never. She was filled with happiness so great, it was as if there were bubbles in her brain that any moment would lift her right off the ground, and allow her to sail right over the steam tables.

Everyone came to congratulate him, even Mr. Davis, who was somewhat annoyed that Frank had invited 160 men from next door without first checking with him. It was very late when they returned to their rooms. Frank told how he and Marco, marooned on the little key after the boat's engine exploded, lived for days on crayfish and coconut milk, then slogged across shallow barracuda-infested flats to the mainland. They had gotten lost for two days in the mangroves only a few miles from U.S. 1, with alligators and snakes for neighbors, and they were found by the police, who took them home after it was determined that they were not saboteurs or Nazi spies sneaking in from a U-boat on a rubber raft.

Inside the box was a baby alligator that Frank said he found in the mangroves, but that he actually had been given at a roadside stand. They decided to call it Alice, and Ilona said they could keep it, with a *caveat.* If it ever came out of the box, she would simply close up their room, nail it shut with everything they owned inside, and ask Mr. Davis for another room.

Later that night, after Frank carried a sleeping Freddie to his own bed and Ilona chased a protesting Hilary to hers, Ilona brought a jar of Noxzema and gently creamed Frank's shoulders and his face, especially his nose. "Well," she said, "did you have a nice vacation?"

"Vacation." He smiled. "With a V."

17

By January, if things were not good for Hilary, they were certainly getting better. Everyone in Miami was singing "I'm Dreaming of a White Christmas," the residents maudlin with nostalgia over snow that they had run away to escape. A rumor spread through Dade County that FDR had been seen at the Florida East Coast train station which was, of course, quickly scotched by pure logic as there had been no mention of a visit in the paper, and news of FDR's doings continued to come from Washington, D.C. The major excitement in the hotel was that Mr. Davis had had some kind of serious accident and was laid up, bandaged and in traction, in St. Francis hospital. Frank went to see him but could not get a firsthand story because Mr. Davis' jaw was wired shut. Marco's explanation was that Davis was the one stealing the meat and selling it on the black market and Lonzo had found out.

While Ilona made Hilary spend much of her free time on the sisyphean sewing of cards that Hazel had sent for Christmas, stupid things where she had to draw a needle and thread in and out of dotted sketches of Dutch girls and windmills, there was a bright side. For one thing, the war news had improved, despite a daily listing in the newspaper of casualties, and photographs of Londoners digging through the rubble for their children. The Russians had broken the Germans' seventeen-month siege of Stalingrad. American troops were landing in North Africa, not

Europe, true, which is where they really wanted to go, but a more circuitous, tangential approach to, at least the right hemisphere, if not the right continent. That meant the MacIntyres would most likely not have to pack up for Cuba, and that Ilona's family would be able soon to leave Denmark.

In addition, Hilary was a few months short of her twelfth birthday, which was bringing her closer to knowledge, power, freedom, brassieres, and her most current life goal, becoming a spy. Finally, and most important, she had Mickey back.

After a placement test had determined that Bill had the manual dexterity to twist knobs without fumbling and a good serial reaction, which insured that he could apply data in an orderly sequence, he had been sent to bombardier school in Midland, Texas, where he practiced looking through a bombsight on top of a twelve-foot platform and aiming at a little black box below, and learning about things like the factor of probable error, and that Texans liked to yip. His abrupt reassignment to the largest state in the Union was the realization of Mickey's worst fear, which centered around the bull's-eye of trust. Trust was what he had asked her to have in him, and what she had almost achieved, trusting him more than any other person in her life, including the mother whom she trusted until the woman became ill. Now, when she had handed herself over—something like walking with a blindfold—he was gone. If that was what trust was all about, she didn't want it. All the love and passion, all the shared experiences which bound them tighter and tighter, had left her in a vulnerable, precarious position, and instead of a bittersweet, clinging, clutching, brave good-bye like those in all the movies, Bill had left on a bad note, with Mickey angry that he had wasted precious leave time on his family in Iowa and him hurt that she did not understand, and did not seem willing to try. So far, Bill had not been able to hitch a ride back in the nose turret of a B-25, as did other trainees on the weekends. There were only so many turrets to go around and long lines for free rides in any direction. The pain and longing of the separation of the first few weeks, caused Mickey, ever prudent, to change her mind about telling Mr. Radner, when he returned, that she was in love with another man.

It was her way of pulling back, of insuring a measure of financial and emotional protection. No one washed out of bombardier school unless he was a total misfit, which Bill was not. This was it.

Bill would be back only a few more weekends at best before he was shipped out. Then he was going overseas, when and where in doubt. The future was uncertain. It was like a snag in a stocking: no matter how much spit you used, you knew it would sooner or later result in a run. Mr. Radner, at least, continued to pay the bills.

January was a good time for picture shows. Most of the good ones, released for Christmas, were still around. After the movie *Casablanca*, Hilary and Mickey rode the bus back to the hotel, sitting on woven cane seats under an advertisement that warned against spreading rumors, as soldiers hung onto the overhead rail and loomed above them.

"Why did Ingrid Bergman love Humphrey Bogart when she was still married to Paul Henreid?" asked Hilary, still trying to get a handle on the dynamics of the thing.

"She didn't see her husband in a long time," explained Mickey. "She was worried about what would happen to her, being all alone and all."

"I would remember whether I loved somebody or not," said Hilary.

"You don't know anything about love," replied Mickey. She looked distracted, her lovely blue eyes following a camouflaged truck.

Hilary did what she always did when Mickey's interest waned, she livened things up. This time she reached into her pocket. "I got a letter from my pen pal," she said.

"Did you tell him you're a kid yet?" asked Mickey.

"Not exactly. You want me to read it to you?"

"Okay," said Mickey. "Shoot."

> "Dearest" [Hilary seemed embarrassed], "Why haven't you written to me? What's wrong? Do you have someone else? North Africa is a very strange place. The Arabs ride around on mules, with these funny hats, like guys going home from a lodge meeting. When we first landed, the people stood around and watched us shooting and all, and then, when things got quiet, they invited us into a cafe for a glass of wine. We're not allowed to speak to any of the Moslem women which is O.K., since they are covered up anyway. I'll

tell you this. From what I can see, they don't look like Dorothy Lamour. Don't drive me crazy. Your Syl."

"I thought you were going to tell him the truth," said Mickey.

"What about you?" asked Hilary. "Are you going to tell Mr. Radner the truth?"

"That's different. That's a different story entirely. He's not a guy on the front line. There is no truth right now. The truth is on ice."

"I don't get that," said Hilary.

"That's because you're a kid. I can explain certain things to you, but certain things I can't explain. You understand?"

"Sort of."

The bus stopped and a score of soldiers jumped off. One of them winked at Hilary from the sidewalk. She watched as he took his folded cap out of his belt and slipped it on his head.

Mickey held out her nails to check her polish. "You see, certain things are plain. Like that chip right there. You can see it. It's a natural fact, just like you should always take mad money so you can get home. Those things are easy to explain. Or when a guy takes you out to dinner, never order chopped steak. Order the most expensive thing on the menu."

"Why?"

"So he gets the idea you're used to the best."

"I don't see how telling the truth is the same as ordering from a menu."

"I wish you'd hurry and grow up. Then we could really have a conversation. Sometimes I think I'm talking to Daffy Duck."

It was unlike Mickey to be caustic. Hilary pursed her lips and looked out the window.

When they got off the bus, Mickey hurried into the hotel to put on her nurse's-aide uniform. She had almost completed training and had found to her surprise that she enjoyed it. The reason was simply one of success. Mickey was good at what she did, so much so that she was frequently held up as an example to other women in the class. "Watch Mickey," "See the way Mickey does it," the instructor said when they were cutting and rolling surgical dressings, or when they were on hospital wards, scrubbing utensils, which Mickey learned to do with her fingers bent backward, changing dressings, or making beds which were still occupied.

Mickey's hands were deft and sure. While she hated illness and everything about it, her hands did what they were supposed to, smoothing linens, soothing foreheads, as if they had ideas of their own.

Hilary stood alone on the sidewalk, still hurt from the Daffy Duck reference. She consoled herself that at least it was not Dumbo. She didn't want to see Ilona, with whom she seemed lately to be at war. The closer she got to her twelfth birthday, the more intense the battle lines. Everything she wanted, Ilona was determined to block. Like a running back, Ilona was there to say no. The latest skirmish had to do with dungarees, the new fashion that had filtered down from high school. All the kids were wearing them after school and on the weekend, navy blue pants made of stiff fabric like the canvas awning over the portico, and over them, all the girls wore their fathers' old white dress shirts, turned back at the cuffs, the long shirttails hanging to their knees.

Ilona said no to the farmer pants, as she called them, and to Frank's shirt, since he had only three and none that he did not wear. Hilary accused Ilona of wanting her to look like a creep, and Ilona said that Hazel had been right and that if she wasn't careful she would wind up behind the bushes with sailors.

"You know what I wish?" screamed Hilary. "I wish you were an American like Mrs. Weiselmann. I wish you were born here. Then maybe you could understand me."

Ilona, wounded, did something she seldom did. She smacked Hilary on the face, then turned and walked away.

After grabbing writing paper from the desk, Hilary cut through the lobby where Lipschutz, wearing a matching maroon silk tie and handkerchief draped in five points from his pocket, and on his way to an audition at the Clover Club, was trying out his new material on Tessie the switchboard operator. Hilary leaned hard on the french doors to get them open, then walked through the windy, chilly patio and onto the beach. The sand, cleaner than it had been in the last few months, trembled in little shivers, puffed up by the wind in moving rills, from which a few grains at a time would scurry, followed by others, to form new puffs. The soldiers next door were firing their Springfield rifles into the ocean with guards posted to insure that no one walk into the line of fire. As an additional precaution a sign stuck in the sand prohibiting swimming, which was all right with Hilary, since the water in January was too cold anyway.

Hilary looked down at her new Poll Parrot shoes, which she had forgotten to remove, at her shorts, purchased two sizes too big so she could grow into them, and her babyish blouse and sweater. No wonder the kids continued to ignore her. She didn't even dress like them.

A rasping from behind that brought goose pimples to her skin caught Hilary's attention. She turned to see Freddie on the seawall, dragging with a rope an orange crate in which the growing Alice was penned.

"Quit it!" she shouted. "My skin can't stand that."

Freddie continued to drag the crate to the end of the seawall, then carried it carefully off and onto the patio. Hilary sprinted from the beach. "Hey, I'm talking to you. That's a dumb thing to do."

"Alice likes it."

Hilary peeked through the slats. All she could see was the alligator's blunt, shovel-shaped nose. "How do you know? You can't know that. She looks pretty tired to me."

"I do so know it. When I said you wanna go for a ride, she smiled."

Hilary walked away with her hands over her ears. She was determined not to get into an argument with her brother. Freddie had gotten into trouble again, this time for lighting matches in the maintenance shack of the schoolground. Mr. Detwiler, who had demanded that both Frank and Ilona come to see him, pointed out that Freddie was developing a record. A record was something no one wanted. It kept you out of work, it kept you out of a lot of things. It could even keep you out of the Army. There was no mention of college. Mr. Detwiler assumed that Frank and Ilona had no such aspirations for their children.

Frank and Ilona accused each other of being alternately too lenient or too infrequently attentive to their younger child. They decided first to be tough, but the launching of their campaign for stringency was obscured in the last gasp of a dying season, one in which Hialeah Race Track announced only three days before it was scheduled to open that because of the new OPA regulations against pleasure driving, it was closing. This knell was followed in quick succession by Hollywood Kennel Club, Biscayne Kennel

Club, and the Latin Quarter's announcements that they too would not open again until the war's end, or until the OPA had loosened its regulation. Everything good was closing down, extinguished like the exterior advertising signs all over the city. Those hotels that were not occupied by the military and had reasonable plumbing, had all the tourists they wanted, but the tourists were beginning to complain that there was no place to go. None of them counted the tent shows of itinerant evangelists who, South for the winter, were now setting up shop all over Miami.

Hilary took her paper and pencil into the lifeguard shack. There, in privacy and solitude, like Emily Dickinson, she could write about the tragedy of being eleven, not twelve.

It was moldy in the shack and cold, the light admitted only in golden patches. Hilary went inside and sat on the mats with her elbows on her knees, gilded on her forehead and nose. It was a good private place to think. A two-inch skink thought so too and scampered into the corner on its tiny legs. She waited for the words. At first they didn't come. Maybe you had to sit awhile. Then, a line popped into her mind, not one word, but a clause, fully formed, dangling, and ready to be rhymed. She wrote it down, "If I could get over being eleven," and a second one flashed into her mind. She sounded it in her head, liked it, and began to write, "I will think I died and went to heaven." It was like getting gum from a machine.

A soldier's face appeared in the crack of the door. He stepped in. Hilary hoped he wouldn't chase her out and she scribbled her second line quickly so she wouldn't lose it.

He closed the door and stood between Hilary and the opening. "Don't scream," he said, "do like I tell you, and I won't hurt you."

Hilary stood up. "What do you want?" she asked.

"Take off your clothes," he said.

"I'm not going to do that," she said. "I don't even know who you are."

He stepped closer, his unrelieved stare clearly menacing. He looked something like Rudy Steinfeld, only much bigger. "Do what I tell you. Go on, now."

Hilary hesitated, then took off her sweater and folded it neatly on the mat. "My father will be very mad at you," she said. "He'll probably beat you up."

"No he won't," he said. "Because you're not going to tell him, see, you're gonna like this so much, you're gonna want to do it again and again, you're gonna be calling me, and coming over the wall, where's B.J., you'll say, I need my B.J. Ol' B.J. knows what's good for little girls."

Suddenly Hilary jabbed at his eyes with two fingers the way the Three Stooges did, and scrambled for the door, but she had only caught the bridge of his nose, and the soldier put out his arm and knocked her to the ground. She lay on the dirt floor, the pain growing on the side of her head like bread dough, the paper nearby in the dust with her sweater. She tried to move her mouth. Her jaw felt broken.

He yanked her blouse over her arms, then her lisle undershirt, mended near the neck, and threw them both on the ground. Ilona would be mad when she saw how dirty they got. Hilary put her arms up to protect her naked chest. He pulled them down, and ran his scabrous hands over her undeveloped nipples.

"Don't do that," she said. "Cut it out. I don't like it."

"That's because you ain't learned yet. Be patient, it'll take time, have confidence in me." He drew her close, kissing her neck, and blowing into her ear.

"Stop that!" She pulled away. "You can get a fungus like that."

He pulled on the waistband of her shorts. "Take these off," he said.

"No."

"I won't look," he said. "See, I'll turn around. I know how shy girls can be." He turned.

Hilary drew her knees to her chest.

He turned again, this time the smile left his face. "I'll give you exactly two seconds to get them shorts off. Don't make me hit you," he said, moving toward her.

Wet was coming from her mouth, like a baby's dribble. Hilary put her hand up and found her lip was bleeding. She brushed away a trace of blood with the back of her hand. "You made me bleed," she whimpered.

The soldier knelt down and grabbed one of her shorts legs and began to pull. "I never had to work so hard for a little loving in all my blame life. Now, help me," he said, "or I'm gonna have to hit you again."

Hilary experienced a wave of nausea. She hoped she wouldn't

have to throw up in front of him. "Daddy," she yelled, "Daddy, come and get me!"

"Daddy," he said, "Daddy, you stupid little bitch, I'm Daddy enough for you. I told you to be patient. Didn't I? Well didn't I?"

He struck her again and again on her face, almost casually, as if swatting a fly, while yanking on her shorts. When they came sliding over her shoes, he reached into the waistband of her cotton underpants that said Saturday and pulled them off as well.

Hilary lay shivering on the floor of the beach shack. She had to go to the bathroom, and she covered her face with her hands. Not even Ilona saw her naked anymore, ever since she was allowed to bathe in privacy. She would never be able to look anyone ever in the face again.

The soldier opened his pants. His member was soft. "You're going to have to do your part. That's what a real woman would do. Now, I want you to take your hand, gentle like," he put it in her hand. Hilary shrunk back and pulled away. The soldier struck her again on her head. "Cooperate, everything will be a lot easier if you just cooperate."

She held it in her hand, something horrible, like the time she and Freddie went to the fishing contest on the pier and the dockmaster slapped a piece of dead flounder on each of their palms for bait.

The sound of scraping could be heard outside.

"Move your hand," he whispered, "up and down. Move your hand."

"Hilary," the voice of Freddie outside the shack.

"Halt," another voice. "The beach is off limits."

"My sister is out here," said Freddie, "but I can't find her."

"Maybe she went to the picture show."

"No. She went this afternoon. I saw her going into the shack."

"I didn't see her, but you can take a look if you like."

"Freddie!" Hilary tried to scream but the soldier put his hand over her mouth. Then he began to adjust himself, closing his pants and tucking in his shirt.

"Don't you say anything about this. If you do, I'll come back and kill you," he said.

With trembling fingers, Hilary put on her shorts and her undershirt, the tears blinding her, picked up her shirt and sweater, and opened the door.

"Halt," said the sentry on horseback. "Who goes there?"

"It's me," said Hilary. She began to cry.

The sentry shined a flashlight on her face. "What happened to you?" he asked.

"That's my sister," said Freddie.

"Nothing," said Hilary. "I fell."

"You sure?"

"I'm sure."

"I thought that's where you were," said Freddie, who followed after her, dragging the orange crate across the patio.

At first Hilary was too numbed and too ashamed to speak. The soldier didn't have to threaten to kill her. She had no thought of telling what happened to her to anyone. This was not something that occurred by accident. This was something she caused, something she was responsible for.

Freddie looked at her peculiarly. "You're all dirty," he said. "And your mouth's bleeding."

"I fell."

"How come he didn't come out too?" Hilary didn't answer.

Freddie poked his face between the slats of the crate. "Alice, you want to eat? You hungry, girl?"

Hilary walked toward the kitchen with her head down. When she saw Frank standing against the french doors smoking a cigar, her resolve melted away. She fell against him and began to cry. He dropped his cigar and cupped her bruised face in his hands, turning it to the soft muted interior light so he could see it better. "What happened?" His voice thundered across the patio. Panic shone in his eyes. "Tell me."

"Hilary was in the shack with a soldier," said Freddie. Hilary started crying again.

Everything that followed was foreshortened, like someone closing up a telescope. Frank ran for Ilona, Hilary was put to bed, Freddie, excluded from the room, was told to get fresh chop meat from Marco for Alice, and Dr. Hershbaum was called. No one else was told anything. Hilary lay on her bed with a cover drawn to her chin, while Ilona gently washed away the dirt.

"It wasn't my fault," she whispered. "Don't be mad at me, Ma, I didn't know he was there."

"Who was he?" asked Ilona.

"I never saw him before."

"You didn't know him?" asked Ilona, her eyes squinted in suspicion.

"No."

"What was he wearing?" asked Frank.

"Soldier pants, and a soldier shirt."

"Jesus, Mary, and Joseph!" shouted Frank. He smashed his fist into the wall. The plaster shattered, but did not fall, instead hung suspended in starlike streaks. "Point him out to me, I'll kill him! I'll kill the son of a bitch with my bare hands! We'll go from hotel to hotel if we have to but we'll find him!"

"What are you saying?" asked Ilona. "How can she go and identify him? And walk past all those soldiers. She'll have to tell what happened, and it will be in the paper." Ilona turned to Hilary. "What did he do?" she asked. "You can tell me. I'm your mother."

"He made me take off my sweater, and then he pulled off my shirt and my undershirt and . . ." Hilary looked around the room, for a place to hide, "then he pulled off my shorts and he punched me."

"Did he touch you?" asked Frank.

Hilary began to cry again. "Sure he touched me. He had to touch me to punch me and get off the shorts."

Ilona pushed Frank out the door. "It's no use. Go outside. I'll talk to her. Did he touch you anyplace he's not supposed to?"

"Yes."

"Show me where."

Hilary pointed to her chest.

"Anyplace else?"

"No."

"You sure?"

"Yes." The schedule of points. Everybody was interested, even her mother.

By the time Dr. Hershbaum came, whistling "Don't Sit Under the Apple Tree," the situation had begun to froth. Frank was in a rage, a blind fury that made him pace and punch. Ilona, a grieving Pietà, said she could cut out her tongue. Freddie had returned, peevish and cranky, with his orange crate and the stuporous Alice, saying that Alice was beginning to get carsick. Ilona allowed him in, saying *sotto voce* to Frank, "You and your *fakokte* alligator."

Dr. Hershbaum gave Hilary a sedative, an injection into her

arm that made her feel as if she were under water. It was in this state that she finally put together the word and its meaning. If that was rape, it was a stupid thing to do to anyone. Did T.H. finally want this? She didn't think so. T.H. didn't act like he was crazy.

"You're lucky," Dr. Hershbaum whispered to Frank. "This could have had a bad ending. As it is, she'll get over it, maybe one or two nightmares. All in all, I'd say you're very fortunate."

"Can you get a disease?" asked Ilona. "From someone's hands?"

"It depends on where he touched her," said Dr. Hershbaum.

"He only touched her on top," said Ilona. "But I thought maybe germs could run around on the skin."

"Not that far," said Dr. Hershbaum, who led them into a corner of the room. "The thing to do," he whispered, "is forget about it. Stop walking around with long faces. No wonder the kid is lying there in shock. If she thinks you're upset, she'll stay upset. Try and act like nothing's happened."

"How can we?" asked Ilona. "The man did a terrible thing."

"The man did nothing," said Dr. Hershbaum, "unless you're not telling me everything."

"We told you all there is to know," said Ilona.

"Well then, don't make a big deal out of it. She's not even twelve yet. She'll forget it, if you will. But if everytime she looks at you you look like someone died, she'll keep thinking of it, and remembering it."

"I'm gonna get that bastard," said Frank. "He spoiled her."

"Forget it, Frank. That's the kind of thinking that leads to nowhere. It's oldtime thinking, Frank, from the last century. He can't contaminate her. He knocked her around a little bit, that's all, but bruises heal. She's not a pitcher of cream. She's a nice little kid that met up with a lunatic and that gags when she sees a tongue depressor. Why don't you take your wife and go to the movies?"

"I couldn't leave her," said Ilona, "not now. All alone after what happened to her."

Dr. Hershbaum closed his bag. "I got my induction notice," he said. No one responded.

When Frank and Ilona tiptoed into their own room, Hilary

called after them with a floppy tongue to leave the light on and the door open.

Freddie stared at her from his bed. "You want to see a star in an apple?" he asked. "I could cut one open and show you." Hilary slid deeper beneath the cover. He continued to stare at her until he fell asleep.

The next day Hilary stayed in bed all day long not speaking to anyone, not even Frank, feeling dirty all over again, even though she took six baths, one after another, and scrubbed her body over and over, especially the places where he had touched her, getting the water as hot as she could, to expunge the feel of his fingers. When she wasn't bathing, she lay with her face to the wall, curled up under her covers. Ilona got her to eat only because she hand fed her tea with orange blossom honey and chicken soup, a posset as golden as Mrs. Steinfeld's earrings, with globules of fat floating on the top that would be scraped away later into the salvage vat earmarked for bullets.

Late that afternoon, Mr. Lonzo came to see Frank. One of the things he asked Frank was a rundown on the situation in the storage locker. Frank replied that in the last few weeks there had been no pilferage of any kind.

"I didn't think you'd have any more trouble," said Mr. Lonzo.

Frank knew enough not to question him further, but he could not keep out the fleeting, tickling thought that Marco somehow was right, that there was a connection between the thefts, Mr. Davis, and Mr. Lonzo. The question was, why? In effect, that meant Mr. Davis was stealing from himself.

Mr. Lonzo read his question. "Some people," he said, in his cryptic manner, "think they're smarter than anyone else. Those kind of people, they underestimate the rest of us, plain guys like you and me, Frank. They think we're stupid. They think because we didn't have much schooling, we don't know anything. You and me, we're up front. These other people, you don't know what's in their minds. They're dogs. It takes a dog to rob that hand that feeds them."

Mr. Lonzo shot his cuffs, then waved a cuff-linked hand to one of his lieutenants, who quickly walked away. "I heard about your kid, Frank."

"What did you hear?" asked Frank, diffident yet courteous.

"It's okay. I'm a family man myself. I understand. You want

help? I could get one of the boys to take care of him. Just point him out, or give us his name. We'll do the rest. Send him to the hospital. Put him right next to our friend. Break both his legs, his jaw. Just say the word. He'll never bother another kid again. We'll even fix it so he'll never bother anybody."

Frank thought about it. The offer sounded good. He wanted to see the man smashed, lying in a pool of blood with bone shards sticking out of his flesh, a heavy boot kicking him in the face, in the balls. This was his fantasy. The reality was that even with remedy in easy reach, he could not do it, primarily because it involved dragging his pigtailed daughter from one hotel to the next.

"It's done," he said. "Believe me, I'd like to kill him, but nothing anyone does to the bastard will change what's done. He didn't actually get her, you understand, but he scared her."

Mr. Lonzo's lieutenant returned carrying a radio, a dome-shaped Philco with a green tuning eye. "Something for your kids. I heard your set broke down."

"Hey," said Frank, accepting the radio, "that's really swell of you. I don't know what to say."

"It's nothing," said Mr. Lonzo affably. "You don't have to say nothing." He snapped his fingers and left his man wheeling after him in a perfect rightface, as Frank carried the radio into their room.

"Well," he said, "what do you think? Hilary, look what Mr. Lonzo brought us." He placed it on the rattan nightstand and plugged it in.

Freddie ran to the radio, turned it on, and after an initial crackle, watched the green tuning eye close on "Amos 'n' Andy." Frank walked out of the room, but not without an anxious look at Hilary.

I bin thinkin' 'bout gittin' a job, Sapphire, but dis ain' de right time.

Is yo gonna tell me January is a slow month like yo' said about December and November?

Honey, it ain' so much de right month as it is de right year. Dis ain' the right year fo' gitting a job.

Freddie turned up the volume, then sat on Hilary's bed, keeping a distance. She didn't say get off and kick her feet at him, which is what she usually did when she was sick and didn't feel good, and so he stayed, flopping on his belly with his hands folded under his chin.

"Lionel is back," he said. "Winona brought him home."

Git yo'self a job or get out.

Honey, I can't git no job right now.

Den git out o' dis house, I can't stand no mo'. Git out! I means it, Mr. George Kingfish Stevens. Git out o' dis house, you big bum!

Hilary turned her face from the wall. Freddie noticed his sister's blackened eye. "You want a pink belly?" he asked.

"I don't want to play like that anymore," she said.

"As long as you live?"

"Never."

Andy, me and de Battle-ax done opened up a second front las' night. To tell yo' de truth, Andy, she done throwed me out on my ear. Course, all my friens' coaxin' me to come stay wid dem. But I figgured dat yo' is my best frien' an' if I went any place else to sleep, yo' would be mad.

I don't git mad dat easy, Kingfish.

The light from the back of the radio played along the wall.

"When I was a little kid," said Freddie, "I thought dust came in a sunbeam."

"I didn't," said Hilary. "I knew dust was everywhere. Even when you sleep, it's going right into your nose."

18

Hilary returned to school, a daily ordeal in which she adopted the wearing of sunglasses, old streaked and scratched Polaroids belonging to Ilona that slipped down the bridge of her nose and made her see double. She could not face anyone and spent whole days staring at her shoes, the perforated toes of which she was really beginning to hate, expecting everyone in school to recognize the mark, whatever it was, that she heard Ilona whisper to Frank that she had.

The kids looked at her peculiarly and so did her teacher, peering at her and her shoes through eyes narrowed like the slats in a venetian blind, which further confirmed Hilary's suspicions that somehow everyone had seen the mark and knew that she had been naked in a lifeguard shack with a soldier.

Now she spent all her spare time in Cimmerian insulation, propped up on her bed, plodding through a distracted melancholy reading of *Treasure Island* and *Oliver Twist* in whose frayed story threads she noted someone was always lurking somewhere to get someone else. The other members of the MacIntyre family did what they could. Freddie bought her a Frank Sinatra record out of his own money, even though they did not have a Victrola and he was still mourning the death of Alice whose fuscous, stiffened body Frank had been forced to pry loose from the orange crate. Hilary's parents had more trouble dealing with the problem. Frank was vigilant, scouring hallway and shack, combing covey hiding places like a carpet sweeper, yet seemed unable to look at her, and when Ilona came to talk to her, sitting gravely on the edge of her bed, it was through veiled and cryptic Austro-Hungarian aphorisms.

"I would like you to get out," Ilona began clearly enough. "I don't like your color."

Color in Miami was a subject on which most people were expert, the gradients and the speed of tan being not only a measure of one's leisure and one's health, but of one's sense. Only idiots got third-degree burns on the first day of their vacation.

"I don't want to, Ma."

"All this lying around inside, it's not good for you. I don't want to force you," said Ilona, when that was exactly what she was prepared to do.

Hilary began to cry, a sudden freshet that stopped as quickly as it started, the lability of which made both Frank and Ilona afraid to say or do anything that would cause its recurrence. "I can't look at anyone," Hilary said.

"No one knows," said Ilona.

"Yes they do. Everyone in the whole world knows."

"You know," said Ilona, beginning the muddy part. Hilary knew this because her mother looked intent, as if she were composing musical notes. "In my village there were always gypsies. Once, in the winter, there was a gypsy woman in labor outside our house. My mother called to her and said, come in the house, have your baby indoors, where you and the baby will be safe and warm. The woman said no, she did not want the baby to get used to a house, for then it could never unlearn soft ways. My sister and I watched from the window. The woman found a ditch and dug it out, the ground was hard, you know, then she lay in it, and had the baby. We didn't see that part, but my sister ran outside and when she came back she told me that the gypsy woman took the new baby and plunged it into a stream of ice water. To harden it, she said."

Why was Ilona talking to her about gypsies dunking babies in water? Hilary hoped she would come to the point. When it was clear that the point was not forthcoming, nor would likely ever come, Hilary turned back to her book to the page she last read where Fagin and the Artful Dodger were teaching Oliver how to pick pockets. "I want to read, Ma," she said.

Ilona sighed and was about to leave when there was a knock at the door, a timid little rap.

"Yes?" She opened the door a crack and peeked out. "What do you want?"

Mickey stood in the doorway, rigged in the raiment of someone about to go out on the town—a strapless black rayon dress, a black satin hair ribbon tied loosely through her hair, her lips outlined in a perfect scarlet bow. "Can I talk to her?" she asked.

"She's tired, and she's going to sleep early," said Ilona.

"I know what happened," said Mickey softly.

"Nothing happened," said Ilona. "Nothing at all."

"I know. Please let me talk to her."

"Let her in," said Frank from the other room. "She might be good for her."

Mickey came in shyly, sat at the edge of the bed, and crossed her legs, arranging them one over the other so that they lay extended and taut, the toes of her feet pointing to the floor like the tail of a bird dog. "Can I talk to her alone?"

"I'm her mother," said Ilona, an announcer at the ball game, calling positions.

Frank shouted that he couldn't find a certain shirt, and Ilona reluctantly, and with a click of her teeth against her tongue, left to help him search.

Mickey's perfume spread over the room like a salve. "Hi, sugar," she said.

Hilary swallowed hard to keep the tears in check. She had not seen Mickey since it happened. Mickey picked up the black Sinatra record and touched its paper label. "I heard this," she said. "He's even better than Bing Crosby. His voice slides right up and down your back."

"I don't care," said Hilary.

Mickey bent down to rub one of her feet. "I walked my tootsies off today looking for a gig. I was all over the city. But with the Latin Quarter closed and a lot of other places closing down, all the girls are scrambling for the same places. The only openings around are in the new review at the Versailles, but when I got there, it was too late. They had everybody already lined up, ponies, horses, specialties. Something might turn up at the Clover Club, though. They told me they'd give me a call."

"I thought you didn't believe in work anymore," said Hilary.

"Well, that's still true. I don't believe in working when you don't have to. I just wanted to see if I could get something. Besides, it's my profession. You have to keep in touch, otherwise they forget about you. Hey," said Mickey brightly, like the sudden flare of a match. "Did you read that FDR and Churchill met in Casablanca? FDR flew five thousand miles across the Atlantic Ocean just to talk about unconditional surrender. Don't you wonder if there really is a Rick's American Café and if they were in it? Probably not. High-toned people like that don't go to clubs. Although once Eddie Rickenbacker sat in the front row of the Pago Pago and the MC made up a cute song about him."

"Who cares?"

There was a pause, heavy and laden like September humidity. Mickey began again, with the crispening edge of desperation. "You want to see Hedy Lamarr in *White Cargo?*"

"I hate her. She looks like Shirley Leone."

"I don't like to see you like this."

"Like what?"

"I'm not blind, honey. You know what I'm talking about. Look, I'll come straight out. What happened to you, it happened to me. When I was nine. I understand what you're thinking now."

For a while there was silence. Hilary continued to swallow hard. "It was awful," she whispered to the wall.

"I know. You never forget it. My uncle did it to me. I still see his face, riding up and down, up and down over me. But you can't let it get the better of you. At first I thought I was a bad girl and I prayed to the Lord Jesus to make me good. But then I thought, much later you understand, that's just how men are. They can't help it any more than we can help being what we are. Look, when I do my lipstick wrong, I wipe it off and start all over again. I cream it all off, so none of the old color shows through. I still remember that I did it wrong. But I don't see it. You have to do the same thing. If you don't, it gets you for the rest of your life. You got to say to yourself, I'm not going to let one person stop me from having fun, no matter what dumb thing he did. The guy, whoever he is, he's not in his room crying at the wall. You understand what I'm saying?"

"I didn't bother him."

"I know. But you were there. And men have this nature. They can't help themselves. When they get hot, they don't think."

First Ilona talking about gypsies, now Mickey talking about being hot, when it was so chilly that day in the shack, she had to wear her sweater. Suddenly the idea appeared, fully formed and dripping. Grown-ups did not talk in code, rather, something happened to them to make them a little crazy, including the soldier in the shack who was the best example of all.

Mickey smoothed one of Hilary's braids, tucking stray blond hairs into the plaiting with her fingertips. "I forget you're not even twelve yet. That's because you're almost as tall as I am. Your birthday's coming along in a few months. This year I'm going to be right on the dot with your present. What do you want?"

"Nothing," said Hilary.

Ilona stood in the doorway with her hands clasped over her waist. "She wants dungarees. What farmers wear."

"Oh," said Mickey, "blue jeans. I used to wear blue jean overalls all the time." She stood up to leave and pulled the bow of her ribbon tighter, then opened her compact to check her nose. "Listen," she said to Ilona, "maybe she could come with me sometime to the hospital. She could help me give out cigarettes."

"She's too young," said Ilona.

Frank stood in the doorway between the rooms, his blond hair brilliantined into a shiny slick the color of sand when the tide pulls out. "What do you hear from the lieutenant?" he asked.

"He's trying to get back for a weekend."

Mickey pursed her bow mouth at the mirror, trilled her fingers in good-bye, and left.

"You should wear your hair like that," said Frank.

"Like how?"

"Loose and ripply with a ribbon. It's pretty."

Ilona stood in the door jamb like someone on a plank. "Do you want me to leave the door open?" she asked.

"No," said Hilary. "Close it."

Hilary remembered most his teeth, yellowed and stained, speckled like an old man's. She yanked the pillow from beneath her head and hit it, tentatively at first, then slapping it harder and harder, finally making a fist the way Gus showed her, her thumb outside, and slamming into the pillow with all her might. "You rotten bum," she whispered hoarsely into the goosefeathers that Ilona had brought all the way from the old country. "You stinking mean bully! I hate you like poison. You crazy moron. I hope you die." She lay back, then turned and struck the pillow one last blow. "Scratch that out about dying," she said. "Just get diarrhea and throw up a lot."

Mr. Radner's bomb part plant was going smoothly, the conversion from pencils that swiveled to lethal weapons a natural succession, like a pupa becoming a butterfly. Even his brother-in-law, usually able to muck things up, was not able to undo the efficient system he had devised. Confident that everything would run smoothly, he left ice-slicked, snowbound Philadelphia and came to Miami for a three-week vacation, accompanied during the first week by his wife. When she left, complaining that most of the good stores on Lincoln Road had closed and that Miami Beach had turned into a military base, he resumed his surreptitious life with Mickey.

She had changed. He put that down to women's glands and took her out to Joe's Stone Crabs, all the way down South Beach near Million Dollar pier, where Lipschutz was now a smash hit, and thinking seriously of getting his nose fixed, a new procedure, as he had explained to Mickey, where some plastic surgeon smashed your nose in with a hammer, then snipped off the excess.

Wearing a cloth bib embroidered with the signature *Claudette Colbert*, Mickey dipped the large cracked claws in melted butter, and popped them, dripping, one after another into her mouth. She was trying to make up her mind whether or not to dip the next one into butter, lime juice, or mustard, when Mr. Radner, his bib reading *Walter Winchell*, suddenly said, "I know about the soldier."

Mickey had expected it, like standing in the wind as darkness thickens the sky, waiting for the first big drops to turn your hair lacquer into glue. It was only a matter of time. Now that it was out in the open, it wasn't as bad as she had anticipated. Still ravenous despite the revelation, she continued to dip her stone crab claws.

"At first I was sore," he said, "sore as hell. I wanted to kick you the hell out. But then I thought, no, she's human, she's got feelings. You were probably lonely for me, doll. I understand that."

Mickey chose the butter, dipped, and swallowed. Her mouth shone with grease.

"So, what do you have to say for yourself?" he asked.

"Nothing," said Mickey. "I have got nothing to say for myself. I don't know what to say."

"You could say you were sorry."

"Sol, I had a few dates. Nothing else."

"My information is different, sweetheart. But that's not the point. It's in the past. The point is, I missed you, baby. Bad. Without you, I don't know, I feel myself rushing ahead to some place I'm not ready to go yet. With you, I feel like a kid. Like life is just beginning. Mickey, I asked my wife for a divorce."

Mickey sat up straight, wiping her hands on her napkin, while the waitress brought them finger bowls.

"Why?" she asked.

"Why? What kind of dumb question is that? So you and I can get married, that's why. Why did you think?"

She had not thought it through that far. Marriage to Sol Radner was not something she had planned. She had hoped that he would have left her with some money, enough so that all the months spent with him had a payoff, a yield, a piece of jewelry she could sell, some stocks she could trade—she knew girls who got certificates—something tangible. The thought of lying beside him night after night and waking up with him at her side as her face creased deeper and deeper like a blouse that never got ironed, was just not something she had thought of.

"Of course, you'll have to sign a prenuptial agreement. It's not unusual for a second marriage. I worked that out with my lawyer. On account of my kids. It's only fair. It's not right that they should suffer just because I don't want to be married anymore to their mother. And then, I want to do right by Doris, her alimony and all, I'm even keeping her moron brother in the business. I'll treat you like I always have, only better. You'll come back to Philadelphia with me, there's not much to stay in Miami for now, but that don't mean we won't come back when it gets miserable. I'll even take you to New York, you can see that Italian singer all the kids are so crazy about, that skinny kid, with the bow tie, I forgot his name."

"Sinatra."

"Well, whadya say? I thought you'd be happy."

"I don't know," said Mickey. "It's a lot to think about."

"Ah, for Christ sake, baby, don't hold a grudge. You see all the guys in here. I bet you most of them smack their old ladies around once in a while." He threw down his napkin. "Jesus, I thought you were gonna throw your arms around me, and we would have a big celebration."

"You want a fresh napkin, sir?" asked the waitress.

He waved her away. "You sure know how to throw cold water in a guy's face." He flipped a box of nylons on the table. "Here. You might as well take them. But I'll tell you something, even if you said yes now, even if you did what I wanted you to do, it wouldn't mean a damn thing, and you know why, because you spoiled it, that's why."

"I'm sorry, Sol."

"I'm sorry, Sol," he mimicked. "Forget it. Forget what I said. You're sitting there with that goddamned dumb expression on your face, is it him?"

Mickey was on thin ice. She had to be very careful, move slowly, and spread her weight. The fact was, the thought of life without Radner was scary. It would put her right back where she started from, which was nowhere.

"No," she lied, "it's not him."

"I don't believe you," he said.

"Honest, Sol." She smiled at him, and took his hand. "I missed you so much. I been so crazy without you, that's the only reason I didn't act the way you expected me to."

"You missed me a lot."

"That's right."

"I'm gonna give you a chance to prove it. Right now. Let's go home." He signaled for the check and Mickey reached beneath the table to slip back the straps of her heels over her ankles. The time was coming for a decision. Soon. She slipped the package of nylons into her purse.

The thefts from the storage locker had ceased, just as Mr. Lonzo had predicted. As hard as it was to believe, the evidence pointed to Mr. Davis, who had returned to work in the front office, a silent wraith with wired molars. Frank figured out that

Davis must have borrowed heavily from Lonzo for his percentage of the hotel and was unable to meet what Frank guessed were heavy interest payments, the reason for selling his own goods on the black market. Although Frank and Marco crewed for other boats in the nighttime search organized by the Coast Guard, the sinking of ships on the Florida coastline was on the decrease, due to the stepped up methods of detecting U-boats, and the fact that most of the German submarines had been called back to the Nordsee where it was determined they would be of better use in the coming counteroffensive against the Allies.

None of these things mattered. Frank's real worry was Hilary, who seemed to be getting life's knocks despite his determination to shield her from them, changing from a lively, playful little girl to the solemn squatter in Hilary's room. Frank was not sure what he wanted for Hilary, in fact, he did not think of her much beyond the present, primarily because he did not think of himself much past that point, but he did not want her afraid of every soldier in Miami Beach. Despite his rage toward the man who molested her, which he could taste every time he saw her face, he entered Hilary's name in the Colonel Pigtail contest sponsored by the Army Air Corps, which was looking for a little girl between the ages of eight and twelve to serve as a mascot. He sent in an old photograph of Hilary at the age of ten with big ears and squinting eyes. Hilary was angry when she learned that her name had been entered, especially with that dumb picture, which the newspaper printed. Frank argued that she had a good chance of winning, reasoning to himself that if she won, it would make her laugh again, and run with Freddie through the hotel, putting jelly on the doors, and to hell with Davis, and somehow reconcile all of them to the armed forces.

Frank was not the only one with active plans for Hilary's rehabilitation. Mickey stopped by almost every day, although it was several weeks before Hilary agreed to go with her to the ultramodern Nautilus hotel—so stellar it had a star over its "i"—which had been converted into a military hospital. There were several on the beach as well as cozy, screened-in blister shacks erected on vacant lots to dispense Band-Aids and aspirin. Ilona, who was afraid Hilary would turn into a bookworm, one of those neutered women who pin their hair into buns and never get married, urged her to go, despite her strong reservations about Mickey.

They went the day after they made the late-afternoon show of *White Cargo*, and images of Tondelayo, gorgeous, elusive, and mysterious, all of which Hilary was sure she could never be, urged her more than her mother ever could, to prepare for a contingency plan. In this case, it was to do good in the world.

Mickey gave last-minute instructions to Hilary, who bent to pull up her socks as they walked down Collins Avenue, where open trucks bounced over potholes, pearly white periwinkles poked through the cracks in the sidewalk, and a mockingbird, flicking its tail from side to side, chattered to them from the curving trunk of a coconut palm.

"Now," she said, "when they ask how old you are, we have to tell a fib and say you're old enough. I'll say you're my sister. And don't be afraid of what you see. I was scared the first day, but I got used to it. Just remember, these boys are happy to see you. All you have to do is hand over Chiclets and cigarettes from the tray. You got that?"

Hilary nodded.

As they approached the circular driveway, Hilary stopped as if shoved back by a gale, the kind of stiff, unyielding wind that sucks away your breath. Behind the driveway on two front porches were men in robes and pajamas, propped up in high-backed wooden wheelchairs like a window display. Some of them wore multicolored ribbons on their chests that Mickey called fruit salad.

"What's wrong?" asked Mickey.

"They can see me without my clothes."

"You might as well get used to it right now. That's how men look at women all the time. It's like they got those dollar glasses you send away for, and so what? You can't stand there all day. We all look the same to them, what you got, I got, only a little more, that's all. They're not seeing something they haven't seen before or won't see again. And I got a little old wardrobe mistress to thank for those words of advice. The sweetest lady you ever want to meet, used to sew up our costumes, she told me that when they wanted me to wear these cherries, like I was a tree. I said I couldn't get out in front of all those people, with the lights and all. And what I just told you, she told me."

Mickey led Hilary upstairs to a closet, where she took out a tray filled with Chiclets and cigarettes to which Hilary immediately clung as if magnetized, having lost all of the bravado of the summer before when she marched into the polio ward of Variety Children's Hospital and pierced through the gristle in Jackie Snyder's earlobes.

She handed a package of gum to Hilary as they approached a room with elaborate yellow stucco moldings that had been converted into a four-bed ward.

"Here," she said, "take this to that guy over there."

Mickey nodded in the direction of a burn case, a blanket covering the man's naked chest, his hands and head bandaged, with only his eyes, nostrils, and lips showing.

"I can't," said Hilary.

"Sure you can."

"I feel stupid."

The men in the ward began to call to Mickey, who smiled in return, with the *noblesse* of the needed. "This is Hilary," she announced. "She's a contestant in the Colonel Pigtails contest."

"She's got my vote," said one man.

"Why'd you have to tell him that?" Hilary turned on her heel.

"Come back here," said Mickey. "Honestly, sometimes I don't know what gets into you. There's nothing wrong with being in a contest. A lot of girls would give their eyeteeth to be in one. Now look here, it's easy as pie. Watch how I do it." Mickey took the package of Raleighs to the burned man, smiling in a perky, winning way that dimpled her cheeks and showed the tiny space between her teeth. "I didn't forget about you," she said. "Last time all we had were Chesterfields."

"You oughta be in the movies," he said, speaking like a ventriloquist without moving his lips. The words could have been coming out of his nostrils.

Two of the other men were griping about the tourists that they could see from their windows. "Now you tell me," said one, "why there has to be all that dancing and music past nine o'clock. What if a fella wants to listen to the radio, or wants to go to sleep. Can't do it. Why? Because some slacker down there's doing a rhumba."

Hilary held the tray and wondered if soldiers were watching the guests dance on the patio of the Flamingo Arms, while Mickey plumped up the pillow behind the last man's head. "Now," she said to Hilary, as they continued into the hall, "wasn't that easy?"

The second room on the floor contained a man in isolation. His quarantine was not the result of infectious disease or of rank, but of what was originally thought to be a lumbosacral strain and had later been diagnosed by the staff psychiatrist as conversion hysteria, camptocormie, in his case, a hysterical bent back. The man was kept segregated to protect him from ridicule, and, more important, to avoid contagion to other suggestible patients.

He swayed toward them, figured like a seven.

"Do you walk like that all the time?" asked Hilary.

"I'm looking for my discharge," said the man.

"How do you sleep at night?" asked Hilary. "Can you straighten out when you go to sleep, or do your feet go up in the air?"

The man looked up at her from beneath bushy eyebrows. "I sleep on my side."

Mickey bent over so he could see her face without having to strain himself. "Would you like something from the tray?"

"Can you help me stand up straight?" he asked.

"No, sir," replied Mickey. "I surely don't think I can do that."

The last room contained two beds and a man flown in from North Africa with fractured vertebrae. He lay on his stomach, sandwiched between two mattress frames, suspended like a hot dog about to be grilled.

"Go on," said Mickey. "See what he wants."

"I think he wants to get out of that thing."

"Never mind that smart stuff. Do like I tell you. Show me you're not a little kid."

Hilary approached him slowly, stopping to flip her braids over her shoulders.

"Don't look at me," he said.

"Don't look at me either," she replied.

The man turned his head in her direction like a mechanical doll. "Things must be pretty bad, they're sending a kid around."

"You want a Chiclet, yes or no?"

"What flavors you got?"

"Spearmint and cinnamon."

"Is that cinnamon red hot?"

"I don't know," said Hilary.

"Well, find out. I don't like it except it's red hot."

Hilary turned to Mickey. "He wants me to test it first," she whispered.

"Okay," said Mickey. "Do like he wants."

Hilary popped a Chiclet into her mouth and chewed it thoroughly, trying to make a serious determination of its degree of bite. She returned to the man suspended between the mattress frames. "It's not red hot," she said, "but it prickles your mouth."

"That's good enough," he said. "I'll take one."

She put it in his hand.

"You ever see a famous person?" he asked.

"I saw Al Capone's house," she said, "and I saw Clark Gable."

"I saw the most famous person you can see," he said. "I saw FDR waving from a jeep, a big smile on his face just like his pictures, that cigarette holder clamped inside his teeth. As near to me as I am to you."

That was about as close as Hilary was to Clark Gable, if one didn't count the height of the tree into which she had climbed, but she didn't say so. This was not the time for contest.

"Was Clark Gable that close to you?" he asked.

"No," she said. "He was pretty far away. About two blocks." The man looked disappointed. "Maybe three blocks," she amended.

"Then how did you know it was him?"

"Someone said, 'There comes Clark Gable.' "

That night, Hilary sat on her bed composing a letter, while Freddie, who had complained earlier that the Lone Ranger was not the real Lone Ranger but someone else, sat listening to Bob Hope. Frank and Ilona were arguing in the next room.

"So I thought," said Ilona, "that if I made another pushke and we saved, each week, a little here, a little there, we could put money aside for a house."

"A house, Ilona, what are you saying?"

"At least it would give us something to plan for."

Frank jumped up. "Jesus," he said. "I just read an ad in the paper that tells you how a man of forty can retire in fifteen years. In a few years I'll be thirty-five and I don't have enough put aside to last two months. I thought you'd be happy that Davis let us keep the two rooms. Now you're asking me to put money aside for a house. You're never satisfied."

Don't make him mad, thought Hilary.

"You can't do this to me. You can't pressure a man like this."

Freddie, with a smile on his face, seemed oblivious to the fight.

"It's not what you think," said Ilona. "A cigar here, a haircut there, I'll make do with all my clothes, you do the same. We don't have to worry about the car for the duration."

"At that rate, we'll have a house when you get rheumatism and can't move your fingers and I'll be six feet under."

"God forbid."

"Look, there's no sense in wanting something we can't have. A house takes money. Keeping it up takes money. Furniture takes money. I see my brother-in-law, he's tied up till the day he dies on payments and mortgages, the same with my old man. It's all we can do to keep our heads above water. A house is a commitment. Worse than even a marriage. It means they lock you up and throw away the key."

"Other people put money aside. Why can't we?"

"Other people get a boost, a leg up, other people are crooked."

"Maybe another job, Frank. People are making lots of money in war work. Winona and her son are going to Detroit to get jobs in a war plant. She says they're going to make a lot of money."

There was silence, then Ilona speaking again, this time more softly. Hilary couldn't hear the words.

"You don't know when to quit." The door slammed.

Hilary wet the end of her pencil and pressed hard on the paper.

Dear Private Farber,

I did a bad thing. The only thing I can say in my defense is that I was too young to know any better. There is no way to tell you except straight out. Here it is. I'm not 22. I'm twelve. Actually, I'm not twelve yet, but I will be soon. Probably by the time you get this letter I will be twelve. I still would like to write to you if you are not too mad at me. The picture I sent to you is not me. It is my best friend Mickey. I probably would have sent her picture to you even if I was 22. I will never be as pretty as Mickey. I am enclosing a picture of me and my brother. I am on the left.

Your friend I hope,
Hilary MacIntyre

Bill and Mickey saw each other for the first time in two months sitting in the Concord Cafeteria, she with a red cross on her sleeve, he in his pinks; they sparred with the elaborate courtesy of a pair of courting egrets.

At first they just looked at each other, checking for remembered features, making tentative, half-finished statements about the springlike weather and the state of each other's health. Then each began to move in closer, relishing the sight of each other, Mickey beginning to feel restored, as if the other half of her had been glued back on again, Bill astonished to see that she was even more beautiful than he had remembered. Leaning on their elbows, their faces inches apart, their causerie progressed to more declarative sentences, Bill saying how glad he was that Mickey was a nurse's aide, and that her work was a real contribution to the war effort. Then Mickey spoke about what was really bothering her, softly at first, purring like a kitten, the way southern women introduce any factious topic.

"I was hoping," she said, "that the major could do something for you, make you an instructor on Miami Beach."

"He probably would have," said Bill, "especially after I gave him Charlene's phone number, if that's what I wanted to do."

"What do you mean, if that's what you wanted to do?" asked Mickey. "I thought we talked about it a lot. That you would be an instructor in OCS, and we could be together."

"Mickey, I want to be with you more than anything in the world. More than even my family. This is my last leave and I'm not in Iowa, I'm here, with you. That should tell you something. But this country needs all the able-bodied men it can get hold of. Everyone's going in the service, even people like Joe DiMaggio, and Glenn Miller. I have to do my duty too. Staying here and being an instructor is not doing my best. That's for some old guy who's too old to fight, or has something wrong with him. I don't have a damn thing wrong with me, except I'm crazy in love, and that's not a condition to keep you out of the service. And, sweetheart, try to see it from my side, I don't want to be out of the service. I want to help end this war as fast as possible."

"But they'll send you someplace far away, and I'll never see you again." She started to cry.

"Hey, that's getting way ahead, and in the wrong direction. First off, the bombardier is always in a good spot. I can see what's coming, so I know when to duck. And then, I'm not going to the moon. We'll be able to write and send pictures. And the way it looks, we're already on the move in North Africa, the whole thing could be over in a couple of months."

"You'll forget me," she said. "You'll meet another girl, someone else who's prettier."

"Is that all you think you are? You're more than just a pretty girl. Sure you're pretty. I'd be 4-F right now, blind as a bat if I said different. You're beautiful. There's no two ways about it, and second, I don't think anyone else could possibly be as beautiful. But third, and it's a big third, there are other pieces of you that make me love you. It's the combination, like this breakfast here. It's not just the bacon, it's the eggs and the hash browns, and this toasted bagel and this witch's brew they call coffee. It's everything. You're soft and tender, and funny and sweet, you got goofy, half-baked ideas about things, that's part of you too, and speaking of eggs, you make the most godawful eggs I ever tasted in my life, but I have a picture of you in my mind, with your eyes all squinted up, cooking over a hot plate to please me. Love is the whole person, especially a person doing something she hates because she loves you."

"How much time do we have?" she asked.

"Thirty-six hours."

She looked into her coffee cup, and tears splashed down her cheeks. "I'm probably wrecking my makeup," she said.

"You look better without it."

"A day and a half," she murmured. "Let's make it last."

"I'll do my best." He leaned across the table, his lips brushing her face. The couple at the next table smiled and looked away. "We can get married. You'll get an allotment that will take care of you."

"I don't know," she said.

"What's stopping you?"

"I don't know, it's just . . ." Her voice trailed like a wisp of smoke.

"It's not what you had in mind, I know. That's another one of your half-baked ideas. It works like this for me, and listen good, because this one's fully cooked. You're the reason I'm going, my family and you, especially you, you give me something to fight for, I know this sounds corny, and you know I'm not a glory hound, but I want to keep our way of living safe for you. You also give me something to live for, to come back for, I dream of coming back to you after this is all over. You understand that?"

"You have pecan eyes," she said.

"Were you listening to me?"

"I have to tell Sol."

"Tell him."

"He's in Philadelphia."

"Don't the phones work? Call him."

"I'm not allowed to call him at home."

"Then I'll call him."

"I'll do it," she said.

Hilary and Freddie were getting ready to take the bus to the Florida East Coast Railway station to say good-bye to Lionel and Winona. Like everything else that involved all members of the family, the event had escalated into a squall. Hilary and Ilona had fought over what Hilary should wear, and Ilona had won. Now Hilary stood in her baby white shirt with the little collar and her jumper, complaining that she was too tall to wear such an outfit. Ilona was impervious to her charge, although not unappreciative that her daughter was feeling well enough to argue the point, and handed them a napkin-lined basket containing two honeycakes and sticky, rock-hard taiglach wrapped in wax paper. "Tell them to be careful of their teeth with the taiglach," she said.

Frank moved in and out of the room behind them, carrying in Dr. Hershbaum's stamp collection, which he had said they could keep for the duration. Confident that the stamps would somehow make up for the deficit in Freddie's learning, Frank, who was as pleased with the offer as he was with the fact that for some reason Ilona had called a halt to her house-buying campaign, which had stalled like events in the North African desert, pointed out to Ilona that having books of stamps at your fingertips was the kind of thing people in houses did.

"How do you like them, Freddie?" he asked. "What do you think? You can see stamps of every country in there."

"It's okay," said Freddie, who stared doubtfully at the massive pile of books, wondering what could be expected of him and certain that somehow his life had taken a downward turn.

Just as Frank brought in the last armload, Mickey and Bill

poked their heads in the door. Bill headed in and roughed up Freddie's hair. "Hiya, sport," he said.

Freddie looked ashamed. "I lost my cap," he said.

"That's okay. You look fine without it."

Frank shook hands with Bill and looked over Mickey with the dedication of a connoisseur checking a burgundy for its glide. "Glad to see you," he said. "Hilary's in the Colonel Pigtails contest. If you get a chance, vote for her."

Hilary realized then that it was hard to die. One could not cause it to happen even though one wished it so hard one's eyebrows touched.

Ilona wiped her hands on her dress and put one out. "I am happy to see you again, Lieutenant. I never really thanked you for your help when my husband got lost. I was a little troubled that day."

"I was glad to help."

"Is it true you pledge to guard your bombsight with your life?" asked Freddie.

"Where'd you hear that?" asked Bill, smiling. "About the Norden?"

"Vera Vague told Bob Hope about it."

"Well, it's almost true but not quite," replied Bill. "I have to get it back under lock and key after I'm through using it. Only we call it the Blue Ox."

"The Blue Ox," said Hilary, running the words over her tongue. "You have to have the Blue Ox."

Ilona gave her a warning look.

"And good night vision," said Bill. "That's important too."

"How do you know how good you are," asked Frank, "when you haven't been on any missions?"

"They give us dummy bombs," explained Bill, "filled with black powder in their tail and sand in their case, then they take a picture of the drop. They can tell by the puff of smoke made by the powder charge how close the hit was."

"How close are you getting?" asked Frank.

"Right on the money," replied Bill.

Frank smiled. "Go get 'em. Give 'em hell and drop one for us."

"Will do," said Bill.

"They have to go," interposed Ilona. "The children. I want them home before dark."

Hilary and Freddie left, carrying the basket. They had turned the corner and were almost into the lobby where Mrs. Templeton was arranging a wooden-horse race, when Ilona yelled down the hall, the way a coloratura socks the balcony, loud enough for the whole hotel to hear, "Don't talk to anybody, and stick together!"

Mickey did it on the telephone. Her resolve to leave Radner did not include the courage it would take to do the thing face to face. No matter. It was still a big step, a plunge into the abyss, a blindfolded run, a leap without a net. She called Sol Radner at home and told him not to get a divorce, that she appreciated everything he had done for her, that she was keeping the fur, and that she was leaving him. He whispered hoarsely that he could not speak at that moment, told her to stay where she was, and called her back from a pay phone from which coins could be heard tinkling, and from which he told her that there were plenty more where she came from, that she could not take the fur, and that she had two days to get out of the room.

There. It was done. She was going to marry Bill someday soon, when he could come home on leave, or the war ended, whichever came first. In the meantime, she had to get a job. She felt giddy, free, like the time she wore shoes that had been too tight, and Bill persuaded her to walk home barefoot, carrying them by the straps.

She and Hilary looked through the newspaper ads for an apartment. They were hard to get. You had to be there first, early in the morning or, like a friend whose cop boyfriend had been on the scene to examine the body of the previous occupant, have inside information.

She found a vacancy in the Drexel Towers, a one-room efficiency with a Murphy bed that pulled out of the wall, that advertised for restricted clientele. Neither knew what that meant, but Hilary suggested maybe it had something to do with the housing shortage. The meaning was made clear when a sign in front, posted on the building, said, "A room with a view, without a Jew." To Mickey it made sense, since some Jews she had known tended to be noisy.

For some reason, just before Mickey was about to give the landlady a deposit, Hilary said, "My mother is Jewish."

"Are you her mother?" asked the landlady.

"Now, how can I be her mother?" asked Mickey. "I'm not old enough, and I sure am not a Jew."

"People will say anything to get an apartment," replied the woman, who added she would think about it.

Where Valentine's Day was fun in the fourth grade, now in the sixth grade it had become a ballot. A big box, covered with red construction paper and little white hearts made from paper doilies sat on the teacher's desk, a grim and lacy reminder of one's worth. The idea was that everyone drop in cards to all the people they wanted to send valentines to.

Hilary sat at her desk with her valentines in a paper bag, waiting with dread for Miss Daly to walk down the aisles so that everyone could drop in their cards.

Hilary had to decide between taking the position of mugwump, sending valentines to nobody, or an active campaigner, sending them to everybody. To nobody signaled her independence and her contempt for the ritual, but to everybody signaled a white flag, an opener, a bid for reconsideration.

She decided to send cards to everyone in the class including, with uncustomary grace, Sorrell Myers, Jack Suga, the tallest girl in the class, Tracey Hollister, and little Pinky Weiselmann. Miss Daly shook the box vigorously, then appointed T.H. and Billy Connaught to be mailmen. The cards were distributed. Hilary got four. She tried not to notice how many other people were getting, but it was too much to ask, like taking only one lick of an ice cream cone. Shirley Leone had a deskful, so did T.H. and his camarilla, while Jack, Sorrell, Tracey Hollister, and Pinky Weiselmann had, like her and other oddlings, a fribbling handful.

Within minutes most were reading the signatures on their cards and giggling. Some of the cards were serious, the early, spraddle-legged baby steps of passion, others were mysterious, signed cryptically From Your Valentine.

Hilary was hoping that perhaps she would have a secret admirer in the class too timid to declare himself or herself, which would be okay, since then she could imagine anyone she liked, but her cards were all signed predictably—Jack, Sorrell, Tracey, and Pinky, youngest in the class by a year.

Mr. Detwiler appeared at the door. They all turned to look, and stopped tearing envelopes with their fingers, then dropped their mouths open, like baby birds waiting for their mother to pop in a worm. There in the doorway, beside Mr. Detwiler, stood Jackie Snyder, her legs in heavy metal braces, a crutch slid beneath each armpit.

"I know," he said, "you are all very happy to see this young lady again."

Jackie clicked her way into class, the heavy metal snapping and grating with each swing of her legs. Some people turned their heads away, but most continued to stare. None of them had ever seen anything like it. Jackie was told to find a seat. She scanned the room and found Hilary, then pointed with a crutch.

"I want to sit there," she said.

Paul was moved to the next row, and Jackie, with gold studs lopsided in her ears, hitched toward Hilary, without speaking to anyone, her face already etched in fine lines, like a cracked china cup.

19

Dr. Weingarten's brown leather waiting room, a gift of the in-laws, was jammed. One of the first of a new breed of specialists, Dr. Weingarten was an EENT man, an eye, ear, nose, and throat doctor claiming as his exclusive territory anything located in the head. His patients occupied every available seat: some with irritated, scratchy throats on the increase now that, in April, the Everglades had begun to burn again; others with impacted ear wax that had to be flushed and syringed out; and six with deviated septums, congenital malformations that produced for their sufferers a chronic catarrh.

Lipschutz was one of the latter, although his interest in seeking medical advice was less in sinus drainage (he had learned to live with the occasional drip) than in the cosmetics of the situation. Lipschutz was meeting with Dr. Weingarten to discuss the possibilities of corrective surgery which would not only straighten out the septum, but shorten his oversized nose as well.

Dressed in a blazer and floral shirt open at his deeply tanned neck, he sat before a coffee table stacked with neat piles of *Reader's Digest*, trying out his new routine, in the melancholy, sardonic humor of which he was coming to be a master, on Hilary and Freddie. In a steady stream of talk he called his monologue, he sounded as Freddie once had when he had the measles and became delirious. Hilary rolled from side to side, clutching herself around the waist as if to keep the top half of her from falling off.

"I can't stand it," shrieked Hilary with her hand over her mouth.

"It's all in the timing," he replied. "You got to know when to make delivery."

Dr. Weingarten summoned his patients himself, poking his head into the waiting room, a bespectacled Gabriel with a chart in his hands. "Mr. Lipschutz," he said. "How are you feeling?"

"Much better, thank you, Doc. The only thing that troubles me is my breathing. I want you to give me something to stop it."

Dr. Weingarten smiled in a benevolent, caring way, untroubled by drollery, concerned only with the issue of an efficient nasal system. "Are these your children?" he asked.

"These are my buddies," replied Lipschutz, reaching out a flowered cuff around each child, collaring them like a yoke.

"They can come in with you," said Dr. Weingarten. "I don't like children unattended in the waiting room."

They followed Dr. Weingarten out of the waiting room, into the narrow corridor. Doctor's offices were locked somewhere in Hilary's and Freddie's dimly remembered past. Hilary had a fuzzy recollection, in bits and pieces like peanut brittle, of being trundled in Frank's arms into a chilly white room, a crying place, but could not bring anything else to mind about why she was there, or of what was done to make her cry.

Lipschutz was asked to sit in a chair with a scrolled metal foot rest like that on the chair of Frank's barber, while Dr. Weingarten, wearing a head mirror like a miner, dug into his nose as if it contained coal. "There's no question that this can be corrected," he said, withdrawing a long, thin speculum. "None at all."

"How will it look after it's over?" asked Lipschutz.

"I'll try to draw a picture for you."

Dr. Weingarten made a sketch of Lipschutz with his long nose that looked like the KILROY WAS HERE signs appearing on sidewalks and telephone booths and toilet stalls all over the city, of a big nose peering over a fence. Then Dr. Weingarten began to scratch over the tip, creating another, shorter, nose, a different Lipschutz, no longer Lipschutz, someone else. Freddie watched in fascination as Dr. Weingarten erased half of Lipschutz's face.

There was something unnatural about the new Lipschutz. The melancholy, sensitive look was gone, in its place, a cocky, confident truncation. How could the tip of a nose make such a difference? Could the doctor sew it back again if Lipschutz changed his mind? "What do you think, Hilary?" asked Lipschutz.

"I don't know. You look kind of mashed in."

"Do you think you can make it like the one Alan Ladd has?" asked Lipschutz, pinning up his nose with his fingers. "Like this?"

"We have to work with what you have," said Dr. Weingarten, spraying something deep into his nose.

Freddie stepped toward the sterilizer with its floating instruments. It reminded him of the dishwasher's big cast-iron tub filled with iridescent, sudsy water in which all the silverware lay soaking.

"Get away from there please," said Dr. Weingarten.

One of the instruments flashed before Freddie's eyes like a fish that he saw once from the dock, silvery and shiny, winking its way back into the depths.

"Young man, please get away from those instruments."

Hilary came to stand beside Freddie. "He said to get away."

Dr. Weingarten looked at Freddie, then turned his attention back to Lipschutz into whose nose he poked a mirror. "Do you always talk to him like that?" he asked.

"Like what?" asked Hilary.

"So that he can see you."

Hilary had not realized it. Now, in contemplation, she saw that he was right, although the fact meant nothing to her. It was just something that she did, like flipping her braids over her shoulder. "Yes," she replied.

"Why do you do that?"

"So he pays attention."

"You mean if you stand over here, where I am, for example, he won't pay attention?"

"Probably not."

"What are you doing up there?" complained Lipschutz, in a whine like a buzz saw. "Taking pictures?"

"I'll be through in just a minute, Mr. Lipschutz."

Dr. Weingarten then lay down his mirror and washed his hands in the little sink.

"What's your brother's name?" he asked.

"Freddie. But he likes it better when you call him Fred."

"Fred," said Dr. Weingarten softly, much more softly than he had been speaking.

Freddie came to stand beside Lipschutz. "How long are you going to have to sit in here?" he asked.

Dr. Weingarten dropped a notepad. It made a sharp slap on the linoleum floor.

Lipschutz jumped up in the chair. "Take it easy on my nerves, Doc," he said. "I have a delicate constitution."

"Has your brother ever been examined by a doctor?" asked Dr. Weingarten.

"Sure he has," replied Hilary. "Lots of times." What did he think they were, hillbillies who used outdoor toilets like those people in South Carolina they saw from the car window?

"What kind of doctor?"

"Dr. Hershbaum, mainly. He's the hotel doctor. He takes care of us when we get sick."

"But has anyone examined him completely, I mean from top to bottom?"

"I don't know. You better ask my mother."

Then Dr. Weingarten said something that surprised Hilary. "Does your family know that your brother may have a hearing problem?"

"I never heard about it, Doc," said Lipschutz. "At least no one ever said anything to me."

"What about you, young lady?"

"What is that, a hearing problem?"

"It means he may have trouble hearing."

"He's not deaf."

"No, he's not deaf, but I wear glasses because my sight is impaired. I'm not blind, but it's less than perfect. It may be the same with his ears. Tell your parents to bring him around sometime, I'd like to examine him."

"They work," said Hilary.

"Tell them there won't be any charge. Tell them that."

"They can pay," said Hilary.

Dr. Weingarten turned to Lipschutz. "You know the parents well?"

"They're great people, Doc. Salt of the earth."

"Well, try to convince these salts of the earth to shake themselves down here."

"Not bad, Doc," conceded Lipschutz.

"And I wasn't even trying," said Dr. Weingarten. "You understand what I'm saying?" he added to Hilary.

"It wasn't a very good joke."

Dr. Weingarten smiled at Lipschutz with the conspiratorial amusement of the tolerant adult. "I want to be sure you understand about bringing in your parents."

"I don't have a hearing problem, if that's what you mean," Hilary replied.

Dr. Weingarten took off his glasses and wiped them, tolerance and amusement gone, while Lipschutz put his bony hand on Hilary's shoulder. "Hilary, the doc is only trying to help."

Then Dr. Weingarten slipped his glasses over his ears and addressed himself once more to Hilary. "Tell them to call the office and make an appointment for your brother, and that I'd like to see both of them if possible."

The suggestion that one of their children was impaired in any way was as embarrassing to Frank and Ilona as Gandhi's fast was to the British. It was even worse than the assault on Hilary. They had nothing to do with that. This had to do with them. The specter of responsibility loomed tall and flapping.

"Who asked him?" asked Ilona. "What is it, his business is so bad he has to drum it up?"

"Doctors are becoming money hungry," said Frank. "Everybody knows that. It has to do with the war."

"Dr. Hershbaum wasn't money hungry," said Hilary. "He gave us all these stamp books. For free."

"He was an exception," said Frank.

"Besides, he would have to pay for storage anyway," said Ilona. "It was nice, but it wasn't that nice."

It seemed to Hilary that they were fleeing from the idea, wildly, blindly, the way a bird trapped indoors darts this way and that, crashing into plate glass, looking only to escape.

"I think he made a test," said Hilary.

"What did the doctor do to you?" asked Ilona of Freddie.

"Who?" he asked.

"He dropped a book," said Hilary.

"You call that a test?" asked Ilona, scorn showing in the corners of her pretty upturned lips. And so on, all afternoon. Then Ilona and Frank began to make their own tests, soft calls and whispers, doors slammed, boxes dropped, to which he sometimes responded and sometimes did not. At first, his reactions seemed random, so haphazard that conclusion could be safely deferred; then, as evidence accumulated came the sickening reality, a feeling of visceral weight, as if what had hidden inside their home, had somehow congealed their intestines.

They worried, consoled one another, and watched him while he slept, expecting the impairment to his ears to somehow generate to the rest of him, as if in sleep he were more vulnerable and needed their guardianship.

Spring and its accessories had something to do with Ilona and Frank finally taking Dr. Weingarten up on his offer. The yellow jasmine and great white lilies heaped in the public flower beds by Jack Suga's father, the tasseled oaks hung with gray Spanish moss swaying with every breeze, and flocks of tiny ruby-throated hummingbirds, massing for their journey North, created an enthusiasm, a promise of change, of possibility. How could anything be wrong at such a time?

It was the third week in April, Easter for Frank and Passover for Ilona, who continued to hope next year in Jerusalem, which didn't really mean going to Palestine, only that her mother and sister and all other Jews fleeing for their lives would be free.

Ilona took both children, scrubbed and shining, dressed in their best clothes, Freddie's golden hair cemented to his scalp with Vaseline hair tonic in neat, glistening waves; Hilary, as tall as Ilona, in a dress she hated, with a sash that Ilona tied into a big bow at the back, anguished, because in addition to everything else, her growing feet made her look like an "L," arguing about her braids; and Ilona, always ready with an answer, countering that Veronica Lake, who was asked by the government to put up her hair because of all the industrial accidents involving women war plant workers whose long hair got caught in the machinery, was now wearing braids on the top of her head. "But not hanging down," said Hilary. It made no difference.

At first Dr. Weingarten just asked Ilona questions that had nothing to do with Freddie's hearing. When did Freddie first sit without support? When did he walk without assistance, speak his first word, pull off his sock? Did Freddie ever rock from side to side, sway? Bang his head against the crib? What about babbling? Ilona recalled that he started it, but unlike Hilary, stopped it. Did he vocalize freely while at play? Ilona asked what he meant. Dr. Weingarten made the sound of a car motor, whrr, he said, choo-choo. No, Ilona did not think he did that. Did he sing or whistle to himself?

"He sings," interrupted Hilary.

"No, when he is by himself."

"How can we answer that?" said Ilona. "If we know it, then he is not by himself."

Dr. Weingarten tried another tack. Did he cry easily? Ilona and Hilary exchanged glances. Yes. Ilona nodded.

Then Dr. Weingarten pulled out a bell, a chime, a clacker, an Ingersoll watch, a tuning fork, and what looked like earmuffs. He asked Ilona and Hilary to wait outside. Alone, he whispered to Freddie, held the ticking watch behind his head, and moved it away to test Freddie's range of high frequency, whispered to him to test his low frequency, tapped the tuning forks and placed them before his ears, clacked and rang the other instruments, then placed little muffs on Freddie's ears, turning some dials and making little notes while Freddie, who had not been told that his hearing might be different from anyone else's, made the observation that the doctor's offices smelled like Winona's cart.

Frank took them to church Easter Sunday. Marco went with them. Hilary wore the straw bonnet she had worn the year before, newly trimmed by Ilona in yellow silk buttercups. Freddie wore his long-lost flight cap, retrieved from under his old tin water chute. Marco had on a polka-dotted bow tie that clipped around his neck. Frank's shirt was laundered whiter and stiffer than any man's in church.

Services were just as Hilary remembered from the year before. She and Freddie bobbed up and down with Frank, although Hilary did not cross herself, believing that if she did, she would cross out Ilona, which, despite their ongoing battle, she was not prepared to do. Priests in satin vestments performed the functions of the mass. Everyone had a job to do. Some were pouring, some were chanting, one was holding aloft a chalice. They seemed to sway from side to side. It was then she realized the major difference between rabbis and priests. Priests were taller. Otherwise, they were pretty much the same, with the exception, Jackie Snyder had told her, that priests weren't allowed to get married.

She looked at Freddie, who bobbed and knelt beside her with relish, and thought of Mr. Samuelson and his big ugly hearing aid with the battery case on his chest that he was always tapping, and of the Civil War veteran she had once seen who held a horn to his ear. Like Ilona and Frank, she began to wish that her brother be a little slow rather than deaf. Let the doctor be wrong, she prayed, not sure in which direction to send the prayer, forward to the priests, sideways to the stained-glass windows with the jewel-toned St. Ambrose and St. Francis streaming with light, or upward to the cross from which Christ hung by his wrists. On impulse, she bent to kiss her brother's forehead.

"Quit it!" he hissed, and swiped at her face with his hand, knocking her bonnet sideways, so that one of the buttercups swung perilously over her ear.

In the next visit, Dr. Weingarten showed Ilona and Frank—he had asked for them both—an audiogram, a chart of horizontal and vertical ruled coordinates upon which was drawn a shallow curve, a graphic representation of Freddie's hearing.

"What does it mean?" asked Ilona, not sure what line to follow.

"It means he has a conductive hearing loss," said Dr. Weingarten. "There is an interference in the external auditory canal that leads to his inner ear. Sound vibrations cannot get in to stimulate the cochlea. He is not deaf, just hard of hearing. His hearing loss is somewhere over forty decibels and under sixty. This means he cannot understand moderate speech. It means he can't get everything his teacher is saying. That explains why he has had trouble in school. But Freddie has learned to compensate. It means he has learned to read lips."

Frank and Ilona stared at one another, then at the doctor, each one wrestling with the private grief that kept them bound to their chairs.

"What caused it?" asked Frank. "No one is deaf in my family."

"No one is deaf in my family either," said Ilona, "except for Uncle Ferry, and he was very old. Does that count?"

"We're not keeping score," said Dr. Weingarten. "Freddie could have been a normal infant, in every way. Forceps could have done it. There's no point in looking for blame. You should be concentrating on what you can do about it."

"What can we do?"

"First, I think you can consider a hearing aid."

Frank sat forward. "You mean those ugly buttons you stick in your ear with the cord hanging down your neck?" Ilona began to cry. If Frank and Ilona had been given a choice, they would have preferred Freddie to be slow in school. They had learned to live with that. A slow student eventually gets out of school and goes to work. Then he's just like everyone else. This was different. This was a handicap. This was a cord hanging down your neck.

"Try the hearing aid first," said Dr. Weingarten. "I don't expect you to rush into things."

Frank heard the angelus, but questioned its ring. "You say first, then what? If you say first, there has to be a second."

"There is," said Dr. Weingarten, slowly, cautiously. "It's new, and yet not so new. There is a procedure, it was done just before the turn of the century, and then discarded. It's being done again, not by a lot of doctors, just a few. With some success."

"What are you talking about?" asked Ilona. She clutched at her purse.

"An operation."

"Let's not talk," she said.

Dr. Weingarten nodded in sympathy. "I can see this is frightening to you," he said. "Perhaps I should explain the procedure. You see, a bone-like tissue has apparently formed around something we call the stapes and the oval window. This prevents sounds from getting in. There is a procedure we call fenestration. We make a little window and bypass the stapes, so that the sound can get in. The problems of such a procedure are two fold. The first, the incision, is of minor importance since it can be concealed by the hair, but the second, and much more important, is that there is a chance that the operation could be a failure, and that hearing in the ear be destroyed totally. Of course, we would only do one ear at a time, to minimize this danger."

"Forget it," said Frank. "I'm not going to risk the hearing he has, and even if that wasn't a possibility, operations cost money. Where would we get that kind of money?"

"I would be willing to work with you on that," said Dr. Weingarten.

"Meaning what?" asked Frank.

"Meaning, I have plenty of other patients who pay me good fees. I can afford from time to time to make adjustments."

"We don't need charity," said Frank.

"Of course not. I wasn't suggesting charity. I would call it a tailoring job, an alteration, you might say."

"Freddie is not going to have an operation," said Ilona, wiping her eyes on a lace handkerchief with tiny silken rosebuds she had brought with her from the old country. "There's no more discussion." And there wasn't.

On the bus ride home, they spoke in whispers as long as the shadows, trying to recall if Freddie had been delivered with forceps. Ilona did not remember, it had all been so awful, she put everything connected to his birth out of her mind. Frank didn't know. He had been in the waiting room, wondering how he was going to pay for everything. He thought he remembered marks on Freddie's face. They all look like that, she said. Frank thought back to Freddie's birth. Instead of a christening party like his sister had, or the bris that Ilona said Jews had, they just took the new baby home. Times were bad. Freddie's birth was unwelcome. No matter how rough things got, though, once you got married, you stayed married. It was a sacrament, even if you didn't get married in the church. Especially after the kids came, he kept his commitment, with one minor lapse, with the same dogged determination that he had seen in his father, even though his father had to get tanked up in order to bear coming home at night. He had even seen it in his crazy brother who hustled his living in pool halls. A man, if he was any kind of man, stuck by his wife and kids, no matter how bad things got. Frank looked at Ilona's face, worries etched around her eyes and forehead, like a peach that has been left out of the icebox. She, in turn, had stuck by him. You couldn't say that about a lot of women. Not these days. Look at Gus's wife, who walked out on him when things began to get a little tough, or all the war widows who went with any kind just to have a good time, while their men were getting their asses shot off. Ilona wasn't like that. She was loyal. She was true blue. He told her so.

The week Hilary was to graduate from North Beach Elementary, they all got an opportunity to see Dr. Weingarten's handiwork. Lipschutz had his nose done. No one they had ever known had done this before. It was a first for everyone in the hotel, as exciting as watching the Frankenstein monster after the lightning bolt. Lipschutz came home from the hospital with eyes swollen and purple, and a little white bandage on his nose that looked like a sock. It was hard to tell what he was going to look like. He was very optimistic.

Everyone stood in the lobby as he stepped out of the cab—Mr. Samuelson; Mrs. Steinfeld and Rudy; two wives of army air corps officers who didn't even know Lipschutz, but who had heard that he was a star; Tessie, the switchboard operator; Mr. Davis, completely healed; Mel, wearing his official civil defense arm band; Hilary in rolled-up dungarees that Mickey bought her; and Freddie, wearing his new hearing aid, with the unplugged cord flopping on his shoulder.

"We're going to have an unveiling in just a few days, folks," said Lipschutz.

"What will it look like?" asked Hilary. "Will it look like that picture, or will it look like Alan Ladd?"

"Whatever it is," said Lipschutz, "it's got to be an improvement."

"I suppose next you're going to change your name," said Mr. Samuelson.

"I don't know," said one of the officers' wives. "It's not good to tamper with nature. God gives us noses for a reason."

"Why should anyone's nose be big?" asked Tessie.

"Maybe Jews need to have more oxygen," said the wife.

Lipschutz put his arm around Mel's shoulder and led him to the bamboo door of the cocktail lounge, while Hilary and Freddie followed after them, hugging the wall and stepping on tiptoes so Mr. Davis would not see them enter the make-believe Tahitian village with the electrified sign of a moon coming up over rippling water.

There stood Mickey, dressed in a sarong and spike shoes, reprieved at the last minute, given a job and a tiny room in the hotel, an inside room without a window, for which she paid by working late afternoons and evenings as a cocktail waitress, making good tips, enough to keep her in clothes and a little in and out money, and getting lots of offers to go out, although she declined them all.

"Jack just mixed a mai-tai," she said. "The customer said it was pretty good."

"Sounds good to me, gorgeous," said Lipschutz. "Tell him to go light on the grenadine, and that I want it in a glass, not a coconut. How's that guy of yours?"

"He's real fine," said Mickey. "He met up with his old buddy, June Bug. He says they fly the milk-run to Tunis together. That's what they call it, but you know what he's really talking about."

"I don't know about Tunis," said Mel, "but he and his buddies are bombing the hell out of Palermo and Naples, really giving it to the northern coast of Italy."

"Bill wrote to me and Freddie too," said Hilary. "His mess hall is in an old Roman ruin. Two thousand years old."

"What does he say about Tunisia?" asked Lipschutz.

"That it's muddy," said Mickey. She didn't repeat the beautiful part of his letter in which he said that some day very soon, the cross hairs of his sight would center the last target, the last train would leave the bay, the last bomb would curve to earth, and then he would return home, wanting everything unchanged, just as he left it, and that she should have her gown and veil ready. Mickey wondered if she could be married in white. They said if you were married before, you couldn't. What if you had been too young to know what you were doing? Maybe then it was okay.

Frank came in and stood before the booth, jerked his thumb over his shoulder. "Out," he said. Hilary slid out of the booth, but Freddie decided to duck beneath the table.

"We were just sitting," she said. "What's wrong with that?"

"Yeah," said Freddie, "what's wrong with that?"

"It's against the law, and I say no, that's what's wrong with it. And stay out. I don't want to catch either of you in here again."

"What if I got something to tell Mickey?"

"Send her a telegram."

Frank took a good look at Mickey's long lovely legs before sliding into the booth beside Lipschutz. "How are you going to breathe with that thing?" he asked.

"I'll manage," replied Lipschutz. "What about your kid? The doc been able to help him?"

"He's fine," said Frank.

"Isn't he supposed to wear a hearing aid?"

"Who told you that?"

The excitement over Lipschutz's new nose almost eclipsed Hilary's graduation. Almost everyone from the hotel went. They took up an entire row—Frank; Ilona; Freddie, minus his new hearing aid, which somehow had gotten lost among his toys; Lipschutz, almost handsome, minus his sock; Mickey, golden and beautiful; Gus; Mel. T.H.'s mother, who had been saving the row with the folding chairs tipped gracefully over, was suddenly face to face with Gus, who said tersely, "Fix the chairs."

"They're reserved," replied Mrs. Dallas, with the bright, intelligent smile of an officer's wife.

"That's not nice," he said, slamming the chairs upright with his hammy fist, and everyone filed in after him, even Mrs. Templeton, who had spent the whole morning teaching Hilary how to sit on a stage. "My good woman," she said, in frosty tones, "you cannot save an entire row. It's just not being done."

The sixth grade paraded into the auditorium to the march from *Aïda*, walking in self-conscious pairs, Hilary and Sorrell Myers, both of whose names began with an "M" marching to the stage together, Sorrell taking it very seriously and stepping with a measured beat, while Hilary skipped beside him to keep in step as shivers from Verdi chased up and down her arms. She had never before in her life felt so wonderful, so tall, so serious, so grown-up. Even the music knew it. The fact that all the good kids were having parties afterward could not smother her buoyance. Jackie Snyder was having one, and Hilary was invited to it, and it didn't matter if she wasn't going to the others, one was enough. When they were seated on the stage, Mr. Detwiler talked about democracy, and how this graduating class would help join the fight to save it.

Hilary thought very seriously then, that when she grew up, she would get a job as an undercover agent. She was very good at finding out things, keeping secrets, and memorizing, which was especially good, since you had sometimes only a peek at secret documents which you then had to either eat or commit to memory.

It was a sunny day. Liz Bonnier, who was taking voice lessons, led the class in the singing of "The Star-Spangled Banner," shrieking out her high notes in the ruthless, self-indulgent manner of all lyric sopranos. Jack Suga's parents sat isolated in the back, until Sorrell Myers's father, dragging his wife by the arm, made a special effort to sit next to them. T.H.'s officer father, with fruit salad all over his well-tailored jacket, came in late. Shirley Leone, who had won the Colonel Pigtails contest somewhat fraudulently, since she wore braids only for her picture, and for the acceptance of the award, was on her way to becoming an acknowledged beauty. Pinky Weiselmann, as predicted by the slam book, threw up. Tracey Hollister had maintained her lead, and, seated, was a head taller than anyone else, on her way to becoming the Cardiff giant of Miami Beach. Because her grades were the best in the class, Hilary was called upon to recite a poem. She chose *Invictus*, over the protests of Miss Daly, who did not like the free thinking represented in the selection, and was trying to push Rudyard Kipling's *If*, or, at the very least, anything by Robert Louis Stevenson.

Having been coached by Mrs. Templeton, Hilary stood, took her place at the podium, looked her audience squarely in their collective eyes, raised her fists, and declaimed with vigor, making artful, practiced movements like a shadow boxer: "'Out of the night that covers me, black as the pit from pole to pole,'" rising to a celebration by the time she got to, "'I am the master of my fate, I am the captain of my soul.'"

Lipschutz said she had natural talent. Mel agreed.

Then Mr. Detwiler called them one by one and handed them a rolled white diploma tied with a ribbon. When Hilary's name was called, Marco stood up and cheered until he was pulled back down by Mel. Afterward, Mrs. Templeton took her aside and said she had something for her. She gave her a dog-eared, yellowed old map of Miami, which she said was one of her personal treasures. It was so old, it didn't even have Miami Beach on it.

The day after graduation, Hilary stood on the beach watching the soldiers next door doing jumping jacks in their gas masks, which Mel said was helping them get adjusted to wearing the masks. Hilary held a rake with which she had just marked her name in huge letters in the sand for airplanes to read. One man collapsed. As Hilary watched him crumple and fall, she felt something funny, as if she had wet her pants. She looked down her leg, and saw a tiny red trickle. Mel had not noticed. Without a word she sprinted from the beach to her room, leaving the rake behind. In the privacy of the bathroom she checked. It was true. It had come. Finally. The start of a brand-new life. She wrote a note to Ilona and folded it over six times, then sent it with Freddie. The note said, "Buy me some Kotex."

Ilona came running. The first thing she did was smack Hilary gently on her cheek.

"Why did you do that?" Hilary began to cry.

Then Ilona, just as unpredictably, hugged her to her small bosom. "It's a custom," she said softly. "My little woman. My mother smacked me like that. Someday, you'll smack your own daughter."

"It's a dumb thing to do. I never heard of it before."

"Who says you know everything?"

"I'll bet Jackie Snyder's mother didn't do that to her."

"Jackie Snyder, nebboch, is a cripple, you," she spit delicately three times, "you . . ."

"Me what?"

"You have such big feet. I just bought you shoes and already its time for another pair!" Ilona went back into her bedroom and emerged with a box of Kotex and a belt. "Take this in the bathroom and put it on."

Hilary locked the door behind her, and tried to figure out the confusion of straps and gauze that was supposed to conform to her body. She heard Ilona yell to Freddie to plug in his battery. While she was trying to untwist a strap from around her leg, clearly not the way the thing worked, she heard Mel ask Ilona what she wanted to do with the rake that Hilary left on the beach and Ilona's reply to please take it to maintenance. After several minutes, Ilona came to the bathroom door and knocked. "What's going on in there?" she asked. "What's taking you so long? It shouldn't take so long."

"I have to get it just right."

"Let me come in and help you."

"No!" said Hilary. "N. O. No!"

"And I hope," Ilona shouted through the door, "big shot, still writes in the sand with rakes, I hope you also have stubborn children who yell at you through the bathroom door."

20

The summer was so hot Hilary's eyes hurt. Not even Ilona's old sunglasses helped. White glare bounced off the water, the sand, the pastel hotels, the cement sidewalks, the victory garden on the roof that had perished in a cataclysm of desiccated beans and radishes that withered as they climbed. With no towering skyscrapers, no hills, no luxuriant, thickening, time-entrenched forest to deflect and block the sun, to shade the broad flat ribbon of beach that was having the biggest summer season it had ever had, the effect was incandescent heat that rose in shimmers.

Freddie in his flight cap, and Hilary, wearing an old one-piece latex bathing suit of Mickey's that jutted over her chest in two cones, ducked, dripping, into the bookie cabana where Mel was sticking pins on a map. Each carried a piece of scavenger equipment—Hilary, an old rusty colander, Freddie, a torn screen that had been bent at the edges, and between them, an old grapefruit sack containing the morning's gleanings, fifty-six cents, mostly in nickels, three tin wrappers, and a cigarette lighter that was jammed shut.

"Put that stuff in the corner," said Mel, "and don't forget to pick it up when you've finished. Last time I sat with your junk for a week."

"Not the money you didn't," said Hilary.

Mickey slipped into the darkened shack wearing dimout anklets made of little white flowers on a white rope that glowed. "I knew I'd find you here," she said. "Whew! It's stuffy. How can y'all breathe?" She turned to Hilary. "I'm going shopping. You want to come?"

"What for?"

"Bill wants me to have a wedding gown ready for when he comes home. I'm going to look for one with a sweetheart neckline."

"When are you kids going to give out those mosquito handbills?"

"Later," said Hilary. "When we come back."

"Don't make it too late. The city printed them up for a reason. I promised I'd cover three blocks in both directions. You don't want all those convalescing soldiers coming down with dengue fever. They got enough to worry about."

The bus ride was a spirited one. Mickey was happy about buying a wedding gown. She had never had one, having been married the first time in a pink rayon dress. Hilary was happy because her ears looked as if they were getting smaller, and Freddie was happy because no one was nagging him to wear his hearing aid. They sang "Deep in the Heart of Texas," until the driver asked them to stop clapping, which of course, was the whole song.

The bridal shop was located on Washington Avenue between a juice stand and an orthopedic shoe store. A saleslady seemed to float to them from the mirrors. She smiled directly at Mickey.

"Can I help you, darling?"

"I'd like to see a gown," said Mickey. "With a sweetheart neckline."

The saleslady turned to another woman who had materialized behind her. They laughed indulgently.

"She thinks it's as simple as that. First we have to decide what category you're in, darling, long or short, summer or winter, traditional or modern, train or no train. It's very complicated, do you want an empire waist, or a princesse style, do you want points on your sleeves, do you want dotted swiss, organdy, tissue faille, lace, satin, taffeta? You see what I mean?" The saleslady took Mickey's arm as if she were demented and led her to the back where ribbons fluttered from a little whirling fan.

"Is he in the service?" she asked.

"Yes," said Mickey. "He's in the Air Corps."

"Then everything has to be just so," said the saleslady.

After much discussion, they brought out a dotted swiss gown with a sweetheart neckline they called their Scarlett O'Hara, and the cap and veil that went with it. Mickey put it on in the dressing room. Although it was clearly too big, she looked glorious as she stepped on a low podium before a mirror while both saleswomen grabbed handfuls of fabric from behind. Miraculously, the gown conformed.

"It's you," said the first one, "I knew it the minute you walked in the door. Sylvia, what do you think?"

"It's definitely her," said Sylvia.

Hilary was awed. Even Freddie stood still long enough to gape. Mickey looked different. Being a bride was different. There was something holy about it. Mickey, who had been transformed in a crucible of tulle, had only ten dollars. They put the gown on layaway and Mickey paid for the cap and veil, the one tangible thing she could afford which would remind her of the crisp, new, white dotted swiss, packed away in a big white box in reams of tissue paper.

On the bus, Mickey talked all the way home of the coming marriage and of Bill who wrote that he hoped she didn't waste time listening to that 4-F Sinatra. He wasn't the only one who didn't like him—all the men in his outfit hated him—and she added conspiratorially that as soon as she knew for sure when he was coming home, she would give them all her records of the Voice. Then she talked of how Hilary would be the maid of honor or the flower girl, depending on how much longer it took, and Freddie could be the ring bearer. The big question was who would she get to give her away. She doubted that her father would come all the way from Georgia just to do it. Maybe Frank, although he wasn't old enough. Freddie suggested Gus. Mickey said the person, whoever it was, should be an American.

They got off the bus as columns of perspiring soldiers marched up Collins Avenue singing "I'm a helluva, helluva, engineer," belting out each *helluva* for the benefit of their drill sergeant, but sneaking sidelong glances at the ocean, as warm as the air, which lay a tempting few yards away. The sergeant blew his whistle, a shrill, piercing shriek that put a margin to the day, and they broke ranks and raced toward the beach, lemmings in fatigues, shouting, crashing, and flopping into the sea.

"You want to go swimming too?" asked Hilary.

They reached the shade of the portico where the bell captain, smiling, met them at the front entrance.

"I got a little package for you," he said to Mickey.

"Where is it?" asked Mickey. "Who sent me a package? I bet it's Bill."

"Someone dropped it off," he replied.

"Well where is it?"

"It's waiting over there." With uncustomary courtesy, he led her to the east wing. Sitting in the corner of an overstuffed Morris chair was a little boy with big solemn eyes. It was the same little boy Hilary and Freddie had seen the year before with the sunburned man, only now just a little bigger. He had a sign around his neck on a string. It said, MARYANN SLADE. FLAMINGO ARMS, MIAMI BEACH, FLORIDA.

"A woman dropped him off," said the bell captain. "She left you this note."

Mickey opened the letter, which obviously had been opened before. "Earl is dead," it read. "I can't take care of Sonny anymore. You're his lawful mother. He is your worry now."

Mickey turned to the bell captain. Her eyes were as wide as the child's. "Where'd she go? I have to find her!"

"She came two hours ago," said the bell captain. "Came, went, left you this little package." His smirk carved up into his ear.

"Didn't she say where she was staying?"

"She came in a truck," he said. "She and the driver. They weren't staying anywhere. At least, not in this town. Looks like he's all yours."

"But he can't be," said Mickey. Her voice rose. "He can't be. No! No! He'll mess everything up. I don't want him. I'm too young to be somebody's momma. I'm getting married. Me and Bill are getting married. I'll send him back. I'll put him on a bus."

Mickey started to cry. It seemed to Hilary that she was behaving the same way Ilona and Frank had when they found out about Freddie. Hilary and Freddie watched the little boy in fascination, Hilary particularly to see if he bore the resemblance to Mickey that she and her brother bore to Frank. His eyes in turn followed their every movement.

Mickey spoke first. "Can you talk?"

"Yes'm." His voice was tiny and muffled, and seemed to disappear into the upholstery.

"Your name Sonny?"

"Yes'm. It's Earl too." His drawl was slow and soft.

"I shoulda known that. You hungry?"

"Yes'm."

"I don't know what to do with a little child. Who asked you to come here?" She directed her anger at him. "What am I supposed to do with him? What a rotten thing to do. She never called me. She never wrote. Just dumped him on my doorstep like a bottle of milk. What a lousy thing to do to someone. Well, he can't stay there all day, that's for sure."

The little boy slid deeper into the chair.

"Now you come out of there," she shouted. "You hear?"

He continued to edge deeper into the cushion, as if he could disappear along with his voice into the upholstery. A pungent smell told everyone why he tried to burrow into the furniture. He had soiled his pants. Mickey threw her hands up. "Lord have mercy." Hilary breathed through her nose. Only Freddie seemed to have an answer. He went for Ilona, who would surely know what to do. She did.

Ilona came running, still wearing her long white kitchen apron. She looked over the situation, the way a chess player assesses his board. With no questions to Mickey, who clearly had no answers, she reached in and gently took the little boy's hand. "Come on," she said. "Someone's going to have a nice bath, a little noodle soup, and chocolate pudding, and then you can listen to the radio with Hilary and Freddie. Won't that be nice?"

"Yes'm," said the little boy. He understood very little of what she said, the accent was one he had never heard before, but he understood her intentions. He slid off the chair, his hand clasped in hers, and walked in the stiff-legged manner of little children whose pants are soiled.

"Who is he?" asked Hilary. The question was rhetorical, she knew who he was, but it required confirmation.

"He's mine."

The realization that Mickey had had another whole life before she met her was like when Hilary found out in school that the music from "The Lone Ranger" was really from the *William Tell* overture, and had been written years and years before there was even radio.

They cleared the lobby, leaving a gaping Tessie; a disdainful Mrs. Templeton setting up her bingo game; Mr. Davis, his arms crossed over his chest, listening to a guest, clad in new-style slacks pegged at the ankles, who told him that Roosevelt and Churchill were in Canada discussing how they would slice up Germany when the war was over; Mr. Samuelson adding that they should cut them up in little pieces. On the arm of the Morris chair, forgotten, lay the cap and veil.

The little boy stood immobile as Ilona peeled off his clothes. "Look," said Freddie, "he has prickly heat." Most of the child's body was covered with a fine pink rash. Ilona set him naked in the lukewarm tub, and he continued to stand as she gently washed him. "Poor bubbie. It doesn't look to me like he's had a bath all year," she said.

After he was washed, everyone except Mickey helped to dry him. Ilona knelt beside him with a can of talcum powder. "You better watch how I do this," she said to Mickey.

"I'm not going to take care of him," protested Mickey. "He's going back just as soon as he's cleaned up."

"Watch," said Ilona. She sprinkled the little boy's body as if she were sugaring mandelchen, patting his buttocks and his small protruding belly with the fine white dust. "How does this feel?" she asked. "Nice?"

The little boy stared at her and said nothing.

"Well one thing," said Hilary. "He's not noisy like some little kids." Then they dressed him in Freddie's old clothes which for some reason Ilona had never thrown away, while his soiled clothes were dumped to soak in the tub.

"Take him to the back door of the kitchen and ask Gus to give you some chocolate pudding and milk," said Ilona. "Then take him outside for a walk on the beach, but stay close to the hotel. Don't let go of his hand and don't take your eyes off him."

Hilary did not have to be told what to do. She had minded Freddie since she was five.

"By the way," added Ilona, "I bought you some bobby socks for junior high school. They're on your bed."

"Me?" asked Hilary.

"Who else is going to junior high school?"

"You can't wear bobby socks with sandals," said Hilary. "You have to have loafers. If I don't get loafers, I don't wanna wear them."

Ilona brushed her hair off her forehead with her arm. "One thing at a time," she said.

They took him by his hand, and led him to the kitchen. Everyone wanted to know whose child he was. When Hilary said he was Mickey's, eyebrows shot up and looks flashed from person to person like an arc of electric current. Gus came from the bakery to stand floured and ghostly before the child to whom he bent down and thundered, "I make you a cookie with your name on it." The little boy cringed. For a minute it looked as though he was going to cry, then Hilary noticed that he was trembling, like when she had a fever and got the shivers.

They took him to show to Frank who was on the receiving dock, talking to the truck driver from Sanitary Fish Market. "They're drafting fathers in October," said the truck driver. "My wife and me are worried sick, I'm not ashamed to tell you that. You being a father with kids of your own, you understand."

Hilary wondered why they were going to draft fathers when the war was going to be over two months later and was about to tell them this, when Frank yelled, "Get that little kid out of here!"

"He's Mickey's," she explained.

"Mickey's? Can you beat that?" said Frank, bemused. "No kidding. That's Mickey's kid?"

"She was married," said Hilary.

"Sure. She ever say anything about him to you?"

"Not exactly."

"Well, did you know about it?"

"Sort of."

"Sort ofs and not exactlies are no kind of answer. I want straight talk from you and don't you forget it. Now get him out of here before he gets hurt."

They took him out in the beach. Freddie's old short pants reached all the way down to his ankles.

"See water?" asked Freddie.

The little boy looked over the broad expanse of sun-dappled ocean before him.

"You want to see it up close?" asked Hilary. "You have to take off your shoes first."

They took off his shoes and socks. The waves lapped over his feet. He remained silent. "I don't think he likes it," said Freddie.

Hilary splashed his feet with her hand. "This is the ocean," she said. "It covers 90 percent of the world."

The little boy scratched his knee. He had nothing to compare this wetness to except washtubs and puddles, which it clearly was bigger than; 90 *percent* and *world* were sounds with no pictures.

They put on his shoes and socks. "You have to put your fingers between your toes," explained Freddie, "to wipe out the sand."

While they were tying his laces, Ilona was teaching Mickey what to do with a small child. She had told her that he had to have three meals a day, twelve hours' sleep, crayons, and a coloring book, that he had to be carefully watched, and that he could get into trouble, or worse, injure himself and that she had to check everything in her room that was potentially harmful such as her nail-polish remover which, if swallowed, would be poisonous to him. "Why would he ever try to swallow nail-polish remover?" asked Mickey. "Because that's how little children are. They're curious. They have to touch, eat, everything they see."

"I don't know what to do with a little child, I was never a mother," sobbed Mickey.

"Nobody was," said Ilona. "But you had a mother."

"She's dead," said Mickey. "She can't help me none."

"But you remember. You remember how she was a mother to you. It'll come back. That's how you will be a mother to him."

Mickey cried for days. Little Earl did not. He was a stoic who had learned to accommodate grown-ups who gave him little or no affection. If he kept quiet, the blows and yells were less frequent. When it became clear, that like sale merchandise, he could not be returned, Frank went to speak on Mickey's behalf to Mr. Davis, who agreed, against what he said was his better judgment, to let the child stay on one condition, that he make no noise. Mr. Davis had nothing to worry about, assured Frank, no one had ever heard the child say anything except "Yes'm."

Hilary and Freddie had fun with him. Suffering the usual boredom during the last few weeks before school started, tired of scavenging the beach, and with no movies worth seeing, they made him a toy, a diversion. They showed him their world, the roof of the hotel with the dried-up victory garden, the plane spotter, the sidewalk in front where they could watch the marching soldiers; they showed him how to do jelly doors; specifically, Freddie showed him; Hilary stood by saying she didn't think that was a very nice thing to do to people; and they took him to the beach to see black, billowing smoke on the horizon. When they left, little Earl bent over to show Freddie that he knew to rub the sand out from between his toes.

They returned him to his mother. Mickey had become a prisoner. Although Hilary baby-sat for her from time to time, and Ilona helped out in the evenings, when Mickey worked, by looking in on him, Mickey was still faced with the never-ending care of a little child.

That night, after sobbing alone on the beach in her cocktail-waitress uniform, she returned to her room to do what she had been putting off for days. She watched him sleep, this small, unwelcome stranger who had put an end to everything.

Not knowing how to explain a four-year life on one sheet of paper, it was easier to do what she did. She wrote to Bill that it was over, saying that she had changed her mind, and could not marry him, and that he should stop thinking about her, since that was what she was doing about him. The ink on the V-mail was blurred with the teardrops that fell. Little Earl stirred in his sleep, beads of sweat dewed on his small nose. "I hate you," she whispered, "I'll hate you till the day I die."

It was a week before school, just when the Allied forces landed near Naples, that Freddie had his accident. The way he got it was that he was showing off for little Earl, who stood on the sidewalk watching as Freddie maneuvered his cart, manufactured by Frank from old roller-skate wheels and pieces of crate, in the street. The show-off part came when Freddie stood on the cart instead of sitting down as he was supposed to. The cyclist rang his bell, even shouted for Freddie to get out of the way, but Freddie never heard him. The collision wasn't hard, at least not as hard as a car would have been, just strong enough to knock Freddie to the curb, where he struck the side of his face, knocking out one of his permanent teeth, and one baby tooth that was coming out anyway. Little Earl continued to stand watching on the sidewalk until some convalescent soldiers from the Lord Feldman brought them both in.

Ilona had been sitting with Frank, one of the few times they had alone together, darning his socks over a wooden egg, her hair loose with a ribbon around it, the way Mickey sometimes wore it, asking Frank to explain what was going on in Denmark, although what she wanted was not explanation, but assurance. There was clearly trouble. The newspapers were full of stories of the Danish underground revolt, public disorders, of Germans sinking Danish and even two Swedish fishing boats, Denmark scuttling its own warships, and King Christian interned, a prisoner in his own castle, and now this latest, and most ominous thing: the Germans had cut the telephone wires to Denmark. Something was happening. Stroking the tendrils that had strayed from the ribbon, Frank said softly that the Germans were getting nervous because with the Allies in Italy, it was clearly a question of only a few more months. He said they were behaving just like the trapped rats they were, lashing out in every direction, and not to worry. That if there were reprisals, it would be against saboteurs, not Jews. He added that, as he had said before, no news was good news. That was borne out by the soldier who carried in Freddie, unconscious in his arms.

"It wasn't the rider's fault," he said. "I saw the whole thing. Me and my buddy. He rang his bell, and yelled for him to get out of the way, but he didn't listen."

Freddie's accident strengthened Ilona's case for a house. It also forced their hand for the operation, which they had put out of their minds. It was clear, and a fact they could not hide from, that Freddie, who would never wear his Sonotone, which now lay rusting somewhere in the rubble of his toy box, could not hear well enough to survive.

While they waited for a hospital bed, Ilona took Hilary and Freddie for the High Holy Days to the little synagogue on Third Street. When they left after what seemed like an interminable service, in which the men below bobbed with striped shawls draped around their necks, one energetic man ducking so fiercely the knotted fringes of his shawl flew like insects, the rabbi greeted them at the door. Hilary's chin was at the level of his eyebrows. He looked up at her. "Shona Tova. When are you children coming to Hebrew school?" he asked.

"We didn't make up our minds yet," said Hilary.

"Still?" said the rabbi. "So what is taking you so long?"

Freddie and Hilary looked at one another. Hilary sighed. She didn't want to hurt his feelings. "We like Catholic better," she said.

"May one ask why?"

"Catholics have miracles," said Freddie.

"What's wrong with the Red Sea?" asked the rabbi.

"That happened a long time ago," said Hilary. "If the Jewish God is so good, why doesn't he do something to help the Jews in Europe?"

The rabbi shook his head. "It's too bad she's a girl," he said to Ilona.

They took Freddie to the hospital the week after Hilary started junior high school and told him the doctor was going to make windows in his ears. Freddie cried when they left him in his room. They cried as they sat in the waiting room. Hours later, the doctor came in to tell them that the operation on the ear appeared to be successful, but there would be no way of telling until he woke up.

They stepped into his room, walking on the edges of their shoes, moving awkwardly and bumping into things. He looked so small and helpless on the big white bed, the bandage covering the incision, his lips parted as if he had a secret to tell. Nobody had any way of knowing whether or not he had lost his hearing entirely in the ear, or whether, let's not tempt misfortune, the unnamable had happened. They hovered about him like smoke over the steam table. When he woke, the first thing he tried to do was fish out the packing in his ear. Then as the day wore on, he became dizzy and unsteady when he tried to get out of bed and threatened to throw up. The first twenty-four hours were difficult for him and for them.

The next day, Dr. Weingarten came into his room and gently removed the packing from his ear, then stood behind him and whispered, "Freddie, you can have anything to eat that you want. What will it be?"

There was silence for a moment. Then Freddie said, "Red."

He didn't hear the question. The doctor shook his head. Frank looked anguished. Ilona bit her lip.

"He means red food," said Hilary. "He hates brown dinners

and white dinners, but he loves borscht and cherry Jell-O. That's what he means when he says red."

Freddie's hearing had been salvaged. Ilona and Frank, weeping, hugged one another, Hilary, Dr. Weingarten, then fell upon the bed.

"Careful," said Dr. Weingarten. "I don't want my patient crushed to death by his own parents."

The improvement diminished the next day, causing everyone, including Freddie, to fall into a deep depression in which no one had anything to say to anyone else nor any inclination to nibble at either the Whitman Sampler brought by Mrs. Templeton, or the giant basket of fruit sent by Mr. Lonzo. They languished in silence until Dr. Weingarten returned to assure them that there was inflammation in the ear resulting from the surgery, which was obstructing the passage of sound, but that it would subside after two or three weeks.

On the sixth day, the afternoon after Hilary, wearing a hairnet, learned in home ec how to line wastebaskets and make butterscotch toast, Freddie left the hospital with only some sterile cotton in his ear, and instructions not to go swimming, or make sudden movements of his head, like looking both ways before he crossed the street, which could make him dizzy.

"You don't have to worry about that," said Hilary. "He never looks before he crosses."

21

The restoration of his hearing was borne with equanimity by Freddie, who considered it with the same dispassion he did the battle-fatigued soldiers returned from overseas to the pistachio-colored hotel next door, who wandered into the water without blinking. It was another event, this muffled, shrouded noise turned suddenly from suggestion into meaning as clear as milk writing held over a flame, not unexpected in a world that was full of surprises. Primarily, it meant to him the convenience of listening to "Fibber McGee" in bed, and not having to sit with his ear to the radio.

When it became clear that the school had been remiss, had somehow sifted Freddie right through their screening program and that his hearing impairment, which they had misdiagnosed, had now been corrected through the miracle of modern medicine, a special tutor was sent to help him catch up in a tailormade remedial course. The tutoring took place in the privacy of the east wing of the hotel when it was rainy, and on the patio when it was sunny, although Mr. Davis said that such arrangements would have to be reevaluated, when the season, which promised to be the biggest ever if the reopening of Hialeah and the Latin Quarter were any indication, began.

As darning needles flashed their iridescent wings and zapped every flying insect that could fit between their mandibles, Hilary had her own crash program, as a novitiate in the world of junior high school, a three-grade curriculum, really a holding tank for the big high school next door with which it shared a common patio and where the seventh- and eighth-graders stood at lunchtime between leggy croton bushes to watch with adoration the big kids, all of whom they could identify by name, dance the lindy hop.

It was here in junior high that the hold of *teacher* was broken, the deadlock of a single powerful, procrustean dame forever splintered, becoming shards of teachers, concepts of *pi* and cubic measurement on one facet, of longitude and latitude on another, no one ever again strong enough to make of an entire school year a misery.

While she carefully wrote down her room numbers and her times in a printed schedule, Hilary knew them all by heart the second day, running through the open, jasmine-scented corridors from one room to the next, passing kids she knew, and others that were strangers, hurrying before the bell rang and she would need a special pass from the principal, to a different teacher for each subject, including her first man teacher, Mr. Cardozo, who taught science.

The class she liked the least, next to home ec, was gym, mainly because she had to undress in a sour locker room, the smell of which stayed in her nose all day long, and shower in front of other girls. Having no breasts to speak of, even optimistically, she was ashamed, surrounded by swelling, budding, peaking classmates, and held a washcloth over her reluctant chest while she managed surreptitious peeks to see what was happening to normal people. The only consolation was Tracey Hollister, as undeveloped as she, except that Tracey was actively fighting it, squeezing her palms together a hundred times a day, even in class. Tracey said she had been doing this for a month and that she was already beginning to see improvement.

Gym was especially difficult on days when Hilary had her period, since she had learned from Tessie that activity on such a day was harmful and would cause her to bleed to death. The gym faculty, who apparently didn't know this, was unsympathetic. When Hilary went to Miss Carney in the second week and confided that she could not participate in field hockey because she fell off the roof, Miss Carney hefted her broad shoulders, resettled them on her collar bones, and gave a lecture to the entire hunter-greenbloomered gym class that what happened to a girl's body was natural and didn't need to be camouflaged with phrases such as, *My grandmother came to visit me,* or, *I'm unwell, I fell off the roof,* or worse, *I got the rag on,* which she never never wanted to hear anyone in her class say.

Neither the mechanics nor academics of junior high school were as complex as its customs and language, myriad dicta, the abrogation of any guaranteed to turn the ignorant or the careless into pariah. What was important was peer opinion. Teachers and parents paled against such an adversary. While learning that one wore cardigan sweaters buttoned only up the back, or said Hey instead of Hi, and knew by heart the words to the top ten songs on the Hit Parade, which changed from week to week, Hilary also was faced with another serious problem that was really not her own. She had gotten a letter from Bill, who asked her to find out why Mickey wouldn't answer his letters and why she wanted to break up with him. This was news to Hilary, since Mickey, her hands full with little Earl, had said nothing about it. Bill wanted to know if Mickey had gone back to Radner and wrote that any information she had would be greatly appreciated. He added that he hoped all was well with her family, that he was near Salerno, that they could not use the nearby airfields because (this part was censored), and that the land was very hilly—not like Iowa, whose hills were blurred and rolling—but sharp, spiny ridges, one after another, and that the people, when they weren't running inside to board up their windows, were very friendly, just like all the people of the hotel whom he asked to be remembered to.

Hilary had a Gordian knot to untie, which arrived on the same day her answers to the *Herald*'s football contest had to be postmarked. The question she contemplated, after she folded the selection sheet, was, should she discuss the letter with Mickey before she replied, or should she say nothing to Mickey and tell Bill what she knew. It certainly had something to do with little Earl. She didn't want Mickey mad at her, but she also felt bad that Bill had no true idea of what had happened.

She went to see Ilona, who was dressing to go somewhere with Frank. Ilona had been told that the New York *Times* ran a small article in which it was reported that Sweden had accepted large numbers of Jewish refugees who had come from Denmark on fishing boats, and her mood was up. So was her guard. The first thing she did was hold up her hand like a traffic cop and say, "No loafers. I told you before you need serious shoes so you can think straight. You got a pleated skirt and a sweater. Be satisfied."

The second thing she did, before Hilary could say that she hadn't come about loafers, or that the sweater, which had been the correct size, and was all wrong, not the oversized sloppy joes that everyone was wearing, was to cup Hilary's chin in her hand and ask, "What's that on your face? Aren't you washing like I showed you? You're supposed to scrub your face until it shines."

"That's what I do."

"Then someone please tell me what that thing is because I don't know. It certainly doesn't belong on a clean little girl."

Ilona opened her purse and checked its contents. It was clear that her mind was occupied with other matters. When she took a bottle of Shinola off the dresser and began to dab her shoes, Hilary knew for sure that the audience was ended. She was sorry that she had come.

The next person Hilary saw who might have helped was Winona, who had returned to the hotel, somber, silent, her skin grayed, grimly pushing her cart. Lionel had been killed in Detroit during a race riot, the issue of which centered, or so everyone had said, over the renting of houses closer to the war plant. The whites were unwilling to allow blacks newly arrived from the South, like Lionel and Winona, the convenience. Lionel had been wielding a pipe when he was rushed by a squad of screaming, cursing men and women and pummeled to his death.

Winona didn't talk about him or Detroit. She just pushed her cart through the halls and sang softly to herself, mostly church kind of music. She had her own troubles. Hilary did not want to add to them. Besides, she didn't think Winona would understand about the complexities of the dilemma that Bill had posed.

Hilary found Frank, who was discussing with Marco the use of POWs in the citrus groves, which he thought was a good idea and a way to relieve the serious shortage of farm workers.

"At least we'll have grapefruit," said Frank.

"If the freeze doesn't get it first," replied Marco, whirling over his head a head of lettuce in a net bag.

Hilary presented her quandary, being careful to avoid the spinning water. "So," she concluded, "I don't know what to do."

"I'm not a traffic light, baby," replied Frank. "I don't have all the answers, stop, go, yes, no. No one has. It's time you learned that."

"Since when did you think you didn't have all the answers?" asked Marco.

"You used to have them," said Hilary, ignoring the salad man as he separated the lettuce, stripping off the outer leaves to reveal crisper white leaves beneath.

"No, you used to think I did," said Frank.

"But I don't know what way to go."

"Pick the one that gives you the least grief."

"Like what?"

"Like, if you tell Mickey, you still got the problem, and you also got another problem, which is, now she's mad at you for getting into the picture. You understand what I'm saying? But if you don't say anything to her, you've solved what's eating Bill, he knows where he stands, he can take it from there, and she's not mad at you."

"But she will be when she finds out I wrote to him without telling her."

"You can cross that bridge when you come to it. I don't say everything on my mind, especially if I know it will make people mad or sad. What's the point?"

"Do you tell Ma everything?"

Frank searched her eyes, so much like his own. "Everything she needs to know. See if she can put something on that thing on your face. It looks awful."

Ilona stood in the doorway, dressed to go out. If she heard anything, she said nothing about it. "I've been waiting in the lobby," she said.

"Okay," said Frank, "let's go." He put his hands in his pockets.

"Where are you going?" asked Hilary.

"We'll be back in an hour," replied Ilona. "Where's Freddie?"

"I couldn't find him," said Frank.

"Don't go to your friend's house until we get back," said Ilona. "And keep an eye out for your brother."

"He can take care of himself, you know, he's ten years old and he hears as good as me."

"Just do what your mother says," said Frank. "Let's not get into an argument."

"But I got to get something into the mailbox," said Hilary.

"Drop it in the slot in the front desk," said Ilona.

"That's no good. It has to be postmarked today."

"What is it that's so important," asked Frank. "A certain letter?"

"No. Something else."

"What then?"

"The football picks."

"When is she going to grow up?" asked Ilona.

It was too chilly to sit on the seawall, her usual place to think when it wasn't warm enough for the sand or the surf. Instead, Hilary sat huddled on the patio, rubbing the extrusion on her chin, as chill winds whisked the sand over the patio, like scouring powder.

Getting married was the most serious, important thing a person could do. What could make Mickey decide not to go through with it when she was in love with Bill and had put down ten dollars on her gown? Little Earl, could it be because of him? He was so cute, it was hard to believe that he could be the reason. Maybe Mickey didn't want to share him with Bill, but if that were true, why didn't she treat him better? Hilary's English teacher told the class that Edgar Allan Poe had married a thirteen-year-old girl named Virginia. Hilary could understand if Virginia, whoever she was, had changed her mind at the last minute; after all, Poe was a very spooky guy, but Bill, Bill was tall, handsome, and brave. Bill was everything.

She decided that Mickey, already frazzled with maternity, didn't need anything else to make her more short-tempered, and that she would tell Bill what he needed to know. After all, it was in Mickey's interest.

Hilary wrote to Bill that she wasn't sure why Mickey broke up with him, but that Mickey's little son Earl was living with her and she was having a hard time learning what to do with him which maybe made her temporarily a little nervous. She added the postscript that Frances Simmons' brother was also in Italy, although he was in the infantry, and Frances said he wrote that the mud was up to his waist during the day and froze at night, and that the Germans' Krupp 88 could shoot around corners, and was that true?

With the dilemma solved, at least for the moment, Hilary attended to the problem at hand, which was the contest for which she had volunteered to make the selections for her home room. She took out the folded newspaper from the pocket of her blue jeans and marked carefully the boxes next to each pair of football teams. Two gave her problems. The Michigan/Ohio State game and Penn State/Pittsburgh. Mel told her that everyone on the Penn State team but the water boy was going to score, and he also told her that Michigan was favored by three points, and that even though she liked the Buckeyes better than the Wolverines, her personal taste should not interfere with her judgment. She picked Michigan.

No matter how heavily Mickey bundled him up, little Earl continued to shiver. She wondered whether he did it for spite. Despite a sweater, the sleeves of which reached past his fingertips and hung almost to his knees, his little face peeked red and rough with cold from the old woolen cap that had belonged to Freddie.

The accommodation between them was bare, just enough to get by. Now they returned from the drugstore where Mickey bought a supply of Vaseline for his chapped face, as per instructions from Ilona. She unpacked the items in their cold, damp room, unheated, as were all the rooms in a hotel designed for balmy tropical weather, and not for the occasional cold snap that could cause the mercury to plummet into the thirties, and send Miamians shivering before electric heaters.

Little Earl stood nearby and watched.

"Take off your hat and sweater," she said. "Do you want me to do everything?"

He did as he was told, wiping his running nose with the back of his hand.

"Are you my new momma?" he asked.

"Don't get yourself attached to me," said Mickey. "You're not staying. Just as soon as I find those rats that left you here, you're going right back to Georgia where you belong."

She had been saying that for weeks. He began to get the idea that it meant nothing, that it was just something she liked to say, as others said land sakes, or gol damn.

His laces lay in a crumpled heap over his shoes. "And didn't I show you how to tie those laces? Look, watch me now. I'm gonna do it one more time. If you pay attention, you can do it by yourself."

He tried to make the bow and knot, but his fingers slipped through the laces as if they were spaghetti.

"Here," she said, twisting off her words with the clipped, sharp voice of impatience. "Let me do it." As she bent over his shoes her hair brushed his nose.

"You smell purty," he said.

"You sound like a cracker. It's pretty, not purty, and it's just my perfume. Didn't you never smell perfume before?"

"No, ma'am."

A sheaf of unopened V-mail lay on her dresser. She looked at it, touched it, turning some of the letters over, and began to think how much she loved Bill, that the only time in her life all the pieces of her fit together was with him, but she squeezed her eyes tightly shut to block out such ideas. They could do her no good. The only thought she allowed herself was a prayer for his safety. She said *darling* aloud, in the soft, slurring drawl that caressed the R and dropped the G and that had made him say once as he held her in his arms, that he had never heard the word before until she spoke it, and that only a Georgia girl should say it.

"Is this good?" asked little Earl. The laces were looped around one another in little coils. Mickey began to cry, deep shuddering sobs that made her lay her head in her arms.

"I can do it better," he said.

There was a knock on the door. Winona let herself in. She held a bundle of clothes in her arms. The skin on her face lay in deep folds, like a football that had lost its air.

"These belonged to my son," she said.

"Drop them on the bed," said Mickey. "I got my hands full. I didn't get to put up my hair in pin curls. Now it looks tacky and droopy and I have got to be at work at six."

"Ain't nothing wrong with pinning it on top of your head. It looks fine that way."

Little Earl listened to them talk, and sidled to the dresser, his eyes on both of them as he reached up and hesitantly touched the white ceramic poodle. It looked like a dog he saw in the lobby with a bow in its hair. When neither Mickey nor Winona said anything, he ventured further, taking the poodle and walking it carefully along the edge of the dresser. Mickey pulled listlessly at her hair, turning her face into the mirror first one way, then the other while Winona put the folded clothes in a drawer. Emboldened, little Earl picked up speed. The poodle slipped out of his hand and fell off the dresser, then hit the foot of the bed, where it broke in half. Mickey let out a shriek. "You damned kid!" she shouted. "Who told you to touch anything on that dresser. Look what you did to my little white poodle, you broke my good luck piece. You bring me nothing but bad luck, since the day I first set eyes on you. You're bad luck." She reached over and slapped the child's hands.

"I never thought I would say this to a living soul," said Winona, gravely, sadly, "but I'm going to say it. As pretty as you are, you're nothing but white trash. Not even a dog treats its puppies the way you treat that little child. You don't deserve him. *Nossir.* You don't deserve him no kind of way."

Winona closed the door behind her as Mickey picked up the pieces of the poodle and began to cry all over again.

Frank and Ilona braved the chill winds to walk to the house across the bridge, Ilona hurrying on ahead, clicking on the pink sidewalk in her heels, and Frank striding behind to keep up. He had never seen the house before. He went because Ilona was restive about the news that surely was to come at any moment, even though he warned her that there was no way for her mother and sister to come to the United States, even if they got a visa, until the war was over. It will be over any day now, she argued, General Eisenhower says so, half of Berlin is in smoking ruins, the Russians were in Poland, and how long can it take the Americans to get from the bottom of Italy to the top? He went because the house had become a focal point for her. If she saw it, he reasoned, it would satisfy her for a while and keep her from nagging him.

It stood exactly as she had described it the night before, the red-tiled front steps, the screen door grilled with iron palms, the fronds of which curled gracefully around its edges, the portholes in the stucco trim.

"There it is," she said, her arm through his. "What do you think?"

A man dressed in a sweater and a golf cap stooped on the front lawn, pulling out weeds. "You looking for someone?" he asked.

Ilona clutched her purse more tightly to her chest. "Where is the FOR SALE sign?" she asked. "When I was here last time there was a FOR SALE sign."

"That must have been a few months back," said the man. "I bought this house last August, me and my wife."

"But that's not possible," said Ilona, "the agent would have told me, he knew I was interested, I told him so. I had this house in mind." Her accent thickened like pudding. "My husband has been putting aside money."

"I don't care what you had in mind, lady. I bought this house. You want to see the sale agreement?"

Frank resisted the impulse to knock the man cold.

"Come on," he said, taking her arm. "Let's go."

Ilona began to cry, softly, quietly, an apologetic weeping that soaked her handkerchief. "It was perfect," she said. "It was just right. I could have fixed it up. We would have been happy there."

"There are other houses," said Frank.

"I gave Freddie a rock from the backyard. I showed him where his room was going to be. He won't believe me anymore. He won't have confidence in me. Children have to have confidence in their mother."

"Kids forget. Anyway, we're so far away from being able to afford a house. If you want to know, I let you show it to me to make you feel good. And that's the truth of it."

"Don't humor me," she shouted. "Make some money instead, so you can take care of your wife and children! Go out and make some money!" She screamed the words. The man pulling up weeds stood up straight as if he would be called upon to defend his property. Frank turned and walked away, his neck pulled into his jacket against the cold. At the end of the block, he turned again and walked back toward her, put his arm around her quaking shoulders, and led her back to the hotel.

They walked for several minutes in silence. The pink and baby blue feathering of the early evening sky stood in frivolous contrast to the bone-chilling cold. Frank wet his finger to test the wind.

"The radio says that if the wind dies down, all the citrus is gonna freeze. The growers can burn all the smudge pots they want, if the temperature gets below thirty degrees and lasts for a couple of hours, it's gonna kill all the fruit. The whole crop."

Ilona jerked free of his embrace. "You worry for everyone but us. You ran around like a crazy man to get into the service so you could fight and get yourself killed, and leave us alone to God knows what. You moped for months because they wouldn't take you, now you're upset about oranges. When will you care about us, Frank? Tell me, when?"

"I thought that's what I was doing," he said, thrusting his neck deeper into his collar.

After Hilary had deposited the letters, one to the sports editor, the other to Bill, she went to her first pajama party at the home of Pinky Weiselmann, who preferred to be called by her real name, which was Rhoda. It wasn't exactly a party, even though Mrs. Weiselmann served them hot dogs, Cracker Jacks, licorice pipes, brownies, and Coke, since Pinky/Rhoda spent the entire evening playing a record titled *Pavane for a Dead Princess,* which made Hilary conclude that Pinky/Rhoda was the kind of girl who probably would have been happy to marry Edgar Allan Poe.

While the Victrola scratched the melancholy dirge, Hilary had time to observe Mr. and Mrs. Weiselmann, plump and content, with their edges blurred, hovering about them like helium balloons, always ready with another plate of licorice pipes or brownies. Hilary wondered if they fought like Frank and Ilona, who had returned to the hotel that evening with their pinched fighting faces. It didn't seem as though they did. Could it be true that fat people were happier than thin people? She would write it down in her new diary under the heading, Thought for the Day.

Frances Simmons announced right before they fell asleep, drugged from a surfeit of glucose, Pavane, and fatigue, that Hilary had a crush on Mr. Cardozo. It was dark in the bedroom, which somehow made the secret larger, looming with clandestine prominence over the beds and cots.

"That's a lie!" said Hilary.

"No it isn't, and you know it," said Frances. "You look at him all the time. You never take your eyes off him. Everyone says so."

"It's still a lie. I don't even like Mr. Cardozo."

No one believed her. There was no response.

Hilary had written a poem to the tall, languid science teacher which was hidden in her diary and which she had shown to no one. She had another piece for her diary. She would head this one, The Secret Is Out. She went to sleep thinking of his hands, lightly veined, with thin black hairs covering their backs, the accidental touch of which, when he handed her a Devonian rock to study its embedded leaf, made her face get hot, as if she had been sunburned.

The next morning Hilary returned to the hotel in time to go to the movies with Freddie and little Earl. Mickey said she didn't want to go, that she needed time alone or that she would go nuts. With little Earl between them, they sat through a pandemic of Saturday films, *The Lone Ranger* and *Tarzan*, a newsreel, and six Tom and Jerry cartoons and the feature, *Guadalcanal Diary*. When they went back to the hotel, Freddie sprinted away without saying where he was going, but slowed when he realized she was watching him. He was up to something. What?

Hilary returned with little Earl to Mickey, wondering if she should tell about the letter. Mickey, still smarting from the white-trash epithet hurled by Winona, lay with two witch-hazel soaked pads over her eyes.

"He liked Tom and Jerry," said Hilary. "Especially the part where Jerry dresses up in a doctor coat and ties dynamite to Tom's tail. I think he laughed."

"What's wrong?" asked Mickey. "You're acting funny."

"Your eyes are closed," said Hilary. "How can you tell how I'm acting?"

Mickey slipped off the pads. "I can hear it in your voice. You're not going to tell me? Okay, then, keep your old secrets. What's that thing on your face? Are you getting a pimple?"

"Well, what am I supposed to do about it?" Hilary felt herself crying, and not knowing why. "I wash my face! I wash it and wash it, and they keep coming every place but my eyeballs."

"Now don't cry, honey. All you need is a boyfriend. Then watch that thing disappear so fast, it'll make your head spin, and that's a natural fact." Mickey slipped off the pads. "What's he doing?" she asked.

"Nothing," said Hilary. "He's just sitting on the bed."

"Make some noise," ordered Mickey in the direction of the other bed. "I can't stand it when I can't hear you. Do like you're told! Say something!"

"Hiyo, Silver," little Earl whispered, a gentle susurrus that rustled to the windowsill.

22

Near the New Year, things seemed definitely on the upswing. Tarawa had been secured, a little coral atoll that Hilary could not even find on the map and that somehow was the key to the central Pacific, had been wrested from its diehard Japanese defenders. Hilary, picking eighteen wins out of twenty games, was announced as one of three tied winners in the newspaper's football contest, making her a hero for the time being and catapulting her and her home room with the trajectory of the new German rockets into instant, if temporary, fame. Bigger kids knew her, some even called her by name, and Frances Simmons, who said she had been keeping an eye on her, invited her to a pajama party.

Then Mr. Davis with his flat, expressionless face, the result of his fractured jaw which clicked when he spoke, told Frank that Hilary and Freddie, costumed at the expense of the hotel association, could ride the float in the Orange Bowl Parade, the theme of which was the association's contribution to the war effort. Its design was actually clever, considering that it had been executed by twenty-three people more assiduous than artful, including Harry Pfeffer from the Versailles, who vetoed every suggestion, and kept insisting that whatever they did had to be a class operation. On top of the float, locomoted by ten people, five pushing and five pulling, was a scaled-down hotel with a model of a B-17 revolving on its roof. Freddie, wearing a scaled-down army air corps uniform was to be the pilot, and Hilary, dressed in a nurse's uniform, was to stand smiling in the entrance.

Mickey, who had turned into a grudging mother, competent in basic skills of washing and feeding, if deficient in more affectionate behavior, was dating. Especially now that Bill's letters had stopped coming, allowing her to forget from time to time, she sometimes even looked forward to dressing up in her new peplum suit with the frilly blouse and the wired push-up bra and waist cincher beneath, feeling pretty again, and seeing how crazy she could get a guy, even if she was tormented by a sorrowful, uniformed homunculus with sandy hair.

New Year's Eve presented Hilary with a conflict. Before she learned that she was to be allowed on the float, she had offered to baby-sit for Mickey. Now she and Freddie would have to wait for Mr. Pfeffer to drive them home and that wouldn't be until late after the float had been hauled into the warehouse. There was a way out. Hilary asked Mickey if they could take little Earl with them to the parade, and Mickey, who would have let anyone take him anywhere, agreed.

Mickey was setting her hair when they left, securing each pin curl with crossed bobby pins. "Smile," she said to little Earl. "When you see all those people, even if you think they can't see you, show your teeth. Let me see how you do it."

Little Earl smiled, dimpling his face like the skin on an orange. Mickey sighed, stood up, clutched her silk kimono about her, and walked into the bathroom. "Come on in here," she said. "I told you to brush real good and you didn't do it. Now I have to do it over. You can't go around showing nasty teeth."

Freddie and Hilary looked at one another, ran their tongues over their teeth, and shifted their feet. When Mickey was satisfied, she pushed little Earl in the direction of Freddie and picked up a silk scarf from the dresser to tie over her head. "And once in a while, remember to wave."

"Yes, ma'am," he said.

Carrying their costumes and holding tightly onto little Earl, Hilary and Freddie pushed through the crowd and found the staging area set behind wooden ramps. Even though a dimout was in force, there was pandemonium, a confusion of a giant Popeye balloon anchored by heavy ropes to four handlers, lights winking and flashing, gadgets whirring, uniformed bands tuning up their instruments, majorettes twirling batons, some of which clattered to the ground, narrowly missing marshals who were running around with route sheets shouting directions, and a generator which provided the light and action for one float beginning to smoke, sending black smoke billowing around the white satin of a screaming majorette.

The hotel association's float, number seven in line, was already staged. Because it was feared that the revolving plane and hotel would not be enough of a class operation, a muzzled greyhound with a racing saddle was placed on one side, with its trainer, who kept scooping up its droppings, insisting that the dog was nervous because of all the people. "He should be used to crowds," said Harry Pfeffer. "We would have been better off with the rabbit."

On the other side of the float, positioned like a picture postcard, were two bathing beauties, tossing a big beach ball back and forth, one continually hiking up a shoulder strap, and in the front of the float, on crepe paper saw grass, knelt Billy Jackrabbit in his Seminole garb, not speaking to anyone, wrestling with the head of a fake alligator, the mouth of which was wired to open and close.

After Hilary and Freddie had changed in a nearby dressing shack each yelling at the other not to look, Freddie was helped up a ladder to the model B-17. The discrepancy became apparent even when he was climbing the ladder. Freddie could barely squeeze into the plane. The only way they got him in was to shove in his arms and legs and force his head over, making him round-shouldered like a shrimp. Worse, when the switch was turned on and the plane began to revolve, Freddie, a foot dangling out each window, got dizzy.

They helped him down. Harry Pfeffer was there in an instant, checking over the situation. With a keen hotel eye that was able to spot a diminishing light bulb at fifty paces, he noticed the little blond boy sitting next to Billy Jackrabbit. "What about the Seminole kid?" he asked.

They had forgotten about little Earl, who, characteristically, had not said a word.

"He's not a Seminole," said Freddie. "His shirt is all one color."

"I'll find out," said Hilary. "You want to go in the plane?" she asked.

"Yes, ma'am."

"Ma'am is what you call teachers, not regular people. He wants to go."

Reluctantly, Freddie lent little Earl his flight cap, telling him to be careful not to get it all dirty and, if he felt like throwing up, to toss it out of the window first. Little Earl was helped up the ladder into the B-17. He fit. They started the motor. The plane began its slow revolutions.

"Are you dizzy?" shouted Mr. Pfeffer.

"No, sir." Little Earl smiled.

"You don't feel like throwing up? If you do, tell us now."

"Throw out the cap first," yelled Freddie.

There was a shriek of whistles. Then Billy Jackrabbit, suddenly and without warning, said he was not going to ride on the float, that they had promised him a real alligator, and that he was not going to wrestle with a toy. Mr. Pfeffer offered him more money, but Billy Jackrabbit slammed his hand into the crotch of an elbow, jumped over the hurdle of the wooden barriers, and disappeared into the crowd. Mr. Pfeffer had the answer again. Freddie, dressed in his army air corps uniform, would wrestle with the alligator head. Even though it was not an accurate representation, there was something eye-catching about it.

The parade began and the float started to roll. The only one at first not happy in her assignment was Hilary, standing in the doorway of the hotel in her nurse's uniform, who said she would rather push the float than hold a hot water bag. She changed her mind when, after she had waved tentatively to the crowd with the back of her free hand, like the pictures of the Queen of England, they waved back, some taking pictures of her, and six kids from school screamed her name, including Liz Bonnier with some eighth-grade girls, a girl in her home ec class who could line wastebaskets with grocery bags in twenty seconds flat, and Sorrell Myers, who kept getting thinner and taller.

Hilary did not see Mickey until three the next morning, when her glamorous friend, who had been out with a captain who had importuned her unsuccessfully with heavy hands and mouth to surrender in the back seat of a Plymouth, returned to her room with her makeup smeared like runny watercolors, and paper streamers strung around her reddened neck.

"How was the parade?" she asked.

"I didn't like it at first," replied Hilary, "but everyone waves and they take pictures of you. The clowns run around alongside the float and there's different music in front of you and behind you, and once the greyhound got loose and jumped off and it took them three blocks to catch him."

Mickey said nothing about the little form sleeping on the next bed.

"He rode in the B-17," offered Hilary.

"Who did?"

"Little Earl."

"Did he mind himself?"

"Everyone liked him the best."

"How do you know that?"

"They kept shouting to look at the little boy in the plane. He was spinning and waving, flashbulbs were popping all the time, once I almost got blinded. He was waving up to the last minute, even when they turned the motor off."

Mickey slipped off her sandals and rubbed her feet. "Did he smile like I told him?"

"He smiled the whole time. He never stopped smiling. He's still smiling."

Mickey glanced at her son.

"How about you? Did you have a good time on your date?" asked Hilary.

"It was a wrestling match. Some men can't take no. They think no means yes. I hate men who think if they paw at you, it'll make you change your mind. Slobbering all over me." Hilary shuddered. "Oh honey, I forgot."

"That's okay. . . . I don't think much about him anymore, except sometimes I still dream about him chasing me, and I can't run, and I wake up all sweaty." Hilary picked up her book from the floor. "There's something I want to know," she said. "How come you're dating, anyhow?"

"I'm lonesome. I got to get out once in a while."

"Won't Bill be mad at you if he finds out?" It was risky, but it was an opening.

"Don't worry yourself, honey, about every little thing. You'll make yourself old before your time."

It was one of the few times Mickey shut her out. Hilary was hurt. She had given Mickey an opportunity to set things right, to tell the truth. For some reason, she did not want to take it. Hilary continued to press. "What does he say in his letters?"

Mickey looked annoyed. "Why do you want to know?"

"Well, for example, does he say anything about me? Or about anyone else? Where is he? What is he doing? You used to tell me. Now you don't. So I want to know why."

Mickey's eyes shimmered with tears. The ice cracked, a spider web of thin, fragile, rimy striations. Now she would tell the truth. She had to.

Mickey sighed. "I'm tired, honey. You know, I worked tonight before I went out, so I'm real beat. Thank you for baby-sitting. And listen, I want to pay you, hear? Just like I'd have to do with a real sitter."

"I don't want money," said Hilary. "We're friends, or I thought we were. Friends don't pay friends."

"A friend can pay a friend for doing them a favor."

"No they can't."

"I'm too tired to argue with you. It seems something made you real testy. Go on, take the money. You earned it fair and square."

"I don't want money from you. If I take money from you, something gets erased."

"Now what in the pluperfect hell are you talking about?"

"About friends. And I'll tell you something. I think you're rotten to him. Everyone on that parade route loved him. He was the star of the whole thing. The least you could do is look at him a little and smile, just like all those strangers did. You used to teach me about winning ways. Who are they for, those winning ways? Can't you spare one for him?"

Little Earl's hands were tucked beneath his face. Mickey unclipped her earrings and laid them on the dresser. "You think it's cold in here?" she asked.

"I can't tell," said Hilary, her hand on the door.

"Well, I do," said Mickey. "I think it's right chilly." She took the blanket and brought it gently up to little Earl's chin.

Frances Simmons' older brother had been blown to bits in Anzio, riding on the old Roman highway in an open jeep. The pajama party, of course, was canceled. His name was put on a plaque and added to the stone memorial in the school patio dedicated to Miami Beach High School graduates who had been killed in action. Everyone put their arms around Frances, some cried when they saw her, and a few kissed her gingerly on the cheek, as if what she had was contagious. There were few families that had not been touched, either directly or indirectly by the war. Who did not have a cousin or an uncle, a friend or a neighbor, who had not lost his life, or was a prisoner of war, like Heshy Levine, a former fullback, whose father owned a local fish market, who was now in a Japanese camp in Burma.

Hilary's family was added to the list. Mrs. Templeton met Hilary in the lobby. The lady was composed, her arms crossed over the expanse of her abdomen, her face serene, even though she had been through a harrowing bingo game in which, among other things, Mr. Salter, a guest from Teaneck, insisted on a payoff when it was clear that he had moved his counter.

"There's been trouble, dear," said Mrs. Templeton.

Hilary's first thought was Freddie, who had been caught the week before smoking behind the seawall. Mrs. Templeton tucked a stray crinkled gray hair into its place, gently, but firmly reminding it where it belonged.

"Is it my brother?"

Mrs. Templeton shook her head. "Your mother has had very bad news, I'm afraid."

Hilary felt sick. "What news?"

"I think she and your father ought to be the ones to tell you."

Ilona was lying on her bed, a crumpled, sodden handkerchief on the sheet beside her. Frank sat on the edge of the bed, awkwardly holding her inert hand. Freddie sat cross-legged on the floor. The air in the room was heavy, the black-damp of a tunnel. Mrs. Templeton discreetly closed the door behind her.

Hilary stood on the worn Axminster carpet over a threadbare and fading rose. For a minute, no one said anything. Frank spoke first, softly, tonelessly. "Your mother got a letter from Sweden. The krauts killed her sister, your aunt Margit. They took your cousin Dieter away, they think to a concentration camp. No one knows where. They were hiding in a shed near the docks. The Germans had dogs. They found them."

"What about my grandmother?"

"She's the one who wrote the letter. She's the one who made it to Sweden. To Malmö."

Ilona curled up like a little baby. Frank began to weep. "I wish

I knew what to do to make it better for you. I don't know what to do."

It was infectious. Hilary and Freddie, who had never seen their father cry, also began to weep. Hilary was frightened and tried to put her face next to her mother's. Ilona didn't seem to know that she was there.

"All gone, all lost," whimpered Ilona.

"Your mother's alive," said Frank. "At least you got that."

"Why?" asked Ilona. "Why me?"

"No one knows that," said Frank. "It's happening to everyone. You're not alone."

Ilona didn't seem to hear him. It was not what she meant anyhow. "My God," she cried, an anguished plaint. "Why was I picked to survive and not her? They didn't want me to come. I deserted them. I left my family and now God has punished me."

"You really think God has nothing more to do than to punish people for every little thing they do or don't do?" said Frank. "I can't believe that. There's just too many people all doing too many wrong things. I'm much worse than you could ever be, sometimes I've been a real bastard, and my folks are still alive. You got to stop thinking that way," said Frank.

"I'm so sorry," continued Ilona. She began to cry again, dabbing at her face with her handkerchief. "And the little boy too. My God in heaven, what do you want with a little boy? They drugged him, my sister drugged him to keep him quiet, a gag in his mouth."

Ilona heaped on the fuel. Everytime they got a breather, there was something new to cry about. Hilary tried to remember what Dieter looked like. The only thing that came to mind was his plastered-down hair and his ears that were big like hers used to be.

"I got to see about something," said Frank. "Sit with your mother."

Hilary took his place on the bed. "Don't cry, Ma," she said. Ilona balled herself up again and began to shiver, then edged away, facing the wall. Hilary tried to put her arms around her, but Ilona shrugged her off and sobbed, agonized sobs that filled every corner of the room. There was no place to hide, no place to escape the wailing, or the sorrow. Freddie, with tears streaming down his face, put his fingers in his ears.

"Why?" asked Ilona.

Another feature of growing up, questions without answers. Hilary moved out of the wet place on the sheet, but Ilona suddenly clutched at her sweater. "Don't go," she moaned, her eyes glazed as if in aspic. "Don't go. Never go. No more. No more."

Frank returned and Hilary slipped out of her mother's clutch to take up a position on the other bed. It looked as though this horror, unlike others in Hilary's and Freddie's experience which were time-limited, like the time the sailors washed up on the beach, would go on forever.

Ilona rolled over on her back, and put her hand over her eyes. "My mother wrote that someone gave her a handbill. She was in Malmö three hours and they gave her a handbill. It said not to talk Yiddish and to keep off the main streets. How long will she be safe there? Answer me that."

It was three days before Ilona came off the bed. There was no funeral, no memorial services, instead, just visitors coming in and out of the room to offer embarrassed and hasty condolences, and to ask one another in the hall when D-Day would finally arrive. Gus was the most timorous of all. "I will never go back to Germany," he said, after waiting in awkward silence behind a cluster of commiseraters for a chance to get close to the bed. Ilona didn't answer him. Freddie did. He shook his big hand. "Thanks for coming, Gus," he said.

Frank felt two things. The feelings were simultaneous and contradictory, like one hand pushing against the other, the dynamic tension of Charles Atlas, only it wasn't making Frank stronger, it was enervating him, robbing him of his starch, like a shirt that has been left to soak. The first feeling was sorrow which permeated everything in their room, even the damp, mildewing draperies. Frank felt pity for his wife; her loss was tragic, especially after the many months of anxious waiting. It pained him to see Ilona wounded afresh each morning, or so frequently, in the middle of the night when she started to recollect, or, with pallid face and eyes almost swollen shut, struggling through routine activities as if trapped in seaweed.

He told her that they would make another effort to save, he would give up going to the barber, she could cut his hair herself, no one would buy anything that they did not absolutely need, they would make do with what they had, and if Mr. Davis could give them a second mortgage, maybe they could swing a house, but that she should remember that a house was also furniture, which they didn't have. Ilona said she wasn't interested. There was no reason for the house. Before they knew it, the kids would be grown up anyway. She was foolish ever to have wanted one.

The second feeling was anger. Frank felt trapped. If he had ever wanted to get away, if he had entertained the idea at all, even fleetingly, he could not do it now. It was hard enough to consider leaving his wife and children, even though he had been laying money aside for that possibility for months, impossible if the wife was grief-stricken. The desire to be somebody, to do something, which could only be done, in his reckoning, alone and unencumbered, was denied to him. He did not accept his confinement cheerfully.

To escape from the helpless rage that sometimes made him want to smash his fist into the peach-colored plaster wall, Frank went outside at night after work and sat alone in the rear of the patio, the only visible sign of him, unless the night sky was cloudless and he was illuminated by the white light of moon and stars, his glowing cigar. There he could sit in private, watch the shadowed figures drift between beach and hotel, and try to sort things out.

One balmy, gardenia-fragrant March evening, after Freddie had come out to announce that he had a Mexican jumping bean that had just leaped seven inches, Frank listened to the surf fizzling on the shore and, as he had done on many nights, watched Mickey cross the amethystine patio on her way back to her room. His inspection was scrupulous and lingered on her legs, which he thought were beautiful, not muscular like some dancers he had seen, but shapely. He lifted his eyes, like the polished curves of her naked shoulders.

"Tips good?" he asked.

"Is that you, Frank? I didn't see you there," she replied. "I didn't really get a chance to count it. What are you doing here all alone?"

"Thinking."

"I'm too tired to think this hour of the night. It's all I can do to get back to my room and get off my feet. What are you thinking about?"

Frank paused, took the cigar out of his mouth, and knocked off the ash. "About how pretty you are."

"You can't see me in the light. If you did, I don't think you would say that." Mickey leaned backward, seeming temporary and flimsy, as if at any moment she would be blown away by the ocean breeze.

"You're beautiful in any light and somebody ought to be around to tell you. Sit with me."

"I have to get back to Sonny."

"I thought his name was Earl."

"It was. But that name just reminds me of his father. Besides, he likes Sonny better too."

"Stay for a minute. I like to look at you. You really are a sight for sore eyes."

Mickey sat down hesitantly. "How's Ilona?" she asked.

"She's still taking it bad. All she does is cry. Not that I blame her. It's a tough way to lose someone. The crying shame of it is all three of them made it all the way to Denmark. When Lipschutz was here to pick up his duds—he's big time now, you know, he's playing at Mother Kelly's—he told me that he read that the Danish seamen who ran the refugee boats to Sweden mixed dried human blood and some drug, and sprinkled it on the deck so when the Germans brought the dogs on board, they couldn't sniff out the people."

"That gives me the shivers. It's easier to find someone, anyhow, than it is to hide, ask me," said Mickey. "I know. Anyway, I thought her mother got out."

"Her mother's still alive, but she's over sixty, and she's been run pretty ragged. Ilona is worried that she won't make it either, that something will happen to her."

Mickey eased her back. "I miss my mother. There's still a lot of things she could have told me. Lord, it's good to rest."

"What do you hear from Bill?"

"That's over, Frank."

"How come?"

"It just is, that's all."

"Does Hilary know? She didn't say anything to me about it."

"I don't want to talk about it."

Frank put out his hand to touch hers, then began rubbing her fingers. When she didn't pull away, he clasped her hand in his own.

"I think you're terrific, baby," he said softly. "I thought so since the first time I saw you. I've known some good-looking, classy dames, but I've never seen a looker like you in person. Only on a big screen."

"That and a dime will get me a cup of coffee." Mickey pulled her hand away. "I got to go, Frank."

"I think I know what's on your mind. Look, what's between you and me is between you and me, nobody else."

"I can't."

"Maybe it's that you don't like kitchen whites. You'd rather have a different kind of uniform."

"That's not fair, Frank. You know that's not it. I think you're swell, Frank. I always have. And I think you're real good-looking too, but Hilary is my friend, and Ilona, she's been wonderful with Sonny."

"What's one thing have to do with another?"

"I don't know. I just can't put the two together. You and them. It's not a fit."

"Okay. I won't press you." Frank leaned back. "I don't believe in pushing myself on any woman. It's got to be a two-way street. It's still him, isn't it?"

Hilary stood at the far corner beside the dispirited blossoms of a hibiscus bush folded for the night, and watched as Mickey ran across the patio and her father crushed his cigar with his heel. Neither saw her. She rolled back the cuffs of her drooping pajama legs and sprinted back into the hotel.

The next day after school and a run-in with her English teacher who didn't like the way she diagramed sentences or the note that she passed to Tracey Hollister in which she described the teacher's nose as a dangling participle, Hilary found her father in the store room counting lettuce boxes. She had been saving her question all day, like an itch that you accumulate before you scratch it good.

"What were you talking about?" she asked.

"Who? When? Jesus, you interrupt me in the middle of a count, now I lost my tally."

"I'm sorry. You and Mickey. Last night."

Frank's eyes narrowed. "What were you doing up so late?"

"I couldn't sleep, and when I can't sleep, I like to see the beach at night. Sometimes the moonlight looks like a ribbon on the water, and sometimes it looks like icing. I wanted to see which.

Last night there wasn't any. The water just looked like that blue stuff you made menus out of. Were you talking about Bill?"

"Yes and no."

"Was she feeling bad about something?"

"I don't know. Why?"

"You were petting her hand."

Frank turned back to his tally sheet. "We were just talking. Nothing more. Nothing less. Don't make a big deal out of it." He pushed the lettuce boxes to the side. "Don't say anything to your mother. She'll take it the wrong way, like you did." Frank patted her cheek. "Don't look like that, sweetheart. Mickey is like a kid sister to me. That's all. Look, you got my word. Okay?"

"Okay, Daddy." Frank had made it all right again. With the nagging worry gone, she went to write a poem to Mr. Cardozo.

By the end of March, when Hilary decided that she was in love with Mr. Cardozo, she could imagine him kissing her near the Bunsen burners, pulling her braids passionately from her head, and that she would be a scientist like Madame Curie. Ilona was back at work, although still in mourning, never bothering with lipstick, or her clothes, and pulling her hair into a careless knot at the nape of her neck.

Hilary and Freddie continued to try to console her. Freddie's brand of leavening was to tell jokes and do things like stand on his head, crack all his knuckles, even those of his toes, and curl his tongue in his mouth. Hilary made suggestions, such as to go see Charles Boyer drive Ingrid Bergman crazy in *Gaslight*, or shop for Ilona's favorite cologne, Midnight in Paris, which came in a box with powder to match. To these things Ilona would shrug.

Hilary persisted, even though she didn't feel like it. "You want to know what I did in school today?"

"Who wants to hear that?" asked Freddie, who walked in with a swagger he had learned from his best friend, Shirley Leone's younger brother, Sheldon.

Hilary pursed her lips and turned doggedly to her mother. "We made a fog in science. We hung a can of cold water over a can of hot water. Mr. Cardozo let me blow through the tube and I made a mist. Then he held a piece of burning cardboard in the mist and it changed to fog."

"Hilary's in love with Mr. Cardozo."

"I am not. Take that back, you lousy brat." Hilary shoved first and Freddie shoved her back in the chest. It was tender and sore. Hilary did not remember hurting herself. "Ooh," she said, "you hurt me." She brushed the tears from her eyes.

"Don't hit Hilary there," said Ilona tiredly.

"I'm trying to talk to Ma. Why don't you go away?"

"It's a free country. I don't have to."

Hilary moved closer to her mother. "I was invited by Tracey Hollister and Jackie Snyder to a party on the same night. What do you think I should do?"

The question was gratuitous. Hilary had already chosen Jackie's party, since a night at Tracey's would be bust exercises and chanting "I must, I must, I must increase my bust," whereas Jackie's party would be gossip, and exchange of items such as who liked who, who hated who, who among the big kids was going all the way.

"Why ask me? I'm a dumb greenhorn. You told me so yourself. Why not ask Rhoda's mother? She'll know what to do."

Ilona would not forget, and she would not let Hilary in. Hilary made a final offer. "If you want me to go to the shul for the Purim carnival, I'll go. So will Freddie. We'll even put on costumes."

"Don't include me," said Freddie.

"And don't do me any favors," said Ilona.

Freddie compounded matters by getting caught smoking behind the seawall. Mr. Davis, who talked about Freddie going bad, as if he were a rotten potato, told Frank, who in turn decided not to tell Ilona. Instead, Frank assigned Hilary, over her protests, to watch him. Three days later, alerted by the sounds of coughing, Hilary caught Freddie in the pool shack with Sheldon, sucking at a smoldering cigarette.

"Phew," she said, "it stinks in here. You want to stunt your growth?"

"Get lost," said Freddie, who continued to pull, although with difficulty because of his overbite.

"Okay. I'm telling Ma."

Freddie passed the cigarette to Sheldon who had to light it all over again. "Go fly a kite. You won't say anything bad to her now and you know it." He was right.

"It'll make you sick," she countered.

"Hilary's getting titties," he giggled to Sheldon, who had become bilious.

"You shut up! I'll tell Daddy!" she screamed.

"And I'll tell about Mr. Cardozo. I love him so much. OOH. OOH. I feel his kisses on my neck." He fell sideways on the floor laughing and rolling in the dirt.

"How did you find my book?"

"Mel found it. Behind the fire extinguisher is not a good place. He told me to tell you."

Hilary dropped her voice to a snarl. "There's nothing worse than reading something private. It's the lowest of the low."

"Oh yes there is."

"Like what?"

"Spying on someone."

"Who's spying?"

"You are. You're always spying on me."

"No I'm not."

"Prove it. Take a puff."

It was a draw. Hilary dropped to the ground to sit in cross-legged resignation between her brother and Sheldon Leone and take a puff of the cigarette, her first. She tried to inhale as she had seen Lipschutz do many times, absently, yet with style and grace. The smoke trickled down into the recesses of her lungs and choked her. After hacking until her chest ached and her throat became sore, she began to like the feel of putting the cigarette to her lips. It was wicked, grown-up, sophisticated, and she was able to take smoke into her cheeks and expel it in a long, controlled stream with only moderate choking. Then she practiced holding the cigarette between thumb and forefinger, between forefinger and middle finger, finally dangling it from her lower lip.

"How do I look?" she asked. "Do I look like Barbara Stanwyck?"

"When do I get a turn?" complained Sheldon. "Your sister is hogging the cigarette."

"What about Claire Trevor?"

The door flew open. It was Ilona. "The bell captain said you were here, but I didn't believe it. Is this what you teach your brother?"

Hilary and Freddie jumped up. Sheldon Leone staggered to the wall; the pack of cigarettes spilled over the ground. "If Mrs. Leone knew, do you think she would ever allow Sheldon to come here again? Would she? You're thirteen years old." Ilona clapped her two hands together and held them there, as if she were praying.

"I can explain," said Hilary.

"Never mind what you can explain. You always have answers. Don't give me any more grief than I already have. Will you please?"

Hilary found Frank in the storeroom. She came to tell him of this recent injustice and that she was convinced Ilona hated her, but Frank was in conversation with a man wearing a suit, who had just told him Mr. Lonzo had been indicted by a federal grand jury, and he waved her away.

That night Ilona initiated a conversation in bed. The light had already been turned out and they were both lying on their backs. "I don't know what I did wrong, Frank. I think that girl hates me. I can't understand it. I loved my mother."

"You left your mother," said Frank.

"What a terrible thing to tell me."

"Don't take it that way, for God's sake, but think about it. You left your mother when you weren't much older than she is. I know you wanted to come to America, but I mean, if you loved her so much, why did you go?"

"You can be very cruel, Frank."

"I'm sorry. I just wish we would say what was what and not walk on eggs. I'm getting tired of walking on eggs."

"Did I ever ask you to walk on eggs? Did I?"

"I'll tell you another thing I'm sick of. I'm sick of the war. It seems like it should have ended a year ago. It just drags on and on. It could last for another ten years at this rate."

"I don't ask you to walk on eggs."

"Go to sleep. I'm beat. You are too. We'll both feel better in the morning."

"What did he want, the man in the vest?"

"He was from the OPA. He came to talk about points."

"Is everything all right?"

"Everything is fine."

Frank was still steaming from the man in the suit, even at midnight when Lonzo's lieutenant knocked on his door to ask if he could use the storeroom for twelve hours, no questions asked. Frank reached into his pants, which lay folded over the chair, and gave him the key. "Fine," he said, with an eye on his sleeping wife. "Just tell whoever uses it to clean it up when they're through."

23

At the same time Tracey Hollister ran the home ec sewing machine needle through her finger while making an apron, Wendell Willkie withdrew as a candidate from the Republican nomination, and the incidence of V.D. in Miami, the highest of any area in the country, forced the military to put a curfew on enlisted men, Hilary learned from Jackie Snyder that Mr. Cardozo was a fairy, a man who liked boys instead of girls, which was borne out by what he said about her poem.

Even as Ilona was giving Hilary prophylactic instructions, primarily not to sit on any public toilet seat, all Hilary could think of was Tuesday, when Mr. Cardozo had told her he knew the poem was from her, even though it was unsigned, and that he did not like girls to write him poems, especially poems that did not scan. It was particularly unfair because the poem did scan, if one recognized trochaic meter which Mr. Cardozo clearly did not.

Ilona had been in Mickey's room waiting for a home permanent to take, neutralizer dripping down her neck, and so could not be reached when she had gotten a long distance call from New York from someone she did not know, with a message from her mother. When Ilona spent most of Sunday at the switchboard with Tessie, frantically trying to get an outside line, Freddie, Hilary, and Sheldon Leone were free to construct a Mexican jumping bean race out of Freddie's beans and a piece of cardboard on which they drew concentric circles, the outer circles marked Win, Place, and Show, and an inner circle marked Start. They took this to the pool patio, packed, in Miami's continuous boom, with service families and war workers seeking distraction from never ending quotas. Freddie first issued the caveat to Hilary that she not show off and tell everyone that the beans were really the larvae of a bean moth. Within the space of two hours, the time it took most sunbathers to tan their bodies both back and front, they made a total of ten dollars and forty cents, which they split, not evenly, since Hilary and Freddie had provided the lion's share of invention and construction, not to mention the beans, while all Sheldon did was collect the bets.

Their timing was perfect. While they were packing up the race in a shoe box, Ilona finally reached the man who had called. His purpose was as mysterious as before. Mr. Rhinegold, someone she had never met, said he had recently arrived in the United States on the Swedish ship *Gripsholm*, and added that he could not discuss on the telephone her mother's message, that it was not a bad message. She was not ill, although she didn't go out much, and if someone could get to New York, since he had no plans for coming to Miami until the following winter, he would deliver the message.

Two weeks later, when Hilary and Freddie had made enough money from the jumping-bean race to buy a war bond each, the tropical easterlies began to battle the wintry westerlies, negotiating for the weather of South Florida. During the interregnum, the season became so dry that ranchers with scorched pastureland and citrus growers with prematurely dropping fruit buds met in worried councils as did the Florida Farm Bureau, which, mindful of the dropping water level in Lake Okeechobee, requested a ban on commercial fishing on the lake.

The hotels tried to do their part. Diners were not served water unless they asked for it, maintenance placed bricks in all the toilet tanks, and guests were asked to forgo baths and limit their showers to five minutes. The visitors were cooperative, most of them transfixed by the two coast guard cutters attempting to cast a net over a mine that had drifted loose from its mooring and was floating toward the shore, or by Miami's red moon and pink sun, the result of the burning saw grass, which some took as a portent of Axis bloodshed.

Ilona met in her room with Mrs. Portman, who was going to New York the following week for her niece's wedding. They tried to speak, sitting side by side on one of the beds, despite the clattering and banging of the maintenance man, angry because he had to work in the evening, who was trying to attach a brick to the toilet tank float, and who lifted a dripping book from the tank which he handed disgustedly to Ilona. Ilona, who didn't seem to care that it was almost time for "Mr. District Attorney," or that a book marked with Hilary's name had been placed in the toilet tank, asked that Hilary and Freddie go and do something somewhere else so she and Mrs. Portman could talk.

Freddie picked up his bean race; then he and Hilary decided to check first on Sonny. They found him still awake, wearing yellow seersucker pajamas printed with pictures of Goofy, playing with a coconut head that Freddie had given him, dragging it about the floor and telling it to, "Hesh up."

Sonny was instantly delighted with the Mexican jumping beans that Freddie spilled over his bed, and dropped the coconut to watch them hop on his pillow.

"You like that, Sonny?" asked Hilary. "They're really the larvae of a bean moth."

"Don't tell him that," said Freddie. "What'd you go and tell him that for?"

"He's got to learn things," said Hilary. "How else is he going to find out? You want one?" she asked.

"Don't just go giving away my beans," said Freddie.

"Yes, ma'am," said Sonny.

"They're my beans," said Freddie. "Sonny, you want a bean?"

"Yes, sir."

Freddie magnanimously handed him a bean and put the rest in his cigar box. "I'm going to the lobby," he said. "A lot of people didn't get a chance to play yet."

"Don't let Mr. Davis see you," said Hilary.

"Mr. Davis doesn't care too much. It's Mel who gets mad."

Freddie closed the door, leaving Sonny staring at the bean in his hand.

"Pretty soon," said Hilary, "the larvae will crack right through the bean."

Sonny threw the bean down, jumped back and picked up his coconut head which he clutched to his chest. "I don't want it no more. Take it away."

"Why not? Don't you want to see it coming out?"

Sonny began to cry.

"I'm sorry," said Hilary. "Look, it won't do it for a few weeks yet." He dragged his coconut head to the corner of the room. "I was only kidding," she said. "Nothing is coming out. Ever. Don't be scared."

"You funning me?"

"Not now, I'm not. Before I was. Here, I'll make sure it doesn't." Hilary picked up a bean and yelled, "You stupid old bean, you stay in there, you hear?"

Sonny smiled, then shouted from the corner, "Stay in there, hear? You don't, I'll whomp you a good one, you old bean."

There were sounds of footsteps coming down the hall, then voices outside the door.

"You're driving me crazy, you know you're driving me crazy."

"I can't help that. I told you before, I can't. I don't want to."

"Maybe this will change your mind."

There was silence. Then Mickey again, "Okay, that was nice, real nice, all right? Please, let me alone, Frank. I like you. I really do. You know I do. But it's no dice."

Hilary, with heart thudding, opened the door. On the other side, her father, his arms locked around Mickey, bent his face to kiss her once more.

Hilary stood there as if in a dream, and watched as her father smoothed his blond hair back from his forehead. Mickey wrested herself from his grasp, and straightened her blouse. "Now look what you've done," she said. "Honey, it isn't what you think."

Hilary brushed past them and walked away fast, her heart hammering against her rib cage, the vision of her father brushing his hair out of his eyes scored on her retina. Frank, the soldier in the pool shack, shoving, grabbing, hurting, all the same. But Frank—she began to cry—why Frank? Why did he want to kiss anyone else but Ilona and her? She hurried to her mother.

She found Ilona talking to Mrs. Portman, who had promised to find out from Mr. Rhinegold what message from her mother could not be written in a letter. Hilary broke into the room, breathless, hurting. One of her braids had come loose.

"Momma," she said.

Ilona was alerted. Hilary had not called her Momma since kindergarten. "What is it?"

Hilary checked herself. She could not tell Ilona what she had seen and heard. "Nothing, I just wanted to find you."

Ilona searched her face. "You knew where I was. Why were you so anxious to find me? Are you all right? Did someone bother you?"

"No one bothered me."

"Then what?"

"Then nothing."

"It's the awkward age," said Mrs. Portman. "They get a little mixed up at this time. It doesn't mean anything."

Hilary sat close to her mother, so close that Ilona was forced to steady herself on the chair. Ilona began to braid the loosened plait and saw that she was trembling. "Are you cold?"

"I don't know." Hilary began to cry.

Ilona went for a cardigan sweater, which she draped around Hilary's hunched shoulders, then reversed it so that the buttons lay down her back, giving it the look of a straitjacket. "She likes it this way," she explained to Mrs. Portman. Mrs. Portman waved her hand as if to say, They're all crazy. Hilary didn't seem to care. Then Freddie came in with his cigar box. He had been chased out of the lobby by Mr. Davis, following the complaints of Mrs. Templeton, who said that the bean race was spoiling the attendance at bingo. Right behind him, running, out of breath, was Frank.

"I think I should go," said Mrs. Portman pulling herself to her feet. "I'll do what you ask. Please don't worry. I'll call you from New York. You shouldn't have a moment's more anxiety than you already have."

"Hilary," said Frank.

Hilary turned away.

"What's wrong," said Ilona. "Hilary, your father is talking to you."

Hilary stood up and went into her room. The sweater fell to the carpet.

"I don't know what's wrong with her," said Ilona.

"Did she say anything?"

"Nothing."

"She said nothing?"

"That's what I'm telling you. She ran in here, sat next to me, that's all."

"Then I'd leave her alone," said Frank. "She'll come out of it."

"I don't think I can take anymore with her," said Ilona. "Let's forget about her for a minute. I want to tell you about a call I got from Mr. Rhinegold in New York." She closed the door.

In the other room, listening to Fanny Brice on the radio which he heard through the murmurs of his parents, Freddie watched Hilary crawl under the covers in her clothes and stare at the ceiling.

Daddy, is this Miss Gooseberry's school?

Snooks, the lady's name isn't Gooseberry! It's Shrewsbury! And I want you to be very careful when we're inside. Miss Shrewsbury doesn't admit every little girl. She's very meticulous.

She very metiklish?

Not ticklish, meticulous. There are one hundred and ten students in her private school.

That ain't so private.

"Aren't you going to get into pajamas?" he asked.

Hilary didn't answer.

"You better not let Ma catch you in your clothes."

"Freddie."

"What?"

"It's so awful."

"I like 'Baby Snooks.' I'm going to listen."

Snooks, we speak of a private school as opposed to a public school which admits anyone. A public school has a large body of students. Miss Shrewsbury has a small body.

Is she a midget?

When the rain began to collect over the Atlantic in the morning and over the Everglades in the afternoon packaged in mountains of cumulus clouds, Mickey went to North Beach Elementary School to register Sonny for kindergarten. She stood in Mr. Detwiler's office wearing a midriff sundress and a ribbon through her hair, clutching Sonny by the hand, and telling Mr. Detwiler, who was straightening his tie, that Sonny knew the words to "Swinging on a Star," although he still had a little trouble getting his laces tied.

Mr. Detwiler did what he seldom did with new mothers. He

came from around his desk to suck in his stomach, stand beside Mickey, and tell her that she was very young to be the mother of a little boy, that if he didn't know any better, he would have thought she was a high school student.

He asked where Mr. Biscayne was, and didn't her husband's people have something to do with the founding of Miami? Mickey replied that she was a widow. Mr. Detwiler said he was sorry, and then, that she had to have a birth certificate and a doctor's certificate stating that Sonny had been vaccinated against smallpox, and all would be complete. He added that he hoped she would become active in the PTA.

The first requirement was easy. Mickey wrote to her father. After several weeks he sent the certificate and the information, that to the best of everyone's recollection, nobody had ever had little Earl vaccinated for anything. Mickey took Sonny to Dr. Weingarten, not knowing any other doctors.

Dr. Weingarten said that Sonny was a little young for boosters, and Mickey said that it was the original shot that he needed.

"I find that difficult to believe in this day and age," he replied. "You mean you were never told by any doctor to have him immunized?"

"We traveled around a lot."

"That's really no excuse," said Dr. Weingarten. But he backpedaled from his Aesculapian position to one more pedestrian when he saw her face. "Of course," he added, "wartime makes all kinds of problems. I can understand how people get uprooted, records get lost. Okay little fellow, put out your arm."

Arms was more correct. They rolled back Sonny's short sleeves, the doctor swabbed both his arms, and jabbed him with different needles, sending inactivated antigens into his bloodstream to protect him against such scourges as diphtheria, whooping cough, and smallpox.

A tear trickled down his face, but otherwise Sonny stood resolute, having planted both his feet as firmly as he did when waves crashed against his shins.

When Dr. Weingarten lay down his needles, Mickey scooped Sonny up into her arms. "Don't cry, baby," she said. "The doctor didn't mean to hurt you. You want a soda?"

"What's that?" asked Sonny, who wondered if you got it in the arm.

"Ice cream soda, with big tall straws, and whipped cream, and a cherry on top. You don't know, do you? Those rotten bastards. If I ever see them again, I'll break their damned necks."

Mickey took Sonny on the bus to the little drugstore on South Beach where she and Bill had gone so often. It looked the same except, in contrast to the year before, it was almost empty.

"What happened to all the soldiers?" asked Mickey. "This place can't be off limits."

The waitress wiped at the place before them, and slapped two napkins on the counter. "South Beach is hurting," she said. "The military has given up a lot of hotels down here. Some of them army air corps people have moved up to North Beach. The rest went to Texas for basic training. Everyone's feeling it, especially the dry cleaners and the barbers, they're feeling it the worst. It has a good side though, I guess that must mean the war is almost over. Mr. Gottlieb, he's the owner, he says they're going to invade France any day now."

"I never heard of anyone taking so long to get from one little place to the other. They better do it before we all get gray and forget why they're over there in the first place. I'll have a Coca-Cola, and he wants a black and white ice cream soda, mind you, don't let the whipped cream drip all over the side, and don't make it too high so he can't reach the cherry."

"And so," said Ilona, "if we can get one thousand dollars to Mr. Rhinegold, he promises to make the arrangements for my mother to get it. He says that's how much it takes to get papers. She already has what she needs for passage."

"You mean fake papers?"

"Whatever. Identity papers, a visa, then, please God, she'll be able to come over."

"Ilona, one thousand dollars, you might as well be asking for fifty thousand. Suppose we had it, to give to some guy we don't even know, we never laid eyes on. It's a racket. A con. He probably calls all over the country doing this, telling people he's met their relatives, and he probably has, that's what makes it sound legit, and telling them, that if you give him money, he'll get them over, can't you see that?"

"Mrs. Portman saw him. She talked to him. She says she will

lay out the money and we can pay her back when she comes back to Miami, or we can send a check."

"All right, so he conned Mrs. Portman. She's a nice woman, but I don't make her out to be a genius. Ilona, try to see it in cold blood, try to see reason."

"All right," she said, pulling at her curls, a habit she had gotten into since the permanent. "Supposing you're right. Supposing even a ninety percent chance you're right, and I'm wrong. Okay, but what of the ten percent chance that he's honest? Can you deny my mother the chance?"

"You really know how to put it to a guy."

"I don't care about the house, Frank, you know that. I'll never ask you for a house again. I'll never ask you for another thing. Just do this for me."

"Jesus, I need time to think."

I couldn't sleep a wink last night, because we had that silly fight.

I thought my heart would break the whole night through.

I knew that you'd be sorry, and I'm sorry too.

"Why the hell does he have to play that radio so loud? Turn that down in there! You hear me, Freddie?"

I didn't have my favorite dream. The one in which I hold you tight.

"I didn't say turn it off. I said down."

It was a jubilant, hopeful week. Mr. Gottlieb, the drugstore owner, was right. The Allies liberated Rome on one day, church bells rang, the pope spoke from his balcony, and everyone came to throw kisses and flowers to the soldiers riding into the city on tanks and jeeps, and most of all, foot soldiers, marching in formation, breaking ranks only to be embraced by enthusiastic Romans. The next day, General Eisenhower led the D-Day invasion which had been anticipated, prayed for, across the English Channel, onto the northern coast of France. In this same week, the most joyous since the war began three years before, Mickey got a letter from Iowa.

It was from Mrs. Wright. At first, Mickey didn't realize who it was. Then it snapped together like a gripper fastener, that Mrs. Wright was, of course, Bill's mother. She wrote that Bill had been wounded during a bombing mission of the northern Italian viaducts and railroads that her husband said were the Germans' supply line, that he had been flown to a hospital in North Africa, where he had been recovering all these months, and that he knew about the little boy, that it made no difference whatsoever—Mrs. Wright underlined whatsoever—and that she and her husband would like for Mickey to come with the little boy to their farm where they would all wait together for Bill's return. Within the envelope was a piece of V-mail, a photograph of the farm, and a little note from Bill's sister, in which she promised to show Mickey pictures of Bill when he was a little boy, especially the one in which he was naked on a fur lap rug.

Mickey opened Bill's letter. He wrote that although there were really sick guys with him who lay quietly in bed and didn't talk to anyone, that most of the guys sat up and called from bed to bed, particularly to each new person who came in on a stretcher and that they cheered each other up; that he had had a bullet near his lung, but that it was out, that they had to wait a long time for scar tissue to form so they could go in and get it; that he didn't know why they had to wake him up at five-thirty every morning—they said it was so morning staff could get on with their chores; that he was lucky—some of the guys were missing arms and legs.

He said that when he first came to, he saw a blond nurse over him, and thought it was Mickey, but realized it wasn't, even though he couldn't make out that her eyes were brown and not ocean blue like Mickey's, when she said, "Don't bellyache, you'd think we never did this before," in a voice as opposite to honey as you could get. He loved Mickey. Thoughts of her heart-shaped face, her sweetness, and her funny ideas kept him going through this whole thing; the little boy made no difference, in fact it gave them a leg up, a head start on a family of their own, which would help to make up for the time they had lost; that the boy would be a little top sergeant to the other children that would follow, and that if he were her child, he would have to love him as he did her, and what was his name?

Mickey's lower lip began to tremble. She tried to catch it in her teeth but it was too late and the tears washed down her face to dampen her collar. "Thank you, Lord," she whispered. "You sure are a sport."

Mickey went to see Hilary, wearing fluffy bangs, a new style she improvised for the occasion. "I need to talk to you," she said. "It's time we squared things between us."

Hilary pivoted in the runway turn she had learned from Tracey and walked away.

"Wait a minute, now listen. This has been going on long enough. You got to listen. What happened between Frank and me, it was nothing, like tasting ice cream. That's all. Not even the whole cone."

"How could you do that?"

"Do what? A little kiss, that's all, just to make him feel good. Your father kisses other women. I saw him give a little peck to Mrs. Portman."

"But I betcha he didn't do it on the lips."

"It doesn't mean anything. It's not a signed and sealed delivery. It's a nice thing to do for a friend, like shaking hands, and if you were listening in my room, I know you heard me tell him no, and I know you know what that means."

"Okay. I listened. Now can I go?"

"No, I got something important to tell you and I need to tell it to someone. I got a letter from Bill's mother. In Iowa. Was it you who told him?"

Hilary folded her arms across her chest. "Why should I tell you? You don't tell me everything."

"Come on, I have to know. Was it?"

"Okay. It was me."

"I figured out he must have written to you. Wait, I'm not mad. I want you to know that."

"How come you didn't tell him yourself?"

"I didn't want him to think I was begging. I love him so much, I was afraid he would say it was off and then I would just die. It was easier this way. I couldn't bear it if he told me it was off. He's been wounded. He's in a hospital in North Africa, that's why his letters stopped coming. I wrote him it was over, you see, but he kept writing. His mother wants me to come and stay with them, me and Sonny, in Iowa. On the farm."

"You gonna do it?"

"I have to think about it. Everything I have ever done has been without thinking. I get an idea, I do it. This time, I want to think real serious before I make up my mind. Their spread sounds a lot prettier than my daddy scratching like a hen on an itty-bitty place no bigger than the lobby. They have nearly four hundred acres; they sent me a picture of it—it's real pretty; I have it here."

Mickey took out the photograph from her purse. "See, this here is rows of soybeans, and between the rows, there's milkweed, that's where the monarch butterflies lay their eggs. I picture Sonny with butterflies over his head, running through that milkweed, and me not having to worry about traffic, and a real house to live in, not a room without a window. And being able to talk about Bill all the time, and see his room and all the things he loved."

"When would you go?"

"I don't know. Two, three weeks, maybe."

"So soon? Things are popping like blisters around here. Why do you have to go now?"

"I thought you were mad at me."

"I was. I am, but you're still my best friend, better than Tracey, better than any of them."

"I'm glad to hear that. I'm thinking to give you my spangled moth costume. It's got sequins all over it, sort of a memento, you know. I don't want you to forget me."

"I don't think I could do that. Anyway, I thought you didn't like farms."

"This is different. It's not all sloppy and run down. This sounds more like a nice house in the middle of the country. No one's sick, and they all sound like they can't wait for us to get there. Plenty of room is the main thing. I keep having to drag Sonny out of the lobby—you know Mr. Davis doesn't like him to play there —and I worry all the time about the swimming pool, and I'm tired of fighting off guys who don't mean anything to me. I forgot. I didn't mean your father."

"Yes you did. It's not your fault anyway. You can't help it if you're so pretty. It's his fault."

"It's no one's fault. Nothing happened, so there's no one to blame for anything. Look, I want us to write so I can hear all about you, the boys you're dating—don't make faces, that's gonna come soon—and I'll tell you all about me and Sonny. You're still mad at your daddy, aren't you, in spite of what I just said?"

"Sure. Wouldn't you be?"

"No. That's because I know a basic thing about men that I been trying to teach you for a long time, but for some reason, you're not about to learn. Men think different than women. They're all the time chasing after women. They need that to feel more like men. But women feel like women anyhow, it's hard for us to forget, so we don't have to chase after men to know it. You don't see women all the time chasing men."

"Boy, I used to think you knew everything. You don't know anything. Tracey Hollister, and Shirley Leone, and Liz Bonnier, they're boy crazy, that's all they ever think about, boys, boys, boys, day and night."

"But they don't go chasing after them, see, that's the difference."

"Who says they don't? Shirley Leone waits for the track team to finish practice, she practices her splits right in their path, then she runs around the field to where the football team crosses the street; she stands there waiting, like a cat. And Liz Bonnier, she waits at the water fountain and presses the lever down for them, and Tracey Hollister, she's the most boy crazy of all, she even calls them on the phone."

"What about you?"

"I don't like boys much; they're stupid."

"Honey, don't stay mad at your daddy."

"That's my business."

"I know it is. Why can't I say what I think? You say what you think."

"You can say what you think, but it's still my business."

Mickey plucked her bangs out of her eyelashes. "Well, I guess I got letters to write."

"I'll help you pack when you're ready."

"That's real sweet of you. I knew I could count on you." Mickey embraced Hilary, enveloping her with her soft arms and her perfume. They were the same height, except that Mickey wore wedgies that gave her a two-inch lift, while Hilary stood in her new penny loafers with no heel at all to speak of.

Frank continued to try to engage Hilary in conversation, without success. Except for answers that required a yes or no, Hilary gave no response. At first Frank was mildly frustrated, then frantic, and finally, he became angry. Once, with one hand barring her exit from the room, he said, "Look, now, this is between you and me, not your mother, not your brother. You're a hanging judge, baby, you know that? You saw, you judged, and you got me strung up."

"I didn't do anything to you. You're the one who did something. You're the one who chased Mickey to her room. It's you. I saw you. Why'd you have to do that?"

"Okay, okay, so I did, let's say I did for argument's sakes. You going to hold that against me after everything else I did good for the rest of my life?"

"Yes."

"You mean, there's no room for a mistake with you. A person can't make one mistake. You make plenty. I forgive you all the time. You know that, don't you?"

"I'm a kid, you're a grown-up, you're supposed to know better. You're my father. I trusted you. Ma trusted you. You know, I used to think you were the most wonderful person in the whole world. Better than God, better than Roosevelt." Hilary put her head down. "Even better than Ma. You're not. You're not at all."

"I'm sorry I'm not better than Roosevelt or God. So now you know I'm human. Look, what can I do to make it better? You know you're the apple of my eye. How can I do my work if the apple of my eye won't even talk to me? What can I do to make it right?"

"Nothing."

That evening, Frank walked the length of Collins Avenue down to Lincoln Road and back, passing trucks of soldiers, thinking of California, where he had heard a person could get a new start and really make a lot of money from a shoestring. The next morning, after telling Marco to run the kitchen, Frank went to the bank and took out the money that he had been saving to give to Ilona so he could go off on his own guilt-free, at least till he made something of himself and could maybe send for them. That evening, he took the money out of his pocket, and handed it to his wife who was brushing through her new ringlets.

"Tell Mrs. Portman to give Rhinegold the money."

Ilona laid the brush down to open the envelope, then ran to embrace him. "Oh Frank, Frank." She covered his face with kisses as if she were blotting him up. "You are the most wonderful husband in the world."

"Wonderful with a W, and tell her to see if she can get a receipt."

Through the closed door, Hilary and Freddie heard Ilona laugh, then silence, interrupted only by murmurs. Hilary covered her ears and took her puckered, dampened diary under the covers to scribble another passionate entry, while Freddie pressed his ear to the door. "I think they're doing it," he said.

As the summer smothered itself with heat, and tanning oils and desiccated shellfish spread a miasma over the sand, Freddie sat at the water's edge and kicked at the waves. He had had disturbing news. Not only had he learned that the Ringling Circus tent, treated with paraffin to make it waterproof, had gone up in flames in Hartford, Connecticut, killing hundreds, which meant that the circus probably wouldn't come to Miami the following winter, but he had read that in July, Lee Powell, the real Lone Ranger as opposed to the fake Lone Ranger on the radio, had died in combat on Tinian Island.

Ilona, still burdened with the anxiety of not knowing if Mr. Rhinegold had kept all of Frank's savings, or had somehow got the money safely to her mother in Sweden, worried also about things closer to home, including the polio epidemic which raged in grim and hidden silence all over the country, and for which she continued to watch the children for sore throats and muscle aches, cautioning Freddie, before she and Hilary left the hotel, not to get chilled, and to keep himself warm. Freddie, who had to dunk his head from time to time to keep cool, thought his mother was crazy, which was consistent with a recent decision about girls.

Other than her concerns about polio, Ilona was no longer worried about Freddie. With his hearing intact and now in his proper grade in school, he was, after all, a boy, which meant he would be all right in the world. Her concern now was for Hilary, whom she regarded in the way a vintner regards a wine that he has been keeping under wraps and that has soured before the bottle is decanted. Naturally, she took full responsibility.

After a discussion with Mrs. Templeton, Ilona concluded that she did not spend enough time with Hilary, that perhaps her attention, as Frank had suggested, had been elsewhere too long, and she decided to make it up to her. They would go for a brassiere and a feathercut, both appurtenances long desired by her strange and moody child who, in addition to hiding books in toilet tanks, was beginning to speak in a mystifying vocabulary.

They went to Morris Brothers' department store in South Beach where, in the foundation department, Hilary tried on a Maidenform A cup brassiere, the smallest brassiere in manufacture, and still too big. Ilona said she would take it up with darts which could be released when the time came or, if Hilary liked, she could stuff it with Kleenex. Hilary also tried on sleazy slips that crept up her thighs like ivy, while calling Ilona, Jackson. When Ilona asked her if she really meant it when she said she wanted to get her braids cut, Hilary replied, "I wasn't clickin' my teeth."

"I wish you would speak English," said Ilona.

The beauty parlor was across the street. Women waited in the storefront window, reading magazines while others sat under machines with wires attached to curling rods on their heads. Hilary and Ilona were assigned to a woman operator wearing a smock. At first, the operator, with an elaborate show of ignoring Ilona's proximity, held out the braids like two ropes, and said to anyone who cared to hear, "This she wants to cut," then, like an executioner, cut them straight across, held them out, and let them splat to the floor. Ilona immediately bent to scoop them up. Then the operator rumpled Hilary's shorn head and snipped, here, there, all over, darting with her scissors like a hummingbird, and dodging Ilona, who stayed at her side, as close as a shadow, until the cut became like feathers. "There's a place over there you can sit," she said.

Hilary smiled into the mirror. Her ears were completely hidden, and she looked like the other kids, except the high school girls who were beginning to wear long pageboys like Mickey's. Ilona cried. Her little girl was gone forever, in her place an adolescent stranger, almost pretty, with pinched and saddened eyes and a crooked smile.

They went to the salvage depot, only blocks away, and Ilona said they had blond braids, of thinner hair and therefore more desirable than brunette, to be used as bombsights, or gunsights, or whatever they did with human hair, to a boy scout behind the desk, who replied, "Okay, lady, fork 'em over."

Ilona changed her mind at the last minute and held one back for a keepsake.

On their way up Washington Avenue, they noticed that the shoe repair shop had a gold star in the window. "I know him," said Ilona. "Wait a minute." She went inside and said something to the shoe repairman, then came out again.

"What's going on between you and your father?" she asked.

"Nothing."

"Don't tell me, nothing. Your father could do no wrong. Now you don't say two words to him. I'm not blind, what is it?"

Hilary scratched her scalp, liking the feeling of unbound hair. A soldier walked by and smiled at Ilona.

"Well?"

"Ma, forget it."

"How can I be a mother to you if you shut me out?"

"I'm not shutting you out. I had a good time today. Thanks for the brassiere and the haircut."

"Did he say something to hurt your feelings?"

"No."

"Then what? He wouldn't give you something you wanted? You know we have very little money now. You know things are tight."

"Nothing like that."

"But it's something. What?" Ilona dug in like a badger. "I think you miss Mickey and Sonny and you're taking it out on your father."

"Why did you mention Mickey?"

"Why not Mickey? What about Mickey? Tell me, what about Mickey?"

"Ma, Ma"—she turned away—"don't make me tell you."

"It's that bad? What is it?"

"I saw him kiss her."

"Oh, I see." Ilona turned her face to the drugstore window. Carter's Little Liver Pills were on sale for twenty-seven cents.

"How come you're not mad?"

"I'm sad, not mad."

"I told you not to make me tell you."

"Come on, let's go in here and sit down."

They sat at the counter and ordered cherry phosphates. "Let me tell you something," said Ilona. "What you saw, it means nothing."

"How can you say that? I don't understand how you can say that!"

"Because I can. I'm his wife, that's how I can say it. Your father is the only man I will ever love. It doesn't matter what he does or doesn't do. It's how I feel about you and Freddie. Lots of times you do things to make me mad at you. But I still love you. That doesn't stop. How can that ever stop? And with your father, the feeling I have for him has nothing to do with a ceremony or a piece of paper, but I'll tell you this, it's what keeps the world spinning under me. I don't know what they teach you in school about what makes the world spin. I can tell you that for me, it's my feeling for your father, and the feeling that I know he has for me no matter what. That's what makes the world go around—love. Someday you will care for someone in the same way, and it will be forever."

"How can it be forever when that person does something behind your back, and with someone else?"

"I have forgiven your father, Hilary, why can't you? Why are you so important that he can't do anything to hurt you?"

Mr. Gottlieb came to stand before them. "Any day now," he confided, "Patton will be in Paris. Then Germany, and then it's all over, right, missus?"

"From your mouth to God's ears," said Ilona.

"Is this your girl?" he asked.

Ilona nodded. "You want to see something? Something new," he said, handing Hilary a strange-looking pen with a rounded tip. "It's called a ball point. You never have to fill it."

24

September brought an acute butter and egg shortage. A hurricane skirted South Florida, then capriciously turned north off Palm Beach, roared counterclockwise toward the Carolina coast, and finally struck New England with hundred-mile-an-hour winds, after snapping the Atlantic City Steel Pier in half. Dewey blamed FDR for Pearl Harbor. Aimee Semple McPherson, an evangelist from California, took an overdose of sleeping tablets.

Pinky/Rhoda, still as obsessed with depression as Tracey was with increasing her bust or as Bette Davis playing Fanny Skeffington was with staying young and beautiful, explained to Hilary that sleeping tablets were the best way to kill yourself, as all other ways, each of which she had examined carefully, hurt. The problem Hilary saw in suicide of any method was that there was no room to change your mind, that once committed, it was like going naked down a greased slide, a fantasy she had had since the second grade. "What if the moment you swallow the pills," she asked rhetorically as she was learning to do in debate when the object is to put the other fellow on the defensive, "you decide you made a big mistake?"

Pinky/Rhoda was prepared. "That's when you fall asleep," she said, "so it doesn't matter. It's too late. That's what's good about suicide. You can't change your mind. It's good for people who are wishy-washy," she added, with the finality of one who knows her point is well taken.

As far as junior high in general was concerned, things were status quo, not wonderful, but dependable, like halvah, except that Hilary could not understand what she had ever seen in Mr. Cardozo the year before, wondering, when he escorted Whoopsie Ferguson out of the creamed-corn-smelling lunchroom for exploding milk cartons, if he always had beads of sweat over his upper lip. And although Hilary missed Mickey, she felt the loss as an occasional ache, and only when she thought about it, like when her twelve-year molars pushed through her gums.

Hilary saw Sorrell Myers for the first time since the spring before in algebra, where they sat side by side because of the spelling of their names. At first Hilary didn't recognize him. Sorrell was tall and slender, not skinny like Marshall Newburgh but wiry, as if someone had wrapped him in cord, and almost handsome, except for an Adam's apple that bobbed up and down his neck like something live, when he spoke.

In the week that Stan Musial hit a homer that gave the Cardinals a five-to-one win against the St. Louis Browns, and National Airlines made a new speed mark of New York to Miami in four hours and thirty-six minutes, Hilary and Sorrell were assigned to construct a sundial together out of cardboard.

The teacher, Miss Fenniker, known for her chronic B.O., instructed everyone to draw a triangle ABX, AB to equal four inches, angle A to equal 90 degrees, and angle B, the latitude of the place where the dial was to be used, in this case, Miami, and to look it up in the Atlas.

"What if we're on Miami Beach?" asked Marshall.

"Miami Beach and Miami share the same latitude," said Miss Fenniker, displaying the fatigue most teachers didn't begin to show until February, "and that includes Sunny Isles, Surfside, Palm Island, Star Island, and the Venetian causeway." Then Miss Fenniker handed mimeographed instructions to each pair and told them to go outside on the patio.

Lizards scuttled to safety as the class trampled through the broad, flat-bladed St. Augustine grass on the way to the flagstones where everyone flopped with their cardboards. With an eye on Sorrell's neck, Hilary read aloud the instructions. "Mark a rectangle ACB plus Y and bend it at right angles along AB."

Sorrell ruled off the lines, then folded back the cardboard. "What happened to your braids?" he asked.

Hilary snorted, a new habit which Ilona said would give her adenoids. "Braids are for little kids. I'm much too old for braids."

"I don't know," he said, "I kind of liked them."

"Observe the shadow," called Miss Fenniker from over the railing. "You're supposed to be observing the shadow."

"I didn't," said Hilary. "I hated them. You know what it's like to have your forehead stretched over the top of your head?"

"No worse," replied Sorrell, "than not being able to see your toes."

"You're not reading your instructions," shouted Miss Fenniker. "I didn't send you out there to play. You're supposed to be doing your work."

Hilary snorted. "Mark in the shadow of the sun every hour," she continued, "and join these markings to B and label each hour line."

Louis Lansky and Norman Nagel darted behind a gardenia bush and escaped, running down the corridor with their cardboard.

"I don't know," said Hilary. "Someone's going to have to do this every single hour. You want to take it home or should I?"

"I'll take it home," he said. "I don't mind. There's a party next week at Liz Bonnier's. You going?"

"Are you kidding?" said Hilary. "Liz is one of my best friends."

"Can I take you?"

"You mean like a date?" she asked. "I don't know if I'm allowed."

"Find out," said Sorrell, rolling up the cardboard, and securing it with a big rubber band.

Mr. Epson, the vice-principal, came striding down the hall, clutching Louis and Norman each by a collarbone. "Two of your people," he called to Miss Fenniker. "They were on their way out the front door."

"So can I go with him?" asked Hilary of Ilona, directing this, as all of her requests, to her mother.

"What do you think?" asked Ilona of Frank in a continuing and dogged campaign to reunite her estranged daughter and husband.

Frank, who was helping Marco and Gus remove boards from the plate-glass windows of the dining room, turned to glance at Hilary, who had not looked directly at him in months.

"You want my opinion? Thirteen is too young. I don't like her even going to a party when there's going to be boys."

"If I have to stay home," said Hilary, "I'll die."

"Hilary is always going to die," said Freddie, pulling out nails with the claw of the hammer which he then dropped into a tin can.

"You shut up," said Hilary, "this doesn't concern you. How come I could go with boys when I was in the sixth grade and I can't do it now?"

"You were little kids then," said Frank.

"I'm in the sixth grade," said Freddie, "and I'm not a little kid."

"Be quiet," said Frank, "this is none of your business. You're growing up too fast as it is, Hilary. Don't rush it."

"Everyone's sitting on me like I'm an egg."

Frank pulled free a board and laid it on the ground behind him. "I don't know why you need my opinion, Ilona, when she's going to give me lip."

"She'll do whatever you say," said Ilona.

Frank's eyebrows sailed up to his forehead. He turned again to Hilary. "I'll come for you after I finish work. Be ready sometime after nine-thirty."

"Nine-thirty! I'll die!"

"Don't argue with your father," said Ilona.

Hilary muttered "God," and walked to the beach to mope under a palm tree. Ilona waited until her daughter was on the sand, her feet coated with damp and clinging grains.

"I don't understand my mother's letter," she confided. "She thanks me for our regards and good wishes, and asking about her health, she says nothing about the money or Mr. Rhinegold."

Frank and Ilona looked at each other. Neither wanted to say what was on the mind of both. The money was gone, with some flimflam man named Rhinegold, or whatever his name was.

Frank yanked free a board. "Those goddamn advisories, they lie like hell to scare you so you board everything up, then nothing happens."

"You mean," asked Ilona, "it would be better if something happened?"

"Don't," he shouted, "don't start. Not with me, not today, not when some bastard is running around with savings it took me five years to collect."

There was no doubt that Liz Bonnier was the most sophisticated girl in junior high school, confident, soignée, wearing her black hair in a long, shining pageboy that swung when she walked, and lipstick, not the pallid shine of Tangee Natural, but real colors, like her newest shade, Pink Lightning, a hue between fuchsia and pink that made her mouth look like a raspberry.

Her mother and father, unlike most of the other parents, went out every weekend and sometimes even during the week, not to a movie, but dressed-up out, good for at least three hours, which made Liz's parties the best. Tonight, suffused in perfume and aftershave, the senior Bonniers were preparing to go to the restricted oceanfront club to which they belonged, and everyone sat in the living room quietly, noiselessly, like toys on a shelf, politely nibbling on pretzels and sipping Coca-Cola, and staring at Mrs. Bonnier's knotted pearls and Mr. Bonnier's sailfish tie pin which drifted in and out of the smoke of his Sano cigarette. They waited with pretzels unswallowed until after the flurry of low-throated, carefully modulated last-minute instructions and the Bonniers' departure, with Marshall Newburgh posted behind the drapes to see the precise moment their Buick left the driveway and had safely turned the corner of the street.

While they waited, the boys tried to see how many pretzels they could stuff into their mouths at one time, and the girls, giggling as regularly as breathing, began to whisper and talk about the pictures of the French female collaborators whose heads were shaved and who were forced to run naked through the streets of Paris. Everyone said that it served the women right, that they shouldn't have collaborated with the Germans. Shirley Leone said they had female collaborators at the Jewel Box nightclub, and Liz Bonnier with a sniff of her aristocratic nose, said they were female impersonators.

"They're gone," called Marshall, from behind damask folds, and everyone began to twitch, twist, squirm, punch, rub, jump, and wiggle on the rattan settees, settling in for a game of post office.

One by one, they slipped from the Florida room as their names were called by Marshall the postmaster, and slunk into the tiny bedroom that had belonged to a maid who left to go into defense work. The postmaster called Sorrell into the room, then came to the door jamb. "I have a letter for Hilary MacIntyre."

Chastened at first into suspenseful silence, everyone started to giggle again, gulping in air like little fish, while Hilary stood, her bobby socks attached to the chewing gum stuck to her ankles, dipping her knees in the way Tracey said models walked, and strolled into the bedroom, her shoulders turning from side to side like Joan Crawford's. With a flinty leer, the result of metal-braced teeth, the postmaster closed the door behind him and Hilary was alone with Sorrell Myers.

He stood a few inches away. "You don't have to if you don't want to, Hilary. It's okay if you got cold feet."

"I might as well. I'm here. Except I haven't done this in a while. I'm kind of rusty."

"That's okay. I've done it three times this summer."

They reached across the space between them, leaning over to touch lips, their bodies apart.

"I want to come closer," said Sorrell whose breath smelled like Sen-Sen.

"You're supposed to," said Hilary.

Sorrell put out a tentative arm around her waist, and Hilary felt a quickening, an intake of her own breath, as though she was scared, but nicer, then he bent his head and kissed her full on the lips, and everything was swept along, her feet, her legs, her stomach, her whole body, like in an undertow. They pulled their faces apart to breathe, and looked at one another's shadowed face in the darkened room.

"I love you," said Sorrell.

"Do it again," she said.

"We're only supposed to do it once," he said.

"Who's going to tell?"

They kissed again, their mouths closed, first gently pressing, then mashing against teeth and gums, and Hilary felt him tremble.

The postmaster slammed the door behind him. "Snap back with

Stanback!" he shouted. "That's not supposed to be a special delivery, Sorrell, and you only asked for one letter."

Hilary and Sorrell were wrenched apart and Hilary came out of the room, her cheeks burning, pushing up the sleeves of her grossly oversized sweater.

"What was in your letter?" asked Shirley, leaning forward with her chest arched like the figurehead of a ship.

"It was in code," said Hilary.

"Come on," said Frances. "Did he try to stick his tongue in your mouth? Did he get a hardon?"

"Was it good, bad, better, or worse? You can tell us that," said Liz. "What's the fun if you can't talk about it?"

"I get so much mail," said Shirley, "I can't keep track of it all."

"Oh, God, Shirley," said Frances, "sometimes you're a pain."

"I'm only saying what's true. You expect me to lie?"

The postmaster stuck his head out. "Special delivery for Shirley Leone."

"See what I mean?" she asked, switching her pleated skirt behind her.

Hilary was waiting for Frank, already standing in the black and white marble foyer when he rang the bell.

"Have a good time?" he asked.

Hilary closed the front door behind her and buttoned her jacket. "Uh huh," she replied.

"What did you do?"

"Hung around, listened to records."

"Anything else?"

"No."

"I wasn't born yesterday."

"Neither was I," she said.

"You sure are a tough nut to crack, you know that? I don't know who you take after with that hard shell you got. You didn't used to be like that. You used to be a little sweetheart. I have to tell you, it's not feminine."

"Ma says I take after your mother. She says she's as set in her ways as a slab of concrete."

"Your mother said that? I don't know why she has to knock my family."

When Hilary got home, the first thing she did was to look in the mirror over the bureau to see if she had changed. Then she slicked her short hair back with the palms of her hands. Her face looked small and vulnerable.

Ilona stood over her shoulder, looming suddenly like an apparition in a shiny pale blue wrapper.

"What are you looking at?" she asked.

"Ma, you know the collaborators, the women in France whose heads they shaved off?"

"I saw pictures," said Ilona.

"If you stayed over there, if you didn't come to America when you did, would you have collaborated?"

"I don't know."

"Not me," said Hilary. "I couldn't."

"You don't know what you could or could not do until the time comes. People say, I could never do such and such a thing, and then when they are faced with the situation, they find it is quite easy. And while we're on the subject, a few months ago you said you could never forgive your father for what you saw. I think it's time you realize that those were only words, not bricks, as you can take them down any time you want. I'm sure if you try, it will be quite easy for you to forgive, and even forget. Hilary, people are dying, millions of people, all over the world, some are in prison camps, some have been wounded terribly, you see the men next door hobbling about, bandaged up with only their eyes showing. Cities wiped off the map. People standing in rubble with no place to go, and everywhere the women cry, for a father, a son, a husband. Suddenly it doesn't seem to be so important, a little kiss."

"You really think that?"

"I said it."

"Okay. I kissed Sorrell Myers. On the lips. In the dark. Tonight at Liz's house."

"Don't do it again."

South Florida responded to a second hurricane alert as a storm hovered over Cuba and poised its inward-spiraling winds to strike at the peninsula before it. Schools were closed, the city once more boarded up, as everyone waited for the big blow to come.

There was a constant roar overhead as military pilots flew hundreds of planes inland, and from the beach one could see craft of every size, military in the lead, civilian trailing in the rear, slipping and weaving through the churning, choppy, dark blue water to the channel of Government Cut, seeking the safety of the narrow, twisting Miami River.

By midafternoon, strong gales were already felt, forerunners of the storm—the kind of early winds that sucked away one's breath and held one like a giant hand—snapping off dried, dead, unyielding tree branches, bending others more resilient, combining with the spray to whip the beach into a froth, and lifting the sea water into giant towering geysers that flung themselves about, sometimes backward, sometimes forward, to smash against seawalls or curl quickly all the way up the beach over patios, running right to the foundations of the hotels.

Most of the staff pitched in to secure the huge expanse of glass that fronted the dining room, especially the glass sliding doors that were already beginning to bow inward, as if in invitation. Ilona, Tessie, and two waitresses held pieces of wood and cans of nails for Frank, Marco, Gus, two maintenance men, and Mel, who was giving even odds on the likelihood of the hurricane hitting Miami squarely.

Freddie came running to tell Frank that the radio just announced that MacArthur had returned to the Philippines. "He's grandstanding," shouted Frank. "Grab some nails and help us board up these windows. Don't look at your thumb and you won't hit it."

Sorrell Myers hovered over everyone's shoulders, as ubiquitous in the last few weeks as the Scarlet Pimpernel, looking, as he always did, for Hilary.

"Go home, Sorrell," shouted Frank.

"I have something to give Hilary," said Sorrell against the wind. His words were carried down the beach like a melancholy drone.

"What? Say it in my ear."

Sorrell spoke again, cupping his hands around his mouth.

"He has something to give to Hilary," shouted Ilona. "Give it to me, Sorrell. I'll see she gets it. Now go home, your mother is going to be worried sick."

"I'd rather give it to her myself."

"What is it?" asked Ilona.

Sorrell looked embarrassed. A palm frond blew up against his legs and clung like a pet dog. "It's an ID bracelet."

"What's that?"

Sorrell took out the box from his pants pocket and opened it.

"That has your name on it," shouted Ilona. "Why would she want a bracelet that has someone else's name on it?"

Before he could answer, a flying coconut smashed against a window on the first floor, shattering the glass, and sending salt spray into the room of a screaming guest. Marco ran with Mel to pull free the rattling shards that bordered the window frame like rays while Sorrell, with wind-driven sand stinging the back of his neck, left the howling patio to look for Hilary inside the hotel.

Mr. Davis stood in the lobby, directing a crew of cleaning and maintenance people who were rolling up the carpet, which they would carry to the second floor in case seawater flooded the lobby.

"What about the chandelier?" asked Mrs. Templeton. "That's Austrian crystal."

"If it falls," said Mr. Davis, "it falls. We can't go up there now to get it."

Mrs. Templeton, in one of her rare breaches, bustled about defiantly, gathering cushions to throw beneath the chandelier. Crystal was crystal. Sorrell found Hilary helping Mrs. Templeton pile up cushions while guests who were planning a hurricane party were ordering ice and scotch from the bell captain.

"Grab a cushion, Sorrell," shouted Hilary. "We're making a big heap in case the chandelier falls."

"Excuse me," said Sorrell to a guest, pulling a seat cushion out from under him. "I have something for you," he said to Hilary.

A wrenching screech came from the portico. "The awning is going!" shouted the bell captain. "It's heading down the street!"

Everyone clambered out the front door, pushing and shoving, to catch the striped canvas which was scraping the length of Collins Avenue, while one of the guests shouted after the bell captain who was in the lead, "What about our ice?" Mrs. Templeton went to get pillows from the warmed seats of those who had gotten up to chase the awning, and Hilary, who could not get enough of kissing Sorrell and of the excitement it caused in her body, took the moment to lead Sorrell into an empty rear office, where Tessie's jammed switchboard blinked soundlessly.

"You think we ought to, here?" asked Sorrell. "Won't someone come in?"

It was like licking the batter from one of Gus's baking bowls:

once you started, you couldn't stop. Hilary pulled him close, not sure if she loved him, for which declaration he continued to press, or just loved kissing him. She had posited this question to Mickey in a letter, and was waiting for an answer. In the meantime, she was determined to kiss Sorrell every chance she got.

When they stopped for a breath, Sorrell pulled out his package and dangled the bracelet.

"That's your ID," she said. "But that means we're going steady."

"I guess it does."

"I don't want to go steady. I'm only thirteen."

"It's okay, Hilary. I'll go steady. You don't have to go steady."

"I don't want to take an ID under false pretenses, and I also don't want any snafus. I mean, I don't want people thinking I'm going steady when I'm not. If I take it I'm going to tell everyone I'm wearing it because we're good friends and I respect you very much."

"You won't hear anything different from me."

Hilary slipped Sorrell's bracelet over her wrist. "I like these chain links," she said. "They're solid. Not flimsy, like girls' bracelets."

"I love you, Hilary."

"Quit telling me you love me. I can't say it back to you. I already told you that."

"You like me, though, you said so."

"I like you. I like you a lot."

"If everyone in the eighth grade was in a sinking ship, and you could save only one person, who would it be?" he asked.

"I don't know."

"Am I one of your choices?"

"Yes. Definitely yes."

"That's good enough for me," he replied.

They kissed again. Hilary felt the steam rising in her shirt, one of her father's old ones with the sleeves rolled up to her elbows. They didn't hear Frank, who came into the rear office, rain-soaked and dripping. His hand was bleeding. "Tessie, Tessie, where are you? The phones aren't working and I need to call the egg man. What are you two doing here? Go home, Sorrell!" he shouted.

"I was just giving Hilary my ID, Mr. MacIntyre," said Sorrell.

"On the mouth? Get out of here! Sorrell go home!"

Sorrell left, dipping past Frank respectfully while Hilary clinked her bracelet and flounced past her father. Frank sucked at his bleeding finger where it had been torn by a splinter. "You're asking for it," he said. "You really are. You're turning into a first-class little bitch, and I don't mind telling you I'm pretty disappointed."

By November, the time of the election, it looked as though the money was gone forever. Of course Roosevelt won. No one paid any attention to the narrow margin predicted by the Gallup poll, since no one in Miami Beach even considered Dewey except Mr. Bonnier and some of his friends, and even they only in idle speculation, since it was well known that Florida, like the rest of Dixie, was staunchly Democratic.

The Germans had a new finned flying bomb, the V-2 rocket, gyroscopically stabilized and moving at the speed of sound, that a rocket expert publicly announced Americans should not worry about streaking across the Atlantic, since he doubted that the Germans had the capability yet. People didn't worry until they read the announcement in the papers and then they rationalized that the Germans would only aim for New York or the oil refineries in Bayonne, as there was no target in Miami, except maybe the blimp base, worth a transatlantic rocket. By December, it was clear that the Germans had dug in, and that the Allies were in for a continued fight. The German generals defending their homeland had proved to be formidable foes, and the end of the war in Europe, which had been predicted by Christmas, was pushed back for several months. Another unexpected event, one even more stunning to Miamians, was the announcement that all horse and dog racing was to end the first week in January which was the beginning of the real big money season. It could only mean one thing. Washington was worried, and since it could not control the black market, sought to conserve what gasoline supplies there were by limiting travel.

Hilary's alliance with Sorrell continued, more or less an egalitarian arrangement, unlike the one she'd had with T.H. Hilary raised her hand in algebra when she knew the answer and frowned when she felt like it. The onus was on Sorrell, whose primary responsibility was kissing, which Hilary exercised as a banker a promissory note.

The discussion of what they were going to be when they grew up took place on roller skates. Sorrell, who skated with a steady, purposeful one-two, said that when he graduated from high school he was going to college, and then medical school, reading his life before him like a map.

"How can you be so sure?" asked Hilary. "I used to think I knew what I wanted to be." She skated backward. "Now I don't know. One day I want to be a comedian like Lipschutz"—she spun around to skate at Sorrell's side—"and sometimes I think I'd like to be a detective."

"Hilary doesn't pick girl jobs," said Freddie.

"I just know, that's all," said Sorrell. "I always knew."

"Maybe I'll go to medical school too," said Hilary.

"See what I mean?" asked Freddie. "She picks boy jobs."

"Get off the sidewalk with those things!" shouted a storekeeper who was lowering his awning for the day. "You can kill someone like that!"

"You can't be a doctor," said Sorrell. One, two, stride, stride.

"Who says?"

"Well, for one thing, I don't know one single lady doctor, do you? And there's a reason for it. Think about it, Hilary, don't get sore. Lady doctors couldn't stand all that blood."

They stepped off the curb. Freddie clacked across the street on his skated toes.

"When Mr. Cardozo cut open the rabbit to show us peristalsis, you were the one who almost threw up. Not me," said Hilary.

"That's because I felt sorry for the rabbit," said Sorrell.

"Boy, Sorrell," said Hilary, "you really know how to throw the bull."

"Honest."

"Pinky swear? On your mother?"

"I'm going to be a bomber pilot," said Freddie.

"The war will be over soon," said Sorrell. "Where will you fly bombs to? You have to pick something else."

"I don't know what to pick," said Freddie. "I don't remember what people do when there's no war."

"Lots of things," said Sorrell. "You can be a basketball coach, a policeman, a lawyer, a railroad engineer, a car mechanic."

"Those are all dumb jobs," said Freddie. "It's no fair. Just when I'm almost old enough, it's over."

"You're not old enough, you're only eleven," said Hilary.

"So? I just need six more years. You can enlist when you're seventeen. I lost my key. Hilary, wait up, loan me your skate key."

"No skates in the lobby," warned the bell captain. Hilary already had hers over her shoulder and was on her way to the front desk.

Freddie rolled onto the marble floor and twirled around the bell captain. "Make me," he said, then skated away while Tessie handed Hilary a letter from Mickey. She tore it open. A photograph fluttered to the marble floor. Hilary picked it up. It showed Mickey on a porch glider, sitting next to an older woman, with a man standing on the step before them with little Earl on his shoulder. Mickey wrote that the picture was taken several months before, that now the snow lay in drifts higher than the porch, and that Bill's father had had to cut a trench between the house and the barn, and that when they went out alone and it was snowing, even if it was snowing lightly, they had to tie a long rope to their waists, especially little Earl, in case it turned into a blizzard, that Mickey missed her and the good times they had together and wanted her to come out someday, that Mrs. Wright fussed over little Earl all the time, that Mr. Wright gave him a pet piglet, that Bill's kid sister sometimes borrowed her makeup and jewelry and forgot to return it, which really burned her up, but that Bill was expected home as soon as he had enough points which was anytime now and then they would get a place of their own. As far as Sorrell was concerned, Mickey wrote, "It doesn't sound like love to me, it sounds like being in like, and that's o.k. Kiss all you want, it's good practice, don't do any French kissing, though, it'll give you trench mouth and then you have to swish pink powder around in your mouth for months."

Hilary stuck the letter in the pocket of her dungarees.

"Remember when we used to do jelly doors?" asked Freddie, clumping down the hall behind her on his skates. They found Frank and Ilona sitting in their own bedroom talking, which was unusual, since it was still very early.

"Hilary wants to go to medical school," said Freddie, attempting a diversion from the skates still attached to his shoes.

"Who's she going to get to pay for it?" asked Frank. "Colleges cost money."

"Never mind that now," said Ilona, who wasn't looking at anyone's feet. "We have good news." Her cheeks were flushed and her eyes luminous. "Wonderful news." She pursed her lips carefully in order to sound the W.

"Did they get Hitler?" asked Freddie who had been slipped a skate key by his sister.

Ilona's words tumbled out in a breathless rush. "It's your grandmother, my mother. She came to New York on the *Gripsholm.* They kept her at Ellis Island for a few days. You see, they were going to send her to Oswego, New York—they have a refugee camp there—but they changed their minds. She's coming to Miami the day after tomorrow, on the Silver Meteor."

At first there was modest excitement. The word "grandmother" pulled strings of warmth and cookies, and soft woolen shawls. Hilary said, "Murder!" and went to hug her mother, while Freddie jumped on and off the bed. Then came the hard, cold light of logistics.

"Where will she sleep?" asked Freddie, standing still on the bed, with the narrowed squint of the prescient.

Ilona answered promptly. Freddie was to be temporarily moved into the room with Frank and Ilona, about which suggestion he began to protest, and Hilary was to sleep with her grandmother.

Hilary was no less upset. "Why me?" she asked. "I don't even know her. I've never been separated from Freddie. Ever, in my whole life. Besides, we like to listen to the radio at night."

"I don't believe my ears," said Ilona, who secretly was glad for the opportunity to separate Freddie and Hilary, whom she believed should no longer be sharing a room anyhow. "Her grandmother has come from the other side, thousands of miles across the Atlantic Ocean through U-boats, and mines, and bombs, and God knows what, survived by the skin of her teeth, and she worries about the radio."

"I'm worried about it, too," admitted Freddie.

"Can you beat this?" asked Ilona, who had already begun cleaning the room, stripping the beds, and ordering Freddie and Hilary to gather up Freddie's belongings, as she disinfected the bathroom with Lysol.

They dragged his boxes into Frank and Ilona's room. The contents of an orange crate, belonging to them both, had to be separated. Freddie took out his old, twisted tin water chute and threw it disdainfully into the wastebasket. "What's this old thing doing here?" he asked. With the beds already upended and stacked against the wall, Ilona instructed Frank to pull up the carpet.

"Why does it have to come up anyhow?" shouted Hilary through the door.

"You have to beat a carpet to get it clean," said Ilona. "I still have my old carpet beater somewhere around here."

"It's no go," said Frank, "it won't budge. The tacks are probably rusted."

Ilona fussed and frowned, then vacuumed the Axminster carpet twice, bumping into everyone's feet and roaring over the faded roses. "It will have to do," she said.

Their last night together was spent listening to the radio and playing Go Fish until ten-thirty, when Freddie fell asleep during Kay Kyser, clutching his cards in his hand. Hilary switched the radio off and wondered if her grandmother snored. Sorrell said his grandmother snored and put her teeth in a glass next to her bed. Hilary thought about what it would be like to wake up every morning and see teeth floating in a glass. Freddie's cards fell to the floor. She picked them up, gave them a rinkadink shuffle the way Mel had taught her, and put away the deck.

They were an hour early for the train, standing in the pale yellow warmth of bridled January sunlight, everyone cleaned and starched, hair slicked back, Ilona nervously folding and unfolding her hands, and cleaning everyone's face, even Frank's, with spit on her handkerchief.

The station was mobbed with vacationers, some wearing fur coats, some carrying golf bags, and men in uniform, a few who had been discharged, standing in the epicenter of embracing knots of shouting, crying relatives, as packages spilled onto the ground and small children clutched at their legs, other servicemen, sent to Miami to recuperate from injuries or to await reassignment, met by no one, carrying their duffel bags over their shoulders.

After what seemed like hours, the Silver Meteor, a bullet of a train, one of the newest and shiniest, hissed into the station and stopped. Porters leaned out to set down stools, and hundreds of passengers spilled onto the platform. The MacIntyre family scanned every woman's face, checking it against Ilona's photograph. No one came close, except for one elderly woman in a fox jacket. Then the platform was cleared, abandoned except for redcaps pulling luggage carts.

"Maybe she's in the station," said Frank.

Ilona was already on her way inside. Within minutes she returned, now frantic. "She's not there either," she said.

"Don't borrow trouble," said Frank. "She probably was asked to get off and give her seat to a serviceman. A lot of civilians get bumped and have to wait for a space. Maybe she'll be on the next one."

They called the hotel. Tessie had no message for them. Ilona decided to stay and wait for the next train, which was not due to arrive for another six or seven hours. Frank said he had to get back to work, and there was no question that Freddie, already stepping pettishly from one foot to the other, would never make a six-hour wait. Hilary offered to stay with her mother. Frank looked at Ilona's pinched and worried face, reached into his pocket, and took out a bill. "Don't make the old lady take a bus," he said. "Take a cab."

"A cab is so much money," said Ilona.

"There are times to pinch pennies," said Frank, "and there are times to pitch them. You have to know which is which."

Freddie looked at him proudly. "You're a sport, Dad," he said.

They settled in to wait on a bench, leaving only to buy a prepackaged triple-decker sandwich, which they shared. Hilary first tried counting every person wearing red, then all the soldiers or sailors with the same insignia, then every man with a mustache, then making up stories about which one was an enemy agent, but soon tired of invention. She leaned against her mother who still clutched the photograph, and they sat silently side by side on the wooden bench marked WHITE ONLY.

It was evening when the next train hissed into the station.

At first they hung back, Ilona clutching the straps of the purse which dangled from her hands, then, as the crowd streamed down the platform, standing on her tiptoes, staring anxiously at each face as she had done for the train before.

"It's so hard to see," she said. "You're taller than I am. See if you can find her."

Hilary saw nothing but a sea of faces, indistinguishable because it was dusk, the only lights the dimmed station lights half taped because of the brownout regulations. The crowd began to thin. Ilona clutched her purse more tightly, the knuckles of her hand strained and taut.

A solitary figure stood alone, a bony woman with a gray knot at the back of her neck, like Ilona, only much older, her face creased like paper that has been folded many times. Ilona stepped forward. "That's her," she whispered. Her voice cut off in a choke.

"Mama!" she shouted, running, running, throwing herself at the body of the woman like a little girl. The woman registered recognition, and wearily lifted her arms. They embraced and cried into each other's necks, their faces contorted by their tears as the Pullman porter handed down Hilary's grandmother's baggage to a redcap below.

Hilary came to stand beside Ilona. She caught the eye of the woman who looked into her own. The woman whispered something to Ilona. Ilona turned and nodded, wiped her eyes, and put her arm around Hilary. "*Mein Kind, Mama, meine Tochter,* Hilary."

The woman looked at first as if she didn't approve, examined Hilary quizzically, then said, "A *langerloksh,*" took Hilary's shoulders, amazing Hilary with the strength of her hands, and reached up to kiss her on both cheeks.

"What did she say?" asked Hilary.

"She said you're a long drink of water."

"*Wo ist dein Mann,*" the older woman asked, "*und dein Sohn?*"

Ilona replied to her in German, then helped her with her luggage, a box tied with rope, an old brown leather valise, and a neatly folded winter coat. They had to wait for a cab. People seemed to come from nowhere to get ahead of them. Finally, when the moon looked like a Necco wafer, Ilona pushed her way forward to the curb, shouting, "I was here first!" No one argued.

The ride home was uneven conversation, a flurry of speech, punctuated by muttered half sentences, smiles, and tears. Hilary could do nothing but try to look friendly.

"How come she doesn't speak English," she asked, already at a loss for how to communicate to her grandmother, the continuous smiling beginning to be a strain. "If I knew I was coming to America, the first thing I would do would be to learn English."

"It's good to know someone in the family has the answer for everything," said Ilona. "That way, we never have to go to the library to look things up."

"Some people have encyclopedias," said Hilary, "in their house.

The whole set. Jackie Snyder, Shirley Leone, all the kids. I'm the only one who has to go to the library."

"*Was hat sie gesucht?*" asked the grandmother.

"Now you upset her," said Ilona. "She thinks we're arguing. Smile."

"I can't smile anymore, my cheeks won't work."

"You better smile," said Ilona cheerfully, gaily, an arpeggio of spoken notes, as if she were trilling a scale. "Smile, or I'll chop up your secret book which your father found frozen in the storage locker and feed it to the barracudas."

Suddenly they both laughed, Ilona hiding her mouth behind her hand, Hilary, in the way she had been laughing lately, hysterical, falling down on the floor of the cab. Hilary's grandmother took Ilona's hand and patted it, then looked absently out the window as Hilary recovered herself, and the half-moon headlights of the cab beamed low on the street before them.

25

The sky was cross-hatched with orioles, bluejays, finches, robins, redwinged blackbirds, and plovers. They rose from the beaches and the spoil banks soon after the first light, casting a feathered net across the sky as they traveled north, to be borne at first by low, easy, gliding currents and then climbing higher into the swifter currents of the streaming altitudes.

Ilona, who could still not believe the good fortune of having her mother safely at her side, had hoped that after two months, everyone would have settled down, but relationships were still just as strained as the first night when she brought her mother home and had to tell Freddie to turn off the radio.

Consanguinity was not enough. It was no one's fault. Everyone tried to oblige the new family member. Freddie didn't walk on his skates, or bang things around when he was mad, or shout through the door to Hilary, or play the radio too loud. Frank said nothing about the serious restriction of his privacy, or the skates that he tripped on each time he walked into the room. Hilary didn't complain about a roommate who snored, who made her bed as soon as she got up in the morning, always folded her towel, made little effort to speak, and stared out of the window through the venetian blinds she was constantly cleaning. She was certainly not the soft and doting grandmother of Sorrell Myers, whose stomach yielded like dough when you were pressed against it. Her presence was felt more keenly, like a knife. Even Ilona was unprepared for the depression that gripped the older woman and caused her to sit in isolated silence for hours at a time, when she wasn't complaining about the way Hilary dressed, or the way she didn't keep her half of the room, or the immodest spangled costume that hung like a lure in her half of the closet. She seemed to like Freddie the best of all of them. While she was civil to Frank, spoke on occasion with Ilona, it was Freddie whose salty brow she kissed. It was to him she began to speak her first words of English.

It was the edge for which he had been waiting most of his life, and he took it. After an argument in which he and Hilary each claimed ownership of a Captain Marvel poison ring which was awarded somewhat grudgingly by Ilona, saying she was too old for such things, to Hilary, because Hilary was able to describe the secret compartment, Freddie whispered his parting shot. "Who cares? Grandma likes me better than you."

It was something Hilary could not deny. She did what she could. She gave up writing in her diary because her grandmother didn't want the light on after nine o'clock, which was okay, since it was impossible to author entries with the woman's solemn eyes upon her. Hilary even tucked Frank's old shirts into her jeans, which no one did, but there was no common ground except genealogy upon which to stand. Hilary's forbearance was three-ply, because of Ilona, because of what she knew of her grandmother's suffering, and because her interest lay elsewhere now that she and Sorrell had graduated to serious necking, with tongues and hot breath and groping hands and Kleenex-buttressed Maidenforms poked out of shape.

Hilary was told by Ilona to take her grandmother out and show her around, but it was difficult to interest a grieving woman in the sights of Miami Beach. The convalescing soldiers distressed her, the MPs frightened her, which eliminated Collins Avenue. She didn't know how to play Mah-Jongg or bingo, and while she could speak to some of the guests in her own language, she declined to do so, which pretty much took care of anything the hotel had to offer. Even the Nikko cruise around the waterfront homes of millionaires who sometimes could be seen on their lawn chairs, failed to arouse her. Frank had the idea that the ocean would be therapeutic. They bought her a bathing suit and finally persuaded her to wear the black-skirted faille garment, which hung to her knees in multiple folds. That was the week President Roosevelt died of a stroke in Warm Springs, Georgia.

No one had thought President Roosevelt would ever die. He seemed immortal, permanent, like the Green Hornet or the sidewalk under your feet. None of Hilary's friends had ever known another President except guys like Lincoln and Woodrow Wilson whom they learned about in history books. Even some of the soldiers in the hotel next door said that they could not remember another President. Everyone, especially the grown-ups, worried that the new President, Harry S. Truman, would not know what to do with the country in the middle of the war. There was talk that with Roosevelt gone, the Japanese were planning another sneak attack, this time on San Francisco. The hotel immediately went into mourning, as did the town. Mr. Davis sent the bell captain to shinny up the flagpole to lower the flag to half mast, as everyone stood in sobbing, whispering clusters. "At least," muttered the bell captain, on his way down the pole, "he should have hung on until Germany got licked."

Hilary's grandmother put away the bathing suit in the box it came in, and expressed her concern to Ilona that now with Roosevelt gone, the Germans would not be afraid to cross the Atlantic, and that they should think seriously of moving inland, away from the coast. Ilona took this information immediately to Frank, who dispatched it, as he did all remarks from his mother-in-law, with a slice of his hand as if cutting through sugar cane with a machete.

"She doesn't know what she's talking about," he said.

"I thought so," said Ilona. "I wanted to be sure, just in case."

On Saturday, the day of Roosevelt's funeral, Hilary and Freddie and Sheldon Leone could not go to the movies to see *The Thin Man Goes Home,* as they had planned to, because all the theaters were closed. They tried to call to find out when the theater would open, but the outside lines were dead. Tessie said there was no phone service anywhere in Miami, and so they stayed in the hotel instead, and listened to the radio with their grandmother and Winona, who wore a black arm band over the sleeve of her uniform. Arthur Godfrey described the funeral procession, telling about the black-draped caisson led by six white horses and a seventh outrider, eyes hooded, stirrups reversed, sword and boots turned upside down and hanging from the stirrups, the mark of a fallen warrior. Suddenly Godfrey's voice broke and he began to sob.

"What's the matter, what happened?" asked their grandmother, leaning forward toward the radio. "What does he say?"

"He said the rider fell off the horse," explained Freddie.

Hilary began to laugh, the falling-down laugh that flung her like a convulsion off the bed to writhe on the carpet. "You ignoramus. That's not what he said."

Her grandmother shook her head in disapproval. "Sha," she admonished, "not nice."

Suddenly Hilary sat up. "What are you shushing me for? You don't even know what he's saying."

"That's no way to talk to your grandmother," said Winona.

"I don't care. I don't care." Hilary stood up. "I'm tired of all this moping around. It's awful. I feel like I'm stuck in cement. I'm alive, and I feel fine, and I don't want to sit around anymore and keep quiet. I don't want to keep quiet another minute." Hilary yanked her shirt out of her jeans. It hung to her knees. "I'm going for a swim."

"You can't swim now," said Freddie. "There's man-of-wars all over the beach."

"Let them watch out for me! Stupid purple things!" She flounced away, the tails of her shirt flapping over her blue jeans.

"What is she so mad about?" asked Sheldon.

"Girls are cuckoo."

"You can say that again."

"Sha," said Freddie's grandmother sadly, "listen." She pointed to the radio and bent to kiss his forehead. He helped by leaning over.

"Did you ever see your sister naked?" asked Sheldon.

"Sure. Lots of times."

"I saw Shirley naked. I'll tell you if you tell me."

A few days after Mussolini had been executed and left to hang upside down in a village square like a side of beef, and Hilary's grandmother finally walked into the surf, there to splash with caution, a daub here, a sprinkle there, as if in baptism, Hilary came home with a paper for Ilona and Frank to sign. It involved a major life decision for her: which track she was to follow for the next four years of school. The academic was college preparatory, the vocational would equip her with the clerical skills to enable her to get a job upon graduation.

The decision of one's high school track was the ultimate divider, even stronger than in kids or out kids, good kids or jerks, the ferry that was to determine the rest of their lives. All of Hilary's friends, except Liz, who was going to Connecticut to a private girls' school, were going into the academic track. She wanted to go with them and she was adamant.

Ilona, who had spent an unsuccessful hour that morning trying to convince her mother that she was not a burden and an old and useless woman, wanted to sign on the vocational side. Its goal was more immediate, and something she could deal with.

"Why prepare for what can never be?" she asked. "College costs money, and you can't count on a scholarship, Hilary. Besides, you'll probably get married soon after you graduate. If you go into the vocational program, at least you will have what you need to make a living if, God forbid, you have to."

Ilona opened the door to the other bedroom and asked her mother what she thought. The older woman had come in from the beach and was tying the belt of a printed cotton housedress that buttoned down the front. She replied that it didn't matter what a girl did in school, that the main things she had to learn she learned at home anyway, for the goal of any woman was to be a homemaker, some man's wife. School was extra, a luxury and, in her opinion, Hilary had not learned the requisite skills of housekeeping. Why push her? Ilona did not translate but it was clear that Hilary's grandmother did not vote for the academic.

"I don't know why you asked her," said Hilary. "She doesn't know anything about it."

"I ask her as a courtesy," said Ilona. "It makes her feel good to be included."

Hilary's grandmother said something else, a remark that had something to do with Hilary, to which Ilona answered with annoyance.

"What did she say?" asked Hilary.

"Nothing."

"I know it was something about me. What did she say?"

"She said you're like I was when I was fourteen, but that's not so. You're nothing like me. I was a responsible young lady when I was your age. When my mother or father told me to do something I did it."

Hilary leaned into the other room. "I'm nothing like my mother. All you have to do is open your eyes to see that."

"Don't use that tone of voice with your grandmother. Now listen, if you knew what you wanted to be, okay, I could maybe understand, but you have no idea what you want to do when you grow up. This way, if you take the vocational course, you don't have to cut ribbons in Woolworth's. You can get a job as a receptionist, after you get rid of those pimples—they only take pretty girls—but the work is clean. You dress up in nice clothes, you're right in the front of the office, and you meet nice men, important men. If you don't want to be a receptionist, you can be a secretary, and then if you're a good one, if you pay attention and learn, you can even be a private secretary—they make a lot of money with benefits. Millie Hankoff's girl supports her mother with the money she makes."

"I don't want to be a secretary," said Hilary. "I want to take the academic course. You study botany and biology, they let you swim with goggles to look at the fishes, and you get to take a foreign language. I want to study French."

"You can't make a living from fish unless you sell them like Mr. Nemser."

"I want to take the academic."

"Why? So you can be with Tracey? Is Tracey's father going to pay for college? Or Rhoda's father? That's not reason enough. Hilary, please, I'm counting on you. I have my hands full here, don't give me any more problems."

"I'm not giving you problems. I just don't want to take the vocational course, that's all."

Frank stepped from the bathroom, wearing freshly laundered kitchen whites, his dark blond hair shining with Vaseline hair tonic. "If she wants to go to college, let her take the college course."

"Frank, how are we going to pay for college? That's only in four years. You gave our savings for my mother. We can't count on Hilary getting a scholarship. That's usually for children, God forbid, who don't have a father. And we can't save enough in four years, not," she lowered her voice, "not with five in the family."

"Maybe she'll work her way through. Lots of people do that. Something will turn up."

"What something? Be practical, Frank. She's got to learn to keep her feet on the ground. Don't give her big ideas."

"She should have a chance at a big idea," said Frank, as he tied his shoes. "What's wrong with a big idea? Everyone should have a chance at a big idea once in his life. You and I never had a chance. They glued our feet to the ground the day we were born."

"Are you saying you didn't have a chance because of me and the children? You want to make me feel bad? All right, I feel bad."

"We're talking about her, not me, not you. What's the difference? Maybe you're right, maybe she doesn't know what she wants. Maybe she'll graduate high school and marry Sorrell Myers."

"I like Sorrell. I don't love him."

"That's the best news I heard all day," said Frank. "Anyhow, let's not make her into a secretary. She'd be a lousy secretary. She wouldn't last a day."

"Why do you say that?" asked Ilona. "Hilary is very smart."

"She's got too many crazy ideas. She opens that yap of hers once, she'll get canned. Hilary's got to study for a career where she doesn't have to talk to anyone. That's the only way she'll ever keep a job."

Frank left to go to work. Ilona reluctantly signed on the academic side, and Hilary ran after him.

"Thanks, Dad," she said.

"Think nothing of it," he replied.

Hilary put her arms around the neck of the person responsible for her manumission.

"Go easy on my jacket," he said. "Does this mean you forgot about that other business?"

"I didn't forget. I just see it differently. Like the kaleidoscope Freddie has. Every time you turn it, the picture changes. What's inside is the same. It just looks different to you, that's all."

"Aren't you afraid I could disappoint you again?"

"I don't need you to be so perfect anymore."

"That's a relief. I hate walking on eggs. What's with you and that kid Sorrell?"

"Nothing. We're very good friends and I respect him a lot."

"I don't want you getting so thick with him you can't back out. You're still a kid. Let's put it this way, I know you're pretty smart about things, I know your mother talked to you, I just want you to save some things for later. You know what I mean? I want you to have some surprises left. I don't want people saying bad things about my girl."

"You're talking about going all the way, aren't you?"

"Jesus, who said anything about that?"

"You did. Don't worry. I wouldn't do anything like that on purpose. You want to know why?"

"I don't think so. Your say-so is good enough for me. You know something, as soon as you start to dress the way normal people do, and put some meat on those bones, you're going to be a real knockout. Take it from your father."

By May, everyone was tired of being polite. Nerves were worn thin, like the splayed frayed cord of an electric wire. Freddie began to shout to Hilary through the door and bang things around the way he used to, play the radio loud, and complain that people were touching his new Monopoly set. Frank had never wanted to get away so badly in his life, except now he had no money to do it. Once, after a free-for-all in which all four doors slammed at once, including those that went to the bathrooms, he even considered going to St. Augustine and staying with his sister, until he remembered his nephew. Ilona, who could have bitten off her tongue every time, found herself in frequent squabbles with her mother, once shouting that she did not want her telling the children stories for which they were too young, like the one about the father who deserted his own son in the barn in which they were hiding, running and leaving the boy behind to save his own life. Most of the squabbles involved Hilary, and the fact that Ilona's mother, with pointed reference to their living conditions, said she had thought in America everyone had it so good, which brought about the most bitter battle of all.

While they were relieved by the news of V-E Day, they were too frazzled, and too involved into their own collateral maneuvers, to give the victory in Europe, the surrender of the Germans, more than respectful attention. As they watched the blackened marquees and billboards and storefronts of Miami Beach quicken into incandescence, the result of the lifted brownout, they knew, as did everyone else that the war was not yet over. The losses in Okinawa, where the news correspondent Ernie Pyle and the maintenance man's son had been killed the month before, were very heavy; the paper said draft calls would continue to be large; Stilwell predicted that the Japanese, with squadrons of suicide pilots and an army still intact, would take years to conquer; and with summer coming on and fresh, cool breezes at a premium, they were, the five of them in two hotel rooms, stifling.

At the end of the month, when Miami was smokebound from the out-of-control Everglades fire, Hilary got a letter from Mickey who wrote that the rivers in Iowa were at flood level because of the unseasonably late snow, but that Bill was coming home, and they were planning a small wedding the twentieth of June. Her major concern, one that caused her to bite off all her nails, was that she hadn't seen Bill in over two years and she worried whether it would be the same between them. If Hilary could come to Iowa, she would be the maid of honor instead of Bill's kid sister, who was acting as if the wedding were hers, and wear pale blue dotted swiss with a garden hat to match. That bothered Hilary more than anything. She should be the maid of honor. She knew just exactly how she would walk down the aisle—proudly, solemnly, gliding in the way Tracey showed her, her head high, a tiny smile at the corners of her mouth, but no teeth showing. She also realized with a sickening, too-late feeling that she would never see Mickey again. There was no way she could get to Iowa. All the planning, all the talk in their last few days together of how they would write every day and see one another at least twice a year, was fiction to help them part, to make their final separation bearable.

Hilary took her diary to the beach to scribble in privacy an entry entitled, "The Best Friend of My Life," but was forced to cut it short because of the mosquitoes, swarming patches which buzzed about her eyes and ears, driven east by the smog of the Everglades. She wrote a letter instead on hotel stationery at the hotel desk, in which she said that she made up with her father and she was convinced Bill and Mickey could fall in love again even if they felt different, for in her experience, love could grow back, like the snapped-off arm of a starfish.

That night, as they all slept under mosquito netting because the screens, which had not been replaced in years, had holes in them,

Mr. Lonzo's lieutenant rapped softly on the door. Everyone was asleep, shrouded in cocoons, as Frank hastily pulled on a pair of pants and opened the door.

Mr. Lonzo's lieutenant handed Frank an envelope saying, "Mr. Lonzo is grateful to you, Frank."

"What's this?"

"His appreciation."

Frank opened the envelope. "What for?"

"For the time you let him use the storeroom, no questions asked, and kept your mouth shut with the heat. Also, he got wind of your mother-in-law living with you and all. Mr. Lonzo is very sensitive to that sort of thing. He wants to help you out."

"How did he find out? I haven't seen him in months."

"Your boy told him. Mr. Lonzo came to talk to Davis. He saw your kids and asked your boy how the radio was, and he told him he wasn't allowed to play it. Your girl is getting to be big, Frank. I almost didn't recognize her." Frank looked at him with narrowed eyes. "No offense, Frank, just making talk."

"I can't take this money."

"Sure you can. There's nothing wrong with it, if that's what you're thinking. I happen to know those particular bills come from blue-chip dividends, so help me, and Mr. Lonzo says that if you like, you can consider this as a loan interest free."

"I sure could use it," said Frank. He closed the door behind him and stood in the hall. "I'll take it, but on one condition, that it's a loan. I'll pay it back. I never owed anyone a quarter in my whole life, except the Singer sewing machine man and that was Ilona's fault. She signed without asking me first. Tell that to Mr. Lonzo. Tell him I plan to pay it back, every penny."

"He knows you're good for it, Frank." Mr. Lonzo's lieutenant flipped the collar of his shirt over his jacket lapels with a snap of his thumbs and left.

Frank held the money in his hand. Enough for a clean break. He thought of leaving—he could have packed everything he owned in ten minutes—of walking out the door while they slept, first bending over to kiss a sleeping Ilona who would murmur and reach for him, and Freddie, who would rub his eyes and ask, "What's the matter, Dad?"

He slipped the money in his pocket and knew that he could never leave. While he might want to be somebody someday, it was just something to think about, a pipe dream of flying high with broads on his arms, making lots of money, sending his family enough to set them up in style, but that he was like Freddie, crouching behind the seawall, making believe he was shooting at Japs. He could never leave his family, because he loved them, and love, for a family man, was not consuming passion, love was staying.

He put on the light and whispered so as not to wake up Freddie who slept with the netting twisted over his legs. Ilona's eyes went wide. "Where did you get that?"

"Mr. Lonzo."

"What for?"

"A favor I did for him."

"Like what kind of favor?"

"Nothing bad. Just a favor. He's a generous guy." Frank turned on his side and stroked the curve of her waist. "But Lonzo is also a shady guy, you know that."

"I know. I also know money is money. Money doesn't have a conscience. It can't help where it goes. Who knows where any money comes from, for that matter? I go to the cleaner and get back your jacket, he hands me change. How do I know a loose woman didn't go in there two minutes before I did and give him the same money he gives me back in change?"

"I have to hand it to you, sweetheart, you sure can make anything come out right."

By early July, the afternoon after Freddie and Hilary had run out just after daybreak with folded film negatives to look at a partial eclipse of the sun, with their grandmother screaming behind them that they would go blind, all of them went to look at the two houses that Frank and Ilona had narrowed from a field of five.

The first one, a moldering pale yellow Moorish facsimile, defended by a high stone wall with bougainvillaea scribbling down its sides, had both a kitchen and a pantry and four bedrooms, but the drains were rusty, and the walls crumbled into grit when you touched them. Frank was afraid that it would fall down around them, while, he predicted, they slept. The second house was ecumenical in design, painted a pale peach with curving red barrel tiles on the rippling roof, french windows that had to be cranked open, and a screen door in front grilled with long-legged flamingoes.

They went inside, first slowly, then spilling in and out of the rooms like water. Ilona was radiant, glowing, and handed them in and out of doorways like an usher. Everyone agreed that it was perfect, except that there were only three bedrooms. This meant the logistics were the same as in the hotel. Hilary and her grandmother would have to share a room.

"What do you think?" Ilona asked her mother.

At first the older woman declined. It was not for her to say. She was pressed. Finally she acceded: "It's small."

"How can you say it's small?" asked Ilona, thrusting an arm through Frank's and forming, between them, a pretzel.

Frank said he would subdivide the master suite, the biggest bedroom of all which would make two rooms, one for Hilary, one for Ilona's mother. Hilary went to pace off the room. She walked the length, measured the midpoint, marked the spot with Sorrell's ID, then lay on the floor to measure it out for a bed. She pointed to herself. "I go over here." She held up two fingers. "Two rooms."

"Good," said her grandmother. "Two rooms." The older woman went to pace the room herself in the measured steps of a slow march. This time it was not evenly divided.

"What's she doing?" asked Hilary. "It's not even. I did it right the first time."

Hilary's grandmother said something to Ilona. Ilona translated. "She says she already stopped growing. You, God help us, have not. You need a bigger room."

Hilary's grandmother looked at her out of the corner of her eyes, like the mockingbird on the top of the royal palm.

Hilary smiled, snapping Sorrell's bracelet back onto her wrist. "Thanks, Grandma," she said, and like the mockingbird, the older woman bobbed her head.

Trouble, when it is finite, is bearable. One has only to see that it has a limit, an end, and one can endure almost anything. It did not matter that they were bursting at the seams or that they stepped on each other and each other's things. It was raining, and Hilary and Freddie played Monopoly with their grandmother, knowing that in two weeks, they would be out of the hotel in their own house with no furniture except a few broken pieces that

Mr. Davis said they could have and a what-not shelf from Mrs. Templeton.

In between moves they talked of the plane that crashed into the Empire State Building and of the atom bomb that was dropped on Hiroshima the day before. Their grandmother rolled the dice and moved her counter.

"Watch me get Park Place," said Hilary. "I already have Boardwalk. If I land on Park Place too, you're blitzed."

"The atom bomb," said Freddie, "is the same as two thousand big bombs."

"It's not just an ordinary bomb," said Hilary, "it's a chain reaction. One atom smashes another."

"Who doesn't know that? You passed Go, Grandma. You get two hundred dollars. Give her two hundred, Hilary."

"I can't be the bank all the time and take care of my moves. It's not fair for me always to be the bank."

"Well, I can't be the bank and help her play."

Hilary handed her grandmother the paper money and rolled the dice. "I wonder what it's like," she said, as she lifted her Chance card from the top of the pile, "to be working at a desk and suddenly a plane crashes into the window? I'm giving myself a hundred and fifty dollars. My building and loan matured. I think I would have seen it coming. I would have heard it for sure. I would have seen it coming and I would have shouted for everyone to take cover, and I would have jumped out of the way and escaped just in the nick of time."

"You wouldn't have seen it coming."

"Oh yes I would."

"You would not. If you're working at a desk, you're looking down, so how could you have seen it coming?"

There came a rapping on the wall and a muffled shout, "Shut up in there!" from someone on the other side. "A person can't sleep in this hotel!"

Hilary's grandmother got up and banged on the wall with her fist. "Nah," she shouted, "a *klop* on the wall for you." She came back to the table, kissed Freddie on the forehead, and rolled the dice.